LIFE IN THE GEORGIAN CITY

DAN CRUICKSHANK and NEIL BURTON

VIKING

VIKING

Published by the Penguin Group
27 Wrights Lane, London w8 5TZ, England
Viking Penguin Inc., 40 West 23rd Street, New York, New York 10010, USA
Penguin Books Australia Ltd, Ringwood, Victoria, Australia
Penguin Books Canada Ltd, 2801 John Street, Markham, Ontario, Canada L3R 1B4
Penguin Books (NZ) Ltd, 182–190 Wairau Road, Auckland 10, New Zealand

Penguin Books Ltd, Registered Offices: Harmondsworth, Middlesex, England

First published 1990
1 3 5 7 9 10 8 6 4 2

Printed in Great Britain by Butler & Tanner Ltd, Frome and London
Typeset in 9/11 pt Lasercomp Sabon

A CIP catalogue record for this book is available from the British Library

ISBN 0–670–81266–8

Contents

List of Colour Plates

Acknowledgements

———◆———

The authors would like to thank the following for their assistance with the production of this book: Charles Brooking for making available for examination items from his collection of architectural salvage; David Jenkins for his drawings of mouldings and house plans; Ian Bristow for advice on paint colours; Hentie Louw for information on exterior paint colours; Peter Hood and John Ashurst for information on traditional materials and finishes; Douglas Blain for sound advice on traditional construction; Andrew Byrne for help with the surveying of No. 15 Elder Street and costing its construction; Dennis Severs for his insights on life in the Georgian town house; David Mlinaric, Jocasta Innes and John Martin Robinson for their advice on internal decorations; Mark Girouard for guidance on local government in the eighteenth-century city; Susie Barson for information on town gardens in Kensington; Ian Lumley for information on Dublin; Sam Anderton for information on Bath; Martin Charles for his photograph of the breakfast room at Pitshanger Manor; Christie's for their help in providing views of modest urban interiors; Penny Wright for help with the preparation of the manuscript; Susie Barson, Glyn and Carrie Boyd Harte, Michael Gillingham, Eric Elstob, Mr and Mrs Enthoven, Martin Lane, the Revd Stride and the Architectural Press for permitting photography in their respective buildings. Also special thanks to Victoria Cruickshank for the support she has given during the writing of this book and for help with picture research.

ILLUSTRATION ACKNOWLEDGEMENTS

For permission to reproduce illustrations, grateful acknowledgement is made to the following:

p. 2 Museum of London; p. 4 Bridgeman Art Library; p. 6 Guildhall Library; p. 7 Bridgeman Art Library; p. 8 British Library; p. 9 Museum of London; p. 11 Bridgeman Art Library; p. 12 Photo Archive, Paul Mellon Center; p. 13 Bridgeman Art Library; p. 14 Yale Center for British Art; p. 15 Museum of London; p. 16 Mary Evans Picture Library; p. 17 Guildhall Library; p. 18 Mary Evans Picture Library; p. 20 Mary Evans Picture Library; p. 21 Guildhall Library; p. 24 Museum of London; p. 25 Museum of London; p. 26 Museum of London; p. 28 (top) Guildhall Library (bottom) Mary Evans Picture Library; p. 30 Bridgeman Art Library (private collection); p. 31 Christie's; p. 32 Guildhall Library; p. 33 British Museum; p. 34 Sotheby's; p. 36 Temple Newsam House Museum, Leeds; p. 39 Bridgeman Art Library (private collection); p. 40 Mary Evans Picture Library; p. 41 Sotheby's; p. 42 Sotheby's; p. 43 Mary Evans Picture Library; p. 44 Mary Evans Picture Library; p. 46 Mary Evans Picture Library; p. 50 British Library; p. 53 drawing by David Jenkins; p. 55 drawing by David Jenkins; p. 56 British Architectural Library, RIBA; p. 57 British Architectural Library, RIBA; p. 58 British Architectural Library, RIBA; p. 59 (left) Dan Cruickshank (right) Architectural Press; p. 62 Museum of London; p. 63 British Museum; p. 66 Guildhall Library; p. 68 Irish Architectural Review; p. 69 Dan Cruickshank; p. 70 Dan Cruickshank; p. 71 British Museum; p. 72 Dan Cruickshank; p. 73 British Architectural Library, RIBA; p. 75 British Museum; p. 79 British Museum; p. 80 Greater London Record Office; p. 81 Bishopsgate Institute; p. 82 Dan Cruickshank; p. 83 Guildhall Library; p. 84 Neil Burton; p. 85 Guildhall Library; p. 86 Guildhall Library; p. 87 Neil Burton; p. 88 Greater London Record Office; p. 90 British Museum; p. 92 Guildhall Library; p. 93 Guildhall Library; p. 94 drawing by John Sambrock; p. 95 Neil Burton; p. 96 British Museum; p. 100 Dan Cruickshank; p. 101 Dan Cruickshank; p. 102 British Architectural Library, RIBA; p. 103 British Architectural Library, RIBA; p. 104 Dan Cruickshank; p. 105 Dan Cruickshank; p. 106 British Library; p. 107 Dan Cruickshank; p. 108 British Library; p. 109 Dan Cruickshank; p. 112 Dan Cruickshank; p. 113 Simon Doling; p. 114 Dan Cruickshank; p. 116 British Library; p. 120 British Architectural Library, RIBA; p. 121 Bath Reference Library; p. 126 Dan Cruickshank; p. 127 Dan Cruickshank; p. 128 British Architectural Library, RIBA; p. 129 Dan Cruickshank; p. 130 British Architectural Library, RIBA; p. 131 Sam Anderton; p. 132 Dan Cruickshank; p. 142 Dan Cruickshank; p. 143 Dan Cruickshank; p. 144 Dan Cruickshank; p. 145 Dan Cruickshank; p. 146 (*left*) Simon Doling (*right*) Dan Cruickshank; p. 147 Dan Cruickshank; p. 151 Dan Cruickshank; p. 152 Dan Cruickshank; p. 153 Dan Cruickshank; p. 154 Dan Cruickshank; p. 156 Dan Cruickshank; p. 157 Photographic Unit of Architecture and Civil Design, Historic Buildings Division, Greater London Council; p. 158 Fairfax House Museum; p. 159 Dan Cruickshank; p. 160 Dan Cruickshank; p. 164 Dan Cruickshank; p. 168 drawing by David Jenkins; p. 169 drawing by David Jenkins; p. 170 drawings by David Jenkins; p. 171 drawings by David Jenkins; p. 172 drawing by David Jenkins; p. 176 British Architectural Library, RIBA; p. 177 British Architectural Library, RIBA; p. 178 British Library; p. 179 British Library; p. 192 Beinecke Rare Books; p. 193 Greater London Record Office; p. 194 British Museum; p. 195 Guildhall Library; p. 196 Beinecke Rare Books; p. 198 National Maritime Museum, Greenwich; p. 199 British Library; p. 200 Greater London Record Office; p. 202 Bristol City Art Gallery; p. 203 Bodleian Library, Oxford; p. 204 Kensington Local History Library; p. 208 Dan Cruickshank; p. 211 drawing by David Jenkins; p. 212 Dan Cruickshank; p. 215 Dan Cruickshank; p. 216 Dan Cruickshank; p. 220 Lambeth Palace Library; p. 221 Dan Cruickshank; p. 223 Dan Cruickshank; p. 224 Dan Cruickshank; p. 228 Dan Cruickshank; p. 230 Dan Cruickshank; p. 233 Dan Cruickshank; p. 234 Dan Cruickshank; p. 235 Dan Cruickshank; p. 236 Dan Cruickshank; p. 238 Dan Cruickshank; p. 240 Guildhall Library; p. 241 Dan Cruickshank; p. 242 Dan Cruickshank; p. 245 Dan Cruickshank; p. 247 Dan Cruickshank; p. 248 Dan Cruickshank; p. 249 Dan Cruickshank; p. 250 Dan Cruickshank; p. 256 Dan Cruickshank; p. 257 Dan Cruickshank; p. 258 (*bottom right*) British Architectural Library, RIBA; p. 259 (*left*) British Architectural Library, RIBA; p. 260 Greater London Council, Historic Buildings Division; p. 261 Dan Cruickshank; p. 262 Dan Cruickshank.

Colour Plates

(*top and bottom*) British Museum
(*top and bottom*) Christie's Colour Library
(*top*) Courtland Institute (*bottom*) National Gallery of Ireland
(*top*) British Museum (*bottom*) British Architectural Library, RIBA
Martin Charles
(*top*) Sir John Soane Museum (*bottom*) Museum of London
Guildhall Library
(*top*) British Museum (*bottom*) Dan Cruickshank

Preface

This work is a joint effort, not a collaboration. When this book was begun some years ago, I had intended to work on it alone. However, as research progressed it became clear that two very important areas had already been well and thoroughly investigated.

Services in the Georgian city and town gardens had become special projects for Neil Burton, who, though he had published no lengthy articles on these subjects, had amassed much information. Very generously, Neil offered to make his research available to me, but, in the circumstances, it seemed best that he should contribute the chapters on servicing and gardens in this book. The other chapters are my work, and any errors of interpretation or faults of fact are mine and not Neil Burton's.

Dan Cruickshank
Spitalfields, London

Introduction

This book has two main purposes: to describe how life was lived in the modest town house during the Georgian period, and to provide information about the construction and decoration of the house itself.

To achieve the first aim, we have relied heavily on contemporary accounts – mostly those of foreign visitors to Britain in the later eighteenth century – so that we can, as far as possible, see the eighteenth-century city through eighteenth-century eyes. Naturally, such an investigation cannot be contained behind the front door. We discuss who slept where and how, the ways in which people ate breakfast and dined, how they cooked, cleansed themselves and their houses, and how they entertained at home. But we have also strayed beyond the strict confines of the house itself and looked at the environs in which it stood.

This book is not a social or political history of the Georgian city, so we have not written of the organization of local government, the role in daily life of institutions such as the almshouse, hospital, workhouse or the Church. We have, however, touched on those things of immediate interest and importance to the humble city resident: how the streets were lit, cleansed and policed. We have also traced the evolution of the town garden, from the cramped and utilitarian yard usual in the early-eighteenth century to the well-stocked miniature pleasure garden of the late-eighteenth century, with its gravel walks and formal planting.

The emphasis of this book has fallen heavily upon London: this was inevitable. London was by far the largest of British cities (its population in 1700 was 674,500 as compared to Norwich, with a population of 30,000, and Bristol, with a population of 20,000), it was almost the exclusive centre of interest for foreign visitors, and virtually all significant developments were pioneered in London. Be it means of financing building speculation and building controls, architectural design, theories and aesthetics, or street paving and lighting, London was always the first testing ground.

A second reason for concentrating on London had to do with one of the main intentions of this book: to get to grips, in detail, with most aspects of urban life at the time. To attempt equal coverage of, say, Dublin, Edinburgh, Bath, Boston or New York could lead only to over-simplification, for conditions and habits in all these cities were profoundly different though superficially similar. To avoid a bland text that irons over differences, we have taken one city – the most influential city in the English-speaking, eighteenth-century world – and examined it in detail.

The second aim of this book, to provide information about the fabric of the Georgian town house, has necessarily had to be tailored to the prime aim of describing life in the house. In the chapter 'Elements of the House' wall treatment, moulding, paint colours and ingredients are all described. This information should not only help give a better understanding of the thinking behind the decoration of the town house – simultaneously revealing something about the way in which life was ordered in the house – but also prove useful to those repairing or restoring a Georgian house.

Finally, a little must be said about the aesthetic and legislative context in which the town house evolved in Britain during the period from 1700 to 1830. The Great Fire of London in 1666 had a profound effect on construction and design – and not just in London. From the 1670s onwards, brick or stone construction became general (though with much timber used for internal partitions, decoration and even for lacing the masonry together), and regulations for controlling urban building were seen as a means of ensuring a city that would be both visually coherent and structurally sound. The London Building Act of 1667 specified that houses should be of four types, that each type had to conform to certain standards of construction and – most important from the point of view of urban design – size had to relate to location. No longer, in theory, could mansions be built in alleys; modest houses were to be placed uniformly in modest streets. Through the first quarter of the eighteenth century external embellishments were gradually banned or regulated (as fire risks), and in 1774 the whole business of controlling construction was given its final eighteenth-century expression by the passing of a massive and comprehensive Building Act. This Act also specified four types of houses and gave, in minute detail, rules for their construction (though abandoned constraints upon location) with immense effect, for, unlike previous Acts, this legislation envisaged strong penalties for non-compliance.

Against this background of increasing legislation must be set the aesthetic development that influenced the town house. In the late-seventeenth and early-eighteenth centuries the English Baroque school of architecture was dominant and produced a modest town house that tended to be flat fronted, though occasionally with a façade articulated by pilaster strips set between windows or framed by giant pilasters, complete with capitals, used merely for decoration and unrestrained by the canons of classical propriety. The only regular embellishment to the façade was the doorcase, which could be of an extravagant and highly individual design. A deep wooden eaves cornice could top the elevation, but these were outlawed in the Cities of London and Westminster in 1707 and quickly fell from use elsewhere.

Windows were generally wide, certainly wider than the brick piers flanking them, though there was a very early-eighteenth-century fashion for narrow windows, with the end windows on an elevation being half as wide as the other windows on the same façade. By 1700 windows were invariably fitted with broad timber sashes set flush with the façade (in 1709 they were ordered to be set back four inches, which rarely happened until the 1730s), bearing glazing bars of broad section. The horizontal hierarchy of window depths was not generally very pronounced early in the eighteenth century, with the ground floor or the first floor containing the main rooms with higher ceilings and so slightly deeper windows.

In 1715 came the Palladian revolution. During the next decade a tightly knit group of aristocrats and architects – Lords Burlington, Shaftesbury and Pembroke, Colen Campbell, William Kent, the cousins Roger and Robert Morris – succeeded in overthrowing the relaxed and inventive English Baroque school in favour of a rule-bound, austere classicism inspired by the works of the sixteenth-century Italian, Andrea Palladio. In Palladio's works, and in Inigo Jones's early-seventeenth-century synthesis of Palladio with English customs and usage, these men (largely Whigs) saw the means of achieving a rational national style and of breaking aesthetic dependence on Catholic France.

To the early-eighteenth-century Whigs, the essence of Palladio was regularity, symmetry, restraint – the logical relation of the parts to the whole. They advanced the creation of a regular structure in which, through certain proportional ratios, the design of the elevation would relate to the interior, the plan to the façade. Essential to the Neo-Palladians was the belief that Palladio had worked in accordance with the classical canons, the 'key of knowledge' of the Ancients, which were derived from a study and understanding of the laws of the universe. As Robert Morris wrote in his *Lectures on Architecture* of 1734, the architecture of Palladio, based on the knowledge of the Ancients, echoed the 'emanation of the harmony of nature'.

When percolated down to the speculative builders – the men who built the Georgian city – Palladio's theories produced buildings in which individuality of expression was replaced by 'pattern-book' detail and in which regularity, repetition and almost dour simplicity became key elements. Certainly the Protestant, indeed puritan, values triumphed over the excesses of the Catholic Baroque.

The Palladian façade, with its first-floor piano nobile and square attic windows, became the standard street elevation for the rest of the Georgian period. The only major change in matters of proportion was that the early-Palladian preference for the Italian practice of making piers between windows wider than the windows themselves (useful in hot climates for creating cool and shady interiors) was gradually and sensibly modified to the British climate, so that window widths and window piers became the same dimension.

The other changes were to do with details. Before the mid century, even the most pedantic of Palladians would indulge in a little Rococo Gothic, or even Chinese when a playful interior was required. After 1760 these whimsical motifs were joined by something far more serious: the fruits of the Neo-classical revolution. In 1762 James Stuart and Nicholas Revett published their *Antiquities of Athens*, which revealed, first to the erudite architect and connoisseur, then to the builder and jobbing craftsman, the unknown riches of the newly discovered

Greek repertoire of decoration and building forms. These motifs reached the street in the 1770s and marked the beginnings of a flood of new decorative devices that broke the Palladian stranglehold on design.

After Greece, there were other revelations about the richness of the classical repertoire, as more sources (unknown to Palladio) were tapped for inspiration. Roman architecture was investigated with new and perceptive interest – an important contribution being made by Robert Adam with his description of the *Ruins of the Palace of the Emperor Diocletian at Spalatro*, published in 1764. Added to this, Gothic was analysed and used in a more correct manner, while, towards the end of the period, exotic and Eastern styles – Hindu and Egyptian – were thrown into the eclectic melting pot.

As far as the town house went, this expansion of the decorative repertoire changed only decorative details: doorcase and fireplace design, cornices, dado rails and the like. The basic structure and form of the house remained the same. This was largely because there was not a corresponding revolution in building materials relevant to domestic urban design; cast-iron was used in warehouse and mill design from the late-eighteenth century, but houses, in the 1830s, were still built largely as they had been a hundred years before.

The internal organization of the modest town house settled down quickly to its optimum form: room front, room back, usually with a closet off the back room, and a dog-leg stair in one of the rear corners – the plan of the 'common house' described by Isaac Ware in his *A Complete Body of Architecture* of 1756. There were regular permutations: top-lit, centrally placed stair between back and front rooms that stretched the full width of the flat; two rooms wide, one room deep, with closet and stair separating the rooms (a form that gave better lit rooms than the common plan); and plans in which the stair rose against the front of the house – a type favoured if fine views could be had from the rear rooms.

But such permutations were limited by the constraints of the standard, narrow city plot (18–25 ft maximum), and even the most adamant of Palladian designers seemed unequal to the task of applying their theories of proportional relationships to the interior when faced by the daunting practical problems of fitting a delicately balanced mix of rooms – kitchen, wash-room, parlour, dining-room, drawing-room, bedrooms, servants' rooms – into a constricted site perhaps no larger than 20 × 40 ft. The way in which this machine worked, how the various uses were shoe-horned in and integrated together, and how all this was done while retaining the sense of classical repose and dignity thought essential for the age, are what this book investigates.

PART ONE

LIFE IN THE CITY

Cheapside, looking west, in 1823. In the City all is animation as shoppers, carters, tradesmen and men of affairs and commerce pursue their business.

Chapter One

— ◆ —

STREET LIFE

THE IMAGE OF THE CITY

The form of the domestic architecture that made up the Georgian cities of Britain not only determined the way in which life was organized inside the home but also had a profound influence on the way the city was perceived. The repetitious nature of the speculatively built terrace house had come to dominate most major cities by 1830 – notably, London, Dublin, Bath, Bristol and Edinburgh. This uniformity and simplicity of design, combined with the dense coal smoke that hung around all cities, created a powerful image of the eighteenth-century city as an unnatural place dominated by inequality, where thousands suffered in anonymous despair.

Among contemporary records this view is best, and most often, expressed by foreign visitors. The reaction of Louis Simond, a French-born American who visited London in 1810, is typical: 'On winter days in London ... the smoke of fossil coal forms an atmosphere perceivable for many miles, like a great round cloud attached to the earth.'[1] Erik Gustaf Geijer, who was in London from 1810 to 1811, criticized the architecture with the atmosphere: 'one passes through houses all alike, all dark and smoke begrimed ... into an atmosphere of smoke in whose twilight move an unending multitude of people', with the city 'an enormous murky lump of brick ... inwardly alive like an anthill and inhabited by a race which, if it ever looks at the sky, finds it made of coal smoke'. As well as being 'all alike', the houses were also, to Geijer, mean in appearance: 'One may say in general that the warehouse gives the character to the whole of London.'[2]

Even natives, not loaded with prejudices against plain brick architecture, despaired of the uniformity and 'extraordinary simplicity of [the] buildings' of the eighteenth-century quarters of the great cities. John Gwynn criticized the new buildings of St Marylebone for giving 'no better idea to the spectator than that of a plain brick wall of prodigious length'.[3] Forty years later Robert Southey would complain in similar vein:

This metropolis of fashion, this capital of the capital itself [i.e., the West End] has the most monotonous appearance imaginable – the streets are perfectly parallel and uniformly extended brick walls, about 40 ft high, with equally extended ranges of windows and doors, all precisely alike, and without any appearance of being distinct houses. You would rather suppose them to be hospitals, arsenals or public granaries were it not for their great extent.[4]

But there were others who appreciated that there was something very special about Georgian domestic town buildings. J.A. Anderson, a Dane who visited London first in 1802,[5] noted the gloom of the houses, but realized this gave even modest domestic buildings a striking 'solemnity'; while Carl Philip Moritz, a foreigner who visited London in 1782, seemed surprised, even confused, by the aesthetic appeal and emotive power of London street architecture: 'The houses in general strike me as if they were dark and gloomy: and yet, at the same time, they also strike me as great and majestic.'[6] There were also others who saw through the reticent and grimy façade and recognized the Georgian terrace house for what it was: a highly ingenious device for making the most of the limited land available for building and of the limited money that the speculative building system allowed for construction and

Despite the evidence, recorded by numerous foreign visitors, that Georgian London was covered with a pall of sooty coal smoke, English painters invariably took a cheerful view, preferring imagined sunlight and blue sky to the reality of black clouds and smog. This painting of c. 1770 shows the City from Somerset House and is one of the very few works that even hints at the presence of a coal-smoke-laden sky. The culprit, according to Paul Sandby who painted this view (only a detail of which is shown), was not the domestic grate but industry on the south bank of the Thames.

decoration (see p. 99). As early as 1727 Cesar de Saussure, a Swiss, had realized that 'it is not possible to make better use of the ground' than in the London terrace house plan,[7] and in 1817 Richard Rush noted that the average London house was 'remarkable for its good arrangement, and economy of space: the most being made for accommodation, in all ways, of the limited ground it stood upon'.[8]

SIMPLICITY AND COAL FIRES

It is understandable that the austere elevations and the smoky atmosphere of Georgian cities should have made an equal and related impression on the foreign observer, for they were both direct reflections of the English character. In the very early seventeenth century the father of English Neo-Palladian design, Inigo Jones, had very nicely summarized the English preference for undemonstrative and uniform elevations to their buildings. Architecture, wrote Jones, should mimic the outward behaviour of 'every wyse man' who 'carrieth a graviti in publicke places', while 'inwardly hath his immaginacy set on fire, and sumtimes licenciously flying out'.[9]

Geijer recognized the symbolic importance of the source of London's grime and smoke, the coal fire: 'The Englishman's house is a sort of sanctuary ... the fire place around which they gather in the evenings is also among the things respected.' The altar-like quality of the fireplace is underlined by the ritual by which it was attended. 'The host and hostess,' continued Geijer, 'have always the places next to the fire ... and only [they] have the right to arrange and poke the fire.' The house was the home, the coal fire its heart.

Coal had been taxed since 1667 (the money going first towards the rebuilding of St Paul's Cathedral and then to the construction of other London churches). It fluctuated in price but was relatively expensive throughout the eighteenth century.[10] Nevertheless, coal reigned supreme as the means of heating and enlivening the home (see p. 76). As early as 1698 the Parisian Francis Maximilian Misson had noted the Englishman's preference for coal. 'None but people of the first quality burn wood at London, and they too only in the Bed Chamber; yet I do not find that wood is very expensive in England.'

The process of making a fire with coal – which could be sea coal, earth coal or pit coal – was unusual enough for Misson to record in detail. 'The way of making a coal fire is thus,' he wrote:

They put into the chimney certain iron stoves about half a foot high, with a plate of iron behind and beneath; before and on each side are bars plac'd, and fasten'd like the wiers of a cage, all of iron. This they fill with coal, small or great, as they run, and in the middle they put an hand-full of small coal, which they set fire to with a bit of linnen or paper: As soon as the small coal begins to burn, they make use of the bellows, and in less than two minutes the other coal takes fire ... The smoke that rises from this is horribly thick ... All things considered, a wood fire must be owned to be much more agreeable.[11]

Foreigners were not only shocked by the 'black smoeks [and] caustic vapours'[12] and the way they 'poison the air we breath',[13] but also, by the fact that, after all this, coal gave off so little heat. As Geijer observed: 'They ... do not know what a warm room means. Porcelain stoves are unknown ... A few forgotten coals lie in the grate when it is cold, but the warmth goes the same way as the smoke and the smell, out through the chimney.'

STREET LIGHTING

If the atmosphere and the austere and dingy elevations of domestic architecture provoked criticism from contemporary observers, the paving and lighting of British cities were generally regarded as amongst the great wonders of the age. This was particularly true of London and its lighting. As early as 1698 Misson could write:

They set up (at every tenth house) in the streets of London (Mr Edward Hemming was the inventor of them about fifteen or sixteen years ago) lamps, which, by means of a very thick convex glass, throw out great rays of light which illuminate the path ... for people that go on foot tolerably well ... They burn from six in the evening until midnight, and from every third day after the full moon to the sixth day after the new moon.

Misson is not absolutely accurate in his report, but he was clearly impressed. In fact, the placing of lights and lighting times were complex matters that varied in the early-eighteenth century from city parish to city parish and from season to season. The system was supervised by the parish vestry, which raised a rate from eligible householders for lighting in the same way as it did for paving, scavenging, watching, and so on. But, from the early-eighteenth century, it is clear that rateable members of certain parishes could avoid contributing to the rate by hanging out their own lamps, presumably under parish supervision. This was provided for by a late-seventeenth-century Act of William and Mary that enforced street lighting from Michaelmas to Lady Day, and then until only midnight. An early local amendment to this was a 1716 Act of Common Council in the City of London, which required householders to hang out lights in the six winter months from 6 to 11 p.m. on dark nights by the calendar, that is, eighteen nights in each moon.[14]

The Edward Hemming mentioned by Misson appears in a tract of 1689 entitled *New Lights in the City of London: The Case of Edmund Heming*.[15] It seems that the hapless Heming set up lights in Cornhill in 1685 in an attempt to raise interest in, and backing for, his project to light London with whale-oil lamps and was immediately opposed by City companies, such as tallow chandlers, tinsmiths and horners, who saw his proposal as a threat to their livelihood. The pamphlet tells the pathetic story of Heming being forced to get up at 'four or five in the morning to trim and order the lights' and consequently facing complete physical exhaustion as well as bankruptcy due to the blocking of his project.

A lamplighter, drawn in 1805 and published in W.H. Pyne's The Costume of Great Britain. *The lamp mechanism is clearly revealed: the oil reservoir and wick are suspended from the upper edge of the glass globe, which is topped with a decorative and well-ventilated metal cap. Typical of the date, the iron of the lamp stand is painted green in imitation of bronze (see illustration on rear of dustjacket).*

Despite Misson's acknowledgement of Heming's pioneering work, it is another man who took most of the credit for creating the prototype of the oil-lamp system that was to light London during the eighteenth century. The historian James Peller Malcolm, in his *Anecdotes of the Manners and Customs of London ...* of 1808, recorded that 'Globular lights were introduced by Michael Cole, who obtained a patent in July 1708.' Malcolm then quoted the 'patent document' for a 'new kind of light, composed of one entire glass of a globular shape, with a lamp, which will give a cleaner and more certain light from all parts thereof'. This lamp was, according to Malcolm, first exhibited at the door of the St James's coffee-house in 1709. Cesar de Saussure, in a letter of December 1725, gave, perhaps, the earliest account of what became a familiar eighteenth-century practice: the suspending of lamps in decorative iron brackets above or beside the front door. 'Most of the streets are wonderfully well lighted, for in front of each house hangs a lantern or a large globe of glass, inside of which is placed a lamp which burns all night. Large houses have two of these lamps suspended outside their door by iron supports, and some houses even four.'

But it was not until after 1740 that street lighting in London – which set the pattern for urban lighting throughout the country – became thoroughly organized through a series of Acts of Parliament. The first of these, which became the model for consequent Acts, was passed in 1736 for the City of London, giving the City the power to rate the inhabitants for lighting the streets throughout the year. This was followed quickly in 1738 by a Watching and Lighting Act for the Parish of Christ Church, Spitalfields. Handing watching and lighting over to the same committee of vestrymen was sensible – both were concerned with security for parish residents and visitors – and became the usual practice after this Act.

The way in which the City's 1736 Act was structured was explained in some detail by Malcolm, who clearly felt that it was the beginning of street lighting as the eighteenth century was to know it. It is worth giving Malcolm's account at length, for it explains how rates were calculated, how the money was allocated and reveals what standard of street lighting was thought adequate.

The aldermen and common council began by determining how many houses there were in the

A glimpse into the Covent Garden Piazza from Paul Sandby's watercolour of c. 1780. The mechanics of the oil lamp – a tray suspended from the cap – are well illustrated. The walkway is neatly paved, the carriageway cobbled.

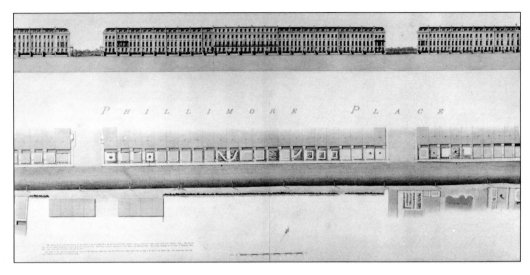

Phillimore Place, Kensington High Street, as recorded by Joseph Salway in 1811. The variety of front garden design and the extent of street lighting can be seen. The lamps, still of the oil-burning type, are placed along only one side of the road.

City, valued them, decided how many lamps were needed and what they would cost to erect and maintain, and then determined what proportion of the total each rateable inhabitant would have to pay. There were, it was calculated, 1,287 houses with rent under £10 per annum; 4,741 with rent between £10 and £20 per annum; 3,045 with rent between £20 and £30 per annum; 1,849 with rent between £30 and £40 per annum; and 3,092 with rent of £40 and upwards per annum. 'In all, 14,014 houses, then inhabited and chargeable.' The reference to rent should not be confused with actual rent paid. Rates were calculated on the value of a house that was expressed in terms of the rent it was worth. This is not to say that the occupier was actually paying that rent: he could have been a freeholder, a most rare thing in the eighteenth-century city, paying no rent; a lessee paying merely a nominal ground rent to the landlord; or a sublessee on a short lease paying a rack rent.

The committee then established that the number of lamps required was 4,200, exclusive of those wanted in 'public buildings and void places'. This was based on the decision that lights should be 'fixed at a 25-yd distance on each side of the way in the high streets, and at 35 in lesser streets, lanes, etc.'. The money was calculated and raised in the following manner.

The several wards of the City agreed for the lighting them at an average of 41s. per annum per lamp, at which rate the expense of 4,200 lamps amounted to £8,610. The fixing of those on posts and irons, averaged at 14s. 6d. each [equalled] £3,045.

The total cost per annum charged to rateable inhabitants was, wrote Malcolm, £5,628. It is a little unclear how this figure was arrived at, but presumably the City Corporation paid for erecting the lights and for maintenance, while the inhabitants paid for only the day-to-day running of them. This £5,628 was raised by fixing the rates as follows: 'Houses under £10 [rent] paid 3s. 6d. per annum; under £20 paid 7s. 6d.; under £30 paid 8s.; under £40 paid 9s. 6d.; upwards of £40 paid 12s.[16]

This rate raised nearly £5,955 on the basis that the more rent your house was worth, the richer you must be. The occupier who paid most towards the rate got the same service as the occupier who paid least. It is possible to test this theory against a little bit of practice to see how the system was applied.

The liberty of Norton Folgate, an extra-parochial enclave of only eleven and a half acres on the eastern edge of the City of London that governed itself through a body of residents or trustees, obtained an Act in 1759 for 'enlightening, cleansing and watching'.[17] At the first meeting to organize the improve-

A typical major London street before the great Paving Act of 1762. This c. 1752 engraving by John Bowles of Cheapside in the City shows a road surface formed with rounded pebble cobbles separated by wooden posts from the flagged pavement. The rough road and the hanging shop signs, a prominent feature of the early-eighteenth-century City, were to go after 1762.

ments, the Liberty Overseer (one of the official posts to which eligible residents were elected annually) reported that thirty-two residents 'had sent their notice in writing of their intention of putting up a lamp at their own expense at their respective houses'. At a subsequent meeting, the trustees resolved on the location of a further thirty lamps to ensure the sufficient 'enlightening of the Liberty'. One, Naboth Farington, was eventually awarded the contract to 'light and keep and repair the lamps' at £1 10s. per lamp per annum, the cost of fixing lamp irons, and 'thirty globular lamps and burners' were £9. So, for an area of eleven and a half acres, sixty-three lamps (a further public lamp was later added to the initial thirty) were provided, with eligible residents of the liberty being rated at 1s. 4d. in the pound to pay for this lighting along with improved cleansing and watching.

The scale of activities in larger parishes is revealed in the notebook of 1773 for paving and lighting St Margaret's, Westminster. Here between 1s. and 1s. 3d. in the pound was raised 'upon all and every person inhabiting, occupying, possessing and enjoying any land, houses, building tenements, etc.'.[18] The number of lamps in this parish is revealed in a lamp report of 1808.[19] It seems that on the night of 5 December the parish had 439 lamps 'up', or burning, 52 'down', with 5 out of operation for

'other' reasons, making a total of 496 for the whole parish. By comparison, the parish of St Anne's, Soho, a more densely populated area, possessed in July 1790 744 lamps. Of these 496 were 'parochiale' and 248 run, apparently, by various occupiers. It cost 15s. per annum to operate each lamp (so £558 total per annum) according to one Jos Hayling, the lamp-lighter contracted by the parish to light and maintain the lamps.[20]

Pierre-Jean Grosley, a Frenchman writing in 1765, both gave an impression of what post-1740 lighting looked like in London and revealed a little more about its organization. 'Two iron pillars ... part of the [area] rails, more or less adorned ... support two lamps that each house is obliged to furnish towards lighting the town.'[21] Grosley is referring to those parishes of west London that were in Middlesex and that continued an improved version of the late-seventeenth-century system where streets were lit by a combination of parish and private lights. Grosley noted that the 'lamps, which are enclosed in crystal globes' were 'lighted ... often half an hour before sun-set', but regretted that they yielded 'immediate light to the foot path, but convey to the middle of the street, only a glimmering'.

This want of penetration was noted in 1810 by Simond, who recorded that the streets of the West

End of London were lit 'at five or six' by lamps 'fixed on irons 8 or 9 ft high, ranged along the houses ... on either side' of the street. However, he regarded these lights as no more than 'little brightish dots, indicative of light, but yielding, in fact, very little'. He thought the problem was the 'want of reflectors' in the lamps. In fact, reflectors had been tried, as Malcolm had explained in 1808, when describing how London had changed since the eighteenth century: 'The only variety that has ... occurred is, the converting of the shape of the lamps from a globular to that of a bell [with] several attempts to introduce strong reflectors [having] failed, as it has been uniformly found that they injure and confuse the light'. The 'several attempts' to which Malcolm referred are probably the experiment of 1803 when Argand lamps – patent oil lamps that were occasion-ally used for interior lighting (see p. 76) – with attached reflectors were set up in New Bond Street.

But more typical than these slightly sour obser-vations of Grosley and Simond are those of Moritz and the German Johann Wilhelm von Archenholz. The former was 'astonished' by the admirable manner in which the streets are lighted up. [They] are so near each other, that even on the most ordi-nary and common nights, the city has the appear-ance of a festive illumination.' Archenholz wrote of London street lighting in the 1780s that 'nothing ... can be more superb. The lamps, which often consist of two, three and sometimes four branches, are enclosed in crystal globes and fixed on posts at a little distance from each other [and stretch along] the great roads within seven or eight miles of town ... the effect is charming.'[22] Archenholz failed to point out the obvious fact that the lamps diminished in number in proportion to the rate-paying popu-lation, so that roads on the edge of London, con-taining few houses, could be extremely poorly lit in comparison with the main streets. This is shown very clearly in Joseph Salway's 1811 'Survey of the Kensington Turnpike Trust Road from Hyde Park Corner to Hammersmith'.[23] In the stretches that were well built up, kerbside lamps were placed on both sides of the street at every third or fourth house, while the lonely tracts of road were only barely lit.

The contribution made by shops also helps to explain why main streets could appear so well illuminated even if equipped with relatively few parish lamps. Shops, like houses (see p. 74), were invariably candle-lit in the eighteenth century and William Hutton observed in the 1780s that he had 'counted twenty-two candles in one little shop.'[24] By the end of the century oil lamps were being introduced into interiors (see p. 76), much to the satisfaction of Malcolm, who noted that the 'store-keepers of London are of infinite service ... by their liberal use of the patent lamps, to shew their commodities'. By comparison with this blaze of light, 'The Parish lamps glimmer ... above.'

By the second decade of the nineteenth century, oil and candle illumination of the streets of London had been replaced by gas. In 1807 experimental gas lights were set up in Pall Mall, St James's, and by 1814 the City of London Gas-Light & Coke Company was in operation, having received its charter in 1812. By 1827 this company, whose works were in Great Peter Street, Westminster, with the South-London Gas-Light & Coke Company on the south bank of the Thames and the Imperial Gas-Light & Coke Company in Hackney and St Pancras, produced annually around 397,000,000 cu. ft of gas, supplying 61,203 private and 7,268 public lamps in the metropolis.[25]

The streets were better lit due to the improved quality and power of the light rather than due to an increased number of lamp standards. In 1827 the parish of St James's, Westminster, possessed 800 gas lamps, whereas the adjacent and comparable parish of St Anne's, Soho, had 744 oil lamps in 1790 (see p. 9).[26]

The manner in which street lighting was arranged in provincial cities is explained in detail by John Wood in his *Essay towards a Description of Bath* of 1742. He notes that Acts of Parliament were passed in 1706, 1710, 1721 and 1739, which together pro-vided for raising money from eligible inhabitants for 'Cleansing, Paving and Enlightening the Streets and Publick ways of the City'. Every householder who was rated as eligible to pay at least one penny a week poor relief, and whose house 'adjoins to any Street, Lane, Alley or Publick Place', was 'Enjoined, from the 14th day of September to the 25th of March ... every Night, to set or hang out Candles, or Lights, in Lanthorns, on the Outside of their respect-ive Houses'. The lights had to be up from when 'it shall grow dark, until Twelve o'clock at Night, upon Pain of forfeiting 2s. for every Default'.

Detail of Antonio Canaletto's view of Northumberland House and the western end of the Strand in c. 1755. This beautifully drawn vignette of Georgian London gives a strong impression of what a stroll through an eighteenth-century city would have been like.

Detail of Samuel Scott's view of Covent Garden in c. 1750 showing Inigo Jones's pioneering uniform terrace of c. 1632. The carriageeway is seemingly paved with pebbles and surface water drains along a meandering central gutter.

PAVING, CLEANSING AND WATCHING

The streets the city dweller walked on or drove through also changed dramatically during the Georgian period. Again, it was a pioneering Act of Parliament for a London district that heralded the changes and that acted as a prototype not only for other areas of London but also for other cities.

The Westminster Paving Act of 1762, like the City of London Lighting Act of 1736, took responsibility for paving from the individual and put it into the hands of commissioners with the power to rate the inhabitants. Previously, all Acts relating to paving had merely attempted to apply more pressure on eligible occupiers to pave and clean a specified area in front of their houses. Typical are the conditions that Wood recorded in his *Description of Bath*: 'as to the Paving of the Streets ... every Occupier or owner of any House ... is required ... within ten Days next after notice given by the Surveyor ... well and sufficiently to pitch or pave ... the Street, Alley or Lane before his or their Houses ... into the

Detail of Edward Dayes's view of Hanover Square, London, in c. 1785. Judging by the location of the sun (it appears to be shining from the north-west!), the painting shows an afternoon scene. Selling milk and victuals was not exclusively a morning occupation, though perhaps the milkmaid is delivering a special order. Note the large smooth stones forming the carriageway.

Detail of a panorama of 1792 (after Robert Barker) showing Westminster and the City from the south bank. To the left are the newly completed terraces of Blackfriars Road; in the centre is Albion Place, designed by Robert Mylne and built 1772–c. 1790; and on the right is Blackfriars Bridge, which was also designed by Mylne and built 1760–69. The organization of the carriageway by use of posts, the lamp-posts and the treatment of the trees are all notable.

Middle of the Street.' The larger London estates, conscious of the advantages of a clean and well ordered environment, usually wrote this obligatiion into the building lease. For example, the Cavendish-Harley Estate specified in 1724 that the lessee

Pave the footway or passage 5 ft wide or there-abouts, and all along the front of the building with good Purbeck stone ... [and] set up good posts of oak on the outside of the paving at convenient distances and pave or pitch with good pebbles, raggstones or flints and gravell all the remaining ground before the said buildings towards the said street. These pavements to be laid at such heights as level as shall be directed.[27]

Specifications as demanding as these were possible only on grander estates during a seller's market such as existed in the mid 1720s, but it should be said that despite the appearance of the 1762 and related Acts, great estates (such as the Bedford Estate in Bloomsbury) continued to enforce their own strict rules for achieving a high standard of paving and cleaning.

It is also interesting that the Cavendish-Harley specifications embody one of the faults that characterized street paving in the first half of the eighteenth century. Saussure observed in 1726 that 'the pavement is so bad and rough that when you drive in a coach you are most cruelly shaken, whereas if you go on foot you have a nice smooth path paved with wide flat stones, and elevated above the road'. Grosley, remembering London before the influence

of the 1762 Act had taken effect, was more specific: 'Pavements in London are formed of stones just as when taken out of the quarry [which] are almost entirely round.' These are the 'pebbles' specified in the Cavendish-Harley building agreement, flanked by slightly raised flat paving. This seems to have been a common enough arrangement for Misson to record that 'on each side of the street there is, almost all over London, a way better pav'd than the rest for foot-passengers'. This view of pre-1762 London is supported by Malcolm, who recalled in his *Anecdotes* that 'The streets of London were extremely inconvenient before ... as the kennels were in the midst, and the stones of the pavements round, nor was there, as at present, a smooth footway for pedestrians.'

The Act of 1762 specified that Purbeck stone replace pebbles in the better streets and that stone kerbs and raised pavement be universal. It also replaced the drainage kennel – dangerously placed in the centre of the street and long a feature of great city streets – with kerbside gutters. This paving of streets remained standard practice until very late in the Georgian period, when street surfaces of tarmacadam and squared granite sets, or cobbles, first appeared. The German prince Hermann Ludwig Püeckler-Muskau, who visited London in 1826 and again in 1828–9, noted the presence of macadam streets in London and described what appears to be cobbling: 'the old pavement has been torn up and replaced by small pieces of granite, the interstices between which are filled with gravel; this renders the riding more easy, and diminishes the noise'.[28]

Crossing a dirty street in c. *1775. The nature of the street surface, formed with small, rounded, pebble-like cobbles, is evident. This type of surface obviously survived in lesser streets in London long after the 1762 Paving Act.*

The Paving Acts of 1762 and later also improved the cleansing of streets and the removal of domestic rubbish, though this latter chore was something in which private estates were also involved. As with paving and lighting, this had generally been carried out by individuals under pressure from the parish. As Wood recorded in his *Description of Bath*:

Every house keeper ... is enjoined, thrice in every week at the least, that is to say, on every Tuesday, Thursday and Saturday, to sweep and cleanse ... all the streets, lanes, alleys and publick places, before their respective houses ... to the end that the filth, ashes, dirt, dust, rubble and rubbish may be ready to be carried away by the scavengers, upon pain to forfeit 3s. 4d. for every offence and neglect.

Street cleansing was achieved by a system of drainage as well as by scavengers paid for by a parish rate. The localized and fairly primitive system of drainage via the sewers was well described by Joseph

Salway, Surveyor to the Kensington Turnpike Trust, when relating how a portion of Knightsbridge was drained in 1811: 'In kennel ... is a grate over a cispool ... that receives [a] drain ... the cispool discharges into an 18-in flat-bottomed arched drain, with which two 9-in square drains from the houses communicate.'[29] Eventually the water was discharged into the nearby Westbourne Brook.

Scavenging seems to have been fairly well organized, if only because street and household dirt could be of some value. For example, ashes collected by the dustmen seem to have been used regularly in the manufacture of inferior place bricks. Saussure recorded that 'carts are used for removing mud, and in the summer time the streets are watered by carts carrying barrels, or casks, pierced with holes through which water flows'.

Malcolm revealed in his *Anecdotes* the demarcation between individual and parish responsibility for street cleanliness suggested by Wood, and that had, presumably, become customary by the early-nineteenth century. The eligible occupant was responsible for sweeping the pavement before his house while the parish scavenger removed the dirt, and that on the carriageway. There were, he noted with obvious civic pride,

Salutary laws provided for the performance of those acts of cleanliness which individuals might neglect. To clean the steps and pavement in front of a house the law commands them to do so every morning under a penalty of 5s. Scavengers are appointed to sweep the carriageways, and carry off the dust ... the publick are very properly forbid to throw any kind of dust into the street, and are ordered to reserve it for the dustman, who is enjoined to call for it frequently ...

and who would come, according to Southey, tolling his bell 'and his chaunt of dust ho!'

Added to the activities of the scavenger were, recorded Malcolm, the 'laudable efforts of the sweepers, male and female, who, stationed at corners and crossings, faithfully remove every appearance of soil from the stones for the casual receipt of a half-pence'. On the minus side was the anti-social behaviour of the *habitués* of the beerhouses – probably mostly unemployed members of the building trades (see p. 122) – who clearly worried Malcolm greatly. 'Beer-houses render our streets extremely

One of the perils of the street: the 'mop trundler' could ruin a man's suit of clothes at the mere flick of the wrist. In this print of c. 1760 the housemaid wears pattens on her feet – presumably to protect her shoes from the wet pavement. She has brushed and mopped the street in accordance with estate or parish requirements.

unpleasant in summer; and delicacy forbids my adding more on the subject. Would that equal delicacy in the keepers would turn their customers backwards.'

This prim observation reveals one of the great problems facing urban reformers in the Georgian period. They could legislate and impose rates and fines for non-performance on docile landlords and lessees, but they could not impose their will or standards of behaviour on the casually employed, the unemployed and workers such as porters and labourers, the impoverished denizens of rookeries, common lodging-houses and unfurnished rooms – in short, the mob that made up a large proportion of a Georgian city such as London. The streets were ungovernable and any behaviour short of absolute riot fell below the field of vision of central authority, which was not equipped with an efficient police force. Malcolm expressed the impotent rage of the wronged middle class: 'The rentors of single rooms, in first, second and third floors, in mean streets, feel themselves above restraint. Those people empty dirty water mixed with their offal into the gutters, the stench of which is appalling.'

Although it could hardly have been appropriate to call out the army to chasten a beerhouse full of drunken builders or to enforce good behaviour on unruly garret dwellers, there was the watch. Like scavenging and lighting, the watch was paid for out of the parish rates, but its job was more of caretaker than law enforcer. Its activities were well described and its limitations implied by Saussure:

London does not possess any watchmen, either on foot or on horseback as in Paris, to prevent murder and robbery; the only watchman you see is a man in every street carrying a stick and a lantern who, every time the clock strikes, calls out the hour, and state of the weather. The first time this man goes on his rounds he pushes the doors of the shops and houses with his stick to ascertain whether they are properly fastened, and if they are not he warns the proprietors.

Substance is given to this observation by the records of the liberty of Norton Folgate.[30] As part of its 'enlightening, cleansing and watching' Act of 1759, a beadle was appointed, at the wage of £20 per annum, to, among other duties, 'keep the liberty clear of vagabonds and people making a shop to sell

A watchman, drawn in c. 1775. He is probably patrolling a late-seventeenth-century City street. Shown here are his standard accoutrements: lamp, rattle, staff and watch. The accoutrements of the street are also typical of the date: timber posts defending the pedestrians from wayward carriages; globular oil lamps on area railings; and a fashionably dressed, if somewhat exhausted, harlot.

fruit, etc.' and to 'set the watch, attend at the watch house [and] to keep the book which of the watchmen's turn it is to be in each stand'.

Six watchmen were employed, at £12 each per annum, and four watch stands built, to guard this enclave of eleven and a half acres. The watch, it was ordered, was to 'beat their rounds every half hour ... from nine o'clock in the evening to six in ye morning from Michaelmas to Lady Day, and from ten in the evening to four in the morning from Lady Day to Michaelmas'. The duties of the watchmen were also specified: 'Four watchmen out of their stand at ye same time, ye other two in ye watch house who relieve those on their stands alternately every hour'. During their rounds these men were to 'apprehend and detain all malefactors, rogues,

The traditional fate of the charley, or nightwatchman, was to be trounced by drunken young blades out on the town. This sketch of 1820 by George Cruikshank shows not only the disadvantages of snoozing in the stand but also the lumbering forms of charleys patrolling the bounds of the City around Temple Bar. By this time of the morning – 6.15 according to the clock on St Clement Danes – private lamps have burnt out.

vagabonds, disturbers of the peace ... deliver to the constable, headborough [both posts held by elected residents of the liberty] or the beadle ... and then with all convenient speed' to 'some justice or justices of the peace to be examined and dealt with according to law'. Perhaps indicative of a special nuisance, the watchmen were also charged to deal out the same treatment to 'any persons casting night soil in the street'.

As with so many aspects of the Georgian city, the effects of the Paving Acts and the behaviour of its inhabitants are best seen in context through the eyes of observant foreign visitors. In 1784 the French writer François de La Rochefoucauld recorded that 'All the London streets are magnificently wide ... all of them have paths on each side for the convenience of pedestrians [and] are usually quite clean',[31] while Meister, who visited London in 1789, felt compelled to describe the paving arrangement in some detail. The pedestrian pavements were, he noted,

raised about 4 or 5 ins, and are of unequal width; in the little streets they are not more than a foot

broad, and from that to 15 or 18 ins, but in Oxford Street they are above 6 ft wide. The flag stones which cover these footways are large and smooth; and, as there is a tax imposed on housekeepers for the pavement, they are constantly repaired as there becomes a necessity.

STREET HAZARDS

Archenholz, writing in 1789, drew attention to another of the provisions of the 1762 Paving Act, one that was to revolutionize the appearance of London and later that of other cities:

About twenty years since [London] ... was the worst paved city in Europe. From almost every house an enormous sign was suspended, which darkened the street, often fell down, and sometimes killed people. Two Acts of Parliament appeared almost at the same time ... the signs disappeared, and the streets of London were covered with a pavement unrivalled in its kind [which allows] ... the passenger, without

*being uncommoded by the horses or carriages, [to]
pass freely along.*

Street signs had been one of the sights of early-
eighteenth-century London. Saussure felt that what
made the Strand, Fleet Street, Cheapside and
Cornhill interesting was the fact that 'Every . . . shop
has a sign of copper, pewter, or wood painted and
gilded [which] hung on big iron branches, and sometimes on gilt ones.' By the mid-eighteenth century
these signs were generally, it seems, regarded as
unsightly and as a health hazard. Not only did
they occasionally crash down upon the heads of
unsuspecting pedestrians but they also interfered
with the circulation of air, and this, to the
eighteenth-century mind, was a terrible crime. Air,
it was thought, made a great, if mysterious, contribution to man's health and well-being: too much
could be bad, so windows would be kept shut to
prevent the miasma of disease flowing into the
home; too little could also be a problem, but worst
of all was stagnant air bereft of its 'vivifying spirit'.[32]

Malcolm painted a vivid picture of street life
under the ominous and sometimes murderous presence of the swinging signs and other impedimenta
attached to roadside buildings. In his *Anecdotes* he
wrote:

*The streets were generally badly paved, very dirty
and not sufficiently lighted: and the signs prevented
a free circulation of the air and views of the streets,
while the posts contributed to impede the passenger.
Nor were the penthouses less injurious, loaded with
flower pots [they] occasioned dangerous hurt by the
fall of the latter and the watering of the plants in
them contributed, with the projecting spouts, in
rainy weather to sluice the citizen, who at the same
time steered an undulating or zigzag way through
the wheel barrows and bawling owners. Another
complaint peculiar to this period was the ambition
of shop keepers, who encroached upon the footways
by bow-windows. When an example was set, the
whole fraternity, fired with emulation, thrust each
new one beyond his neighbour. Such were the
impediments to walking so recently as 1766. The
reader may imagine how a Londoner must have felt
during a high wind and shower; a thousand signs
swinging on rusty hinges above him, threatening
ruin to his person at every step, and a thousand
spouts pouring cascades at his luckless head.*

London, as befitted the commercial centre of the
kingdom, again led the way in legislating out the
anti-social side of trading with the Paving Act of
1762, which forbid hanging signs in Westminster.
Quite why this legislation was ignored by inns is not
clear, but the generality of shops did turn to the use
of fascias above the shops' windows such as remain
with us today.

In 1765 the same committee that reported on
street signs and water spouts arranged a plan, wrote
Malcolm, 'for inscribing the name of streets, lanes
and alleys on their corners'. In addition, he recorded,
'the nobility introduced brass plates or door plates,
with their names engraved on them; [while] the
numbering of the houses completed this portion of
the great work of amendment'. It is hard to say how
quickly this practice spread through London, let
alone other cities, but Archenholz could remark of
London in 1789 that 'Every street, whether large or
small, courts, alleys, etc., have their names painted
at each corner. All the doors are numbered and . . .
generally have the names of their owners engraved
on a brass plate.'

To complete the list of threats from theoretically
inanimate objects that attended a stroll through a
mid-eighteenth-century city, it is only necessary to
add some observations made by Meister:

*you must be careful not to forget, as you are passing
along, that you approach, every moment, the brink
of a precipice. Here it is a hole of some coal vault,
there the passage, or rather stairs, into a kitchen,
workshops, or cellar for foods, or where wine, beer
or cider are sold. These little abysses are sometimes
shut up with an awkward kind of rail, or ill made
door, but in the day time are for the most part open;
and the danger of stumbling into these pitfalls is the
greater as some of them advance further on the
pavement than others.*

As well as dodging the inanimate objects that
threatened his destruction, the man in the street also
had to contend with the extraordinary behaviour of
his fellow-pedestrians. Two accounts give an idea of
the hazards of using London streets in the eighteenth
century. Saussure recorded that

*sedan chairs . . . are allowed to be carried on the
footpath and when a person does not take heed, or
a stranger does not understand the 'Have care', or*

'*By your leave, Sir*', *of the bearers and does not make room to let them pass, he will run a great risk of being knocked down, for the bearers go very fast and cannot turn aside with their burden. I went through the experience on first coming to London. Not understanding the 'By your leave' addressed to me, I did not draw aside, and repented quickly, for I received a push which hurled me four feet further on.*

Chairmen and porters were obviously terrors of the street. James Boswell, in his *London Journal*, remarked that the only advantage of being confined

to his lodgings was that he avoided being troubled with dirty streets and jostling chairmen,[33] while Georg Christoph Lichtenberg, a German who was in London in 1770 and 1774, gave a fine description of the porter in a remarkable vivid vignette of street life:

You stop and bump – a porter runs against your shoulder. 'By your leave', after he has knocked you down. In the road itself chaise after chaise, coach after coach, cart after cart. Through all this din and clamour, and the noise of thousands of tongues and feet, you hear the bells from the church-steeples,

MISERIES OF LONDON.

Above: *One of the miseries of London, according to Thomas Rowlandson, was heavy traffic and the consequent disruption of private life. The pair in the carriage on the left, stuck in an 1807 traffic jam, are late for a dinner engagement.*

Opposite: *The parish and the government appointed tax collectors to gather (often on a quarterly basis) their respective rates or taxes from eligible city dwellers. These visitations were, of course, unpopular, particularly when further taxes and higher levels of taxation were introduced to cope first with the American and then the Napoleonic wars. This cartoon of 1806 by James Gillray records some of the things then taxed. Details to note are the unsatisfactory nature of the yard surface and the exposed oil reservoir and wick of the shattered oil lamp.*

postmen's bells, the street-organs, fiddles and tambourines of itinerant musicians, and the cries of the vendors of hot and cold food at the street corners. A rocket blazes up stories high amidst a yelling crowd of beggars, sailors and urchins. Some one shouts 'Stop, thief', his handkerchief is gone. Every one runs and presses forward, some less concerned to catch the thief than to steal a watch or purse for themselves. Before you are aware of it a young well-dressed girl has seized your hand. 'Come, my lord, come along, let us drink a glass together', or 'I'll go with you if you please.' An accident happens not forty paces away. 'God bless me', calls one. 'Poor fellow', cries another. A stoppage ensues and you look to your pockets. Every one seems intent on helping the victim. Then there is laughter again: some one has fallen into the gutter. 'Look there, damn me', cries a third, and the crowd passes on. Next comes a yell from a hundred throats as if fire had broken out, or a house was falling, or a patriot had looked out of a window. In Göttingen you can go anywhere and get within forty paces to see what is happening. Here, that is at night and in the City, you are lucky to escape with a whole skin down a side alley until the tumult is over. Even in the wider streets all the world rushes headlong without looking, as if summoned to the bedside of the dying. That is Cheapside and Fleet Street on a December evening.[34]

Chapter Two

WORK AND PLAY

WAYS OF LIFE

One of the intriguing aspects of eighteenth- and early-nineteenth-century urban life is the timetable of daily activities; when did journeymen arrive for work, when did people dine, when did evening entertainments such as the theatre begin? The answers are a little complex, for not only did habits change in the hundred years after 1714, but the different classes pursued different regimes, rising and eating at quite different times. Also, in London there was an added complexity, for, in their social habits, the City and Westminster were worlds apart. The social and architectural contrasts between these two adjoining cities fascinated visitors to London, and their attempts to describe each, and the differences between the two, provide much information about both the social habits and the appearance of London.

Christian Goede, a German who was in London from 1802 to 1804, painted a pair of excellent portraits of these two faces of London. He visited the city on a spring morning. At six o'clock he found the streets perfectly empty; then a few people appeared, 'such as carpenters, brick layers then going to their several occupations'. At eight o'clock, 'city shops are opened ... hackney coaches begin to rattle ... the unmarried man calls for his breakfast at a coffee-house'. At nine o'clock, 'rich merchants come to their counting houses from their country box's, in elegant equipages: and all the streets near the Thames are crowded in the extreme'. At one o'clock, 'everything is alive. Carriages from the West End begin to crowd the city ... The foot-pavement all this time is so thronged that it is difficult to get along

... men of business now go upon "Change".' At three o'clock, 'The fashionable have finished shopping ... and now the Bank and Exchange closes and the merchants repair to dinner.' At five o'clock, 'The City coffee-houses fill with company, and avenues adjacent to the Thames are quite deserted ... Towards dark the shops displaying their elegant lamps are in such profusion as to produce a very brilliant effect ... And now thousands of unfortunate women begin to infest the street, to the convenience of some and annoyance of others ...' At ten o'clock, 'the shops close; the streets consequently darken, and the crowd gradually disperses. Now gamblers, house-breakers, and robbers of all descriptions steal from their haunts ... but the public streets are ... much frequented till after midnight, and so well guarded by the common watchman and the police.'

Of the West End, Goede observed that, till eleven in the morning, 'all the streets in ths part of town are still and desolate ... a groom here or there ... or tradesmen attending for a commission; but otherwise not a soul is visible'. At one o'clock, 'The street begins to fill with carriages and saddle horses and now the people of fashion begin to move. The ladies form parties to go shopping and the gentlemen, accompanied by a single groom, sally forth on a morning ride. In the meantime the square fills with ladies in their morning dress, presenting lovely groups to the observation of the passengers.' In Bond Street women shop, while 'the gentlemen pass on horseback up and down the street, to see and to be seen. [The] foot-pavement is so perfectly covered with elegantly dressed people as to make it difficult to move.' At three o'clock, 'all the world hurries to Hyde Park, where the procession returns between

Portland Place, looking north, c. 1800. The grander streets of west London were free of commerce and trades, and were enlivened spasmodically by visitors calling on residents, street vendors calling their wares, shopmen delivering their goods or servants taking messages. In contrast, the City was all animation, (see page 2).

four and five and thus the morning concludes'. 'This part of town at night appears more gloomy than the City for want of the illumination from the shop windows, but there are regular rows of lamps ... we shall scarce meet a creature [in the streets] unless it be some fair nymph prowling for a hard-earned supper.'[1]

Other observers both confirm and extend Goede's analysis of the differing quality of life in the City and Westminster. In 1789 Archenholz noted that 'shops are open by eight o'clock every morning in the city; all is then in motion, everybody at work, while on the other hand, at the west end of town, the streets are empty ... and even the very domestics are asleep.'[2] Anderson, who was first in London in 1802, noted that the 'fashionable streets at the west end of town' were 'perfectly undisturbed by the noise of carts, waggons or fishermen, dustmen, etc.' until noon, when 'footmen ... partly half dressed, and some in full dress, were seen hurrying in various directions; and female domestics came out with chil-

dren to take the morning air'.[3]

Moritz painted a pretty picture of West End life in the 1780s: 'In the morning, it is usual to walk out in a sort of négligé or morning dress, your hair not dressed, but merely rolled up in rollers, and in a frock and boots. In Westminster the morning lasts until four or five o'clock, at which time they dine; and supper and going to bed are regulated accordingly.' Of the other side of town, Moritz observed that 'the further you go from court into the City, the more regular and domestic the people become, and there they generally dine about three o'clock, i.e., as soon as the business or "Change" is over'.[4]

Sophie von la Roche from France lodged in Portland Street, Marylebone, in 1785 and Louis Simond near Portman Square, also in Marylebone, in 1810. Both their accounts are interesting because they make it possible to see, if only dimly, a Georgian street through Georgian eyes: they also hint at the sort of noises that filled the background and explain

A collection of beaux and belles in Bond Street c. 1820. Bond Street was the fashionable place for afternoon parade – the place to see and be seen in Regency London.

what the few people visible in their fashionable West End streets were actually doing. Sophie first:

I was already dressed when I saw the first workmen passing and heard a young voice calling 'chimney-sweep, chimney-sweep' and perceived a tiny chimney-sweep boy, six years old, running along barefoot at his master's side, his soot bag on his back, shouting for all he was worth; then I saw the milk-maid calling in the district, and some youths from the apothecary with china pans, and the maids coming up from the basement through the railings in front of the house to buy their milk.[5]

This reference to the use of steps in basements as a means of getting goods into the house is most important, because there is little archaeological evidence that basement steps were supplied regularly before about 1770. Richard Rush, who also lived in Marylebone, recorded a similar event in about 1817: 'You perhaps saw nobody before noon, unless ... a butcher's boy with tray in hand issuing here and there from an area.'[6]

Louis Simond's account reveals that little had changed in Marylebone in the quarter of a century that separated his residence from that of Sophie von la Roche:

Not a mouse stirring before ten o'clock [then] milk-women with their pails perfectly neat ... ring at every door, with reiterated pull, to hasten the maid servants, who come half asleep to receive a measure as big as an egg being the allowance of a family ... milk is not here food or drink but a tincture – an elixir exhibited in drops, five or six at most, in a cup of tea; morning and evening ... The first considerable stir is the drum and military music of the guards, marching from their barracks to Hyde Park, having at their head three or four Negro giants ...

About three or four o'clock the fashionable world gives some sign of life, issuing forth to pay visits, or rather leave cards at the doors of friends ... to go to shops, see sights or lounge in Bond Street. At five or six they return home to dress for dinner [now] the noise of wheels increases: it is their dinner hour ...[7]

Jane Austen, describing street noises in Bath in about 1815, confirms that the Georgian city was far from quiet; she noted the dash of carriages, 'the heavy rumble of carts and drays, the bawling of newsmen, muffin-men and milkmen, and the ceaseless clink of pattens'.[8]

Grosley was explicit about the timetable of activities for Londoners in the 1760s:

Regarding Bankers, Merchants, lower Physicians, and all citizens in general [in London] ... They rise a little of the latest, and pass an hour at home, drinking tea with their families; about ten they go to the coffee-house, where they spend another hour; then they go home, or meet people about business; at two o'clock they go to the Change; on their return, they lounge a little longer at the coffee-house, and then dine about four. Thirty years ago two was the hour of dining, and before that one: the hour of going to Change interfered with dinner time, so that the merchants thought it most advisable, not to dine till their return from Change. Since this arrangement, dinner concludes the day, and they give the remainder of it to their friends ... About ten at night they go home to bed [if been out] after taking a slight repast.[9]

Malcolm gave what appears to be the definitive breakdown of the social habits of the four classes of London in the early-nineteenth century: 'journeyman', 'tradesman', 'opulent tradesman and merchant' and the 'nobility':

The usual time of rising with the class of Journey-man is between five and six in the morning. At the latter hour they commence their daily labour and work till eight; an hour is then allowed for breakfast, and from twelve to one for dinner; and the business of the day concludes at six; but some industrious men work many extra hours ... The Tradesman and his lodger generally rise about the same hour, from six to nine o'clock ... Tea, coffee, cocoa, roll and toast, and bread and butter, form the breakfast

Bloomsbury Square in 1787. West End squares, tranquil, pleasingly planted (indeed bucolic) and well inhabited, were popular places for elegant parade. Note the profusion of lamps on area railings, the paving of the carriageway with large stones and the gutter drainage.

of this class of the community [tradesmen]; and the hours of dining vary from one till half past four ... Tea etc. succeeds from five to six o'clock and a slight supper at nine. The evening is variously spent, on visits, at the Playhouse, or with the eternal use of cards.

The opulent Tradesman ... and the Merchant, live much in the [same] manner [as ordinary tradesmen] in many respects; but, as the family never do anything themselves, a cook, a house-maid, a Nursery-maid, and a foot-boy, or foot-man become necessary ... [They] ... breakfast at nine, ten and eleven, dine at four, five or six [when] several hours elapse in drinking wine ... the Ladies retire to cards till the Gentlemen are summoned to tea. Supper ensues and the bottle finishes the scene at a late-hour.

Among persons of ancient families ... and the nobility ... early rising is neither necessary, nor is it universally practised. Breakfast often makes its appearance at the Tradesman's hour of dining. Novels, newspapers, magazines and reviews ... are spread abroad on the breakfast room, and offer amusement and conversation while the languid operation of eating is performed ... Five, six, seven is dinner. Tea and coffee generally make their appearance before the wine and fruits are removed, but there are some who retire to the drawing room for the use of those refreshments ... supper may be introduced from ten o'clock till two in the morning.[10]

BREAKFAST

This somewhat glib description of the community of the Georgian city can be usefully checked and enlarged by reference to other contemporary accounts. Grosley implies that breakfast was about nine o'clock for 'Bankers, merchants, etc.'; Malcolm said this class breakfasted at nine, ten and eleven. La Rochefoucauld stated that 'throughout England it is the custom to breakfast together' and that 'the commonest breakfast hour is nine o'clock'.[11] He clearly included the journeyman class in this sweeping statement. Geijer confirmed that nine o'clock was the breakfast hour, and that it was a social event of some importance: 'the whole family gather

for what is here called breakfast, that is to say round the tea-table'.[12]

The food consumed during the breakfast hour and the behaviour of the participants clearly surprised foreign observers in the eighteenth and early-nineteenth centuries, though they seem unexceptional enough today. La Rochefoucauld noted that 'Breakfast consists of tea and bread' and that 'the morning newspapers are on the table ... so that conversation is not of a lively nature.' The character of the fare was so unusual to Moritz that he felt obliged to describe it as if he were writing from some distant and alien land: 'a kind of bread and butter [is] usually eaten with tea, which is toasted by the fire, and is incomparably good. You take one slice after the other and hold it to the fire on a fork till the butter is melted, so that it penetrates a number of slices all at once; this is called toast.' Also present on the breakfast-table could be, as Boswell wrote in 1763, 'that admirable viand, marmalade'.[13] Of tea, the foreign visitor recorded that it was a passion amongst Englishmen of all classes. 'Throughout the whole of England,' wrote La Rochefoucauld, 'the drinking of tea is general. You have it twice a day and, though its expense is considerable, the humblest peasant has tea twice a day just like the rich man.' Geijer too recorded that 'Next to water tea is the Englishman's proper element.'

The accoutrements and rituals of breakfast were best described, if in a somewhat exaggerated manner, by Southey in 1807.

The breakfast-table is a cheerful sight ... porcelain ... is ranged on a Japan waiter ... the hostess sits at the head of the board and opposite to her the boiling water smokes and sings in an urn of Etruscan shape. The coffee is contained in a smaller vase of the same shape, or in a larger kind of tea-pot wherein the grain is suspended in a bag ... [The tea] is made in a vessel of silver, or of fine black porcelain; they do not use boiled milk with it, but cream instead in its fresh state, which renders it a very delightful beverage.

Bread, according to Southey, was eaten 'either in thin slices, or toasted, or in small hot loaves, always with butter'.[14]

The breakfast of the common working man – the journeyman – eaten at around eight, after about two hours' work, was of the same substances. It could,

as Malcolm suggested, be had from 'Public houses [which] will either send tea and bread and butter to the Journeyman for breakfast, or provide it for him at the house'. Alternatively, the working man could purchase a breakfast with tea from a street stall: 'If one is out on the London streets early in the morning,' wrote Geijer in 1809, 'one may see in many places small tables set up under the open sky, round which coal carters and workmen empty their cups of this delicious beverage.' Benjamin Franklin, who worked as a printer in London in 1725, painted a lurid picture of the English working man's breakfast, which took the form of 'a pint of beer before breakfast followed by a pint with bread and cheese for breakfast'. For himself, Franklin obtained 'a good basin of warm gruel, in which was a small slice of butter, with toasted bread and nutmeg'. This cost him three halfpence.[15]

DINNER

The hour for dinner was even more susceptible to class differences than was breakfast. Dinner was the main meal of the day. Indeed, it could be the only real meal, as breakfast consisted of nothing more than tea and toast, and supper was an optional meal that, if taken, comprised a light repast of cold meats. Lunch in the first half of the century was an informal midday snack. The 1765 edition of *Dyche's Dictionary* defines it thus: 'Nunchion or Lunchion: a meal between the set time of dinner and supper'. In Dr Johnson's dictionary it is described as 'a piece of victual eaten between meals'. Quite when this casual repast – also referred to as 'Nooning' by Susanna Whatman in 1776[16] – became elevated to a formal meal is not clear, although the increased importance of the midday snack must reflect the tendency during the eighteenth and early-nineteenth centuries for dinner to be taken ever later in the day, moving

from around two o'clock in 1700 to five o'clock in 1800.

In 1710 the German Z.C. von Uffenbach visited London and identified dinner time as 'towards two o'clock';[17] in about 1714 J. Mackey, a Scot who had spent many years abroad, wrote that 'at two we generally go to Dinner';[18] and in 1727 Saussure explained that 'Dinner is taken at two or three o'clock, sometimes even later, and there is no supper.'[19]

Grosley and Moritz observed that bankers, merchants 'and all other citizens' dined between three and four o'clock because they were occupied until then with business in the City. This point is confirmed by Goede, who noted in 1802 that at three o'clock 'the Bank and exchange close [and] the merchant repairs to dinner'.[20] Boswell recorded in 1763 that 'our time of dining is three o'clock', while Southey wrote in the early-nineteenth century that 'the labouring part of the community dine at one, the highest rank at six, seven or even eight', but that 'the dinner hour is usually five'.

La Rochefoucauld had already noted in 1784 that 'five o'clock . . . is the dinner time'. But even amongst the middle classes in late-eighteenth-century London the dining hour was not absolutely fixed, for, in the same decade, Sophie von la Roche was still able to conclude of the English that 'they eat at three thirty here' and in 1809 Geijer – clearly confused – wrote both that 'between one and two o'clock dinner is eaten' and that 'The order of a day in London . . . one gets up at nine o'clock, greets people with a good morning up till five in the afternoon, when one eats dinner and goes to bed between twelve and one at night.' Even Jane Austen, in *Northanger Abbey*, begun in 1797, had dinner starting at both five o'clock and at four o'clock.[21] Rush (who had been the United States Ambassador to England from 1817 to 1825) gave a timetable for an exceptionally grand London dinner: the invitation was for seven o'clock, before eight dinner was announced, soon after nine the ladies left table, and before ten

Opposite, top: A familiar morning scene: a watchman in his stand, a woman selling salop, and her customers. From W.H. Pyne's The Costume of Great Britain, *1805. Charles Lamb, in his essay 'The Praise of Chimney-sweepers' of 1822, describes salop as made of 'sweet wood 'yclept-sassafras . . . boiled down to a kind of tea, and tempered with an infusion of milk and sugar'.*

Opposite, bottom: Breakfast in the street for the early-rising working man and the pauper. Note the mechanism of the early gas lamp. This scene of 1825 is by M. Egerton.

A table laid for tea: detail from Johann Zoffany's painting c. 1770 *of the de Broke family. The tea urn is particularly fine. The china stands on a Pontypool tin tray and the teapot on its own special saucer. In the background is a hob grate, seemingly with stone cheeks and iron bars, of the type that preceded the later-eighteenth-century cast-iron mass-produced hob grates of Coalbrookdale and Carron.*

the gentlemen followed. The company then 'broke into knots, or loitered through the drawing rooms' and left at eleven. At another dinner Rush recorded that 'ten o'clock arriving, with little disposition to rise from table', the gentlemen played Twenty Questions. This lasted until twelve when they rose from table and went upstairs for coffee.

The process as well as the hour of eating dinner varied from class to class and could be more or less elaborate depending on the degree of formality demanded by the occasion. 'The Journeyman and Labourer,' wrote Malcolm, 'sometimes eat ... on the spot where they work; others return to their homes to dine; and others eat at the Cook's-shop at which they may have what quantity they please of baked and boiled meat ... and pease pudding, at a very reasonable rate.'

The cook-shop was one of the institutions of London most appreciated by the natives of all classes and much puzzled over by foreigners. Misson

The ritual of taking tea: from the heated urn hot water is poured into the teapot. Thomas Rowlandson, c. 1795.

deemed the cook-shop and its services worthy of detailed description:

There are cook shops enow in all parts of the town, where it is very common to go and chuse upon the spit the part you like, and to eat it there. A Frenchman of any distinction would think it a great scandal in France to be seen to eat in such a place; and, indeed, custom will not allow it there; but in England they laugh at such niceties. One of the first

Lords of the court makes no scruple to take a Hack, if his coach makes him wait too long; and a Gentleman of 1,500 livres a year enters a cook's shop without fear of being at all despis'd for it, and there dines for his shilling to his heart's content.

Generally four spits, one over another, carry round each five or six pieces of Butcher's meat (never anything else; if you would have a fowl or a pidgeon you must bespeak it). Beef, Mutton or Veal, Pork and Lamb; you have what quantity you please cut

A busy city chop-house in the 1790s drawn by Thomas Rowlandson. Dining here would have cost 1s. a head.

off, fat, lean, much or little done; with this, a little salt, and mustard upon the side of a plate, a Bottle of beer, and a roll.[22]

Samuel Johnson used such an establishment when he came to London in the 1730s: 'I dined (said he) very well for 8*d.*, with very good company, at the Pine-Apple in New Street [Covent Garden] ... it used to cost the rest 1*s.* for they drank wine; but I had a cut of meat for 6*d.*, and bread for a penny, and gave the waiter a penny.'[23] The seating arrangements of such establishments were described by Boswell in his *London Journal 1762–3* when praising a beefsteak-house, which, like a chop-house, was a slightly more comfortably appointed cook-shop: 'You come in thence to a warm, comfortable large room, where a number of people are sitting at table. You take whatever place you find empty; call for what you like, which you get well and cleverly dress-ed.' Boswell wrote that this type of meal – 'beef, bread and beer and [a penny for the] waiter' – still cost a shilling in 1763. Moritz, twenty years later, also paid a shilling in an 'eating house' for 'some roast meat and a salad'. He objected to having

to give nearly half as much to the waiter. These observers must have been using very superior cook-shops, for there was most certainly another world of dining-cellars where the journeyman, earning at most three shillings a day wages (see p. 121), would have dined. Their sort of dinner is hinted at by Daniel Defoe in his novel *Colonel Jack*, published in 1722. The pauper hero, having unexpectedly come into a few guineas, followed the frugal habits of the poor of London and 'went to a boyling house ... and got a Mess of Broth, and a piece of Bread, Price a Half-penny', with an occasional halfpenny worth of cheese and 'very seldom any meat'. The eating expenses of Defoe's hero 'did not amount to above 2*d.* or 3*d.* a week'. John Macdonald, in his *Memoirs of an Eighteenth-century Footman*, recorded that in 1745 in Scotland, 'a working man could dine well for two-pence',[24] with his meal consisting of bread, meat and broth.

The presence of fast-food eating shops catering for all classes suggests that the average city dweller did not generally eat dinner at home. Indeed, this idea is supported by Misson, who recorded of Londoners that 'they do not invite their friends to eat

A coffee-house in Cleveland Street, Fitzroy Square, London, drawn in c. 1825 by George Scharf. Coffee-houses, chop-houses and cook-houses of this modest scale, created within the ground floor of a standard domestic terrace house, nourished much of the population of Georgian cities.

at their houses so frequently as we do in France'. This custom is explained partly by the fact that many people dwelt not in houses but in parts of houses, in lodgings or in furnished rooms that could be far from presentable (see p. 60). It is also explained by the fact that, as well as economically priced cook-shops and eating-houses, there were taverns and coffee-houses providing accommodation more comfortable, convenient and commodious than the generality of lodgings could offer. Misson praised coffee-houses, for 'you have all manner of news there: you have a good fire, which you may sit by as long as you please: you have a dish of coffee: you meet your friends for the transaction of business, and all for a penny, if you don't care to spend more'. Samuel Johnson confirmed the role of the coffee-house as a surrogate home when he told Boswell how, in the 1730s, an Irish painter had assured him

that £30 a year was enough to enable a man to live [in London] without being contemptible. He allowed £10 for clothes and linen. He said a man might live in a garret for 18d. a week; few people would inquire where he lodged; if they did, it was easy to say, 'Sir, I am to be found at such a place.' By spending 3d. at a coffee house, he might be for some hours every day in very good company; he might dine for 6d., breakfast on bread and milk for a penny, and do without supper. On clean-shirt-day he went abroad, and paid visits.[25]

A middle-class family at dinner in 1783. The artist, Robert Dighton, entitled the view Master Parson with a Good Living. *The liveried servant, pulling the cork from a bottle of wine, certainly singles this parson out as someone special.*

Even if dinner was taken at home, a householder, as well as a lodger, was quite likely to have had the food sent in ready-cooked. Misson observed that 'as to eating [in London] there are many ways for that, including . . . having victuals brought to your lodgings' and John Macdonald recalled that in 1773 his master, who lodged in Pall Mall Court, 'had his dinners from the Star and Garter'. Boswell, in his

London Journal 1762–3, revealed one of the reasons for this course of action: 'Temple and his brother and I dined in their chambers, where we had dinner brought, thinking it a more genteel and agreeable way than in a chop-house.' In 1807 Southey, describing the morning scene in London, mentioned 'the porter-house boy [coming] for the pewter pots which had been sent out for supper the preceding night'.

No matter where the food and drink came from, if it were to be taken at home, and the occasion was in any manner formal, then the business of dinner was lengthy. 'When you live in a provincial town,' La Rochefoucauld observed, 'and are invited out to dinner, it is customary to start at three o'clock [and] stay until ten, for in no circumstances will an Englishman hurry over his food and drink.' La Rochefoucauld was undisguised in his horror of the ordeal: 'Dinner is one of the most wearisome of English experiences lasting, as it does, four or five hours.'

However, the lengthy dinner ritual was made bearable by being broken down into a series of digestible portions. The first event was the gathering. This seems an indistinct event, only on the periphery of the ritual of dinner, and it receives scant mention in otherwise highly detailed accounts of dinner parties. Indeed, it is possible that the guests sometimes met in the dining-room, or dining-parlour, and sat straight down at the table. There is certainly very little evidence to suggest that the formal procession from drawing-room to dining-room – which was an important part of country house life from at least the mid-eighteenth century – was undertaken in the town house at the same period. Even on the rare occasion when pre-dinner gatherings are mentioned, processions are not. For example, La Rochefoucauld merely said: 'At four o'clock precisely you present yourself in the drawing room [and] strangers go first into the dining room and sit near the hostess.' Similarly Anderson, who visited Edinburgh in the very early years of the nineteenth century, described dining with a laird, implying that the event took place in the city, and recorded that 'we were ushered into a magnificent drawing room where we found the laird' and his family and were 'shortly afterward ... summoned to dinner'. James Boswell, when he dined in the City of London in 1776 with Dr Johnson and John Wilkes, recorded in his *Life of Johnson* that they all gathered in the drawing-room until the 'cheering sound of "Dinner is upon the table" dissolved the reverie'.

Tobias Smollett gave slightly more detail in his novel *Roderick Random* of 1748. Here he suggested that men gathered before dinner and met the women in the dining-room. Random, invited to dine in a house in Bath, was 'very kindly received by the squire, who sat smoking his pipe in a parlour, and asked if we chose to drink anything before dinner ... We sat down ... and entered into conversation, which lasted half an hour ... when ... a servant coming in, gave us notice that dinner was upon the table.' Random then 'ascended the staircase' – revealing that in Bath, as in London, it was a custom to have first-floor dining-rooms (see p. 54) – and met the daughter of the house for the first time that evening or, as Smollett put it: 'When I entered the dining room, the first object that saluted my ravished eyes, was the divine Narcissa.' Jane Austen, in *Emma*, also has her dinner guests gather in the drawing-room before dinner, and then return to it afterwards for tea.[26]

If a formal progress was called for, the order in which the guests were dispatched from the drawing-room determined their placing at the table, and that women sat together at one end and men at the other. John Trusler, in his *Honours of the Table* of 1788, explained:

When dinner is announced, the mistress of the house requests the lady first in rank, in company, to show the way to the rest, and walk first into the room where the table is served; she then asks the second in precedence to follow ... bringing up the rear herself ... the master of the house does the same with the gentlemen ... when they enter the dining room, each takes his place in the same order; the mistress of the table sits at the upper end, those of superior rank next to her, right and left, those next in rank following, then the gentlemen and the master at the lower end.

Trusler pointed out that precedence was worked out on the basis that 'women have here always taken place of men, and both men and women have sat above each other, according to the rank they bear in life. Where a company is equal in point of rank, married ladies take place over single ones, and older ones of younger ones.'[27]

The Dinner Locust, *engraved in c. 1815 after E.F. Lambert, shows a modest urban dining-room. The pair of bell pulls flanking the fireplace, the reeded fire surround, and the overmirror are typical. The dining-table stands on a protective crumb cloth. Note the use of the table-cloth as a napkin.*

The frictions caused by the practice of precedence were revealed by Jane Austen in *Persuasion*, where two of the female characters fret over the loss of precedence that followed their changing stations in life: one feared losing the right to walk 'immediately after Lady Russell out of all the drawing-rooms and dining-rooms in the country', while the other felt that her status as daughter-in-law prevented her getting the 'precedence that was her due'.

More typical, perhaps, of urban dining is J.T. Smith's description of a dinner party that took place in about 1780 in Nollekens's terrace house in Mortimer Street, London: 'Before the company sat down, they were requested to walk upstairs for a moment to see Angelica Kauffman's portrait of Mrs Nollekens.' This certainly suggests that, in Nollekens's house at least, it was not the custom to gather in the first-floor drawing-room before dinner.

Presumably guests sat or stood in the dining-parlour until the party was complete and the food announced, when, as Smith wrote, 'there was a great rustling of silks for preference of places'.[28]

Smith's further observations reveal more information about how a dinner was conducted in a modest town house: 'Two tables were joined; but as the legs of one were considerably shorter than those of the other, four blocks of wood had been prepared to receive them.' Though Smith made this practice sound ridiculous, it was usual; until the late-eighteenth century or early-nineteenth century it was not customary to leave a large dinner-table standing in the centre of the dining-room. If a gateleg table was used for dining, it would be folded after use and placed against the wall in the dining-room, in the hall or in an adjoining room. If it were a table formed with leaves, then after use the ends of the table could be placed against the wall as pier tables, and the extra leaves and pedestals stored or used in other rooms as occasional tables.

This system of furnishing was mentioned by Jane Austen in a letter of 1800. Describing a table, she wrote, 'The two ends put together form one constant table for everything, and the centre-piece stands exceedingly well under the glass.' Both tables were covered with green baize.[29] The advantage of this type of table was that the dining-room could double as a sitting-parlour, while the disadvantage was indicated by Smith. If a large party of people were to be accommodated – in Nollekens's case twelve – and a large leaf table was not available, then one standard gateleg table was not adequate and rarely did two gateleg tables match absolutely in height or width. The tables, when joined, were covered with a damask table-cloth. This practice was illustrated by William Hogarth in his *Election Entertainment* of 1755, where a rectangular and a round table were butted against one another, each covered with a separate cloth.

The table-cloth was an item of some importance. Not only did it protect the mahogany and hide the joins between tables, but its removal at the end of the main course signalled a change in the nature of the dinner. Before its removal, the business was eating; after, the business was drinking. Also, to the dismay of foreign visitors, the cloth stood in for napkins. In 1789, Meister remarked that the 'large table-cloth which covered the dining-table [was] used to wipe your mouth and fingers in the place of napkins',[30] while also in the 1780s Archenholz observed that 'Napkins, which have been disused for twenty years, are beginning to be introduced. Those who are attached to the old customs ridicule the use of them ... they ... cover themselves with the table-cloth, which is of extraordinary length.' That this habit was regarded as a national custom – and a sign of independence from foreign influence – is supported by Sophie von la Roche: 'The table was covered with a fine big damask cloth, on which we all wiped our mouths in old English style.' The desirability of removing the cloth at the earliest possible moment, even if somewhat inconvenient a task, is obvious.

As for other items on the table, Smith recollected that 'the knives and forks matched pretty well, but the plates of Queen's ware had not only been ill-used by being put on the hob, by which they had

lost some of their gadrooned edges, but were of an irregular size'. Hobs were the flat metal plates flanking the coal basket and gave their name to the grate that was commonly used in town house interiors. The function of these hobs, as revealed by Smith, was for keeping plates of food or kettles warm until needed. The knife and fork, innocent of any deep significance even to the keen-witted Smith, were, nevertheless, redolent of English oddness to many foreign observers.

In 1784 the Frenchman Barthélemy Faujas de St Fond thought English usage of these instruments worthy of lengthy description:

I do not like to prick my mouth or my tongue with those little sharp steel tridents which are generally used in England ... I know that this kind of fork ... [is] ... only intended for seizing and fixing the pieces of meat while they are cut, and that the English knives being very large and rounded at the point, serve the same purpose to which forks in France are applied, that is, to carry food to the mouth ... the fork, whether steel or silver, is always held in the left hand and knife in the right. The fork seizes, the knife cuts, and the pieces may be carried to the mouth with either. The motion is quick and precise. The manoeuvres at an English dinner are founded upon the same principles as the Prussian tactics – not a moment is lost ... In France ... when meat is cut to pieces, the knife is laid down idle on the right side of the plate, while the fork on the other hand passes from left to right.[31]

Archenholz in the 1780s also noted the English use of cutlery: 'the fork is always on the left, and the knife on the right, hand. They do not use these instruments indifferently in either hand, as other natives of Europe.'

Smith related that the guests sat 'five on a side', with, presumably, Nollekens and his wife at either end. But he did not mention if the women were seated alternately with the men. Traditionally men sat in a group at the lower end of the table and were presided over by the master, and women in a group around the mistress at the upper end of the table. However, custom, wrote Trusler in 1788, 'has lately introduced a new mode of seating. A gentleman and a lady sitting alternately round the table, and this, for the better convenience of a lady's being attended to, and served by the gentleman next her.' But, 'not withstanding this promiscuous seating', he pointed out the ladies were still to be 'served in order, according to their rank and age, and after them the gentlemen, in the same manner'.

Toasts and challenges conducted with wine, like big damask cloths and no napkins, were regarded as peculiarly English practices. Goede, first in London in 1802, gives us a glimpse of an old-fashioned dinner 'peculiar' to the 'class denominated citizens' (i.e., merchants) in which 'many of the old English customs still have existence'. Needless to say, there were no napkins and, explained Goede, 'each lady must be solicited to drink wine by a gentleman, who first drinks to her, then to the hostess and master of the house; and so on until he has gone through the whole company. It would be undecorous,' wrote Goede, 'to touch a glass with your lips previous to such challenges [and] healths.' This unfamiliar formality obviously made Goede uncomfortable: 'When a stranger does not recollect the names of all around him, he is ... exposed to great embarrassment.' But, he thought, 'the habit of calling on the company to sing after supper is cheerful and pleasing.' At Nollekens's house there were, wrote Smith, 'no challenges at dinner ... nor do I think wine was mentioned until the servants were ordered to "take off" [the cloth]'. Smith suggested that the absence of challenges conducted with wine, and the absence of wine generally until the table-cloth was removed after the main course, were unusual and a sign of Nollekens's legendary meanness.

In the 1780s Trusler observed in his *Honours of the Table* that the old English custom of drinking toasts was being challenged as a meal-time activity: 'Drinking of healths is now growing out of fashion, and is very impolite in good company, [where] the improved manners of the age, now render it vulgar. What can be more rude or ridiculous, than to interrupt persons at their meals with unnecessary compliments.' Challenges, on the other hand, seem to have continued until the end of the Georgian period. The difference between a toast and a challenge, and the vital importance of the latter, was described by Prince Püeckler-Muskau:

It is not usual to take wine [at dinner] without drinking to another person. When you raise your glass, you look fixedly at the one with whom you are drinking, bow your head and drink with great gravity ... It is esteemed a civility to challenge anybody in this way to drink ... If the company is small, and a man has drunk to everybody but happens to wish for more wine, he must wait for the dessert, if he does not find in himself courage enough to brave custom.[32]

If Smith's account makes an English dinner party seem somewhat mean and seedy, Saussure's description of a typical London dinner not only makes the affair sound a little more wholesome but also reveals how challenges and toasts were administered when still in fashion and when the host was not so mean with his wines:

An Englishman's table is remarkably clean, the linen is very white, the plate shines brightly, and knives and forks are changed surprisingly often, that is to say every time a plate is removed. When everyone has done eating, the table is cleared and a bottle of wine with a glass for each is placed on the table. The King's health is first drunk, then that of the Prince of Wales, and finally that of all the royal family.

The disposition of the food upon the table and the manner in which the diners were served with it were noted by Trusler in *Honours of the Table*. Rather than being presented with a dinner composed of portions of all the dishes served, the diner bespoke his meal, choosing a selection from the dishes that were placed on the table itself or on the sideboard.

The mistress ... should acquaint the company with what is to come ... or if the whole is put on the table at once, should tell her friends they 'see the dinner', but they should be told, what wine or other liquor is on the side-board. Sometimes a cold joint of meat, or a sallad, is placed on the side-board. In this case it should be announced to the company.

The diner's selection would be made up by the servants waiting at table, although women guests would also be served by their male neighbours if seated in the new custom of men alternating with women. Anticipating problems for those men inexperienced in making up women's portions, Trusler warned: 'Eating a great deal is deemed indelicate in a lady (for her character should be rather divine than sensual), it will be ill manners to help her to a

A York dining-room in 1838, drawn by Mary Ellen Best. Although early Victorian, this table arrangement is still in the late-Georgian manner. The mistress of the house would sit at the top (right) of the table and serve the soup; the man would sit at the lower end (away from the door) and carve. The hob grate and fire surround are of the 1780s.

large slice of meat at once, or fill her plate too full.' Trusler continued, 'When you have served her with meat, she should be asked what kind of vegetables she likes, and the gentleman sitting next the dish that holds those requested should be requested to help her.'

Püeckler-Muskau, writing roughly forty years later, gave more information about Georgian dining habits and hinted at the changes that were to come:

When you enter, you find the whole of the first course on the table, as in France ... every man helps the dish before him, and offers some of it to his neighbours; if he wishes for anything, etc., he must ask across the table for it: a most troublesome custom, in place of which, some of the most elegant travelled gentlemen have adopted the more con-venient German fashion of sending the servant round with the dishes.

J.E. Austen-Leigh, in his *Memoir* of Jane Austen, remembered not only 'the custom prevalent in my youth [he was born in 1800] of asking each other to take wine together at dinner' but also the time 'when our dinners began to be carved and handed round by servants, instead of smoking before our eyes and noses on the table'.[33]

Eating in this manner could take two hours according to La Rochefoucauld, who noted that this part of the four- or five-hour dinner ritual concluded with an unsavoury display:

after the sweets you are given water in a small bowl of very clean glass in order to rinse out your mouth –

a custom which strikes me as extremely unfortunate. The more fashionable folk do not rinse out their mouths, but that seems to me to be even worse; for if you use the water to wash your hands, it becomes dirty and quite disgusting.

Simond observed a permutation of this cleansing ritual in 1810 and was equally shocked:

Towards the end of dinner, and before the ladies retire, bowls of coloured glass, full of water, are placed before each person. All (women as well as men) stoop over it, sucking up some of the water, and returning it, often more than once and with a spitting and washing sort of noise, quite charming, the operation frequently assisted by a finger elegantly thrust into the mouth. This done, and the hands dipped also, the napkin and sometimes the table-cloth are used to wipe hands and mouth.

This complete, the end of this part of the dinner ritual is at hand. 'This ceremony over,' wrote La Rochefoucauld, 'the cloth is removed and you behold the most beautiful table that it is possible to see.' The exposed table is then 'covered with all

kinds of wine [and] a small quantity of fruit, a few biscuits ... and some butter.' St Fond commented that the table was mahogany, appearing 'in all its lustre', that the wines came in decanters (an English invention) and that the collection of delicacies laid on the mahogany could include 'comfits, in fine porcelain or crystal vases' and 'elegant baskets' – presumably of china, and possibly French, for the fruits of different kinds.[34] Püeckler-Muskau noted that 'three decanters are usually placed before the master of the house [which] generally contain claret, port, and sherry or madeira'. These were passed from right to left by being 'pushed ... on a stand, or in a little silver wagon on wheels'.

La Rochefoucauld wrote of the meal's end with some relief: 'The ladies drink a glass or two of wine and at the end of half an hour all go out together. It is then that real enjoyment begins – there is not an Englishman who is not supremely happy at this particular moment.' Thus the third phase of dinner begins – the sexes separate and the women retire to the drawing-room to talk and supervise the making of the tea and coffee that will eventually be consumed when men and women reunite.

This division of the party did not surprise most

Four gentlemen dining in 1821, drawn by George Cruikshank. The fireplace arrangement – mirror overmantel and bell pull – are characteristic of the period.

The Shelley family, painted in c. 1740 by Charles Phillips, taking tea in a Palladian interior of c. 1725–30. The room is particularly remarkable for the austerity of its furnishings: few chairs, no paintings, window curtains or carpets.

foreign observers – indeed it was a custom not peculiar to Britain and clearly provided a welcome change of pitch to the proceedings. But the abrupt nature of the split seems to have been shocking to some. Saussure observed in 1727 that, after the toasts, 'the women rise and leave the room, the men paying them no attention or asking them to stay ... this custom surprises foreigners, especially the French'. The French-born Simond, on the other hand, noted merely that 'after dinner the ladies retire, the mistress of the house leaving first, while the men remain standing'. But this was eighty years later, by which time, it seems, Englishmen had learnt to stand in honour of the ladies' withdrawal.

La Rochefoucauld explained what happened after the ladies departed:

Everyone has to drink in his turn, for the bottles make a continuous circuit of the table ... after this has gone on for some time ... drinking of 'toasts' [begins] ... This is the time I like best ... conversation is as free as it can be, everyone expresses his political opinions with much ... frankness ... Sometimes conversation becomes extremely free upon highly indecent topics – complete licence is allowed.

So much did the Englishmen enjoy this part of the dinner that, to Archenholz at least, it seemed that the earlier part of the dinner was hurried so that 'they may sooner indulge this passion [when] politics immediately commence and healths continually go round.' This welcome escape from the polite

Ladies and gentlemen relaxing, perhaps in the drawing-room after dinner; painted c. 1735 by Joseph Highmore. Certainly the gaming and the tea-drinking were after-dinner activities, although the floor – if marble and not a fine floor cloth – suggests this is a hall rather than a drawing-room.

formality of mixed sex gatherings took three quarters of an hour; or, according to La Rochefoucauld, two to three hours. It ended, recorded Anderson, at 'about eight o'clock', when the men 'proceeded to the drawing-room'.

But even this convivial entertainment contained elements that amazed foreigners. As La Rochefoucauld wrote: 'The side board is furnished with a number of chamber pots and it is common practice to relieve oneself whilst the rest are drinking: one has no kind of concealment.' While La Rochefoucauld took this in his stride, Simond seemed much affected by this English peculiarity: 'Will it be credited that in a corner of the very dining-room there is a certain convenient piece of furniture to be used by anybody who wants it? The operation is

performed very deliberately and undisguisedly, as a matter of course, and occasions no interruption of the conversation.' The maintenance of this tradition for uninhibited behaviour in male-only company – long ago abandoned in polite society in France – was, thought St Fond, 'one of the reasons why the English ladies, who are exceedingly modest and reserved, always leave the company before toasts begin'. Eventually, 'a servant announces that tea is ready and conducts the Gentlemen from their drinking to join the ladies in the drawing room, where they are usually employed in making tea and coffee.'[35]

Thus the penultimate phase of dinner was reached. It is hard to imagine how the men composed themselves for tea after an hour or so of drinking, and how they conducted themselves as participants in this feminine phase of the evening. The drawing-room – light in colour, comfortable and fashionable – was the woman's realm, as the dining-room – darker, old-fashioned and redolent of ancestry – was the man's (see p. 70). The administering of tea and coffee presented an opportunity for feminine display. As La Rochefoucauld wrote, now was the chance to show a 'magnificence in the matter of tea-pots, cups and so on, which are always of the most elegant design based on Etruscan and other models of antiquity. It is also the custom', added La Rochefoucauld, for the 'youngest lady of the household to make the tea'.

The tea was likely to be excellent (see p. 27), but the coffee, as visitors remarked, was likely to be awful. 'Those who wish to drink coffee in England,' wrote Moritz, should 'mention before hand how many cups are to be made with half an ounce; or else the people will probably bring them a prodigious quantity of brown water'. Archenholz attempted to explain this: 'The impost of [tax on] coffee is great

... [This] does not, indeed, lessen the consumption, [but] occasions it to be drunk very weak.'

The manner in which the company arranged itself for tea seems to have been to scatter around the room; as Southey wrote: 'Tea is served between seven and eight, in the same manner as at breakfast [see p. 27], except that we do not assemble round the table.' Jane Austen, in *Emma*, has her men join the women after dinner in a most informal manner, sauntering into the drawing-room from the dining-room singly rather than in a body. The manner in which the men integrated themselves with the women is described thus: 'at last the drawing-room party did receive an augmentation. Mr Elton, in very good spirits, was one of the first to walk in. Mrs Weston and Emma were sitting together on a sopha. He joined them immediately, and with scarcely an invitation, seated himself between them.'

During, or immediately after the tea, pleasant and communal activities could be pursued if the company was still sober. 'Often we read aloud,' recorded Geijer, but he was lodging in a clergyman's house; Anderson was subjected after tea to a

Home amusements in 1821: dinner has been cleared, the cloth has been removed from the dining-table to reveal a green baize cover on which have been placed drinks, fruit and dessert. The walls are purple, a favoured early-nineteenth-century colour.

Family relaxation in what appears to be a modest interior. Here the ubiquitous pedestal table supports candlesticks and the snuffer necessary for keeping the candles as bright as possible. The fact that the Rococo wall sconces do not bear lit candles suggests that it was the usual practice, for informal family gatherings at least, to carry candlesticks from room to room as needed rather than to light the whole house. The scene dates from 1783.

daughter of the house singing 'a Scottish air, accompanied by herself on a piano', while La Rochefoucauld noted that 'after tea one generally plays whist'.

SUPPER

The final event of the evening seems to have been optional. Anderson, after listening to the daughter on the piano, took his leave at about nine o'clock. On other occasions guests stayed on to enjoy a light supper. As La Rochefoucauld recalled: 'at midnight there is cold meat for those who are hungry'. This could be followed by more alcohol – all seems to have become very informal. Southey explained that 'supper is rather a ceremony than a meal' and was followed by 'wine and water, or spirits'. This was, to him, the 'pleasantest' hour of the day.

The status – indeed the very existence – of supper had been uncertain from at least the late-seventeenth century. This, to foreign observers, produced an unfortunate imbalance in the Englishman's eating habits and led Misson in 1698 to characterize the English as 'Gluttons at noon, and abstinent at night'. James Beeverell, in his *Pleasures of London*, stated plainly that 'It is not customary to eat supper in England' and informs us that, instead, 'in the evening they take only a certain beverage, which they call Botterdel [which] is composed of sugar, cinnamon, butter and beer brewed without hops; this is put in a pot, sat before the fire to heat, and drunk hot'.[36] This curious drink was presumably the precursor of cocoa and chocolate as the hot drink before bed. Saussure wrote of London habits that 'If you wish to eat or drink in the evening you can do so, but supper is not considered a necessary meal' and Sophie von la Roche did not subscribe to the English habit of considering tea parties as supper and greatly surprised her landlord by wanting more to eat. On the other hand Boswell spoke quite clearly of supper parties in his *London Journal 1762–3*. For example, in January 1763 Lord Eglington asked him to sup, with others, at his Queen Street house in Marylebone. Boswell arrived at nine, stayed until three and was 'really uneasy going home [because] robberies in the street are now very frequent'. At roughly the same time William Hickey, in his *Memoirs*, stated

categorically that, after dinner, activities such as billiards and taking tea or coffee in the drawing-room were pursued 'till ten, at which hour supper was served'.[37] Earlier in the century Benjamin Franklin, when working as a printer in London, used to share supper with his landlady, and this 'consisted only of half an anchovy a piece, upon a slice of bread and butter, with half a pint of ale between us'.

Long dinners and later suppers meant that English cities stayed awake later than was usual on the Continent. Plays began between four and five[38] but also, if the theatre had an evening licence, as late as nine o'clock – allowing adequate time for an abbreviated dinner before – and were 'generally over by eleven o'clock'.[39] Shops, as we have seen, would stay open until about ten o'clock in the livelier parts of the town, and routs in private houses (see below) 'commenced after the opera, that is at midnight'[40] and lasted two hours. Goede, describing the day of a young man of fashion in 1802, has him go to the play at nine, then on to a rout, a ball, the 'faro bank of some lady of distinction' and to bed at four o'clock. Lichtenberg, when he arrived in London at midnight in April 1770, was amazed by the night life: 'the noise in the street was as great as in other places at midday. This is not surprising, when you think that eleven p.m. or half past is the regular supper time in many genteel families.'[41]

THE ROUT

The rout was a private entertainment of some significance, because it seems to have had a direct influence upon the design of large town, as well as country, houses. Certainly, Isaac Ware suggested this was the case in his *A Complete Body of Architecture* of 1756, in which he also implied that routs were then a recent development:

In houses which have been some time built, and which have not an out of proportion room, the common practice is to build one on to them: this always hangs from one end, or sticks to one side, of the house, and shews to the most careless eye, that, though fastened to the walls, it does not belong to the building. The custom of routs has introduced this absurd practice.

It is curious that all accounts of routs adopt the sour disapproving tone of those who have waited long, and in vain, for an invitation to the party. In launching his attack, Ware went for the old English gambit:

Our forefathers were pleased with seeing their friends as they chanced to come, and with entertaining them when they were there. The present custom is to see all at once, and entertain none of them; this brings in the necessity of a great room ... This is the reigning taste of the present time in London, a taste which tends to the discouragement of all good and regular architecture.

La Rochefoucauld confirmed that 'it is customary, when one gives a party, to invite the whole town', but the best description of routs comes from very early in the nineteenth century, when the fashion seems to have reached its peak. Goede attended one in about 1802:

One of the social pleasures of London is a rout ...

a colossal caricature of an assembly ... When the apartments are not sufficiently capacious for the company, temporary rooms are created in the yard, and most elegantly fitted up. The scene in the street serves as a prelude to that within doors; a long range of carriages fills up every avenue, and some times a party cannot get up to the door for an hour or two. Having, however, accomplished this arduous task, on entering the temple of pleasure, nothing is presented to the view but a vast crowd of elegantly dressed ladies and gentlemen, many of whom are so over-powered by the heat, noise and confusion, as to be in danger of fainting. Everyone complains of the pressure of the company, yet all rejoice at being so divinely squeezed. The company moves from room to room; and the most an individual can do, on meeting a particular friend, is to shake hands as they are hurried past each other. The confusion increases when the supper rooms are thrown open. The tables, it is true, are laid out with Asiatic profusion ... but not one fifth part of the guests can be accommodated. Behind each chair, are ladies standing three or four deep;

This print of 1770 shows a rout of sorts. Most interesting is the variety of lighting devices, including a candle sprouting from the stairs in an up-turned glass bell.

others are enclosed in the doorway, unable to advance or retreat.

It is clear from Malcolm's *Anecdotes* that this type of entertainment was attempted in even the modest London houses. See, he wrote, a West End house:

confined to an ichnography of 25 × 40 ft prepared for a rout: the floor is painted in graceful figures and flowers with coloured chalks for dancing; girandoles and lustres of splendid cut-glass with numerous wax-candles lighted exhibit the lady in her jewels ready to receive her guests equally resplendent. Ay, but the number – what say you to an hundred, two hundred? There is pleasure, there is amusement, and the inexpressible delight of languor, even fainting through exertion, heat and suffocation: the company endeavours to compress themselves for obtaining a space to dance in, and afterward they crowd to the supper table sparkling with polished plate; and loaded with every delicacy; there the amusements of Tantalus are renewed.

Simond's experiences supply a few further details. He noted that all but ornamental furniture was carried out of sight to make way for the guests, who were 'received at the door of the principal apartment by the mistress of the house'. Also, as indicated by Goede, the company was in constant, if congested, motion, making a circuit of the main rooms of the house, very much as in a country house entertainment of the day: 'No cards, no music, only elbowing, turning and winding from room to room.' A detail that particularly struck Simond was the determination to make this private entertainment as public a display as possible. Not only was attention drawn to the house by 'immense crowds of carriages', but 'every curtain, and every shutter of every window [was] wide open, shewing apartments all in a blaze of light, with heads innumerable in continual motion'. Simond discovered that 'this custom is so general, that having a few days ago five or six persons in the evening with us, we observed our servant had left the windows thus exposed, thinking, no doubt, that this was a rout after our fashion'.

PART TWO

LIFE IN THE HOUSE

Life in the House

The architect, the client and the workman: from John Crunden's Chimney Piece Maker's Daily Assistant *of 1766.*

Chapter One

THE 'COMMON HOUSE'

PUBLIC GRAVITY, PRIVATE GRACE

Simond's first impression of the English town house is revealing. When in 1810 he arrived by coach at Hyde Park Corner, the hub of west London, he recorded that 'we were soon lost in a maze of busy, smoky dirty streets' in which the exteriors of the houses presented 'a sort of uniform dingyness'. But 'most opposite to this dingyness' were the glimpses Simond caught of the interiors of the houses. Here 'everything was clean, fresh and brilliant'.[1] The contrast between the exterior and interior of the Georgian town house was often remarked upon by contemporary observers (see p. 4); the former grimy, austere, repetitive, the latter clean, richly decorated and full of variety.

But, to judge by the reactions of foreign visitors, the difference between the gloomy exterior and bright interior was only one of the town house's remarkable characteristics. The general cleanliness excited great comment. Grosley wrote in 1765 that the English had the habit of washing out rooms once a week, but he disapproved because he thought it 'dangerous and unnecessary', since it caused dampness and produced rheumatism and cold;[2] in 1784 La Rochefoucauld observed with surprise that 'houses are constantly washed inside and out, generally on Saturday',[3] and when Sophie von la Roche visited London in 1785, she noted that beyond the plain, uniform brick façade was a stair 'clean, well lit and carpeted'.[4] Her observation not only records the cleanliness of the interior but also hints at the differences between the English and Continental manner of living in the city.

The difference is explained very succinctly by Simond, who seems generally to have approved the English system of urban living.

Each family occupies a whole house, unless very poor. There are advantages and disadvantages attending this custom. Among the first, the being more independent of the noise, the dirt, the contagious disorders, or the dangers of your neighbours' fires, and having a more complete home. On the other hand, an apartment all on one floor, even of a few rooms only, looks much better, and is more convenient.

Simond, like several quizzical foreign visitors, described the English town house in detail. He was not specific about the activities that took place on the various levels. He merely noted that 'every apartment [was] in the same style – all is neat, compact, and independent' and that 'the narrow houses ... with two rooms to each storey' were 'three or four storeys high', with floors used 'one for eating, one for sleeping, a third for company, a fourth underground for the kitchen, a fifth perhaps on top for the servants'. Simond, as a Frenchman, could not help gently mocking 'the agility, the ease, the quickness with which the individuals of the family run up and down, and perch on the different storeys [giving] the idea of a cage with sticks and birds'.

But on what plan was the house based and what happened in each room? The answer is given by a designer of eighteenth-century town houses, Isaac Ware, when describing in 1756 what he called 'the common house in London'. He wrote in *A Complete Body of Architecture* that it was 'the general custom to make two rooms and a light closet on each floor',

each house being five storeys, including basement
and dormer-lit garrets in the roof space.

THE LOWER STOREY

'The lower storey of these houses in London,' wrote
Ware, 'is sunk entirely underground for which
reason it is damp, unwholesome and uncomfortable'. But, despite these reservations, Ware
stated firmly that 'the front room below in London
is naturally the kitchen; the vault runs under the
street with an area between, in which is to be a
cistern [see p. 248] and there may be behind other
vaults beyond another area'. If the garrets were too
small to serve as servant accommodation (see p. 58)
or the servants too numerous, 'a bed for a man or
two maid servants is contrived to be let down in the
kitchen'. But, Ware pointed out, 'the necessary care
of those people's health requires it should be board-
ed'.

The practice of banishing the servants below
stairs to work and occasionally to sleep is confirmed
by numerous foreign visitors. Saussure noted in 1727
that

*in all the newly built quarters the houses have one
floor made in the earth, containing the kitchen,
offices and the servants' rooms. This floor is well
lighted, and has as much air as the others have
[because] a sort of moat, 5 or 6 ft in width and 8 or
9 deep, is dug in front of all the houses, and is called
the 'area'.*

Saussure also revealed that as early as 1727 coal was
stored in 'cellars and vaults ... built beneath the
street'.[5] Unfortunately, he did not say how the coal
was put into the vaults, but coal holes in pavements
seem to have been of mid-eighteenth-century origin.

Grosley observed in 1765 that town houses had
'a subterraneous storey, occupied by kitchen and
offices' and stated that this was 'a uniform arrangement'. According to Sophie von la Roche, 'the
basement [of London houses] contains not only the
cellar but also kitchen, bake house and servants'
quarters', while Archenholz in 1789 thought that
'New west end houses ... have each of them two
storeys under ground to which sufficient light is

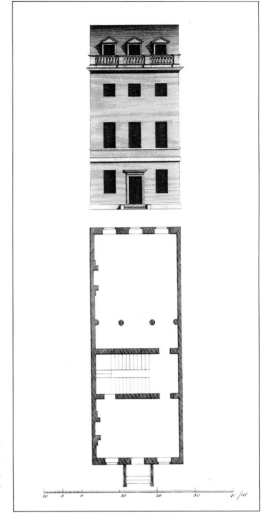

*Isaac Ware's vision of the London terrace house as
it could be, from A Complete Body of Architecture
of 1756. Ware argued that town houses would look
more noble if the door were centrally placed and if
the garden were reached from the rear basement
room rather than by passing through the ground
floor. This rearrangement would have had a profound influence on the ground-floor plan. The front
of the house was given over to a generous hall rather
than a passage and small parlour, while a large
formal dining-room could be created in the rear.
Apart from the central door, the elevation, with its
string-course and square attic windows, is a good
example of the Palladian astylar town house.*

communicated by means of a fore-court'; in them 'the servants are lodged, and the kitchen, store-rooms, etc. are placed'.[6] Ware believed that this arrangement was due to the fact that 'the ground rent is so dear in London that every method is to be used to make the most of the ground plan'.[7] Grosley thought it was simply a device to give 'the ground floor all the salubriety of the first floor', while Archenholz observed that this practice of burying the servants in the ground left 'the rest of the house … entirely at the disposal of the master'.

Whatever the reason for this arrangement, there were those who disapproved. Malcolm, writing in the first decade of the nineteenth century, recognized the convenience of Georgian interiors but wished 'that the kitchen might henceforth be created behind the house that no human being should be immersed in damp, and blinded with darkness, as our servants are, 7 or 8 ft below the surface of the street'.[8] A compromise solution – rarely practised – was to place the kitchen below ground level but not beneath the house. This arrangement allowed the kitchen to be a little better lit and ventilated and commodiously

planned. The designs of c. 1775 for No. 28 Soho Square[9] (see p. 56) display such an arrangement. But this plan also shows that this reorganization was not undertaken for humanitarian reasons, for the subterranean rooms beneath the houses were still used for servants' accommodation.

This practice is described by Rush, who rented a house in Baker Street, London, in about 1817. He depicted it thus:

The kitchen was underground, on the space in the immediate rear of the house, which space was roofed over with a flat roof covered with lead, light being admitted below through sky lights … In the basement, under the main body of the house, were a house keeper's room, butler's pantry, and other apartments, deriving light from the area upon the street, or the sky lights in the leaden roof.[10]

This was not a large house, according to Rush, possessing a 30-ft frontage and a depth of 50–60 ft. It probably had been built between 1789 and 1800, as had most of Baker Street.

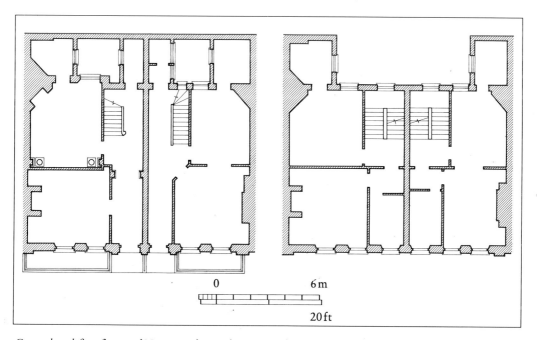

Ground and first floors of Nos. 6 and 7 Frith Street, Soho, 1718. This plan, with room front, room back, dog-leg stair and rear closet, became the usual urban type after c. 1720 and is cited by Ware in 1756 as the plan form of the 'common house'.

THE GROUND FLOOR

Turning his attention to the ground floor, Ware stated that 'In common houses the fore parlour is the best room upon the ground floor; the passage [from front door to the staircase set against the back wall] cuts off a good deal from this, and from the back parlour, this usually running strait into the opening, or garden as it is called, behind' (see p. 190). Describing the parlour in a small private house, Ware confirmed that it was 'a very convenient room', but 'not the apartment of most shew'. In placing the parlour on the ground floor, Ware followed Richard Neve's 1703 description of a parlour as 'a fair lower room'[11] – indeed, a parlour was a ground-floor room almost by definition. Thus for Ware, in accordance with the Palladian principle that the piano nobile should be the first floor (see p. 137), the ground floor should not contain the most important formal rooms.

However, the relationship between the ground and first floors remained ambiguous throughout the Georgian period. This was partly because there were always very sound functional reasons for making the ground floor the major floor (for example, if the house were only three storeys above ground, with the first floor having to serve as bedrooms) as well as a positive preference for a ground-floor piano nobile in the 1720s and in the early-nineteenth century. But a major contributory factor to the unsettled relationship between ground and first floors was the fact that the location and status of the formal dining-room and of the formal drawing-room with which it was balanced were unresolved until the late-eighteenth century.

The idea of having a fixed location for dining – possibly with a large and permanently placed dining-table and related furniture – seems to have been an innovation of the 1730s or 1740s. Before that, and until the 1790s, the common practice was to turn one of the lower rooms into the dining-room – as was convenient – by opening up a gateleg table.[12] When the dining-room did arrive, it would have seemed sensible to locate it on the ground floor near the kitchen. But in the early-eighteenth century it was just as likely that the dining-room would be located on the first floor – probably in the back-room if the house was large enough to contain one of sufficient size. At No. 25 Brook Street, Mayfair,

an early-eighteenth-century house inhabited by Handel, the eating-room was on the first floor,[13] while at No. 29 Grosvenor Square, built in 1728, the dining-room is recorded as being on the first floor in 1746 but on the ground floor in 1757.[14]

This relocation could involve some major work. At No. 43 Brook Street, built in 1725, the dividing wall between back and front ground-floor rooms was replaced later by a columnar screen, the rear room being reduced in size.[15] But if moving the dining-room from first to ground floor was a thing of fashion, then the fashion does not seem to have been followed universally. Ware could still write in 1756 that 'The first floor in the common house consists of the dining-room over the hall or parlour', and a lease of 1773 for No. 11 Queen Anne's Gate, Westminster, has a plan and schedule attached[16] (see p. 246) that make it clear the ground floor contained 'front' and 'back' parlours, with the dining-room being located in the first-floor front-room.[17]

There are numerous descriptions of late-eighteenth-century houses with dining-rooms on the ground floor[18] and accounts by such as La Rochefoucauld, who insisted that the ground floor was 'always lived in since it contains the best rooms' including the 'dining room, which is always large', above which was 'the drawing room which is always the same shape and reached by a spotlessly clean staircase'. In fact, La Rochefoucauld went so far as to say: 'It is a general custom in England, which would not be liked in France, to have the dining room below and the drawing room above; people find this more convenient for the servants and make no trouble of going up a staircase of twenty steps or so.' The 'trouble' must refer to having to ascend to the drawing-room. This view was partly supported by Southey, who also observed that 'one of the peculiarities of this country is that everybody lives upon the ground floor' with 'one room on the first floor ... reserved for company'. Southey's description of a London town house included a dining-room, a drawing-room and a breakfast-parlour, and implied that the parlour, where informal, day-to-day family life was lived, was on the ground floor.[19] So where was his dining-room – on the ground floor? Not necessarily; Southey's phrase 'Breakfast parlour' suggests that a parlour could also be used for eating, at least for informal meals.

Large town houses could contain both types of eating-room. A building agreement and related documents for No. 10 St James's Square, built in 1734,[20] indicate that the house possessed a 'best dining-room' as well as an informal eating-room – both on the ground floor; the plans of *c.* 1775 for No. 28 Soho Square[21] show a formal dining-room in the first-floor back room and a dining-parlour in the ground-floor front room – an arrangement also shown in town house plans in John Crunden's *Convenient and Ornamental Architecture* of 1770.

The arrangement for dining in the more modest town house was, perhaps, typical of that followed in the late-eighteenth century in the London household of Joseph Nollekens, the miserly and mean-spirited but talented sculptor whose life was written by J.T. Smith. The 'drawing room' was on the

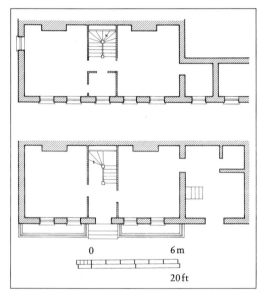

Ground- and first-floor plan of No. 36 Elder Street, Spitalfields built in 1725: an example of the plan type in which two rooms per floor, separated by closet and staircase, are aligned parallel with the street façade. This particular example is not typical, for the house occupies a corner site and possesses an additional closet over a ground-floor yard. Usually light would flood into the rooms from both back and front windows, with chimney-breasts on flank walls. In this house the absence of a stair window is compensated for by top-lighting the staircase. The void between the stair and the rear wall permits a shaft of light to penetrate to the basement.

first floor, with the 'dining parlour' adjacent to the sculptor's studio – therefore fairly certainly on the ground floor; and when this parlour was to be used for dining, 'two tables were joined' and covered with a damask cloth to form a dining-table.

THE FIRST FLOOR

According to Ware, the first floor of the common London house contained, beside the dining-room, 'a bed-chamber over the back parlour and closet over its closet'. However, he also stated that 'in a house something better than the common kind, the back room upon the first floor should be a drawing-room, or dressing-room, for the lady; for it is better not to have any bed on this floor'. It is interesting that Ware should consider drawing-rooms a luxury – presumably feeling that their function could be quite properly fulfilled by the ground-floor parlours, while dining-rooms were, apparently, essential. Ware was clear about the role of the dressing-room:

in the house of a person of fashion [it] is a room of consequence, not only for its natural use in being the place of dressing, but for the several persons who are seen there. The morning is the time many choose for dispatching business [and so must] admit [people] while they are dressing.

A letter of 1748 written by Mrs Edward Boscawen supports this description of life in the dressing-room: 'I saw company in my dressing-room for the first time since its being furnished ... and everyone admired my apartment.'[22]

La Rochefoucauld also located bedrooms on the first floor but said that they were at the front of the house, implying that the 'drawing room, which is always above the dining room' were both at the back of the house – as at No. 14 Queen Anne's Gate in 1776 (see p. 268). He said, 'above the entrance hall is a bedroom and sometimes an apartment or two'. Indeed, he confirmed this rear location for drawing- and dining-rooms by noting that 'Three houses out of four have a little turret at one end which adds space to the dining room and drawing room. The rooms are given a very pleasant shape

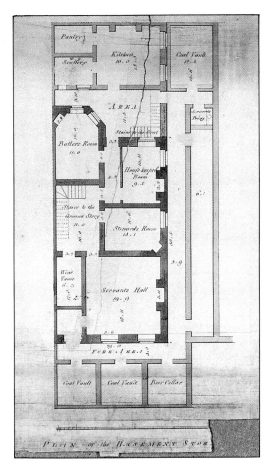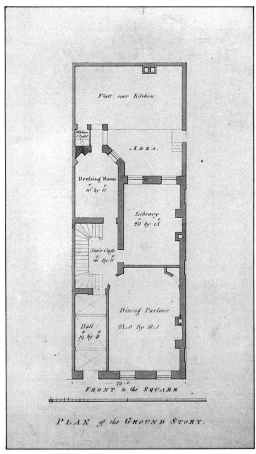

Above and opposite: *Plans, elevation and section of c. 1775 of the now demolished No. 28 Soho Square. This house represents a skilful use of a corner plot and is a trifle more ambitious than the standard terrace house. The room descriptions are important, for they reveal where different activities were located. Particularly interesting is the basement plan showing the location of the servants' privy in the area, the kitchen below a lead flat with servants' accommodation below the main house. The ground floor, like the first floor, possesses a guest or family water-closet and a dining-parlour, as opposed to a dining-room, that is located on the first floor adjoining the drawing-room. The main bedroom, complete with bed alcove, is in the second-floor back room. The top floor is subdivided to create five or six rooms, some lit by the lightwell above the lantern of the top-lit staircase.*

and more light is admitted.' These turrets are the semi-circular, half-hexagonal or elliptical bays that were often added to the rear of terrace houses in Dublin in the 1760s and in Bath, London and Edinburgh after the mid 1770s.

It should be said that the word 'apartment' seems in these various accounts to mean an individual room, although it could also mean a suite of rooms of different sizes and uses interlinked and forming a distinct component within a house plan. Indeed, a floor of the sort described by Ware – a large front room, a slightly smaller back room and a small closet – could be regarded as an apartment in itself, the rooms being used in the manner of early-eighteenth-century country houses as sitting-room/ drawing-room, bedroom, and cabinet/closet/

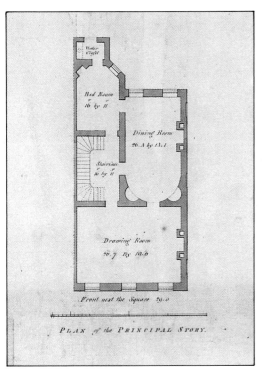

Front next the Square 29.0

PLAN of the PRINCIPAL STORY.

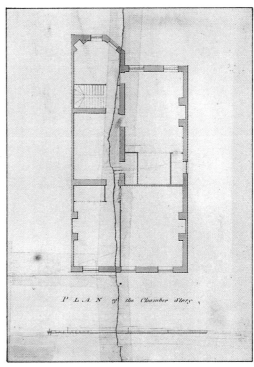

PLAN of the Chamber Story.

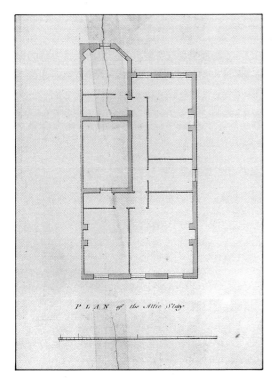

PLAN of the Attic Story.

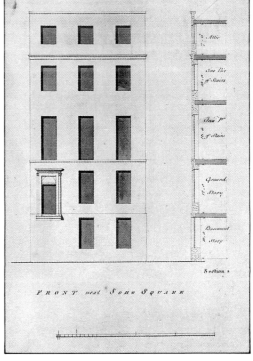

FRONT next Soho Square

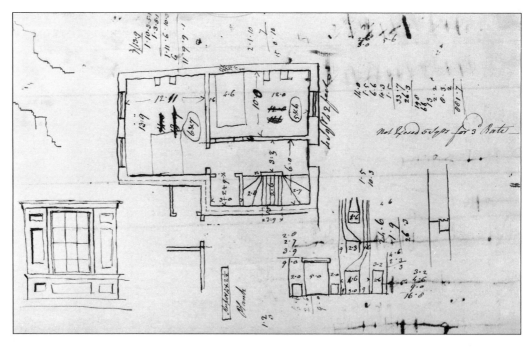

Sketch plan details by George Dance or James Peacock in the Dance scrapbook in the RIBA Drawings Collection. The plan, perhaps for a Finsbury Square house of c. 1780, catches the late-eighteenth-century architect in the act of designing a modest house. Note floor plank dimensions considered, flue placing tested, bed locations envisaged and rough cornice profiles and window compositions.

dressing-room by one member of the family occupying the house.

This pattern of use is supported by evidence surviving in No. 79 Berwick Street, Soho. This house, built in about 1736, possesses a first-floor closet lined with raised and fielded panelling, while the large room it adjoins contains inferior ovolo panelling (see p. 150). Clearly, the closet was not merely a humble and utilitarian anteroom but, on the contrary, could be the very focus of the piano nobile. It was, presumably, where the master of the house entertained his most choice guests in a rich yet intimate setting.

ABOVE THE FIRST FLOOR

As for the rooms above the first floor, Ware wrote, 'The two rooms on the second floor are for bed-

rooms, and the closets being carried up thus far, there may be a third bed there. Over these are the garrets, which may be divided into a larger number than the floors below, for the reception of beds for servants.' Simond also observed that servants were lodged in the top of the house, as did John Wood, who noted that 'garrets [were] for servants'.[23] And James Peacock stated that 'the dormitories for the servants [are] in the attic storey or roof'.[24] But, as we have seen, Ware, Archenholz and Saussure all recorded that servants also dwelt in the basement.

Although evidence is slight, there are indications that servants were parcelled around the house in a most ad hoc manner to suit the convenience of the family. *The Gentleman's Magazine* of 1746 recorded that Matthew Henderson, a footman who had murdered his mistress earlier that year, said in confession that he 'went up into the back-parlour where he used to be, and let down his bed'.[25] Small closets were located off the half landings between first- and second-floor level at Nos. 5–13 Queen Anne's Gate

No. 79 Berwick Street, Soho, 1736. View from the first-floor rear closet into the back room. The distant room has ovolo panelling on its walls, while the closet possesses superior raised and fielded panelling, suggesting that this little room held an important position in the hierarchy of the house.

Two early-nineteenth-century 'exquisites' taking tea in a London garret. The regular recurrence of this image – overdressed youths presenting an affluent appearance and indulging in a few fashionable luxuries while living in pathetic squalor – suggests that it may, in reality, have been a fairly common condition. Note the turned-up bed and the ingenious disposition of domestic necessities.

(see p. 237). One of these (in No. 13) was lit by a round window that borrowed light from the top-lit staircase. This was probably a closet for a close-stool but could have been a servant's bedroom. At the Christ Church minister's house, No. 2 Fournier Street, Spitalfields (see p. 227), built between 1726 and 1731 to the design of Nicholas Hawksmoor, there were small closets contrived beside the main stair on first- and second-floor levels. Cramped, though well lit by windows in the flank façade (the house is an end of terrace), these were perhaps servants' bedrooms. Carlisle House, at No. 24 Cheyne Row, built about 1708, also possessed a closet between the second and third floors that was lit by a window, suggesting possible use as a servant's bedroom.

Closets came in two types: the light closet, which was agreeable to inhabit, and the dark closet, that was not. The Queen Anne's Gate closet was probably a dark closet of the type referred to in an inventory of 1756,[26] because it is small and windowless. The light closet, which Isaac Ware mentioned in his description of the 'common house in London', was an extension off the back room and well lit by windows. This type of light closet could be used as a dressing-room cabinet or small bedroom and, in larger terraces, as a location for a secondary staircase by which servants could remove dirty clothes and night soil with maximum discretion.

OCCUPANTS OF THE HOUSE

The number of people – family and servants – that were fitted into the ten- to fifteen-room house seems to have been around eight to twelve. Certainly the 1801 census suggested an average of eight to nine people per house in London. Isaac Ware wrote that the 'common house', with five storeys and about fourteen rooms of various sizes, was 'for the reception of a family of two or three people, with three or four servants'. Earlier Nicholas Barbon had stated that a Mr Grant reckoned that there were about eight people per house in the City of London – a figure that Barbon argued should be increased by a third for a true figure.[27] This calculation may have been prejudiced by the fact that Barbon was a speculative builder promoting the idea that more housing was needed, but his figures seem to be supported by other evidence. When in 1763 Lady Molesworth's 'small' house at No. 49 Upper Brook Street, Mayfair, burned down one night, between seven and ten people perished, with several being saved,[28] while in 1726, at No. 52 Grosvenor Street, Sir Thomas Hanmer had fourteen servants in addition to his family.[29] This, admittedly, was one of the largest houses on the Grosvenor Estate, but its massive total of eighteen or so people was supported by Malcolm in his *Anecdotes*: 'Fashionable and opulent inhabitants of Westminster often occupy a house [25 × 40 ft] calculated for the reception conveniently of the Master and Mistress, two or three children, a nursery maid, a groom, a coachman, a butler, three footmen, a cook, and two or three house maids, governed by a house-keeper, and a governess.' Some of these sixteen to eighteen people would, presumably, have slept outside the main body of the house in the stable or outbuildings.

THE HOUSE DIVIDED

The common perception of a Georgian town house is that it was occupied by one family. This is under-

standable enough, for its compact plan and its single basement kitchen suggest single occupation. But the fact is that vast numbers of inhabitants of the great cities lived not in whole houses but in parts. Indeed, the houses they occupied were often rambling pre-Georgian buildings, but it is clear that the terrace house, with its two or three rooms per floor (see p. 51), was commonly occupied by several independent tenants.

The 1801 census provides dramatic evidence both of multiple occupation and of the manner in which densely tenanted houses could relate to those occupied by single families. For example, a block of five-storey houses, built on the corner of Broadwick Street and Berwick Street, Soho, was complete by early 1737[30] and included a new smaller street, off Berwick Street, called Bentinck Street. In 1801 most of these Bentinck Street houses contained four, five or six families, while the Berwick Street houses built at the same time, for example No. 79, contained a single family of three.[31] Clearly Bentinck Street, containing stabling as well as houses, had become a refuge for poorer families, while adjoining Berwick Street retained its gentility. This juxtaposition of wealth and poverty is typical of Georgian cities.

The manner in which the terrace house was tenanted survives in the practice still followed in London's Inns of Court. The hall, stairs and landings were common areas servicing the sets of rooms or apartments on each floor. These sets could, in particularly poor circumstances, be subdivided, with a lodger or family in the front room and another in the back. However, the vertical divisions of the terrace house were often breached to meet the contingencies of multiple occupation. If a family needed, and could afford, another room, a door could be knocked in a party wall to possess any vacant space available in the neighbouring house. In early-eighteenth-century houses in Spitalfields, evidence survives of lateral connection between houses that were built for independent occupation.[32] But, though the potentially inhibiting form of the narrow terrace house could be adapted to meet the organic demands of sprawling multiple occupation, its design and construction did prove to be the source of major problems.

Malcolm, in his *Anecdotes*, noted the 'discontent and altercations ... between the landlord's family and the lodger' that were a common consequence of multiple occupation. The single basement kitchen 'used in common by both parties [is a source] of discontent; the cleaning of stairs ascended by all the inhabitants of the house another; and the late hours of the latter a third.' Clearly the tight planning of the terrace house and its generally flimsy construction (particularly the $\frac{1}{4}$-in-thick panelled partitions of early-eighteenth-century houses) did not allow for much breathing space or sound insulation between families.

The reasons for multiple occupation were simple: either the tenant chose it, or it was forced upon him. For the thousands of visitors to the great cities – be they foreign travellers in London or seasonal tenants in Bath – and for the unmarried man, it was the natural manner of living. For others, such as the families of journeymen artisans, it was the inevitable consequence of high rents and low wages. Or, as Malcolm put it: 'Persons with small incomes [are] compelled by great rents and heavy taxes, to occupy furnished and unfurnished first and second floors.'

Misson in 1698 confirmed that, for foreign visitors such as himself, 'the way of lodging ... is to take a room, ready furnished at so much a week'.[33] With this type of lodging went a certain way of living, with food and entertainment being found outside and the apartment used only for sleeping (see p. 32). As Saussure pointed out, 'men, and more especially foreigners, live in furnished apartments, and take their meals in eating houses'.

In his *London Journal 1762–3* Boswell gave an excellent account of a well-to-do lodger's life in London. He took lodgings in Downing Street 'up two pairs of stairs [i.e., second floor] with the use of a handsome parlour all the forenoon ... for £40 a year' – soon reduced to £22 per annum. The second-floor rooms Boswell referred to as his bedroom and dining-room. The parlour was, presumably, the ground-floor front room, which was also used by the family of the house after midday. As for eating, Boswell agreed with the landlord that he could dine with the family whenever he liked for a shilling a time, although he more usually ate out. His breakfast was served in his rooms, where he would occasionally be joined by a companion. There was no question of compromising his dignity by pursuing his romances in his lodgings, a rented room in a tavern being used for the purposes of pressing the issue with a particular lady.

The way in which this apparently convenient and economic lodging ended is interesting, for it high-lights one of the frictions of multiple occupation. Boswell and two men friends spent an evening in the parlour (where he should not have been according to the agreement), 'drinking negus and frolicking'. The landlord, exasperated, 'bawled' at Boswell and called the watch, and charged them 'with riot, and would send [them] to the roundhouse'. The landlord relented, but Boswell left two days later.

The rent charged for a furnished room or apartment varied greatly depending on quality, size and location but was generally recorded as high. Saussure noted that 'you can have rooms from 6d. to half a guinea a head' – presumably this was a weekly rate. Boswell paid 16s. (reduced to 10s.) weekly, and in 1782 Moritz 'procured an apartment for 16s. a week'. This was in George Street, Strand, with the landlady being a tailor's widow who lived in the rest of the house with her two sons and a maid. For this rent Moritz got 'a large room in front on the ground floor [which was] very neatly furnished; the chairs are covered with leather, and the tables are of mahogany. Adjoining to this I have another large room.'[34]

The furniture of an apartment could be peculiar to the circumstances, for the spread of high-density occupation generated ingenious types of hybrid furniture. As Malcolm observed, a landlord and his lodgers often rose in the morning from 'the same description of turned up bedstead, and beds enclosed in resemblance of chests of drawers and book cases'. But this type of 'unwholesome contrivance' was peculiar to those more desperately crowded lodgings where it was necessary to accommodate 'many persons in a space calculated for very few'. In the furnished apartments occupied by such as Boswell and Moritz, Malcolm noted that 'four post bed-steads and elegant curtains are constantly provided'. Indeed, in his *Journal* Boswell mentioned having a 'handsome tent-bed with green and white check curtains'.

Those forced into multiple occupation by poverty occupied the terrace house in accord with a strict hierarchy that reflected both physical and design considerations. As Francis Grose explained in 1793, the poorest tenant in a house occupied the cellar or basement, often reached directly from the street via a hatch or, in larger houses, by way of an area stair. From this location

we take our flight to the top of the house in order

A Grub Street writer straining at his garret desk, while his wife is startled by the milkmaid's unpaid tally. A picturesque but evocative image by William Hogarth dated 1740 of the family life of the majority of city dwellers who could not afford a house of their own.

to arrange in the next class the residents in garrets; from these we gradually descend to the second and first floor, the dignity of each being in the inverse ratio of its altitude, it being always remembered that those dwelling in the fore part of the house take the pas of the inhabitants of the back rooms, and the ground floor, if not a shop or warehouse, ranks with the second storey.[35]

This hierarchy of occupation is explained by the design of the house: rear rooms were generally smaller than front rooms and so less desirable, cellars were dark and damp, garrets draughty and cramped and so the least favoured areas of accommodation, while the first floor was removed from street noise and, in accordance with Palladian proportioning principles, possessed the highest ceilings and stretched the full width of the house. These qualities made the first-floor front room the best lodging in the house. In 1801 T.A. Murray noted that 'in a large proportion of the dwellings of the poor a house contains as many families as rooms'

and that 'on the ground floor resides almost universally the master of the house with his family, which, if pretty numerous, sometimes occupy the whole of that floor; if not, the back room is tenanted by another family.'[36] This universal practice of the landlord occupying the ground floor probably confirms, rather than contradicts, the pre-eminence of the first floor, which was, no doubt, regarded by the landlord as too valuable an asset to be squandered on his own family.

Before the great rise of prices after 1795 because of inflation, the rents of this type of accommodation were 1s. to 1s. 6d. a week for a cellar or garret (see p. 33) and 2s. to 3s. 6d. a week for a furnished or unfurnished room.[37] In 1725 Benjamin Franklin lodged with a widow in Duke Street for 3s. 6d. a week; this was reduced to 1s. 6d. after he threatened to leave. The house, recorded Franklin, 'was kept by a widow, who had a daughter, a servant, and a shop-boy; but the latter slept out of the house ... in the garret of the house there lived, in the most retired manner, a lady seventy years of age'.[38]

Life below stairs in 1772, drawn by John Collett. The most accurate detail is, no doubt, the scene on the far right.

To put these rents in context, it must be remembered that up to about 1800 the average journeyman worked a five-day week for at most 3s. a day (see p. 121), giving him an annual income of around £40. Set against this, his rent at, say, 2s. a week would have been £5 4s. per annum, or about one eighth of his income. But the proportion could be far higher, for it was not unusual for journeymen to be unemployed for a large part of the year. As Robert Campbell wrote of journeymen bricklayers in 1747, 'they are out of business for five, if not six months of the year; and, in and about London, drink more than one third of the other six'.[39]

ROOMS OF THE HOUSE

The Kitchen

Kitchen quarters can be reconstructed by contemporary accounts, illustrations and inventories that often go into obsessive detail. An inventory attached to a lease of 2 April 1718 for a late-seventeenth-century London house in Red Lion Square, Holborn, gives a list of the basic items found in a basement kitchen:

two dressers, three shelves; an oven, a lid of iron to it; two stoves and broglers; chimney piece with rack for spits; two cupboards; large firegrate, iron back to the chimney, iron crane, a fender, a pair of iron racks; a leaden cistern lying on a thick plank over a stone paved sink with leaden pipe; a cock for New River water to come into it; two windows with double iron bars in them and one iron casement; window shutters with bars and staples; kitchen paved with Purbeck stone.[40]

Further items are mentioned in the schedule of fixtures attached to a lease of June 1756 for a house in Northumberland Row, Tottenham. This includes: 'one leaden pump, one leaden sink' and 'one shelf for pewter, one dresser, one iron crane, two pot hooks, two staves, one trivet, one iron range'.[41] A lease of May 1760 for No. 36 Dover Street, Mayfair, lists the sort of accoutrements that would accompany a kitchen in the basement of a larger town house. There was a 'lodging room for servants' (see p. 56), wine vaults, servants' hall, laundry with 'two large dressers and four turned feet', 'butler's pantry – wainscotted about 5 ft high; one Portland stone chimney piece ... one dresser'; two larders with 'two dressers and two turned feet'; wash-house with 'one dresser and turned foot; one window half glazed and half wired, one leaden pipe and cock'; scullery with 'one leaden sink, pipe and cock'. The water supply that served these rooms was in the back area, which contained 'one large leaden cistern and framed front in wood, and cover to ditto; one leaden pipe from the tree in the street to the cistern, one stop-cock and brass cock in the cistern; one cock under the cistern and leaden pipe and a stack of leaden water pipes'.

The kitchen itself contained: 'one large elm dresser and two turned feet and three drawers; one deal dresser, two turned feet and potboard ... one leaden sink and pipe and cock, three stoves and boiler'.[42] Sophie von la Roche noted that the basement of the London town house contained not only cellar, kitchen and servants' quarters but also a 'bake-house'.

Different functions – preparation, cooking, storage – were allocated to different rooms in even relatively small houses. At No. 11 Queen Anne's Gate a schedule attached to a lease of 1773 (see p. 245) reveals that the cooking took place in the front basement room, which did not possess a sink, while the wet kitchen business took place in the rear 'wash room'. Storage was a 'pantry' occupying part of the space between the two.[43] Southey's 1807 description of a kitchen demonstrates this split of function very well. After describing the front kitchen and its range, on which the cooking was done (see p. 79), he wrote: 'There is a kitchen in which all the dirty work is done, into which water is conveyed by pipes. The order and cleanliness of everything made even this room cheerful, though under ground, where the light enters only from an area, and the face of the sky is never seen.'

Some of the items mentioned need explanation. It is quite clear from these inventories – and from illustrations such as George Scharf's watercolour of his London kitchen in about 1830 – that pride of place in the kitchen was given to the dresser, on which were displayed china, copper and pewter.[44] Southey described a kitchen dresser thus: 'a dresser as white as when the wood was new, the copper and tin vessels bright and burnished ... the plates and dishes hanged in order along the shelves'. This description is interesting, for it reveals that the top of the dresser, at least, was unpainted, scrubbed wood – usually deal, though elm was mentioned in the Dover Street schedule. The rest of the dresser – the shelves, back, brackets, legs and drawers – was generally painted.

Dressers could be quite elaborate pieces of furniture and, as their presence in inventories explains, were invariably fixtures, embedded in the walls. As the Dover Street schedule shows, the legs on which the board and drawers were supported could be turned – usually in the form of small Tuscan or Doric columns, on plinths. Such a dresser survives in the kitchen of No. 15 Elder Street, Spitalfields, built in 1727 (see p. 219). A similar type of dresser seems to have been installed in the nearby Christ Church minister's house, No. 2 Fournier Street (see p. 232). This, according to the account books, was a 17-ft double deal dresser with three turned bearers $3\frac{1}{2}$ ft sq. and 2 ft high. It cost 1s. per foot to make – not a cheap price, representing about six days' work for a joiner[45] (see p. 232). The dresser for the kitchen of the minister's house at Wapping, constructed between June 1729 and March 1731 by John Balshaw, joiner, was even more expensive: 'of deal', with 'six fir turned legs' at 1s. 8d. each – a total cost of £1 12s. 3d.[46]

The other large and recurring item is the lead cistern, which was often located in the front or back kitchen but could be in the front or back area (see p. 82). These cisterns were handsome objects, embellished with strap work and bearing the initials and coat of arms of the landowner or developer and the date of its, or the house's, erection. A cistern of this type, located in a front kitchen, survived little altered until recently at No. 23 Queen Anne's Gate, which had been built in about 1704. This cistern, complete with a water cock (a later addition), sat upon a brick stove that could be used to heat the water and faced a large copper bowl, similarly heated, in the opposite corner. The water to fill these cisterns came from one or other of the water companies (see p. 87) and was delivered via elm pipes located in the street – the 'tree in the street', mentioned in the Dover Street schedule.

If these cisterns were not in the kitchen, then the water they contained was drawn via a pump that could also be used to raise water from basement level, where it entered the house, to a higher level where it could be stored (after about 1820 water was available at sufficient pressure to reach higher floors without pumping). A pump is mentioned in the Northumberland Row schedule of 1756 and in the account books of the minister's house for Christ Church, Spitalfields. These list a 'pump with iron work, bucket and sucker, £3'.

The 'broglers' mentioned in the 1718 Red Lion Square inventory may have been vessels for cooking or keeping eels.

The description 'chimney piece with rack for spits' in the same Red Lion Square inventory is significant, for it suggests that the racks were designed as part of the fire surround. This is confirmed by a late-eighteenth-century spit rack that survives at No. 21 Grove Terrace, Highgate, where the rack forms part of the overmantel.[47] The 'trivet' mentioned in the 1756 Northumberland Row schedule was, perhaps, a tripod for supporting a pot or kettle over the range or, more likely, a bracket with three projections for fixing on the top bar of the range.

The sinks mentioned in the inventories are both of stone and timber lined with lead, but those cut out of a solid piece of stone are not uncommon survivals.[48] The account book for the Christ Church minister's house in Fournier Street records 'three sink stones one shilling each' and the Red Lion Square inventory implies a combination of stone and lead when it states that the sink was 'paved' with stone.

Not mentioned in any of the inventories or schedules are those slightly more complex kitchen fittings such as clock spits (a spit turned by clockwork and hung from the chimney lintel) or the dog wheel. This latter device was described in detail by Southey:

The enormous joints of meat which come to an English table are always roasted upon a spit [which is] now turned by a wheel in the chimney which the smoke sets in motion but formerly by the labour of a dog who was trained to run in a wheel. There was a peculiar breed for the purpose, called turnspits from their occupation, long-backed and short legged; they are now nearly extinct. The mode of

teaching them their business was more summary than humane: the dog was put in the wheel and a burning coal with him; he could not stay without burning his legs and so was kept upon the full gallop.

Southey went on to describe the modern kitchen range – and kitchen – which puts some flesh on the bare bones of fittings offered by the inventories and schedules:

the kitchen-range ... has been constructed upon the philosophical principles of Count Rumford [see p. 79] ... a philosopher, the first person who has applied scientific discoveries to the ordinary purposes of life. The top of the fire is covered with an iron plate, so that the flame and smoke, instead of ascending, pass through bars on the one side, and these heat an iron front, against which food may be roasted as well as by the fire itself; it passes on heating stoves and boilers as it goes, and the smoke is not suffered to pass up the chimney till it can no longer be of any use. On the other side is an oven heated by the same fire, and vessels for boiling may be placed on the plate over the fire. The smoke finally sets a kind of wheel in motion in the chimney, which turns the spit. I could not but admire the comfort and cleanliness of everything about the kitchen ...

Against Southey's cheerful picture can be set La Rochefoucauld's most odd description of the town house kitchen, which becomes a metaphor for the English character. He began by admitting that 'the cleanliness which pervades everything is a perpetual source of satisfaction' and that

at first I was quite astonished at all this and did all that I could to make sure whether the cleanliness was natural to the English and so pervaded all their activities, or whether it was a superficial refinement. I was led to see quite clearly that it was only external ... to give a simple instance, I need only mention the kitchen which, amongst people who have a natural instinct for cleanliness, ought to be spotlessly clean. But the worst thing that could befall you would be to go into the kitchen before dinner – the dirt is indescribable. Women are usually employed and are as black as coal; their arms bared to the elbow, are disgustingly dirty; to save time, they handle the portions of food with their hands.

This is surely a rogue description, because other observers, both foreign and native, were, like Southey, fulsome in their praise of English cleanliness. Typical is Saussure's account:

The amount of water English people employ is inconceivable, especially for the cleaning of their houses ... Not a week passes by but well kept houses are washed twice in the seven days. All furniture, and especially all kitchen utensils, are kept with the greatest cleanliness ... and every morning most kitchens, staircases and entrances are scrubbed.

The Hall and Staircase

The attention lavished on the entrance hall seemed to astonish foreign visitors. Isaac Ware referred to it as merely the 'passage' but to foreign visitors it was amongst the wonders of the English house. Even La Rochefoucauld was forced to admit that the 'entrance hall' was 'always very clean and more like a room than one of our vestibules [in Paris], which are always dirty'. Likewise, Simond wondered that 'instead of the abominable filth of the common

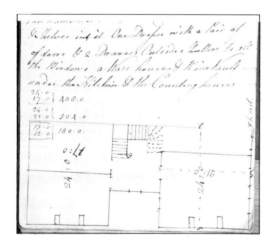

The London Assurance survey plan, made in 1747, of a merchant's house at Dolphin Court, near the Tower of London. The plan is typical of late-seventeenth-century houses built on congested City plots. The front door appears to be top right, in which case the passage to the centre of the house runs in an awkward manner between the winding flight of the staircase.

entrance and common stairs of a French house, here you step from the very street on a neat floor cloth or carpet, the walls painted or papered, a lamp in its glass bell hanging from the ceiling'.

The staircase that lay at the end of the hall also made an impression on the foreign visitor. Two descriptions from the 1780s tell more or less the same story. Archenholz observed that 'the staircase, whilst it is covered with the richest carpets, is supported by a balustrade of the finest Indian wood, curiously constructed, and lighted by lamps containing crystal cases. The landing places are adorned with busts and pictures and medallions'. La Rochefoucauld described the progress to the first-floor drawing-room and wrote that it was 'reached by a spotlessly clean staircase; the hand-rails are of mahogany in beautiful condition; the stairs, like the floor, are made of boards of fir or pine-wood, fitted together as exactly as a mosaic work'. He also observed that in the terrace house 'you are upon mats and carpets everywhere' and 'there is always a strip of drugget on the stairs'.

The Formal Rooms

One of the earliest, and best, descriptions of the formal rooms in a town house was published by John Wood in the 1749 edition of his *Essays towards a Description of Bath.* His account is somewhat suspect, however, for it is meant to reveal the squalor of Bath in the 1720s in contrast to the elegance that the city achieved – largely due to Wood himself – after 1740:

About the year 1727, the Boards of the Dining Rooms and most other Floors were made of a Brown Colour with Soot and small Beer to hide the Dirt, as well as their own Imperfections; and if the Walls of any of the Rooms were covered with Wainscot, it was such as was mean and never Painted: The Chimney Pieces, Hearths and Slabbs were all of Free Stone, and these were daily cleaned with a Particular White-wash, which, by paying Tribute to every thing that touched it, soon rendered the brown Floors like the Stary Firmament: The doors were slight and thin, and the best Locks had only Iron Coverings varnished: With Cane or Rush-bottomed Chairs the principal Rooms were furnished, and each Chair seldom exceeded three half Crowns in

Value; nor were the Tables, or Chests of Drawers, better in their Kind, the chief having been made of Oak; The Looking Glasses were small, mean, and few in Number; and the Chimney Furniture consisted of a slight Iron Fender, with Tongs, Poker and Shovel all of no more than Three or four Shillings' Value. With Kidderminster Stuff, or at best with Cheyne, the Woollen Furniture of the principal Rooms was made.

The interior that Wood described is essentially that of a modest, late-seventeenth-century country-town type – not exactly vernacular but decidedly provincial. It is, therefore, interesting to compare this description against other, more fragmentary evidence about the appearance of formal rooms in the modest town house in the first half of the eighteenth century.

In the 1718 lease for the house in Red Lion Square (see p. 63), the two parlours on the ground floor are merely described as wainscoted and painted, with marble jambs, chimney-pieces and brass locks to the doors. Articles of agreement dated May 1736 for repairing nine late-seventeenth-century houses in Essex Street, Strand (see p. 150), mention that the rooms on the ground floor and the 'one pair of stairs' (first floor) were 'to have new wainscot in the several rooms as before were hung' and new marble chimney-pieces, while others were to be 'altered and set with Dutch tiles' and all door-frames and wainscoting painted in oil.[49] The replacement of wall hangings, a seventeenth-century fashion, with panelling is particularly intriguing, because within a few years the fashion reversed, panelling being covered over with scrim – a hessian painted with undercoat – which formed a flat base for wallpaper (see p. 163).

Surveys of 1747 by Thomas Stubbs for the London Assurance paint a tantalizing picture of a merchant's house in the narrow Dolphin Court, near the Tower of London. To judge by the ground-floor plan sketched by Stubbs, this brick house was of the late-seventeenth century. The rooms in the 'attick storey' were lined 'with green Bayes: the south room hung with ordinary'. This presumably is a survival of the seventeenth-century fashion for hangings. The chimney is described as 'with tiles' – no doubt Dutch Delft tiles. The walls were 'painted in oil; the stairs wainscoted rail high with square deal work'. The stair landings, on the other hand, had 'square deal

work to the top'.

The dining-room seems to have been on the second floor, because this merchant's house, like many in the City, had 'Ware house and Wine vaults under the kitchen and counting house' that were on the ground floor. This general raising of the uses one storey above their conventional position also meant that the parlours were on the first floor. But the location of the dining-room was not its only notable feature. It was 'part wainscotted to the top and about one third with paper above the surbase' (the surbase is the dado rail). There was also a 'purple marble chimney piece . . . set with blue and white tiles'. The 'one pair of stairs' was wainscoted to the top [with] round work and plain pannels' (see p. 150). 'The back parlour' was 'wainscot'd surbase high and with India . . . above the surbase' and had a 'marble chimney piece . . . set with white dutch tiles'.[50] 'India' was Chinese wallpaper (see p. 162).

John Wood complemented his account of a typical 1727 Bath interior with a good description of the formal rooms of a new, or newly fitted up, town house of the early 1740s. As the new buildings of Bath advanced, wrote Wood,

Carpets were introduced to cover the Floors, though Laid with the finest clean Deals, or Dutch Oak Boards: the Rooms were all Wainscoted and Painted in a costly and handsome Manner; Marble Slabbs, and even Chimney Pieces, became common; the Doors in general were not only made thick and substantial, but they had the best sort of Brass Locks put on them; Walnut Tree Chairs, some with Leather, and some with Damask or Worked Bottoms supplied the place of such as were Seated with Cane or Rushes; the Oak Tables and Chests of Drawers were exchanged, the former for such as were made of Mahogany, the latter for such as were made either with the same Wood, or with Walnut Tree; handsome Glasses were added to the Dressing Tables, nor did the proper Chimneys or peers of any of the Rooms long remain without Well Framed Mirrours of no inconsiderable Size; and the Furniture for every Chief Chimney was composed of a Brass Fender, with Tongs, Poker and shovel agreeable to it.[51]

What Wood omits from this description is as interesting as what he includes: no mention of dining-tables as such, though he does mention tables

Entrance halls and staircases. Above: No. 12 Merrion Square, Dublin, c. 1765. Opposite: No. 58 Grafton Way, London, 1793. At both large and small scale these clean and elegant entrance passages and staircase halls impressed foreign visitors to Britain.

Ground-floor dining-room at No. 29 Percy Street, London. Although the house was built c. 1765, this floor is still panelled (in the manner of the 1740s), while the drawing-room above has fashionable plastered walls.

of mahogany in general, and no mention of any wall covering other than wainscot 'painted in a costly and handsome manner'. In London and most provincial cities the days of wainscot as the preferred wall covering for major rooms were waning in 1742, and all but over in 1749 (see p. 155). However, it must be said that the dining-room, as the location for family portraits and silver, seemed to have been consciously old-fashioned in comparison with the drawing-room.[52] The dining-room could be dark, perhaps panelled into the 1760s, and very much the masculine room – the symbol of the family's pedigree and a repository of values transcending fashion. The drawing-room in contrast would be light, the height of fashion, the feminine room, with walls of painted plaster or hung with paper or fabric. This was where women retired after dinner to make tea, while the men stayed on in the dining-room to drink and talk politics (see p. 41). This allocation of different wall treatments to different types of room is explained by Ware: 'For a noble hall, nothing is

so well as stucco [see p. 165], for a parlour wainscot seems properest; and for the apartment of a lady, hangings.'

As well as these somewhat technical descriptions of the formal rooms and parlours in the town house, there are also a few livelier contemporary observations on furnishing. In *Persuasion*, Jane Austen offered a delightful description of the changes overtaking the decoration and organization of the formal room:

the old-fashioned square parlour, with a small carpet and shining floor ... the ... daughters of the house were gradually giving the proper air of confusion by a grand piano forte and a harp, flowerstands and little tables placed in every direction. Oh! could the originals of the portraits against the wainscot .. have seen what was going on, have been conscious of such an overthrow of all order and neatness: the portraits themselves seemed to be staring in astonishment.

A Bloomsbury drawing-room c. 1830: George Scharf's sketch of his own drawing-room. The house was built in the late-eighteenth century, although details shown in this view (especially the fire surround with corner roundels) indicate an early-nineteenth-century refitting. Characteristic is the small drugget in front of the fire to save the main floor carpet (not shown) from wear and the elaborate curtain arrangement with a continuous valance.

Southey made more detailed comments about the ground-floor front-parlour. He found it very inconvenient, because it meant 'living on a level with the street: the din is at your very ear, the window cannot be thrown open for the dust which showers in, and it is half darkened by blinds that the by-passers may not look in upon your privacy'. Notwithstanding this basic flaw, 'the common sitting room' is an excellent example of

an Englishman's delight to show his wealth ... the whole floor is fitted with carpeting, not of the costliest kind ... This remains down in summer and winter ... before the fire is a smaller carpet of different fabric, and fleecy appearance ... a fashion of late years which has become universal because it is at once ornamental, comfortable and useful, preserving the larger one, which would else soon be worn out in that particular part. Of the fire place ... the frontal is marble, and above is a looking glass the whole length of the mantelpiece, divided into three compartments by gilt pillars which support a gilt architrave. On each side hang bell ropes of coloured worsted, about the thickness of a man's wrist ... which suspend knobs of polished spar.[53] *The fender is remarkable; it consists of a crescent basket work of wire painted green, about a foot in height, top't with brass, and supporting seven brazen pillars of nearly the same height, which are also surrounded by a band of brass. This also is a late fashion, introduced in consequence of the numberless accidents occasioned by fire ... The chairs and tables are of a wood brought from Honduras, which is in great request here.*

This room clearly also doubles as a breakfast-parlour, for it contains:

our breakfast table ... oval large enough for eight or more persons, yet supported upon a claw in the centre ... Here also is a nest of tables for the ladies, consisting of four, one less than the other, and each fitting into the one above it; you would take them for play things, from their slenderness and size, if you did not see how useful they find them for their work. A harpsichord takes up the middle of one side of the room, and in the corners are screens to protect the face from the fire, of mahogany, with fans of green silk, which spread like a flower, and may be raised or lowered at pleasure. A book-case standing on a chest of drawers completes the heavy furniture, it has glazed doors, and curtains of green silk within.

Southey described window furniture in detail and suggested that blinds, shutters and curtains were all used in conjunction to ensure privacy and security.

The plan [of the blinds] is taken from Venetian blinds, but made more expensive, as the bars are fitted into a frame and move in grooves. The shutters fit back by day, and are rendered ornamental by the gilt ring by which they are drawn open: at night you perceive you are in a land of housebreakers, by the contrivances for barring them, and the bells which are fixed on to warn the family, in case the house should be attacked. On each side of the window the curtains hang in festoons, they are of rich printed

cotton, lined with a plain colour and fringed, the quantity they contain is very great. Add to this a sconce of the most graceful form, with six prints in gilt frames, and you have the whole scene before you. Two of these are Noel's views of Cádiz and Lisbon; the others are from English history, and represent the Battles of the Boyne and of La Hogue, the death of General Wolfe at Quebec, and William Penn treating with the Indians for his province of Pennsylvania.

Southey went on to describe the dining-room:

Here the table is circular, but divides in half to receive a middle part which lengthens it, and this is so contrived that it may be made to sit any number of persons from six to twenty. The sideboard is a massive piece of furniture; formerly a single slab of marble was used for this purpose, but now this is become one of the most handsome and most expensive articles. The glasses are arranged on it ready for dinner, and the knives and forks in two little chests or cabinets, the spoons are between them in a sort of urn; everything being made costly and ornamental.

Second-floor front room at No. 58 Grafton Way, Tottenham Court Road, of 1793 showing bed alcove.

The 'single slab of marble' formerly used as a sideboard is the buffet that crops up occasionally in town house inventories; for example, the lease of 1756 for the house in Northumberland Row, Tottenham, mentions several 'beaufets' and 'beaufots', some with doors, in both first-floor and ground-floor rooms.

Southey's description of the drawing-room is brief: it

differs chiefly from the breakfast-parlour in having everything more expensive, a carpet of richer fabric, sconces and mirrors more highly ornamented, and curtains of damask like the sofas and chairs. Two chandeliers with glass drops stand on the mantelpiece ... in this room are the portraits of [the master of the house] and his wife, by one of the best living artists.

The Bedrooms

Southey's picture of his bedroom is a vivid representation of such rooms at this time:

It is on the second floor ... my bed, though neither covered with silk nor satin, has as much ornament as is suitable; silk or satin would not give the clean

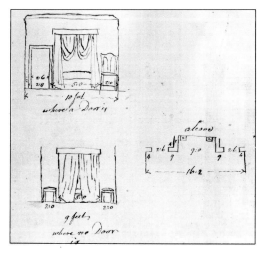

Late-eigthteenth-century sketch by George Dance or James Peacock in Dance's office scrapbook showing bed alcove and bed arrangement in a small bedroom.

appearance which the English always require ... hence the damask curtains which were used in the last generation have given place to linen. These are full enough to hang in folds; by day they are gathered round the bed posts, which are light pillars of mahogany supporting a frame work, covered with the same furniture as the curtains; and valances are fastened round the frame, both withinside the curtain and without, and again round the sides of the bedstead. The blankets are of the natural colour of the wool, quite plain; the sheets plain also. I have never seen them flounced nor laced, nor even seen a striped or coloured blanket. The counterpane is of all English manufactures the least tasteful; it is of white cotton ornamental with cotton knots, in shape as graceless as the cut box in the garden. My window curtains are of the same pattern as the bed; a mahogany press holds my cloths, an oval looking glass swinging lengthways stands on the dressing table: A compact kind of chest holds the basin, the soap, the tooth brush, and water glass, each in a separate compartment; and a looking glass, for the purpose of shaving at (for Englishmen usually shave themselves), slips up and down behind, the water jug and water bottle stand below, and the whole shuts down a-top, and closes in front, like a cabinet. The room is carpeted; here I have my fire, my table, and my cassette.

Sophie von la Roche echoed Southey's portrait of the clean and comfortable bedroom. When staying at an inn in Ingatestone, Essex, she noted that the rooms were 'well papered and carpeted' and 'fitted with every possible comfort'. Unlike Southey, she rather admired the bedcovers, which she described as being 'of a white cotton material with fringe decoration woven in' and, like 'everything ... spotlessly white'.

Not mentioned by Southey is the practice of placing beds in alcoves created against one wall of the bedroom. This enveloping of the bed within curtains, and then within an alcove, has its roots in the medieval practice of creating a private, draught-proof bed-enclosure within a room in common use. It may seem curious that this habit lingered on in the eighteenth-century town house, but there are enough examples, both surviving and in plans, to suggest that the bedroom alcove was a fairly common device.[54]

Chapter Two

SERVICING THE HOUSE

In eighteenth-century houses most rooms were serviced only to the extent of having an open fire and a candlestick. Things began to change after the mid-eighteenth century, and more rapidly after about 1780, but the brightly lit, well-heated house with more or less odourless drains was really a Victorian creation.

For the purposes of analysis it is convenient to divide services into two groups: those coming into the house and those going out. The principal items coming in were fuel, food and water; the outgoing items rubbish and sewage of all kinds. In addition there was lighting, a relatively straightforward subject that can be dispatched fairly quickly.

LIGHTING

For the whole of the Georgian period, right up until the accession of Queen Victoria in 1837, the principal means of lighting rooms was by candles, rush-lights or lamps. These light sources were governed by a strict social hierarchy. At the bottom were rush-lights, made by dipping the stripped pith of common rushes into hot animal fat. Gilbert White, the Vicar of Selborne, recorded that thrifty countrywomen used the skimmings of their bacon pot for this purpose. The lights were held in adjustable holders that consisted of a simple clip mounted on a stand. An average rush 2 ft 4 in long would burn for just short of an hour. White described with irritation how the poor preferred, for merely snobbish reasons, to burn tallow candles rather than rush-lights, which made them the very worst of

economists. For while eleven rushes could be bought for a farthing and would burn for ten hours, a tallow candle costing a halfpenny would last for two hours at most.

Tallow candles made of rendered animal fat, usually mutton fat, were by far the most common source of light for the artisan and middle classes, and in ordinary town households were universal. They were smelly and burnt badly, requiring constant snuffing to prevent pieces of charred wick falling into the tallow and causing guttering, which literally means forming a gutter down which large amounts of molten tallow would run. Their light output was poor to begin with and decreased rapidly with burning.

At the top of the social scale was the beeswax candle, which cost a good deal more than tallow but had a higher melting-point, smelt less and could be left unattended for longer periods. The rich used wax candles whenever the occasion might be held to justify such extravagance; those less wealthy only on very special occasions. Wax candles had considerable advantages when used in chandeliers and other inaccessible locations, where snuffing was a difficult operation; perhaps this is the reason that chandeliers were an exclusively upper-class fitment.

Prodigality with lighting was not the Georgian rule and the average room was very underlit by the standards of both the nineteenth and twentieth centuries. Inventories of the contents of modest eighteenth-century town houses seldom record more than two candlesticks in a room, while contemporary paintings of interiors at night show that it was not at all uncommon for a room to be lighted with a single candle. Placed on a table, its light was sufficient for all the family to read or work, while a

Scharf's sketch of the interior of Mr Barron's hardware showroom near Charing Cross in 1830. Barron evidently ran a reputable business, as witness the fashionably dressed couple deliberating over the purchase of an elaborate cast-iron grate. It is instructive to see the variety of grates offered for sale: some of those on the shelves to the right are late-eighteenth-century types; those at floor level are the more modern all-in-one variety. Against the rear wall are various kitchen items, including a cooking range and a clockwork turnspit, while the table in the foreground holds Argand oil lamps with their distinctive reservoirs.

glass globe full of water could conveniently concentrate the strength of the single flame to permit fine work like lacemaking. The most frequent inventory reference to lighting is to 'a pair of sconces', that is, wall-mounted candles, probably with mirrors behind them to increase the light. In ordinary rooms such sconces were almost invariably mounted on the chimney-breast, often flanking another mirror.

For some reason oil burning lights were not nearly so widespread in eighteenth-century England as they were abroad, where fish and vegetable oil were in regular use. The commonest form of Continental burner differed little from Roman versions, with a twist of material for a wick, fed by capillary action from the reservoir below. A revolutionary improvement in this arrangement was effected by Ami Argand of Geneva, who evolved a tubular wick that allowed air to be drawn up through the middle of the flame and added a glass chimney to improve the draught. In 1783 he demonstrated his lamp, which had the light output of ten wax candles, to the French Academy of Sciences, but the Academicians were much more interested in Montgolfier and his hot-air balloon. Disgruntled, Argand brought his invention to London, where it was taken up with enthusiasm by Matthew Boulton and others (in fact, his French demonstration had not gone wholly unnoticed and lamps to the Argand pattern were soon being produced by the Frenchman Quinquet under his own name). Colza oil lamps with Argand burners could be found in many of the wealthier late-Georgian households. Before 1798 they had had to have an oil reservoir above the level of the burner because the oil (almost invariably the heavy and viscous green Colza oil, made from the same oil seed rape whose bright-yellow flowers now cover much of the summer countryside) required a gravity feed. The reservoir obscured one side of the lamp, casting a heavy shadow, and for this reason it became common practice to have twin lamp-burners, fed by a common central reservoir. After 1798 a little clockwork pump was available to force the oil upwards, though it was not very reliable.

Argands were expensive to buy and expensive to run. Candles were simpler and more economical and remained by far the most common source of lighting until the mid-nineteenth century. With the arrival of paraffin oil from Pennsylvania in the 1860s things began to change.

Gas lighting was not a feature of the Georgian house. In the first decades of the nineteenth century coal gas came into wide commercial use. In 1805 it was installed in a cotton mill in Halifax, and, by 1823, 215 miles of London streets were lighted by gas (see p. 10). But although a few lonely pioneers, including Sir Walter Scott, had gas lights installed in their homes, the vast majority of the population distrusted the new invention. They had good reason to do so, because the early gas burners were not very reliable and were safest burnt in a large or open-air location. The distrust persisted and as late as 1846 a Mr Rutter, Engineer to the Old Brighton Gas Company, observed the 'remarkable circumstance connected with the progress of gas lighting that while many thousands of persons had availed themselves of gas, never doubting that it was indispensable in their business transactions, so small a proportion had thought it equally necessary to the comfort and convenience of their families'.[1] Rutter was writing just as the tide of opinion was beginning to turn, and the installation of gas light in the new House of Commons in 1852 must have reassured many people as to its safety.

HEATING

The heating of Georgian town houses was effected by coal. Some aristocrats may have burnt wood for snobbish reasons, but they were only a small minority. Smaller inland towns might also have used wood, but larger towns were all coal-fired. Already by the mid-seventeenth century this was the principal fuel in London, and virtually every foreign visitor to the capital in the eighteenth century was struck by the black pall of smoke that hung over the capital (see p. 3). The main reason for this pall was the inefficiency of the average domestic fireplace. In the seventeenth and early-eighteenth centuries most fireplaces were really wood-burning arrangements, with a roomy brick or tiled hearth and a wide chimney. The coal was placed in a free-standing iron or steel basket, usually with an iron fireback behind. It is often assumed that firebacks belong to the seventeenth century, but they occur regularly in both country and town house inventories well after 1750. Smoke eddied about in the wide chimneys and often came back into the room because of down-

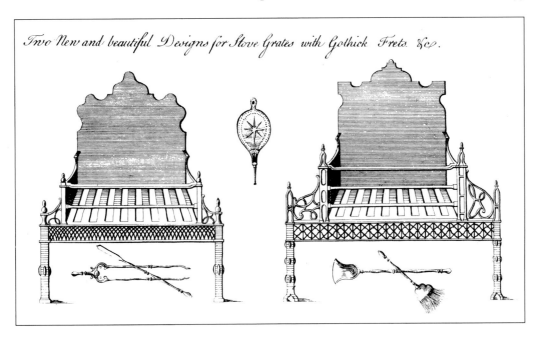

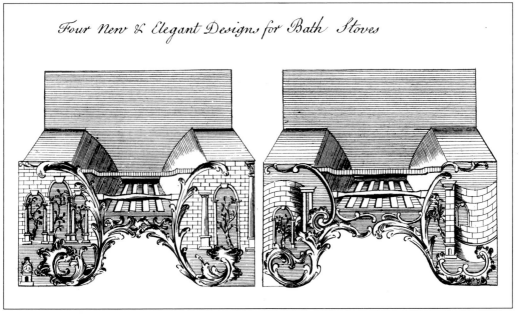

Top: *A plate from* The Smith's Right Hand *by William and John Welldon, which appeared in 1765. The plate shows a grate in the Gothic style. Although it was evidently intended for coal, this is still essentially a wood-burning apparatus. It has a large open basket with an integral fireback, and the two front legs are clearly derived from the old-fashioned fire-dogs used to prop logs. Grates like this were placed free-standing in the tall openings typical of mid-eighteenth-century hearths, and must have been chronically inefficient.* Bottom: *The Welldons' designs for Bath stoves, a type of hob grate.*

FIGURE 16.4
"The Comforts of a Rump ford."

A satire on the fundamental improvements in domestic heating made as the result of Count Rumford's experiments.

draughts, while much of the heat went straight upwards, taking with it a quantity of unburnt coal dust, which formed the famous London pall.

Remarkably little chimney equipment from the first half of the eighteenth century has survived, but it seems that during these years it became usual to unite the three separate pieces of equipment in the hearth – namely the coal basket, fireback and firedogs – into one unit, which was commonly called a 'stove grate'. The only practical advantage of this development was that the coal basket was raised up somewhat higher, but such grates afforded wide scope for ornamental decoration. Some idea of the variety of stove grates available in and after the mid century can be gained from two contemporary pattern-books: *The Smith's Right Hand* of 1765 by William and John Welldon and *The Stove-Grate Maker's Assistant* of 1771 by W. Glossop. These pattern-books have a close family resemblance to the books of designs for houses and garden orna-

ments produced by writers like Batty Langley and William Halfpenny in the hope of attracting a wealthy client, and the ornamental stove grate was very much a fitment of the homes of the upper and upper-middle classes. Leading designers like Thomas Chippendale and later Robert Adam provided their own designs for individual clients, often with brass inlay and a great deal of pierced ornament. Grates for the wealthy were of a good size and capable of holding a large amount of burning coal, but the basic design was inefficient.

The first main improvement in this state of affairs was the introduction of the cast-iron hob grate in the years after the mid century. Primitive hob grates, in which iron fire bars were set between stone cheeks, can be found in fairly modest houses of the 1720s and 1730s, and even then must have been more efficient than basket grates. At least the coal baskets were smaller and the fires must have been more economical with fuel. The cast-iron version, which seems to have made its appearance in about 1750, combined the advantages of a small basket with those of a wholly cast-iron front, which radiated a great deal more heat than a fireback. The most substantial parts were the top or hob itself and the front, which was made of a single iron casting, usually with some simple decoration. The Coalbrookdale Company at Ironbridge in Shropshire produced a particularly pleasing design that portrayed the iron bridge itself. The rest of the grate was made of thin sheet-iron. These things were cheap to produce and much more efficient than an open fire. They very soon became virtually standard equipment in ordinary town houses, and also in the smaller or less important rooms of grander mansions. Besides space heating, the hob grate served other functions: the hob itself was useful for keeping things warm, and indeed such grates doubled as a cooking stove in many poorer Georgian homes.

After the introduction of the hob grate, the most significant improvement in domestic fires was effected by Benjamin Thompson, Count Rumford, the polymathematical founder of the Royal Institution. On a visit to London from mainland Europe in 1796 he was so appalled by the foul air and the draughts of the average English drawing-room that he wrote and published a small pamphlet called *Chimney Fireplaces*, which pointed out that a narrow chimney throat would improve draught and lessen smokiness.[2] Two years later he had taken up residence in London and at his own house in Brompton Row, Knightsbridge, he installed new grates to his own design in which a further improvement was made. The source of heat was brought forward from the back of the chimney opening, and the sides were canted to increase radiation. These 'Rumford Stoves' soon became fashionable. Lord Palmerston had them, as did Sir Joseph Banks, Lady Templeton and the Marquis of Salisbury.

Rumford's design, with some improvements and modifications, was essentially the same as the all-in-one iron fireplace that is now in common use, but it was a long time before this arrangement became pre-eminent. Stove grates and hob grates were still being made in the 1820s and 1830s, often to patterns that had been current in the 1780s. Versions of all these grates can be glimpsed in George Scharf's 1830 view of Mr Barron's showroom in Charing Cross, along with clockwork spit mechanisms and reflectors for speeding the cooking of meat.[3]

COOKING

Kitchen stoves seem to have been a late-eighteenth-century introduction. Domestic cookery for most of the eighteenth century was done with the aid of an ordinary fire in an ordinary grate. Food to be cooked was heated in a pan, boiled, or roasted on a spit. Roasting in the modern sense, which is really a baking process, was not usually an option, because satisfactory ovens were unavailable to most people. Here again house inventories are probably the most reliable source of information about the stock of kitchen equipment. In 1722 a publican named Claudius Gulland of Soho had in his kitchen: 'a wind-up jack compleat, a fire range complete with pot hangers, two gridirons and two trivetts, three brass potts, and one iron pot, three sauce pans, one stewpan, two spitts, one chafing dish, a pair of doggs, a tin dripping pan and other tin ware'.[4] The word 'range' here is deceptive, because ranges as we now understand them, made entirely of cast-iron with integral ovens and sometimes even an arrangement for producing hot water, do not seem to have come into use until the 1780s. In October 1780 Thomas Robinson took out a patent for a range

that combined an open fire with spits and an oven. The spits were turned by a smoke jack, which was a fan in the chimney turned by the current of hot air rising from the fire. Smoke jacks required a strong current of air to turn a heavily loaded spit, ovens heated on one side only were of limited use, and altogether the eighteenth-century cooking stove was a clumsy device.

Here again Count Rumford was one of the catalysts for improvement. In his essay 'Of the Imperfections of the Kitchen Fireplaces Now in Use' he described the customary arrangements for cooking as follows:

The Kitchen Fireplace of a family in easy circumstances in this country consists almost uni-

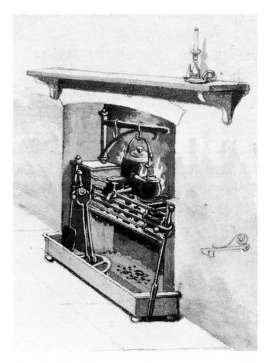

A modest late-Georgian cooking range. It is similar in general arrangement to eighteenth-century domestic grates but with a slider on the right-hand side to adjust the size of the fire for the required number of pots. The other obvious addition is the swinging crane. In this example the crane holds a large pot with a tap, which gave a constant supply of hot water.

A kitchen in Leadenhall Street, London, formed out of a medieval undercroft. Apart from its medieval setting, the kitchen follows the normal arrangements, with a cooking hearth and copper. Attached to the grate bars is a trivet with a pot, and another trivet stands in front. On the chimney-breast above is the mechanism for a smoke jack of the kind that Count Rumford so heartily detested.

versally of a long grate, called a *Kitchen-Range*, for burning coals, placed in a wide and deep open chimney with a very high mantel ... At one end of the grate there is commonly an iron oven, which is heated by the fire in the grate; and sometimes there is a boiler situated in a similar manner at the other end of it. To complete the machinery (which in every part and detail of it seems to have been calculated for the express purpose of devouring fuel) a smoke-jack is placed in the chimney.*

Rumford despised smoke jacks for their wastefulness: 'No human invention that ever came to my knowledge appears to me to be so absurd as this ... incomparably less labour will be required to wind up a common jack than to bring coals to feed the fire that is requisite to make a smoke jack go.' He considered that

The great fault in the construction and arrangement of the Kitchen of private families now in common use ... is that they are not closed. *The fuel is burnt in a long open grate ... over which the pots and*

kettles are freely suspended, or placed in stands; or fires are made with charcoal in square holes called stoves, in a solid mass of brickwork, and connected with no flue to carry off the smoke ... The loss of heat and waste of fuel in these kitchens is altogether incredible.[5]

The only answer was to redesign the apparatus for cooking, with small enclosed fires placed directly underneath the ovens or plates. Rumford put forward a series of improvements of this kind, which were taken up with alacrity. As early as 1802 the Exeter ironfounder George Bodley introduced a kitchen range, owing much to Rumford, that can be taken as the prototype of all nineteenth-century kitchen ranges. Rumford's contribution to domestic comfort was widely recognized:

Lo, ev'ry parlour, drawing-room I see
Boasts of thy stoves, and talks of naught but thee
Yet not alone My Lady and young MISSES,
The cooks themselves would smother thee with
  kisses.

A late-nineteenth-century drawing of the basement kitchen at No. 30 Spital Square. The house was built in the late 1730s, and since the lead cistern is dated 1739, this view probably shows the original arrangement. The kitchen was in the front basement room overlooking the front area. Under the window was a stone sink, and immediately next to it the lead water storage tank. Presumably the tank was fed through the pipe running up beneath it, with the water supplied, most probably, by the New River Company. The massive cooking hearth must be original, but it has had a smaller grate inserted to make it more economical. All in all, a typical eighteenth-century London kitchen.

Yes! Mistress Cook would spoil a goose, a steak
To twine her greasy arms around thy neck.[6]

Fuel

Before the maid brought her scuttle of coal to fuel all the various fires in a town house, the coal itself had to be ferried from the nearest wharf and stored in a convenient place. The average house might have two or three fires burning during the day, consuming coal and producing ash, and considerable volumes of both needed to be kept. Space in town houses, especially the smaller ones, was always at a premium and the most common solution to the problem was to store both the coal and the ash in vaulted cellars extending under the street at basement level. Such vaults are virtually standard in Georgian town houses after about 1740, and there are many earlier examples, although houses of the 1720s and before might be built in a countrified fashion, with no basement. In such cases the coal must have been stored under the stairs or in the backyard.

Vault-building became an important part of the whole process of laying out streets, because the brick arches formed a firm foundation for the roadway

between the houses. In better-class developments the gap between the ends of vaults was soon found to be a convenient place for a brick sewer.

Coal was usually shot into the vaults by way of a hole in the pavement. These holes were presumably covered, but, without exception, the present coal-hole covers in London are of nineteenth-century date, usually with the names of their makers round

Above: *A rather crude view of a late-eighteenth-century London coalman, similar in almost all respects to modern equivalents. It is a great pity that the coal-hole cover itself is not shown, because information about eighteenth-century coal-plates is curiously hard to come by.*

Opposite: *Two views in the kitchen of No. 23 Queen Anne's Gate, Westminster, a house of c. 1704. The arrangements are very similar to those at Spital Square, with a sink and tank next to the window, the tank fed this time by a pipe from above. The cooking hearth has a late-nineteenth-century cooking range in which the fire is totally enclosed. Next to it is a copper with its own small grate for heating the washing water.*

the rim. Their huge variety is a startling indication of the great number of small iron-founders in the capital during the nineteenth century. For original eighteenth-century coal-hole covers one must go to Bath, where in Trim Street and South Parade can be seen square openings in the street surface covered with large blocks of stone or with square iron plates.

Between the coal vaults and the basement proper, which in town houses was the most common location for the kitchen, scullery and servants' accommodation, was often the narrow yard commonly called the 'area'. Early-eighteenth-century houses in London, Bristol and other towns, as well as houses in suburban locations or of low social status, were often built with no area. If there was a basement, the windows of the front basement room gained their light through sloping embrasures cut down from the street. This was clearly an unsatisfactory arrangement: it limited the free circulation of air that was needed to disperse cooking smells and prevent them percolating up the stairs to the rooms above; at the same time it did nothing to prevent damp from the street penetrating directly through the wall of the house. Even in the eighteenth century proper ventilation was an important consideration. It is surely significant that in early-eighteenth-century house descriptions the area was usually called the 'airy', which suggests that its ventilating function was primary.

ACCESS FOR SERVICES

In many houses the area also afforded the space for a servants' or tradesmen's stair leading directly to the kitchen, but it would be wrong to assume that such stairs were standard in the eighteenth century. Indeed, it seems more likely that they were a mid-eighteenth-century development. The earliest front areas, like those in Queen Anne's Gate, where the houses on the west side date from about 1700, almost certainly did not have steps. By the 1740s they could be found in the best houses. The original building accounts for both No. 44 Berkeley Square, built between 1742 and 1744 for Lady Isabella Finch,[7] and No. 10 St James's Square, built in 1736 for Sir William Heathcote,[8] mention the provision of stone

A stone coal-hole cover in Gay Street, Bath. For some reason, perhaps because of paving regulations, there are apparently no surviving eighteenth-century coal-hole covers in London. All date from the nineteenth century or later and most are of cast-iron. By contrast Bath streets still exhibit many examples of eighteenth-century stone covers with a simple central hole for lifting.

steps in the front area. But ordinary town houses, even quite substantial ones like those in South-ampton Place, Bloomsbury, were still being built without steps. By the 1770s they were much more common: all of Robert Adam's town houses had them; so did the speculative terraces in Gloucester Place (1790s) and York Street on the Portman Estate and those in Montague Street (1800) on the Bedford Estate in Bloomsbury. But on the adjoining Found-ling Hospital Estate, which was developed at about the same time, some houses had area steps and some did not. There seems to be no obvious explanation for such differences, nor were they confined to London. Many of the houses in fashionable Bath had no front steps, but instead were provided with a lifting gate in the area railings, so that supplies could be lowered down in a basket. In a few places a simple crane was provided. Where there were no steps and no lifting gate, all the provisions must

have been brought through the front door and taken down the inside stairs. Some confirmation that this was common practice is provided by the large numbers of eighteenth-century tradesmen's cards that have vignettes showing fish and other goods being sold at the front door. Indeed, there are appar-ently no cards showing deliveries being made via the area.

WATER SUPPLY

Besides fuel and food, the most important of the incoming services was water. The most primitive means of supply, but the commonest outside London, was the public conduit or fountain, often erected over a spring or stream at the expense of a

J.C. Nattes's view of a front area. This example is much wider and more spacious than the usual poky arrangement and evidently belongs to a grand town house. Nevertheless it has the customary ingredients: iron railings round the top with a gate opening on to a flight of stone steps, a door opening into the vault under the street (which was used variously to contain coal, ashes, the water tank or even the water-closet) and a pierced stone cover for the drain hole.

One of Francis Wheatley's glamorized 'Cries of London', showing a mackerel seller. It is interesting to see fish, one of the smellier commodities, being delivered to kitchen staff through the front door of what is evidently a fairly large town house. The inference is that there was no direct access to the basement kitchen by way of the area, whose railings appear on the left, and underlines the point that area steps were by no means universal.

Bath still has many examples of front areas with gates in the railings but no steps. At Alfred House, No. 14 Alfred Street, the reason for this arrangement is made clear by the survival of a crane and winch. It is usually said that this was used for the hoisting up of sedan chairs, but it was probably used much more often for the hoisting of groceries. The Alfred House railings also preserve their lamp bracket and extinguisher.

private benefactor, from which water could be carried away in jugs for private consumption. Few early conduits survive in anything like their original form (Hobson's conduit in Cambridge is a notable exception); many were converted to more mundane but economical pumps in the nineteenth century and even those have mostly gone. But a great number of English towns have streets whose names commemorate long-vanished water sources: London has Conduit Street, White Conduit Street, Lamb's Conduit Street and Sadler's Wells; Oxford has Holywell; Bristol has Jacob's Wells Road; Nottingham has St Ann's Wells Road.

Another free source of supply was rain-water. The London Building Act of 1724 made it compulsory to have drain-pipes on the fronts of houses, and in many cases the water was led down into a butt or tank in the front area. A very substantial number of town residences also had their own private wells in the basement or backyard. All the houses in Inigo Jones's 1630s Covent Garden Piazza were originally supplied in this way[9] and most of eighteenth-century London south of the Thames, but town wells were very unpredictable: their water might be suddenly drained off by the wells of other houses near by, and in the later Georgian period they must have become increasingly polluted by the seepage from cesspools.

For a small fee, water was available from the carts of water-carriers, but undoubtedly the most convenient, although the most expensive, arrangement was to have a piped supply. In the Georgian period this was almost exclusively a metropolitan option. Piped systems did exist elsewhere in the country, but they were of very limited extent. A piped system was initiated at Derby in 1692, but a hundred years later there were only six and a half miles of pipework in all. Bristol, one of the largest Georgian towns, was worse supplied with water than any other city in England. As late as 1846 only 5,000 out of the 70,000 houses in the town had a piped supply.[10] Eighteenth-century London was served by several private water companies, and by the first decades of the nineteenth century their number had risen to eight. These included the New River Company, which had been bringing fresh water from Hertfordshire to Sadler's Wells in Islington since the beginning of the seventeenth century, the Society of Hampstead Aqueducts, established under Queen Elizabeth I, which supplied much of the Holborn district with water from ponds on Hampstead Heath, and the London Bridge and Chelsea companies, which drew their water from the Thames. In the first half of the eighteenth century the New River and Hampstead supplies depended on gravity, but from the 1760s the New River Company was using a steam pump. Water was conducted under the streets in wooden pipes made from the trunks of elm trees and connections were made to the homes of those customers who paid the appropriate fee by small pipes, or 'quills'.

The supply of water was regular but not constant. In the 1760s, for example, the New River Company had four mains to the west part of London; the Soho

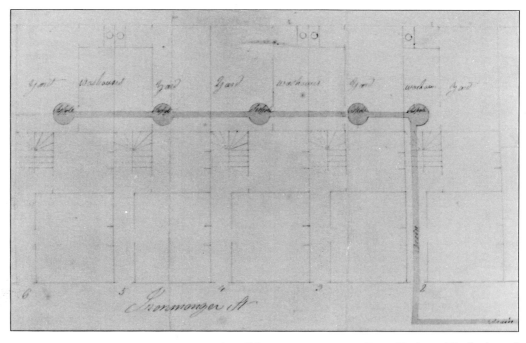

The drainage arrangements for a terrace of small houses in Ironmonger Row, Finsbury. The back yards contain a privy and wash-house, the latter draining into a cesspool immediately outside the back window. Small houses like this probably lacked a constant water supply, and the cesspools would have been offensive.

main was filled, or 'charged', for seven hours on three days a week; the Oxford Street and Portland Street mains were charged for fifteen and six hours a week respectively; while the Grosvenor main that served the richest private houses was charged every day for a total of twenty-four hours a week. A similar class bias was operated by the Chelsea company, which supplied Pall Mall and Whitehall daily, but the rest of its district less frequently.[11] Intermittent supply made a large cistern absolutely necessary, and the commonest sort was the large lead box, of which many examples still survive. The strapwork decoration on the front of these cisterns, often with the date and the initials of their owner embossed in the centre, changed little during the course of the century. They were often placed in the front area, where they could also receive rain-water from the down-pipes, but they could also be found in the vaults under the street, in the backyard or in the kitchen itself.

From the cistern a supply could be pumped to a higher level. There are examples of roof-level tanks well before the Georgian period. Of these, the cistern that Samuel Vincent placed on the roof of Buckenham Hall in Norfolk in the 1680s sounds the most entertaining. His house was described as 'a neat pile of brick, on the summit whereof is a lofty lantern or turret, and on the top of this house he (being a very great humorist) erected a fish-pond, with a bason of lead to contain the water, and had pipes of lead which brought water by an engine from a canal in the gardens into every room (it is said) of the house.'[12] A more modest example of town house arrangements is contained in the building specification prepared by the architect Roger Morris and the builder Benjamin Timbrell for a house in the Strand in 1736-7.[13] On the ground floor there was to be 'a flat out of the back room and a water closet in the south east corner' and 'over this water closet a cistern of oak 6 ft by 5 ft by 4 ft deep, lined with lead, which will hold nine hogsheads of water, to supply this water-closet and the wash-house and kitchen'. In the back room on the first floor there was to be 'a leaden pipe brought up in the wall, in case a water closet should be required'.

In the eighteenth century piped water was something of a luxury, on a par with the telephone before the Great War. The records of the various water companies are difficult of access at present, and it is not easy to make any sort of useful estimate about the numbers of houses supplied, but it seems likely that most of the houses in the West End had piped water, as well as quite a few in the City. The West End had the peculiar advantage of being so sited that its houses could take water from several different companies, and it is clear that some households solved the problems of an intermittent supply by having pipes laid in from every available main. In 1718 the speculative builder Thomas Barlow described the arrangements at a house he was constructing in Great George Street, off Hanover Square, for the first Earl Cowper: 'as to the pump thear is a very good one alredy fixed in ye stable yard: and the Cundit water may be layd thear: and ye Hampstead waters forward: and we may expect the new revir will soon be layd down becaus it is allred layd down to som of ye new houses at the uper side of ye square'.[14] In other words, water from the City's Conduit Mead supply in the stable yard, water from Hampstead Ponds in the front basement kitchen, and the possibility of water supplied by the New River Company from the Sadler's Wells reservoir in the near future.

The old wooden mains pipes were sleeve jointed, and not at all watertight. They were tolerable when the water was fed by gravity, but, on the arrival of a steam pump at Sadler's Wells in the 1760s, it was found that these pipes could not withstand the high pressure of which the pump was capable. As a result the pressure had to be restricted, and for the whole of the eighteenth century none of the water companies could provide a water supply above ground-floor level. William Chadwell Mylne, Surveyor to the New River Company, remembered that 'in 1810 the Company could not serve above the ground floor in any part of the town . . . because their works were all in wood, and the mains were shut off at night to preserve water. Since 1816 when iron pipes were introduced, the Company could serve the top floor of any house in the district, and the pipes are always full.'[15]

Although some iron pipes were in use as early as 1740, they were an expensive capital item and all the water companies shied away from wholesale installation. But leakage from the wooden pipes wreaked havoc on the surfaces of London's streets and pavements, and as the number of pipes increased the damage increased in proportion. In 1817 Parliament passed the Metropolitan Paving Act, which compelled all the companies to lay their pipes in iron, and by 1820 wooden pipes were a thing of the past.

Following these improvements there was a massive increase in consumption. Mr Knight of the West Middlesex Waterworks, commenting in 1821, put it down to 'the luxury of the times, there is a vast number of water-closets and baths used that never were used in 1810'.[16] In order to limit consumption and to prevent the total drainage of their reservoirs, the water companies introduced a dual tariff. Most customers contented themselves with the ordinary supply, or 'low service', in which the water could be laid to the ground floor but no higher. An extra payment permitted the 'high service', in which water could be laid to the top of the house. It remains something of a puzzle as to how the companies discriminated between the two sorts of users, since there was only one set of mains. One side-effect of the dual tariff was to hinder the installation of water-closets and bathrooms on the upper floors of town houses.

DRAINAGE

As far as outgoing services are concerned, the most important was undoubtedly drainage. Modern drains, underground pipes carrying off all sorts of household waste in a constant flow of water, are a Victorian creation. Their principal requirements are a constant supply of water and a supply of cheap watertight pipes, neither of which was available before 1800. Most accounts of drainage take the nineteenth-century improvements as their starting point, and ignore the fact that most Georgian houses were equipped with some form of drainage, even if it was not very efficient by modern standards. Drainage and water supply have always been interdependent. The earliest British drainage plan is probably that showing Prior Wibert's water and drainage arrangements at Christ Church, Canterbury, in 1160, where a stream was diverted to serve

The back of our house, the second beyond ours, being repaired, in Francis Street

April 1844. morng 8 o'clk.

the various fountains, and then led back to its course by way of the privies.[17] Outside such controlled environments things were rather different; even medieval towns like Southampton and Exeter, where the water supply was well organized, were rather perfunctory about drainage.

Towns sited by water, and especially tidal water, took advantage of natural flushing. Perhaps the most memorable example was Dick Whittington's late-medieval Long House in London, a public lavatory built at his expense over a tidal inlet of the Thames, with seats for sixty-four men and sixty-four women and an almshouse on the upper floor.[18] In Georgian Bristol all the drains led directly into the Avon, which was reasonably satisfactory until the Floating Harbour was created in 1805. As part of this work the river was dammed, and for the next fifteen years the sewage flowed into a virtually stagnant piece of water. As so often, London was different from other towns. Since the sixteenth century it had enjoyed a better water supply than most, but this also created problems of disposal. The first attempt to deal systematically with the problem was made in the time of Henry VIII, when the town and its hinterland were divided into seven areas, each controlled by a different commission of sewers. For the next 300 years the commissioners controlled the drainage of their districts. Their principal concern was the disposal of surface water, and their main sewers were mostly natural streams, like the Fleet River, the Walbrook or the Westbourne. In some areas secondary sewers were built to improve local drainage, and builders and house-owners were permitted to make a private connection with these sewers on payment of a fee. Secondary sewers were built only where there was an obvious drainage problem, and connection was not compulsory. As a result the drainage of Georgian houses was unpredictable: some had main drains, some did not. New developments, especially those on well-managed properties like the Grosvenor and Bedford Estates, always provided a sewer under the street. The older and poorer parts of town were less well provided. As late as 1834 Cheapside, one of the main streets of the City

of London, was not provided with a sewer, and none of its houses could have drains: 'Its night soil is kept in poisonous pools, of which the inhabitants pump out the contents into open channels in the streets at night'.[19]

Until the mid-nineteenth century both main sewers and individual house drains were built of brick, and there were constant problems with seepage. Another perennial problem was blockage. With sewers being built in such an ad hoc fashion, there were many instances where the builders followed the lie of the land without properly considering the gradient required to ensure a steady flow in one direction. Only the natural streams forming the main sewers had a constant flow of water. The secondary sewers carried merely what was put into them. In dry weather there was no flush to speak of and solid deposits could build up rapidly, which eventually led to a very unpleasant kind of flooding. For this reason solid waste was officially prohibited and connections from privies were specifically outlawed, but the minutes of the various sewage commissions show that these prohibitions were constantly flouted. In June 1717 the Holborn and Finsbury commissioners heard that 'several persons in Baldwin's Gardens ... do permit excrement and noysome filth coming from their several houses of office to issue and run into the common sewers ... And that the said sewer is thereby stopped and clogged up.'[20] The culprits were fined £2 each. Nowadays this restriction seems unbelievable, but it was real enough. Matters began to improve only after the Napoleonic War, when several of the commissions obtained private Acts of Parliament to allow privy connections to the sewers.

CESSPOOLS

The existence of a rudimentary sewage system in London is something of a deception, because the great majority of London houses led their household

Opposite: A rare view of the back wall and yard of a modest town house in Francis Street, Tottenham Court Road, built in 1772. The yard itself is hardly more than 10 ft long, with the coal bin and privy built against the back wall. A lead water pipe snakes above the scullery window to supply the wooden storage butt. Immediately to the left of the butt is the pipe from the sink inside, discharging into a small open drain. The drain must either have run back under the house into a street sewer or directly into a cesspit.

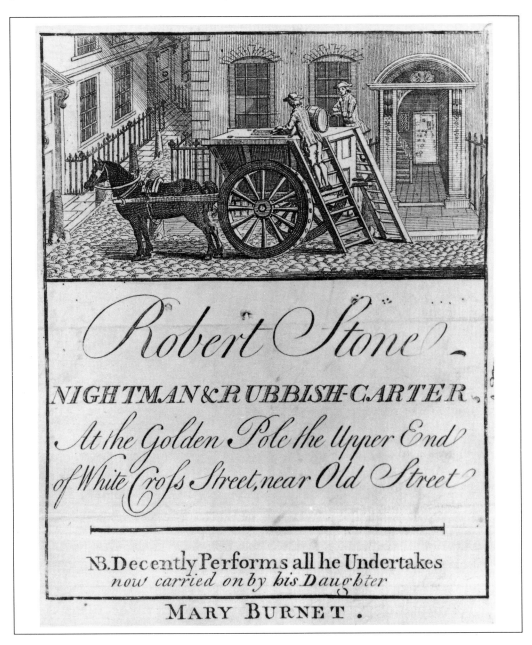

A highly informative representation of a nightman (or rather nightwoman) on the trade card of Mary Burnet. The card is undated, but it was probably issued c. 1750. Through the open door of the house can be seen the front hall running back to the garden behind. At the far end of the garden is a little wooden hut that obviously contained the privy. The two men are using a wooden tub to ferry the excavated contents of the privy's cesspool to their wooden tanker cart parked outside. It is clear that their route lies through the main part of the house, and it is easy to see why this smelly business had to be conducted at night when everyone was well out of the way in bed.

A much more elaborate trade card of Samuel Foulger, Nightman. The rule, square and other implements shown in the Rococo border suggest that Mr Foulger also traded as a building craftsman of some kind, though the usual secondary employment for nightmen was as chimney-sweeps. The text refers to a 'New Invented Machine for the Quick dispatch of Business', which sounds fascinating, but the illustration shows only the conventional equipment of wooden tubs and tanker carts.

drains into a cesspool. In the better houses, and where a sewer was near by, the cesspool acted as an intercepting trap for solid matter, and the liquid was allowed to run off into the system (this is the arrangement illustrated in Ware's *A Complete Body of Architecture*). Cesspools of this type had both an inlet and an outlet pipe, the latter usually about 6 ins lower. But the most common type of cesspool had no outlet. Primitive versions were simply excavated from the earth and most of the liquid matter was expected to percolate into the ground. This was obviously a danger to health when drinking water was drawn from wells, but it persisted well into Victorian years. In the late-eighteenth and nineteenth centuries cesspools were lined mostly with brick and often given a domed top. Information about them is hard to come by. Most were filled in when main drainage arrived, and those that do survive are usually taken for ice-houses.

Cesspools required periodical emptying. This function was carried out by the nightmen, so-called because they were compelled by law to operate between the hours of midnight and 5 a.m. (most doubled as chimney-sweeps by day). Nightmen excavated the deposited matter and laboriously carried it by the bucketful from the house to their tanker-carts. The night-time was busy in Georgian towns, as we know from Southey: 'Besides the regular annoyances (of the watchmen, whose business it is not merely to guard the streets but to inform the good people of London every half hour of the state of the weather) there is another cause of disturbance ... the clatter of the nightmen has scarcely ceased before that of the morning carts begins.'[21]

Since the main function of the urban cesspool was to take the filth from the privy, it was often built directly underneath. Privies were pretty smelly, and were usually placed outside, where there was direct ventilation. The most common location, especially in smaller houses, was across the backyard, as far from the house as possible. Ware, a thoroughly Palladian architect in his love of symmetry, suggested that the backyard privy be turned to aesthetic advantage. In *A Complete Body of Architecture* he wrote of these yards: 'The best method is to lay the whole with a good sound stone pavement, and at the further part to build the needful edifice, that cannot in London be removed farther off; and something of similar shape and little service opposite.'

In larger houses the privy for the family was often built adjoining the rear wall of the house. It is often assumed that the small projections called closet wings at the rear of many early-eighteenth-century houses were for privies, but there is no real evidence to suggest that they were anything but small retiring rooms. Confusingly, the larger rear wings of late-eighteenth-century houses did often contain the water-closet. There was very often a second privy for the servants in the front basement area, or even in the vaults under the street, but there were no hard and fast rules about cesspool location. It was not unknown for one to be excavated in a basement room. Arrangements such as this caused dire problems when, as often happened, a cesspool was forgotten and overflowed.

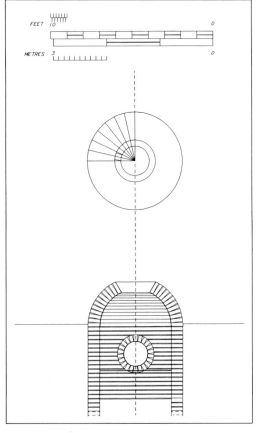

A measured drawing of the Holland Street cesspit showing the size of the brick inlet hole.

The domed top of a disused eighteenth-century cesspit in the back garden of a house in Holland Street, Kensington. The pit is immediately next to the rear wing of the house, one of the preferred locations for a privy. In this case there were both inlet and outlet pipes in the straight wall of the pit. The large hole at the top covered by a stone slab was for the periodical emptying.

WATER-CLOSETS

Finally, something must be said about the domestic water-closet. Although plenty has been written about the history of the water-closet as a mechanism, there is not much information about the speed at which the invention was adopted for common use. A water-closet in the eighteenth century meant a lavatory-pan that could be flushed with water, usually from a tank but sometimes directly from a water pipe. It seems pretty clear that water-closets were not unusual in Georgian town houses of both the upper and middle classes. In 1733 Lord Chesterfield's house at No. 45 Grosvenor Square had a water-closet on the first floor in the small rear wing, and in the kitchen area there was 'a pipe laid from the Cistern to the force pump in the garden to convey the water into the Cistern at the Top of the Water-closet'.[22] The location here is significant, because the first floor was the principal reception floor. Most of the household probably made more use of the bog-house in the garden. Lower down the social scale and only four years later, Benjamin Timbrell's relatively modest houses in the Strand, with shops on the ground floor, were to have one water-closet from the start, with provision for another. It is probably safe to say that the majority of fashionable town houses would have been equipped with at least one water-closet by the 1780s. All of Robert Adam's fashionable town houses of the 1770s and 1780s had a water-closet as standard, usually hidden in a corner off the back staircase.

* * *

Although we would probably find them draughty, dark and smelly, Georgian town houses probably worked fairly well as machines for living. There does not seem to have been much grumbling about living conditions from the occupants and, despite their various strictures on other aspects of English urban life, most foreign travellers agreed on the high level of domestic comfort. The trouble is that so much of the factual information about things like water supply and drainage comes from sources that record only abuses of the various systems, and from the mid-nineteenth-century commissions of inquiry. By the time these commissions were convened, the rapid growth of population in the towns had made the Georgian systems appear hopelessly inadequate.

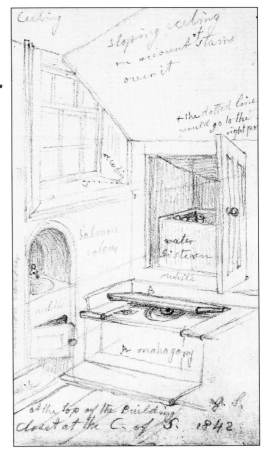

A drawing by George Scharf of 1842 showing the sanitary arrangements at the top of his house. They look remarkably civilized, with a lavatory and wash basin both supplied with water from the cistern. There is nothing to indicate whether the cistern was filled by means of a 'high service' water supply; probably the water was pumped by hand from a ground-floor tank.

PART THREE

THE HOUSE

A late-Georgian street under construction: Beaumont Street, Oxford, in 1825.

Chapter One

CONSTRUCTION AND SPECULATION

EVILS OF THE LEASEHOLD SYSTEM

Isaac Ware recognized the intimate connection between the speculative building system and poor construction:

The nature of tenures in London has introduced the art of building slightly. The ground landlord is to come into possession at the end of a short term, and the builder, unless his Grace tye him down to articles, does not chuse to employ his money to his [the landlord's] advantage. It is for this reason we see houses built for sixty, seventy or the stoutest of this kind for ninety-nine years. The care they shall not stand longer than their time occasions many to fall before it is expired; nay, some have carried the art of slight building so far, that their houses have fallen in before they were tenanted.[1]

Ware's opinion was by no means unusual, being shared by all manner of eighteenth-century and early-nineteenth-century observers of the building trade. Indeed, those who bothered to record their views on the subject displayed a remarkable and persuasive consistency. Grosley confirmed that 'the solidity of the building is measured by the duration of the lease' and revealed that the manufacture of materials as well as the construction of houses suffered through the speculative building system in which all costs were ruthlessly minimized: 'the outside [of the houses] appears to be built of brick, but the walls consist only of a single row of bricks, and those being made of the first earth that comes to hand, and only just warmed at the fire'.[2]

Malcolm made similar observations in 1808 about the evil influence the leasehold system had upon solidity of structure and blamed the abundant use of dirt in mortar for 'the horrid effect produced by the fall of frail houses'. To emphasize the urgency of the problem, he calculated that 'there are at this moment at least 3,000 houses in a dangerous state of ruin within London and Westminster'.[3]

Simond gave a foreigner's view of London building practice. Writing of brick-built terrace houses newly erected in London, he observed that 'as if to destroy the little solidity of which such thin walls are capable, they generally place windows above a pier below, and a pier above the window below ... I am informed that it is made an express condition in the leases of these shades of houses that there shall be no dances given in them'.[4]

So far the blame for poor construction has been laid firmly on the speculative system and the inability of builders to resist the forces pushing them towards cheap and shoddy construction. But central and local government, estate owners and their agents, stewards and surveyors also bore responsibility. From 1667 various Building Acts were passed in London (and gradually imitated in other cities) to regulate construction. Inspired by the spectacle of London burning in 1666, these Acts were aimed mostly at making houses, particularly elevations and party walls, as incombustible as possible and ensuring that the thickness of façades and party walls was related to the height of the structure. Key Acts were passed in 1707 and 1709, when wooden eaves cornices were outlawed and wooden box-sashes were orderd to be set back from the façade in 4-in reveals. But the most important act was passed in 1774.

Part of the south side of Fournier Street, Spitalfields. Built 1725–31 by a number of different speculators, the terrace contains houses of various sizes and quality.

Montague Street, Bloomsbury. Built in 1800 by various builders working to an elevation agreed between the head lessee, James Burton, and the landowner, the Bedford Estate. The variety of the early-eighteenth-century terrace has given way to rigid uniformity.

This was a massive affair that attempted to combine all the major controls passed since the 1667 Act and, like that Act, related size of house to thickness of wall construction. Henceforth there were to be four rates of building for houses; each rate was determined by size and expense of construction, and every house, when it fell within a certain rate, had to conform to the structural requirements specified in the Act for that rate. Hence a large dwelling house worth at least £850 and exceeding nine 'squares of building' (a 'square' was a hundred sq. ft) had to comply with the constructional standards imposed on first rate buildings. Another relatively minor consequence of this Act was that after 1774 box-sashes not only had to be set back from the façade by 4 ins but also placed well out of harm's way by being concealed behind the brick or stone window jambs.

Although sound in their aims and generally influential on the superficial appearance of buildings, these Acts were remarkably ineffectual when their demands clashed with the economics of speculative building – and nowhere was this clash of interests stronger than over construction. The practice of the

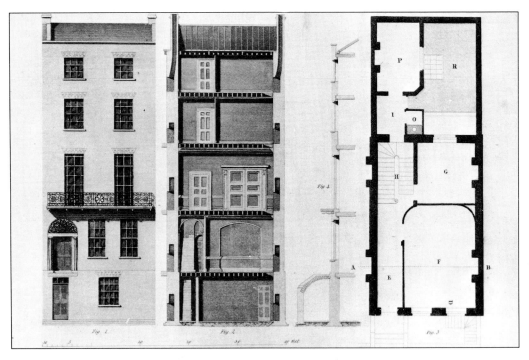

The Building Act of 1774 specified that urban housing should conform to one of four rates, or sets of specifications, according to size and cost of construction. Illustrated is a second rate house as published in Peter Nicholson's New and Improved Practical Builder *of 1823. Typical of the informality of the early-nineteenth century, the vertical alignment of windows has been abandoned so that the ground-floor front room can be well lit; the house is starting to be designed from the inside out, with practical and functional considerations outweighing formal concerns.*

speculative builder was, it seems, simply to ignore those aspects of the Acts that got seriously in his way. Setting box-sashes back 4 ins as required by the 1709 Act was awkward, for it meant that the wall had to be thicker to accommodate the internal window shutter-box, or that the panelling or shutter-box would have to be built out into the room. These were both potentially expensive and inconvenient solutions, so box-sashes simply stayed set flush until the 1730s, by which time it had become hopelessly unfashionable (and hence uncommercial) to continue to build houses with archaic-looking flush sashes. If such an open violation of the Acts as this could be practised, then it comes as no surprise to discover that abuses that were easier to conceal, such as undersize or ill-constructed party walls and façades, were regularly perpetrated. In short, the Acts proved impossible to police in the

hostile and unresponsive world of speculative building.

Various private estates did invoke the Building Acts in their building contracts with developers as well as specifying their own minimum standards for construction. But, as we shall see, these were usually imprecise, indeed were intentionally so, to allow leeway for negotiations between estate and builder if the going got tough for either party.

So it was a combination of unpublic-minded landlords, profiteering builders (aided, when necessary, by unscrupulous architects) and weak legislation that created and fuelled the speculative system. Yet, for all its evils, this was the system that created much of what was great in Georgian urban design. It is clear that the speculative builders, being aware of market trends, were intensely aware of the changing nuances of fashion and followed closely (if often

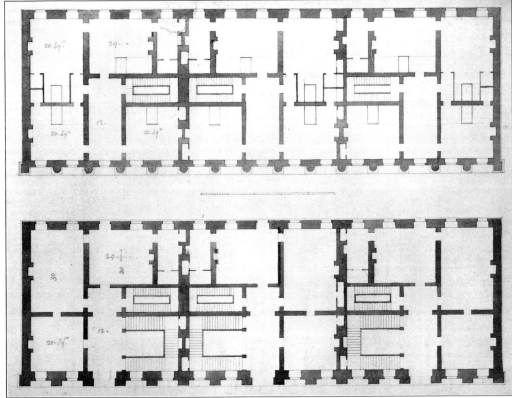

Elevation, first- and ground-floor plan of Colen Campbell's design of 1725 for part of the east side of Grosvenor Square. This is one of the earliest eighteenth-century designs for a uniform terrace, where the individual houses are united behind a palace front. The first-floor plan is interesting, for it shows bed locations and bed alcoves. This terrace was never built.

a little clumsily) the developments produced by leading architects of genius. The apparent conflict between mean intentions and noble realizations is one of the many subjects touched upon by Sir John Soane in a hard-hitting lecture delivered to the Royal Academy between 1809 and 1836. As Soane explained: 'Grosvenor Square and the streets surrounding and leading thereto, were among the first grand essays of the speculative system of building … In them we trace an imitation of Palladio, in them we see that Inigo Jones was not quite forgotten.' But, continued Soane,

All these appearances quickly faded and our hopes of better architecture were destroyed by the monotonous houses forming many of the streets and squares, which have been built since that time. These will be found to consist, not only of thin, flimsy walls, perforated for use, so many brick-heaps piled one after the other, but in many cases, so far in open defiance of the principles of sound construction that our ephemeral publications are constantly recording the melancholy events occasioned by their instability. Such have been the effects of the speculative system of building; a system which in its progress has swept away so many of our ancient and extensive mansions by holding out to their owners the prospect of increasing the value of their property by miserably parcelling out the inheritances of their Ancestors, into streets of monotonous, and it may be added of ill constructed, houses. If this system be continued, it will eventually destroy all relish for substantial construction, and finally root out every vestige of good architecture. I am sorry to have to add that some architects have materially assisted in establishing this revolutionary system in architecture, by prostituting the credit of their profession, sometimes by taking large tracts of ground and parcelling it out to the tradesmen employed by them, and at other times by taking the ground and becoming builders themselves.[5]

CONSTRUCTION

To understand the underlying causes of the evils catalogued by Soane and the other observers, it is necessary to look more deeply into the close relationship between building speculation and the Georgian construction industry.

BRICKS

Since the Middle Ages bricks have been the basic building material for much of Britain and reached their apogee in the late-seventeenth and early-eighteenth centuries, when they were cut and laid beautifully and with great skill. But, as the remarks of Grosley and Malcolm reveal, they were also victims of some of the greatest abuses of the speculative system. Batty Langley, in 1748, pointed out the evils

Section through a 13-in façade in Albury Street, Deptford, c. 1710. Clearly shown is the snapped header construction in which fine face bricks do not bond back into the place brick pier behind.

to which cost-cutting could give rise in brick walling. Most notable is his observation that brick façades were often 'not only a very great deceit, but ... dangerous' when the bricklayer, 'for the sake of saving about 400 Grey-stocks in a rod of work, whose value is not half a crown', would run up a façade with snapped grey stock headers facing, but not bonding into, the cheaper place bricks behind (see p. 215).[6]

Although Langley publicly chose to criticize this structurally dangerous type of two-skinned walling, he must have known that theory was well detached from common practice. Undaunted, he offered a price for 'common front walling; as fronts of dwelling houses' composed of grey stock bricks and place bricks regularly bonded together. There were, wrote Langley in his *London Prices of Bricklayer's Materials*, three ways of increasing expense:

1. *Those laid in the same thickness of mortar as Place-bricks, viz. four courses to one foot, and jointed [i.e. pointed] in common manner.*

2. *Mortar laid so much thinner with four courses rising 11 ins and jointed as aforesaid.*

3. *That whose courses of mortar don't exceed $\frac{1}{4}$ in [with] eleven courses to the foot and with tuck-and-pat joints.*

Mortar was made with burnt lime and sand mixed with water;[7] tuck-and-pat jointing was an expensive type of pointing in which thin and delicate pointing was applied over flush pointing coloured to match the bricks. This false tuck joint was formed with white lime putty mortar made of lime slaked with water but no sand (see p. 238). Langley priced these three types of face walling at £5 12s. $\frac{3}{4}$d., £6 1s. 10$\frac{1}{4}$d. and £13 16s. 6$\frac{1}{4}$d. per rod respectively. A rod was 272$\frac{1}{4}$ sq. ft of walling at one and a half bricks thick, and the last extremely high price reflects the expense of tuck-and-pat pointing.

The method for bonding grey stock bricks with place bricks described by Langley was clearly a traditional piece of good practice (the bonding technique was illustrated by Peter Nicholson in his

Pointing on Nos. 7 (left) and 9 Elder Street, Spitalfields, of 1725/6. On the left is flush pointing, grooved or penny struck. This was the standard Georgian brick joint. On the right is tuck-and-pat pointing: a false white lime putty joint laid over a flush joint of brick-coloured mortar. This was expensive but a favoured method of giving standard brickwork the appearance of fine and regular jointing.

Mechanic's Companion of 1825 when common practice was still no better), but it demanded more time and more regularly sized place bricks than the

two-skinned type of speculator's walling. Langley described the method in *London Prices*:

If every front course be laid with headers and stretchers ... which is called Flemish bond and which is very strong and beautiful, then the number of Greystocks to the place bricks will be as four is to five and therefore 2,000 of Grey-stocks with 2,500 of place bricks will do for one rod of walling.

Flemish bond was universal during the Georgian period, although usually wrought with snapped headers set between stretchers.

Another idealized account of construction is given by Nicholson in his *Mechanic's Companion*. This, which purports to be a blow-by-blow account of the building of a house, is particularly interesting for the emphasis it places on the use of timber within, and beneath, the brick and masonry building. Nicholson recommended timber piling to strengthen the foundations of the walls (common practice in larger, expensive buildings) and cross bearers, or sleepers, to provide a substructure for timber planking of the ground floor. He then warned that 'all timber whatever, of which the thickness stands vertical [i.e., timber laid horizontally in the building] being liable to shrink, will also make the building liable to crack, or split, at the junctions with the return parts [that is, the corners]'.

Having warned that timber used structurally was liable to 'crack' the building by movement, Nicholson went on to explain how timbers were built into brick walls to prevent damage by settlement:

In cases where the ground is not very soft, a balk [large, square-section timber beam] is sometimes slit in halves, and then either laid immediately at the bottom, or at heights of two or three courses, and this will frequently prevent settlements, which are occasioned by an irregular pressure on the piers, and the intermediate brick-work or masonry under apertures.

Plate from Batty Langley's London Prices of Bricklayer's Materials *of 1748 showing different methods of brick bonding. Top (figs. I–II) is Langley's economical solution for the problem of constructing 13-in Flemish bond using more place bricks, which were cheaper, than stock bricks. In this piece of walling only twelve stock bricks (hatched) are used to fifteen place bricks. The other fig. shows the method of English bond (figs. III–V) and header bond (figs. VI–VIII).*

This seems to be a reference to building soft wood bond timbers into the place brick piers set behind the 4-in skin of facing bricks. This practice, which in theory should be detrimental to the stability of the walls (soft wood is corroded by the lime in the mortar and tends to wet and dry rot, leading to

The substance of speculator's Flemish bond revealed: a house at Aberavon Road, Bow, of c. 1825 after the 4-in skin of facing brickwork had been removed. At ground floor the skin was backed by, though hardly bonded into, a panel of place bricks. At first floor the wall was a mere 4 ins thick over lath and plaster.

compression and failure of the pier), was clearly regarded by Georgian builders not as shoddy but as proper. Quite why is not clear, although Nicholson gave a couple of good clues:

When the bricklayer has got to the top of the first window, the carpenter may lintel the window; but if the joisting of the next floor is laid upon the lintel the wall-plate and lintels will form one continued length of timber, which will be much stronger than lintels, having only 9 or 10 ins of bearing upon the walls ... in carrying up the second storey, bond timbers must be introduced opposite to all horizontal mouldings, as bases and surbases. It is also customary to put a row of bond timber in the middle of the storey, of greater strength than those for the bases and surbases.

The implication is that timbers were built into brick walls merely for the convenience of fitting embellishments such as skirting and dado rails to rooms, and because it was 'customary' to do so. The name, 'bond timber', suggests that the intention behind planting these little potential time-bombs in the structure was, arguably, to hold the structure together. Perhaps they were introduced to stiffen the brick structure, while the slow-drying lime mortar hardened. But what is certain is that timber was regarded as an essential addition to a brick structure. As Campbell explained in his *London Tradesmen* of 1747: 'the carpenter, by the strength of wood, contributes more to the standing of the house, than all the bricklayers' labour'.

However, as used in the Georgian period these timbers can have had very little use in bonding the building together. Typical is the case of No. 15 Fournier Street, built in 1725 by a joiner called William Tayler. Bond timbers appear in the place brick piers between the windows. On first- and second-floor levels, the piers are even built off a softwood beam that stretches the full length of the façade and is located just below windowsill level. The presence of these timbers might appear to be related to the fact that this is a corner house, so that they in some way tie the façades together in the manner of a timber frame house. In fact, the timber, though continuous, is formed by several short lengths merely butted together and so incapable of exercising any restraint. Clearly the timber used here has a very limited role; perhaps building off these timbers was a way of levelling the structure as it rose. If they were meant to stop settlement, as Nicholson suggested, then it was a fairly feeble gesture; the 4-in skin does not contain bond timbers, so even the eighteenth-century builder must have realized that the two skins would behave in different ways. If the outer skin moved and the inner one did not, then the small structural link that was made between the

Plate from Peter Nicholson's Mechanical Exercises *of 1812 showing timber floor construction. Fig. 1 shows a 'floor where the joists would have too great a bearing without a girder'. The girder (D) is placed diagonally so that it bears into a pier rather than sitting above a window. Fig. 2 shows a 'double floor' with binding joists (a, b) and bridging joists (c, d).*

Brick piers at first-floor level at No. 15 Fournier Street, Spitalfields, 1725. Soft-wood bond timbers not only run the width of the piers but provide the footing off which the piers are built.

two (an occasional header bonding back from the face skin) could have been quickly and easily severed. However, that bond timbers were regarded as a hedge against settlement – even as rudimentary expansion joints absorbing vertical movement that would have cracked brickwork – was not implied by Nicholson alone.

In 1796 the surveyor to the Foundling Estate, Bloomsbury, then being speedily covered with speculative housing, noted his anxiety that insufficient bond timbers were being used in the speculatively built houses he had inspected. He feared that this omission would result in the houses not holding together and that they would settle with the two skins of the façade separating.[8]

STONE

Stone construction was, in cities like Bath and Edinburgh, subject to similar abuses brought about by the financial exigencies of the speculative system. Stone could, like brick, be of varied quality, laid with more or less skill and used only as a veneer over inferior materials to which it was bonded in the most casual manner. In Bath it was usual for stone blocks 6 to 8 ins thick to face piers of about 18 ins thickness – constructed of rubble walling with, later in the eighteenth century, soft place bricks being used to construct thin party walls. This double-skinned wall could be given added thickness and solidity by having the cavity between ashlar and rubble grouted with stone chippings and lime mortar, forming a sort of primitive concrete. Ashlar was laid to present a pattern of wide and narrow blocks on the same course – rather like headers and stretchers in Flemish bond brickwork – but, as with speculators' brickwork, only a few of these 'header' stone blocks actually bonded back into the rubble walling behind.

This type of rubble and ashlar walling, with its soft-wood lintels and perhaps poor mortar, was by no means the last word in slight construction in Bath. From the late-eighteenth century it became increasingly common for speculators to indulge in single-skin construction and give their houses façades formed with ashlar blocks only 6 to 7 ins thick. In this type of construction a timber wall plate or bressummer, supporting floor joists and spanning from party wall to party wall, could be set into the thickness of the single-skin wall and limewashed to make it look like stone. The rear elevation of the east side of St James's Square, built in about 1790, and Great Stanhope Street, built during the 1770s, are of this single-skin construction.

The building process in early-eighteenth-century Bath involved the facing stones being worked into ashlar blocks at the quarry and then transported by lumbering cart to the building site in the city, where rough walling masons would incorporate them with the rubble walling. John Wood the younger revealed that masons in Bath were paid $1\frac{3}{4}d$. for every foot superficial in 1781. This price included 'cleaning down' by the mason, which involved combing the façade with a special saw-like tool that removed excess mortar from the joints and filled in any small irregularities of the surface.[9]

In Edinburgh a sandstone far harder than Bath limestone was available for building. This stone, though more difficult to carve, did hold its embellishment far better than soft, and quickly weathered, Bath limestone. Consequently Edinburgh masons developed a wide variety of patterns of tooling, or texturing, the surface of cut stone. Many houses in the first New Town, particularly in Queen Street of the 1770s and 1790s, possessed stone façades that displayed three or four different types of stone construction or methods of tooling: for example, random or coursed rubble (and occasionally rock-faced ashlar) for basements, rusticated ashlar ground floors, then a band of smooth ashlar between ground and first floors, with the rest of the façade being formed with boldly tooled ashlar.

A problem facing masons was that not only could stone be of poor quality for building, but even good stone could last no better than bad if laid incorrectly. To avoid rapid corrosion by weather and delamination, stone should generally be laid on its natural bed. A skilled mason would be able to identify the natural grain of the stone and make sure that it was cut and used in the correct way – usually naturally bedded for facing ashlar block and edge-bedded for window lintels, sills, voussoirs, string-courses and blocking-courses above cornices. An inferior mason, working quickly and with dubious stone, could wreak havoc.

Tobias Smollett, writing of Bath in 1771, gives some idea of the consequences of speculation upon both the appearance of Bath and the stability of its houses and shows that, in many respects, one speculatively built city was much like another:

The rage of building has laid hold on such a number of adventurers, that one sees new houses starting up in every out-let and every corner of Bath; contrived without judgement, executed without solidity [and] built so slight, with the soft crumbling stone found in this neighbourhood, that I should never sleep quietly in one of them.[10]

SPECULATION

The speculative building system was very straightforward in theory but highly complex in practice, being tailored to fit the many different circumstances of landlord, builder and occupier. However, in essence it was a system of building that was meant to benefit mutually all three parties and that generated wealth while fulfilling the worthy purpose of providing housing.

THE LANDLORD

Ideally, the landlord had his estate developed for minimum outlay, and, although he received only small ground rents during the period of the first lease (usually sixty-one or ninety-nine years), he possessed an asset of great value, because the houses and their fittings reverted to his ownership at the end of the lease, when he could redevelop or relet them at higher prices. So the landlord's prime concern was to safeguard the quality of the development. This often meant a delicate balancing act between enforcing high standards that would serve his long-term interests (well-built houses of a quality and size to attract high-class tenants who would maintain or raise the tone, and hence the value, of the estate) while, at the same time, attracting developers with different sets of short-term interests (houses built quickly and cheaply for immediate profit during the 'life' of their leases). If the estates

were in fashionable parts of town and a building boom was under way and houses were selling well, then the estate-owner had a good chance of acquiring the sort of high-quality development to which all aspired.

The legal formula for doing this was to insert conditions to do with size and construction of the house into the lease and building contract, and to include restrictions on undesirable uses. In London, for example, the Grosvenor and Cavendish-Harley Estates in the 1720s, and the Christ's Hospital and Bedford Estates in the late-eighteenth century, all included prohibitions on certain noxious trades being carried on in the major streets. Typical of the uses banned by all these estates were butchers, tallow chandlers, soap-makers, tobacco-pipe makers, brewers, distillers, pewterers, fishmongers, bagnio-keepers, dyers and blacksmiths.

Having achieved the type of development it required, the estate then had to preserve the buildings until they fell into its ownership. Again, the instrument for this was the initial lease, which could specify maintenance and, more important, make it clear that valuable fittings within the house belonged to the estate and not to the lessee. For example, a building contract of 1777 between the Duke of Bedford and the builders William Scott and Robert Grews to build in Gower Street, Chenies Street and Store Street, Bloomsbury, specified that after the expiration of the 99-year lease the occupiers of the houses (who would inherit, and be bound by, this contract) were to surrender up the premises with 'doors, wainscott ... keys, bolts, bars, staples, hinges ... marble and other chimney pieces, mantels, piers and chimney jambs ... window shutters, partitions, pumps, pipes, posts ... anything fixed or fastened'.[11]

In Edinburgh, as befitted a country with a separate legal system, different social traditions and the recent experience of unsettling rebellion, speculative building took a different form – especially in relation to the landowner. In the New Town, laid out to a competition-winning design of 1762 by James Craig, the various estate-owners feued land to builders who either built houses or tenements on speculation or, more rarely, to order for an individual. In this system the landlord was paid a significant amount of money for the plot. He retained feudal rights over this, which took the form of payment by the house-occupant of an annual feu. Unlike in England, the

Above: *St Anne's Place, Bath, built c. 1760, showing an exposed timber bressummer running above the ground-floor windows. This construction detail was usually, though not always, associated with walls one ashlar block thick. The wood was traditionally lime washed a stone colour to merge with the masonry.*

Opposite: *Detail of the elevation of a house of c. 1790 in Queen Street, Edinburgh. Craigleith sandstone of differing qualities has been used in four different ways: on the first floor the ashlar has been tooled; the ashlar between string-courses is smooth; the ground floor is rusticated; and the basement is constructed with squared rubble.*

Section through a Bath terrace: Widcombe Parade was built c. 1770 and, typical of that date, the front wall was the thickness of only a single ashlar block. The rear wall was of random rubble construction.

Scottish landlord never regained possession of the land or house built upon the land, but, instead, got a large capital sum initially and a regular income from feus that, unlike English ground rents, were far from token sums. It seems common that sums of £15 to £25 a year were paid in the early-nineteenth century as annual feus.

In Dublin the London and Edinburgh systems were combined. Landlords let house plots – but for 999 years. Consequently, since he could not look forward to the reversion of the house for the benefit of his family, the landlord sold the lease for a relatively large amount of money and charged a high annual ground rent.

THE OCCUPIER

The occupier benefited from a flexible housing market, which offered him a roofed and floored shell that he could complete to suit his own taste and pocket. In this transaction it was usual for the occupier to buy not only the house but also the remainder of the lease from the builder. In return for this fairly large initial capital outlay, he had to pay only a relatively small annual ground rent to the landlord. Another possibility was to buy from the builder a sublease on a fitted-out house, in which case the occupier would pay out less initially but would have to pay a higher or 'improved' annual rent, part of which would be pocketed by the builder or head lessee and part of which would be paid as ground rent to the landlord. There were also many permutations of short-term renting, where the occupier would take a very short lease on whole or part of a house from the head lessee or landlord and pay a rack rent that would be subject to regular increases.

Speculating in property was clearly something of a national pastime in the Georgian period – a pastime made possible by the lack of control on subletting. A speculator with a building lease on a piece of land would readily grant a sublease on part or all to other builders. Similarly an occupier with a lease on a house would happily act as a landlord, subletting part or all at will, for as much profit as possible until the lease reverted to the landlord. During this process the head lessee, like the landlord, would attempt to pass on to the sublessees all responsibility

for maintenance and for paying all rates and taxes on the house.

THE SPECULATIVE BUILDER

The speculative builder came in many guises during the eighteenth century. There were the polished architects such as Robert Adam with his ambitious but misjudged Adelphi development of 1768–72, Sir William Chambers with his more modest and successful Berners Street development of 1764–70 and the more businesslike John Wood of Bath. Then there were the building tradesmen who – a few plots at a time – developed such areas as Spitalfields, and at the end of the eighteenth century men like James Burton of Bloomsbury, who undertook to organize the development of entire streets and sections of estates as one building operation.

Roger North, a lawyer, amateur architect and associate of Wren, recorded in the late-seventeenth century that Nicholas Barbon had pioneered the system of large-scale speculative development that rebuilt London after the Great Fire of 1666: 'He was the inventor of this new method of building by casting of ground into streets and small houses, and to augment their number with as little front as possible, and selling the ground to workmen by so much per foot front, and what he could not sell build himself. This has made ground rent high for the sake of mortgaging.'[12] This speculative system, refined by Barbon no doubt but certainly not invented by him, was inherited by eighteenth- and nineteenth-century builders of both great and small means.

Large and small speculators had many important things in common: the length of lease of the building that they obtained (usually sixty-one years in the early-eighteenth century and ninety-nine years at the end), the possibility of bartering amongst themselves rather than dealing in cash, and the various options in the way the house might be finished.

The small-time speculative builder, who was characteristic of the early-eighteenth century, could set up in business with virtually no ready cash at all. He would acquire the option on a building lease on a small piece of land directly from the landlord and raise money on this agreement, or mortgage the land

A pattern-book detail from William Pain's Practical House Carpenter, *dated 1789. This type of plate gave a competent workman enough basic information to proportion and detail a fashionable doorcase.*

to buy materials to build the house. He would then build the shell and hope to sell it on – roofed and floored – before the peppercorn period of the lease expired. To ease the builder's lot, all estates guaranteed a peppercorn period in their building leases – usually one, two or three years, or as much as five – during which no ground rent was payable. The shell, if all went well, would be quickly sold to the first occupier for a sum covering building costs plus profit. If the builder was rich enough not to need a return on his capital as quickly as possible, he might sublease the house to the first occupier (in which case the builder would have finished the house completely himself) and charge him an 'improved' rent that would be substantially higher than the ground rent due to the landlord.

This tendency to sell on shells explains why, in areas of cities developed in the early-eighteenth century, variety of parts triumphed amongst the basic regularity of façade widths and heights, and why, within one street, there must have been a striking social mix. Typical are Fournier Street and Elder Street, Spitalfields. Both were developed during the 1720s by a variety of builders who preferred to build pairs of houses at a time (see p. 208). But, in Fournier Street in particular, large, richly fronted and expensively fitted-out houses stood cheek by jowl with smaller, much humbler houses – each reflecting the wealth and social status of its first occupant. By the end of the century this mix was still present in Georgian town-planning, but it was expressed in the contrast between streets on an estate rather than between houses in a street.

Harder to comprehend than the original social mix of an early-eighteenth-century street is the way in which the humble builder acquired the art and knowledge so often displayed in even the smallest terrace house. Much of the well-mannered uniformity was dictated by building economics and technology. A house could be built only three or four storeys above ground level before the walls and foundations would have to be constructed in a more substantial, and so expensive and time-consuming, manner. The width of the house was determined by the spans that could be achieved with readily available timber beams. A tree trunk squared roughly to a 12-in section could comfortably span 20–25 ft, hence the average width of the terrace house. If the house was wider, internal load-bearing walls or stout stud partitioning (an extra expense)

were necessary to break the span of the beams.

But the details and proportions of these humble houses are another matter. From the very beginning of the eighteenth century, pattern-books had been available that listed and described decorative details such as doorcases and panelling, as well as recommending means of construction. These, no doubt, were of great use even to the unlettered builder, because the drawings and plans were easy to scale off from and copy. But it was the average builder's very simplicity of character and his readiness to copy rather than indulge in weird decorative invention that gave Georgian architecture its reputation for good taste. The builders of Georgian cities were highly conventional men; they were not imbued with the spirit of individuality and would happily copy whatever detail was fashionable at the time. Thus virtually all London houses of the 1720s have segment-headed windows, while virtually all before and after this decade have square-headed windows.

The design vocabulary of the builder was based on observation as well as on the pattern-books. Ideas were culled, often a little misunderstood and always late, from the works of leading architects of the day, or even of the previous generation – certainly the red brick arches, red brick window reveals and segmental window arches of the Spitalfields houses of the 1720s are in the 1690s language of Wren.

Campbell made an interesting comment on the competence of the builder to design houses: 'Though I scarce know of any in England who have had an education regularly designed for the profession, bricklayers, carpenters, etc., all commence architect, especially in and about London, where there are but few rules to the building of a town house.' A master bricklayer, continued Campbell, thought himself 'capable to raise a brick house without the tuition of an architect. And in towns they generally know the just proportion of doors and windows.'[13]

INSURANCE AND CONSTRUCTION COSTS

Organized house insurance was one of the great legacies of the Great Fire of London and made a considerable impression on foreign visitors to

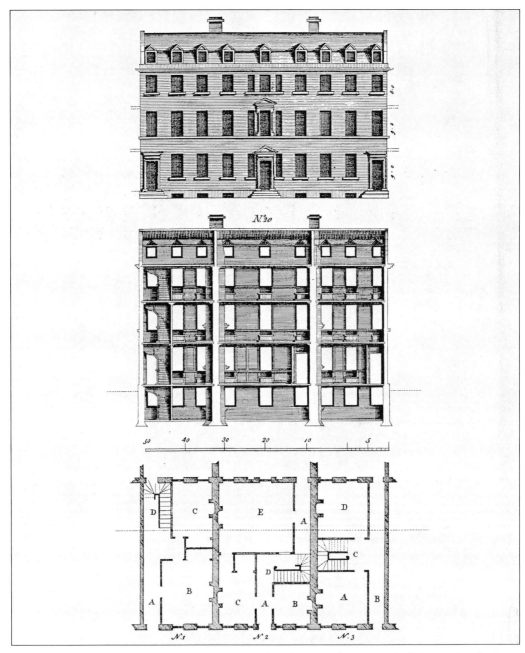

Complete houses could be plucked from pattern-books. This example is particularly interesting, for it was designed by the Palladian theorist Robert Morris and published in William and John Halfpenny's The Modern Builder's Assistant *of 1747. Morris shows three permutations of plan, including the common form with a dog-leg stair (house No. 1). All the main ground-floor rooms are panelled and called 'parlours', with the recesses in back and front parlours in house No. 1 described as 'Beaufets'. These three houses measure 21 squares (i.e., 2,100 sq. ft) and, wrote Morris, would cost £840 to build.*

England. Nicholas Barbon, who made his name and fortune (and eventually lost both) in house speculation after the Fire, is credited as the initiator of fire insurance.[14] Barbon insured 5,650 houses between 1686 and 1692 with premiums of $2\frac{1}{2}$ per cent for brick-built houses and 5 per cent for timber.[15]

Misson observed of London that 'there are two societies of insurers, that for so much in the Pound upon the rent of the house, are obliged to rebuild or repair such as are destroyed by fire, or demolished to stop the progress of it'.[16] The rent to which he referred is the notional rent worked out to reflect the value of the house and used for assessing various rates (see p. 8). Archenholz gave a little more detail: 'They are careful in England not only to insure their houses and their shops but even public buildings ... a mere trifle is given for the risk; it is usually no more than in the proportion of half a crown for a hundred pounds.'[17]

By the late-seventeenth century numerous insurance companies had been formed: the Phoenix, the Hand in Hand, the Sun. Most of these operated their own fire services in an attempt to prevent their clients' houses burning down and so save on insurance payments. Thomas Stubbs's surveys of 1747 for the London Assurance give some idea of how houses were assessed:

£400 on his dwelling house being brick ... except about one fifteenth part being timber situate on south side of Mulberry tree in Nightingale Lane surveyed May 1747 ... Mary Stileman £600 on her dwelling house in Charter House Square, brick situate on west side surveyed 1747 ... Laurance Williams of Dolphin Court, Tower Street, Merchant, £600 on dwelling house being brick ... Robert Ratcliffe of Whitechapel, wineworker, £150 on his dwelling house being timber situated on north side of Whitechapel Road. Sept. 11 1747 ...[18]

Many of these brief valuations and descriptions were accompanied by schedules describing the house room by room and listing fixtures such as fireplaces and panelling but not furniture. Occasionally, a rough floor plan was included.

The insurance valuations quoted by Stubbs were, presumably, the sums needed to rebuild the house if it were destroyed by fire, and so give a good idea of the value of a mid-eighteenth-century London house. This value of between £150 and £600, reflect-

ing the initial building cost, is borne out by detailed analysis of building costs (see pp. 213–18 and pp. 237–45) and by other insurance material. For example, in 1718 Sir James Bateman insured the newly built Nos. 6–10 Frith Street for £2,000 with the Hand in Hand.[19] Nos. 6 and 7 (now numbered 5 and 7) survive as good substantial houses valued then at £400 and £300 respectively – a figure that is probably a true reflection of the rebuilding cost of the time.

Construction costs of London houses before the great rise in prices in 1793, brought on by the desperate war with France, are indicated by the estimate of £180 to £200 for No. 15 Elder Street in 1727 (see p. 218). By contrast the larger No. 2 Fournier Street cost £1,461 15s. in 1726–31. This house was far more substantial, and hence expensive, than the usual speculative terrace house (see p. 227). On the Grosvenor Estate in the 1720s and 1730s smaller houses were being sold for around £200 to £300 and were rented for around £25 per annum. Slightly higher prices were those charged for No. 52 Davies Street (£500) and No. 54 (£550) in 1725.[20] These houses, demolished in the nineteenth century, were relatively modest, with 20-ft frontages.

Auction details for the sale in September 1811 of a group of modest, uniform houses in Upper Dover Street, Bath (now long destroyed), reveal the cost of a small house in early-nineteenth-century Bath. Described as 'compact new-built freehold dwelling houses with suitable conveniences', the houses were noted as worth a yearly rent of £14 14s. and valued at £190 each.[21] This sum is a trifle less than fourteen times the rentable value, which was the formula for relating rents to house value given by Ware (see p. 219). This shows that by 1811 inflation had made even modest houses expensive.

The sale price must not be confused with the construction cost, but it does give an indication. More revealing, perhaps, is the information that one developer, constructing a house in Mount Street, Mayfair, was required by the estate to spend £300 within two years and another £200 within twelve months.[22] This range of costs is supported by Ware, who explained that in 1756 a five-storey, three-bay 'common' London brick house cost between £600 and £700 to build – a figure supported by the costs of Nos. 5–13 Queen Anne's Gate, built 1770–71: each house cost an estimated £550–£650 to build.

In Bath construction costs seem to have been

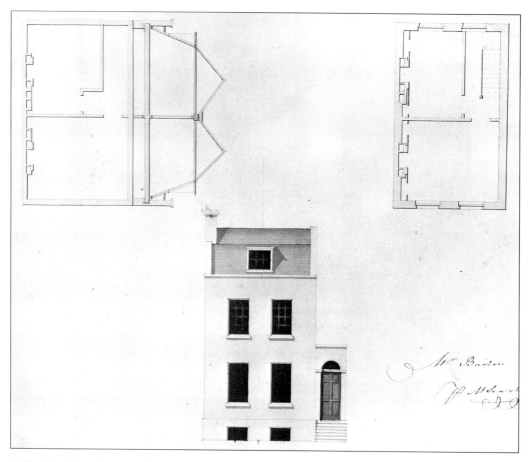

Michael Searles's drawing of c. 1790 for a modest house. The plans, roof section and elevation shown here are probably design and working drawings combined and represent all the information (if accompanied by a cost plan) that a competent Georgian builder would have needed. Details like window joinery and brick arches would have been executed as tradition and good practice dictated.

relatively higher than in London: partly because stone was more expensive than brick and partly because of the uncertain nature of the city's building industry. Bath, unlike London, was particularly subject to unsettling booms and recessions at irregular intervals, for its prosperity was based on the vagaries of the eighteenth-century tourist industry. Certainly John Eveleigh's ledgers, covering the years 1790–94, reveal the cost, in more ways than one, of building in Bath. Eveleigh was one of the leading Bath architects of the late-eighteenth century and, as well as being an able designer in the standard late-eighteenth-century Neo-classical mode, was

also capable of some originality. In about 1788 he designed Camden Crescent for a consortium of developers and produced a handsome elevation still in the Palladian manner inspired by Wood's Queen Square. At about the same time he speculated in his own right at Laura Place, Bathwick, where he worked to elevations designed by Thomas Baldwin. As the ledgers reveal, Laura Place eventually proved to be Eveleigh's undoing, for the collapse of 1793 caught him in the midst of his Bathwick speculation, leading to his bankruptcy in November of that year. His bankruptcy hearing and disclosure of assets, noted in the ledgers, reveal that he sold a house

Queen Square, Bath, drawn by Thomas Malton in c. *1784. On the right is the palace-fronted north side, begun by John Wood in 1728. On the west side is a pair of houses united beneath a common pediment.*

in Laura Place for £2,500, which included £317 profits (or about 14.5 per cent) over building costs and interest charges on a loan, and that another of his speculations – a five-bay house in Grosvenor Place, London Road, of about 1791 – cost £3,000.[23]

WAGES

Throughout the eighteenth century, until the rise in prices during the 1790s, journeymen members of the building trade were paid around 3s. a day in London and a little less in the regions. Journeymen were those members of the building trades who were paid a regular salary, usually at a daily rate, by a master, though they were offered no security. Building labourers were paid between 1s. 8d. and 2s. a day in London. These figures are stated very clearly in the Church Commissioners' accounts recording the building of ministers' houses in the 1720s.[24]

Elizabeth Waterman Gilboy, in her researches into wages in eighteenth-century England, examined the bills handed to Westminster Abbey stewards for repairs carried out on the abbey itself and to abbey-owned property in Westminster. These are interesting not only because they confirm the general level of wages while reflecting the sharp increase in prices in the 1790s, but also because they record minor fluctuations: general labourers received 1s. 8d. per day from 1700 to 1787 (when records cease) but with a drop to 1s. 7d. in 1701 and 1702 and 1s. 6d. in 1714 and a rise to 1s. 10d. in 1761. The daily wages for journeymen – bricklayers, masons, plumbers – range from 2s. 6d. to 3s. through the eighteenth century. Carpenters earned a little more: 2s. 6d. to 3s. 4d.

Gilboy also analysed bills for construction in Southwark and found that bricklayers' bills remained constant through most of the century: 2s. 8d. per day in 1708, 3s. in 1717, until 1790, when they rose dramatically to 3s. 4d. a day. Likewise, carpenters' wages in Southwark ranged from 2s. per day in 1708 to 3s. in 1727. They remained fairly constant until they rose to 4s. between 1790 and 1800.

In the North Riding of Yorkshire, Gilboy discovered that masons' and carpenters' wages were similar at around 1s. 6d. per day until 1760, rose to 2s. 3d. in 1773 but then settled at 2s. per day until the end of the century. In the West Riding, labourers' wages were 8*d.* per day until the early 1740s, then 1*s.* until the early 1780s, rising to 1*s.* 2*d.* per day at the end of the century.[25]

A little flesh is put on these figures by Campbell. Journeymen stonemasons, he wrote, 'make 3*s.* a day, or at least 2*s.* 6*d.* but are generally idle about four months of the year'. Of bricklayers he wrote: 'a Journeyman-Bricklayer has commonly half-a-crown a day, and the Foreman of the works may have 3*s.* or perhaps a Guinea a week: But they are out of Business for five, if not six months of the year; and, in and about London, drink more than one third of the other six.'

Journeyman carpenters, recorded Campbell, were paid 'from 12*s.* to 15*s.* a week'; journeyman joiners 'generally 2*s.* 6*d.* a day; but in Piece or jobbing work 3*s.*'; journeyman plasterers and paviors 'from 12*s.* to 15*s.* a week' but the plasterer was 'out of business about four months' a year; the plumber earned 15*s.* to a guinea a week. A glazier earned the 'common wage of 12*s.*' per week, the locksmith 9*s.* to 14*s.* or 15*s.* per week.

The daily rate was for ten hours' work, the journeyman's day beginning somewhere around six o'clock in the morning (see p. 27). These hours are confirmed by a note in William Pain's *British Palladio* of 1785, in which he recorded that the price for carpenters' work was 3*s.* 4*d.* for each man per day or 4*d.* per hour. More senior members of the industry, architects' draughtsmen, surveyors and the like, were paid on a very different basis with more security, dignity and regularity. For example, Robert Mylne recorded in his pocket-book in June 1764 that he paid his clerk '£40 per annum with breakfast and lodgings'.[26]

THE MORTGAGE SYSTEM

The most common way of raising money for building operations was, as already discussed, by borrowing against the security of the offer of a piece of ground or by mortgaging the lease itself. On the Grosvenor Estate in the 1720s the majority of mortgages were for amounts ranging from £100 to £500, chiefly at 5 per cent interest, which was the maximum then allowable by law.[27] In the late-eight-

eenth century the Bedford Estate lent money on very favourable terms to builders working on Bedford Square and Gower Street. No interest was charged for the first year and thereafter at only 4 per cent. By the end of 1782 the Estate had lent, mostly in mortgages for Bedford Square, £22,500.

Apart from providing the essential ready cash that most builders were short of, the mortgage system could also have a direct influence on the plan of the town house. This was particularly true in the early-eighteenth century, when builders of limited means operated on small sites. As observed on p. 124, ground rents were calculated on the width of the building plot's main frontage. What this means is that, since the ground rent was not based on a plot area but on the width of its main frontage, the wider the frontage the higher its rent. The higher the rent charged on a plot, the greater its value, and the more money it could be mortgaged for. Consequently in early-eighteenth-century streets such as Elder Street houses one room wide and two rooms deep stood side by side with houses two rooms wide and one room deep. The wider houses offered no more accommodation than the ones with narrower frontages, although they occupied plots of larger size. The profligate use of land seems to be economically unsound, until the logic of mortgaging is understood. The point of building one wide house on a double plot, instead of two narrow, deep houses, was that twice as much mortgage money could be raised for a house with a wide frontage than for a house of the same size with a narrower frontage.

If money was not raised by mortgage, and the builder did not have ready cash and could not do all by barter with other builders, then he would have to rely on short-term credit for materials and sometimes even labour. All would be well with this barter system if the house was completed quickly and sold successfully. If not, then the builder would frequently end in a debtors' gaol. Well-established speculators, in the possession of leases or valuable land and in command of a certain income in rents, had other options for raising money for further building operations. They could, as the wealthy Thomas Barlow did on the Grosvenor Estate (see p. 124), acquire annuities that could be paid back out of their rents or profits, or borrow against future rent revenue.

The sort of people who lent the money to builders, the mortgagees, were of an unexpected variety. The

Elder Street case study (see p. 210) reveals that money for building Spitalfields in the 1720s came from local tradesmen with a little cash to invest or from potential occupiers who advanced the builder money to construct the house.

The *Survey of London* suggests that when the Grosvenor Estate was being developed in the 1720s, these same types of mortgagees were included in the wider spectrum of investors that one would expect to find involved in the development of a fashionable West London estate:

The mortgagees came from a variety of stations in life, one of the largest sources of capital on the Grosvenor Estate [being] solicitors and barristers. Widows and spinsters were prominent in providing the small sums necessary to maintain the essential flow of cash to builders, but a high proportion of mortgagees were tradesmen living or working in the several Westminster parishes ... there were also merchants [and] several instances in which builders obtained mortgages from timber merchants, brick-makers or even fellow-craftsmen.

The builders who worked on the larger scale – undertakers who were responsible for the development of entire urban components – must be considered somewhat differently, because thay had a vision that they alone could realize. Speculative builders of Barbon's generation did not attempt to organize their developments to create coherently composed street elevations. Even major undertakings like Bloomsbury and St James's Square (1661 and 1665 respectively) were only decently, not rigidly, uniform, with no attempt to govern the individual houses into palace-like compositions, as Inigo Jones had done in the Covent Garden Piazza of the 1630s.

But after 1725, this was to change, with the undertakers striving, in their various ways and with more or less success, to realize the vision of the palace-fronted terrace.

INDIVIDUALITY TO UNIFORMITY

The first significant eighteenth-century attempt to unify individual terrace houses into a palace-fronted composition was Colen Campbell's design of 1725

for the east side of Grosvenor Square. This grand Palladian design, in which a giant order rose from a rusticated ground floor to embrace the first and second floors and supported a full entablature, seems to have fallen victim to the speculative system. Simmons, the builder who eventually developed the site, was presumably unwilling to go to the trouble and expense of constructing this noble elevation, and the estate was clearly unwilling to make him.

It was in Bath that the vision of urban uniformity and the demands of the speculative building system were first reconciled. The north side of Queen Square, designed in 1728 by John Wood, is the realization not only of Campbell's design for Grosvenor Square but a textbook example of Neo-Palladian urban design. Unlike Campbell's design (but like Henry Aldrich's pioneering Palladian elevations to the Peckwater quadrangle at Christ Church, Oxford, of 1706–13) the Queen Square palace front possesses a mighty central pediment that crowns the five-bay-wide centre house. Also at Queen Square the pair of end houses were designed as terminal pavilions and possess an attic storey above the entablature.

The financial arrangement behind the creation of this handsome composition of seven houses is well described by Walter Ison, who reveals that Wood's aim as a developer was not to secure an immediate return on capital by selling on the leases of shells, but to create an annual income for his family from rents charged on the individual houses.[28] To be able to do this – to accept relatively small payments over a long period rather than the quick recouping of capital sum plus profit – the undertaker had to be a man of some substance with a well-organized cash flow.

Wood's method of development at Queen Square was to take a series of 99-year leases from the ground landlord Robert Gay on various plots of land around the proposed square. This phasing of land acquisition must have reflected both Wood's financial limitations at this stage in his career and his unwillingness to take on building land until he was sure that there was a demand.

The first lease was granted by Gay in November 1728 and was for two plots, on the south and east sides of the square: each had a 100-ft frontage and a depth of 150 ft. The annual ground rent for these two pieces of land was £20. The convention in the eighteenth century was to calculate the ground rent of a piece of land by fixing a rate per foot and then multiplying that rate by the width of the site's main frontage. It is apparent that Gay was charging a rate of 2s. per foot. This was only twice as much as was being charged in Elder Street at the same time, though charges for plots on Grosvenor Square in the 1720s were 6s. per foot.

Between September 1729 and September 1731 Wood granted 98-year subleases to builders for the erection of houses on both these sites. During the four years after 1728, Wood leased the rest of the land around the square from Gay and, again, sublet plots to various builders. The north side, providing the ground for the palace-fronted terrace, was leased from Gay in October 1732. This plot, with a 206-ft frontage and 150-ft depth, with a smaller plot (101-ft frontage on the east side of the square), was worth a ground rent of £32 14s. The building subleases for the north side were granted between January 1732 and July 1734, with Wood building some of the houses himself – notably No. 24, which had a remarkably rich interior and which was built not as a speculation but for a particular client.

By 1736 all twenty-seven houses on Queen Square were completed and entered in the city rate books. Wood's ambitious designs for the square were only partially realized, however. He achieved the palatial north side, but he also intended that the east and west sides would be uniform if less grand, forming a sort of palace forecourt for the north side. The east side was carried out more or less as envisaged, but the west side fell victim to the sort of pressures and changing circumtances that so often defeated projects of similar ambition in London. The building on the west side finally took the form of a large central mansion set back from the building line, flanked by a pair of houses treated as grand pedimented single compositions. In some respects this west elevation, with its somewhat informal grandeur, became, if only unwittingly, a challenge rather than a foil to the regimented, formal north elevation.

When the Queen Square development was complete, Gay and his heirs were in possession of ground rent worth £137 per annum and would gain possession of the houses themselves in ninety-nine or so years. Wood and his heirs possessed 'improved' ground rents of £305 1s. per annum. Gay's sum, though substantially less than Wood's, was the profit of a transaction carried out with little effort

or risk on Gay's part. Wood's rent was earned by much energy and risk, and it represented the increase over the basic ground rent that Wood charged those to whom he sublet building plots.

If Wood's improved rent seems rather high in comparison with the ground rent, it was not in any way out of the ordinary when measured against the profits that were being made by some of his successful contemporaries in west London. For example, Thomas Barlow, the Grosvenor Estate surveyor and speculative builder, took a 99-year lease in 1721 on six acres of estate land at a ground rent of £67 per annum. He then divided the land into plots and sublet building underleases on leases of eighty years at most but generally on leases of sixty years. From these he obtained about £280 per annum in 'improved' rents above the £67 he had to pay to the estate in ground rent. He also got a further £160 per annum in rack rents from buildings held directly by him. When his properties were auctioned in 1745, they realized £7,000.[29]

The means by which Wood imposed his uniform elevations on those builders to whom he guaranteed subleases is a fascinating issue – particularly since his contemporaries proved such spectacular failures in this sphere of operation. When, for example, the east side of Grosvenor Square was developed, not Campbell's uniform columnar elevation but an astylar terrace was gradually erected between 1725 and 1753 by the speculator John Simmons. In this terrace Simmons acknowledged Campbell's palace front so far as to place a pediment on the centre house and an extra storey on the end-of-terrace houses to form terminating features. Such was the then prevailing standard that even this modest attempt at coherently designed street architecture caught the eye of John Soane a hundred years later and received praise in his Royal Academy lecture (see p. 104).

Wood probably obtained, and enforced, uniformity by getting the various builders to work to an agreed design drawing – perhaps that later reproduced by him in his *Essay towards a Description of Bath* of 1742 – which would have been part of the legal documentation accompanying the lease. Certainly this is how uniform developments in both London and Bath were later achieved (see p. 130). The alternative to a drawing was a written description or specification, and words are always liable to a certain amount of interpretation and manipulation – not that a builder needed much ingenuity to subvert to his own ends the usually very imprecise design description generally contained in building agreements.

Typical is the description in a 1724 specimen 'contract for building' for the Cavendish-Harley Estate in Marylebone. This contract contains much on the subject of construction, uses permitted and responsibility for paving and maintaining the pavement but very little on design. The signee was merely obliged to complete, by an agreed date, with 'good and substantial materials ... good and substantial double brick messuages or tenements to contain an uniform and continued building or buildings upon the whole front ... to be built with Red and Grey Stock bricks with straight or compass [segmental] arches and the returns or jambs of the windows to be rubbed brick or stone'.[30] This suggests that the estate required that groups of houses built by different developers should possess façades of at least rudimentary uniformity and be designed in the current fashion. It does not, however, aim at a very high level of architecture, nor does it even hint that the various elevations should be organized into a balanced and unified urban composition. It was this sort of uninspired building contract – imposing bland uniformity but not realizing the potential offered by estate control – that produced the kind of street architecture that depressed John Gwynn so much in the mid-eighteenth century. Gwynn, in his visionary *London and Westminster Improved* of 1766, observed that the 'new building' in Marylebone gave 'no better idea to the spectator than that of a plain brick wall of prodigious length'.

But even those later-eighteenth and early-nineteenth century developments in London, Bath and Edinburgh that were uniform or organized as a single composition were developed under agreements that were hardly any more strict than this Cavendish-Harley contract. What seems clear is that elevational uniformity, when it was achieved, was brought about because the chief undertaker desired it, and he desired it because it became increasingly obvious during the Georgian period that the illusion of living in a palace was highly marketable.

The records of the Bedford Estate in Bloomsbury provide an intriguing insight into the way in which elevational uniformity was achieved in late-eighteenth-century London, and by whom. Bedford Square was the first London square in which the Palladian palace-front ideal was finally realized – albeit in a somewhat compromised manner (see p. 126). The four sides possess uniform elevations, each with a pedimented centre – stuccoed and dressed with pilasters – and end pavilions that break forward slightly. But the documents that controlled the development say little directly about how this palace front was achieved. The building contract of 1776 for the south side of Bedford Square simply required that the builders 'erect, build and completely finish [within five years] one uniform row of houses to front north ... agreeable to an elevation for the same signed by ... Robert Palmer, William Scott and Robert Grews and deposited in the Steward's Office of Bedford House'.[31] Palmer was the estate surveyor, but this statement is ambiguous enough to leave doubt as to whether he was the designer or merely, like the two builders, a signatory to a legal document. By signing the drawing, the three agreed that the design was the model that was to be worked to. It was, presumably, in similar manner that Wood organized the development of the north side of Queen Square, Bath. The written specification gave no idea of the palace-fronted nature of the design it controlled. Floor-to-ceiling heights for the various storeys are given (see p. 137), and it was ordered that Scott and Grews should undertake to 'build all the houses with hard place bricks with good grey stocks in uniform colour with the walls of all the houses to be flushed solid with good mortar and to be carried up and continued in every respect agreeable to the Act of Parliament lately passed'. The only real puzzle in the contract is that, despite this general if vague attempt at uniformity, a clause is inserted giving the 'occupier' freedom to lower any windowsill to floor level if desired (see p. 139).

Bedford Square was built in the usual manner and suffered those problems so often visited upon ambitious, large-scale speculative developments. Scott and Grews, though contractually responsible for building the whole square to the agreed elevations, sold subleases on several of the plots to other builders. Scott and Grews built the whole of the south side and individual houses on the other three sides, but also active were John Utterton (see p. 128) and the architect Thomas Leverton. Leverton built the large centre house on the east side (now No. 6) and a house for himself, No. 13, which lies just

The east side of Bedford Square showing the centre house designed in the late 1770s by Thomas Leverton. The centre house's generous five-bay width permitted the creation of a classically correct pedimented and pilastered design. First-floor windows of different depths may be an original feature of the square.

outside the formal palace front of the east side of Bedford Square.

The fact that the execution of the square was in several hands, and ruled by the exigencies of speculation, is revealed by the different designs of the pedimented central feature. On the north and south sides the two three-bay centre houses are united behind a stucco façade and beneath a four-bay pediment. Unfortunately a six-bay centre feature can end only in tragedy, or rather farce, if it is crowned with a four-bay pediment and embellished with five pilasters. This arrangement resulted in

a painful solecism, with a pilaster, not a space, occupying the centre of the temple-front composition. This must have been 'the spirit of speculation' that Soane saw at work in the square and noted in his Royal Academy lecture (see p. 104) and that was referred to in particular by Thomas Malton in his *A Picturesque Tour through the Cities of London and Westminster* of 1792–1801: 'the pediments extend over two houses and have a pilaster in the middle; destroying that appearance of unity which is the characteristic of a pediment. It is scarcely to be imagined that such a fault could be committed,

The north side of Bedford Square showing the unfortunate classical solecism of the centrally placed pilaster,
where speculative builders tried to make a classical composition out of two standard three-bay houses.

at a time when architecture has been so much studied and improved.' The problem was avoided on the west side, where a single three-bay house sported a pediment that acts as a somewhat reduced, but more classically correct, central feature. On the east side more thought was given to the problem: the central house, built by Leverton, was five bays wide. Therefore, he was able to escape the Scott–

Grews problem (turning a pair of three-bay houses into a central feature) and avoid their clumsy solution. He merely needed to add a sedate and classically correct three-bay pediment to his five-bay elevation.

Bedford Square – with its ambitious if flawed uniformity – was a special case. More typical of late-eighteenth-century speculative terrace buildings is the slightly later Gower Street. Nos. 15–49 Gower Street comprised a terrace that achieved a high level of uniformity, but where no attempt was made to organize the three-bay houses into any sort of coherent palace-front composition. There were no pediments or stucco-frontis pieces, no articulation of the façade and no end pavilions. Most of the leases on these houses were granted for ninety-nine years from 1781, and many were made out to John Utterton, builder, who worked regularly in association with Alexander Hendy. These leases allowed the builder a generous five-year peppercorn period – by the end of which they were contracted to have completed the houses – and required the payment of a ground rent of £9 18s. per annum for the 22 × 120 ft plots (that is ground rent at the rate of 9s. per ft frontage).

A 'contract for building on the East and West sides of Gower Street', dated 15 February 1783, reveals that, as in the early-eighteenth century, uniformity of appearance was not achieved by the use of legally binding words, for virtually nothing is

written about the appearance that this terrace was to have. [32] This 'article of agreement' was between the trustees of the Duke of Bedford, his surveyor Robert Palmer and John Utterton, and devolves responsibility on Utterton for supervising the erection of the two long blocks each side of Gower Street between Store Street and Chenies Street. Like Scott and Grews in Bedford Square, Utterton sublet plots to other builders, who then obtained their own leases from the estate. The 'article of agreement' confirmed that construction was to be completed by the end of the peppercorn period (five years from 1781) and specified the ground rent payable (£125 on one side of Gower Street and £145 on the other). As to appearance, the document merely required that Utterton build 'in a good and workmanlike manner and of the best materials one uniform row of houses to front Gower Street'. The uniformity that resulted reflected the public's taste for austere and repetitive façades (speculative builders always had to be sensitive to public taste), as well as the

Michael Searles's design of 1795 for the centre-piece of Surrey Square. The centre house is only three bays wide (revealed by the roof parapet), with each of its neighbours possessing one bay of the centre-piece.

economic advantages offered by mass-produced architecture. Coade stone, the material that epitomizes the role of mass production in late-eighteenth-century architecture, was used to good effect in this Gower Street terrace. It was employed here not for the door frames, as at Bedford Square, but for the bold guilloche pattern of the continuous first-floor sill course.

It is instructive to compare the buildings undertaken on the aristocratic Bedford Estate – characterized by simplicity, repetition and uniformity – with contemporary developments on more humble estates in London and the provinces. Not exactly typical, but highly attractive, are the works of Michael Searles undertaken for a number of modest south-east London estates and landowners.

Searles, a surveyor, architect and developer, showed remarkable skill in the design of modest urban housing. Using a limited vocabulary of standard architectural motifs and devices – characteristically round-headed windows linked by impost blocks to form arcades and judiciously placed string-

and sill-courses – he was able to enliven long runs of terraces by introducing subtle central and intermediate emphasis. Notable is Surrey Square, Walworth, which he built between 1791 and 1795. The square possessed one long terrace on its northern side and individual houses, built later (and now demolished), on the other three sides. It seems that Searles undertook the development of this terrace on a lease from the head lessee (the land had been acquired on a 99-year lease in 1763 by bricklayer Thomas Clutton from the estate of James Brace) and strove to give his design a uniform and well-organized appearance.[33] The nine-bay centre group was embellished with a five-bay pediment, while the centre three houses of the long flanking terraces were emphasized – like the three centre houses below the pediment – with arcaded ground floors.

No doubt Searles let or sold plots to other builders, and he controlled their activities with the use of elevational drawings that, as at Bedford Square, the various parties to the development were

The centre-piece of Surrey Square as built: the central porch has been moved to the side to create a standard plan, with entrance passage flanked by parlour.

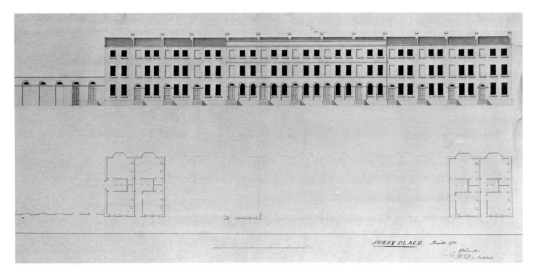

Surrey Place, Old Kent Road, built in 1784 to the design of Michael Searles. This austere elevation has been enlivened by the judicious use of standard elements – arcades, blank windows, string-courses – that gave the elevation a sense of rhythm and focus. The centrally placed and top-list stairs allow the generous-sized rear rooms to be fitted with an elegant bow.

probably contracted to follow. Certainly a series of elevations for Surrey Square survive amongst a large collection of Searles's drawings at the RIBA.

In Bath the Palladian palace-fronted terrace, pioneered by Wood, entered the local building vernacular, and it became a matter of course to organize terrace developments so that they possessed uniform façades with the centre at least emphasized. Typical is Sion Place (or Sion Hill Place, as it is now called), which was built around 1812 in the form of an austere, four-storey terrace framed by end houses treated as full-height three-bay bows, and with a three-bay centre house emphasized with a pediment. Documents granting leases show that individual builders not only had to pay an annual ground rent of £2. 13s. 4d. to three different people (Caleb Hillier Parry, the landlord, William Cowell Hayes, the head lessee, and to a George Watts) but also had to agree to erect the building to conform to an elevation and block plan designed by architect John Pinch, which was attached to the lease.[34] Again, the evidence is that elevational uniformity, when it was achieved, was via the simple and relatively objective medium of an agreed and legally processed design drawing. Interestingly, in the case of the three-bay pedimented

centre house (now No. 5), built by Daniel Aust on a lease dated 24 June 1812, the lower left-hand corner of the pediment was actually the responsibility of the builder of the neighbouring house, so close co-operation between overseeing architect, landlord and the different builders was clearly essential for a successful result. This lease also makes it clear that, upon non-payment of ground rent, the offended parties had the power after twenty-one days 'to enter and distrain for such several rents respectively'.

In Edinburgh the palace-fronted terrace did not arrive until the early 1790s, when Robert Adam's Charlotte Square was begun. This was, no doubt, due to the fact that building in the New Town in the 1760s and 1770s was a far from certain speculation, with the town council being loath to inhibit builders by imposing demands for uniform or regularly composed elevations. Indeed, in 1768 the town council went so far as to obtain an Act that gave individuals the right to design in any manner they chose, 'as people's taste in building is so different, that it is not possible to lay down a fixed and determined rule'. However, by 1782 the town council clearly felt more able to impose uniformity.

John Pinch's design of 1812 for the centre feature of Sion Hill Place, Bath. This drawing was attached to the lease, and its execution formed part of the legal agreement for building on the site. Thus were individual builders compelled to conform to a uniform palace-front elevation.

An Act of that year, re-enacted in 1785, demanded amongst other things that 'no feus shall be granted in the principal streets ... for houses above three storey high exclusive of garret and sunk stories', that houses in lesser streets should not exceed two storeys and that no 'feu to be granted, until such time as a plan and elevation of the intended building, signed by the person applying, be given to the committee and approved by them'.[35]

This type of specification led to the creation of Charlotte Square, after which all major New Town developments displayed marked uniformity and a concern for balanced, unified compositions.

CONSTRUCTION TIME

Most of the leases and building agreements contained clauses that forced the builder to complete construction within a certain time. This building period was usually linked to the peppercorn period (see p. 117). This type of clause was essential from the landlord's point of view, for otherwise he could find himself with an estate let to builders who preferred to raise money from mortgaging their interests in his land and to use the money to build elsewhere.

The centre-piece of Sion Hill Place as built.

Indeed, most estates built in strict requirements about performance. The Grosvenor Estate confirmed its grant of leases on the ground only when builders had reached certain stages of construction; for example, within forty days of the first and second floors of the houses being laid or within forty days of tiling in. At Bedford Square, the Bedford Estate agreed to grant the leases to Scott and Grews or to 'such person or persons as they shall name' only when the houses were complete. This was usual practice and a very powerful incentive to complete the works, because until the builder was in possession of the lease he could not sell on or let the house he had built. Generally speaking, it was to the builder's advantage to complete construction as quickly as possible and, indeed, actual construction time could be much less than the length of the peppercorn. On the Grosvenor Estate the usual peppercorn period was two to three years, but some building contracts specified that houses should be complete within six months or, for the larger houses in Grosvenor Square, within twelve or eighteen months. There is, however, no evidence that laggards were penalized.[36]

The speed of construction directly reflected the individual builder's resources; construction time could drag on if he could afford to employ only a few men and had little ready cash, and so had to barter his service for those of other builders. But when the developer had adequate resources, construction could be surprisingly quick. For example, the five large houses on the south side of Queen Anne's Gate, built in 1771 (see p. 244), were completed, it seems, in eight and half months, including a certain amount of interior fitting out.

That construction was usually fast is supported by observations made by various foreign visitors. Geijer noted that 'they build a small brick dwelling of this [flimsy] kind in fourteen days, within a month it is all finished'.[37] This incredibly fast construction time was confirmed by Pückler-Muskau when he claimed that a collapsed house in St James's Street would be rebuilt in a month by speculative builders, 'although perhaps no safer than before'.[38]

But the most convincing and evocative account is by Goede, who gives a sense of what it must have been like to live in a Georgian city in the throes of expansion. Goede lived in Bloomsbury at the time when Russell Square was being built, and the great early-nineteenth-century expansion of the Bedford Estate was under way:

I resided in Southampton Row, Bloomsbury, near which the Duke of Bedford is engaging in very extensive building, and has some thousands of workmen in constant employment ... I remember that on my return to town after an absence of some months I could scarcely believe myself at home. On reviewing the neighbourhood I could have fancied myself transported into a fairy world, where by the power of a magic wand palaces and gardens had suddenly found existence. I ... asked myself whether I had not previously seen that new street, new square, new garden; in a word this city; or whether in reality the heaps of stones and rubbish which I had left piled up from the material of old houses, had been metamorphosed into new and elegant buildings ... People crowded along the well-lighted pavement ... everything bore the appearance of enchantment. The opposite side of Southampton Row, late an open space, was not only built upon but inhabited: a coffee house was open and some very handsome shops exposed their merchandise for sale. Tavistock Square ... and streets intersecting each other, were novelties that raised new wonders in my head.[39]

Chapter Two

PROPORTION

PALLADIAN THEORISTS

Georgian theories of proportion found only limited expression in the modest town house. Even the proportioning of the openings in the façade – the most obvious manifestation of the Georgian concern for proportional relationships of parts – could be affected by the exigencies of the speculative system and the demand to maximize the accommodation built on the site. Significantly, Ware, authoritative on all aspects of design and construction, was uncharacteristically relaxed when confronted with the problem of proportioning the parts of a town house. In his *A Complete Body of Architecture* he merely noted that 'as the fixed point, in the matter of general proportion, is not known, there is no other guide ... but a natural judgement and practice'. Not a particularly helpful analysis, although Ware did hazard a further opinion: 'What we understand by the general proportion of an edifice, is its uniformity, or proper agreement, in length, breadth and height.'

The most coherent theory of proportion held in the Georgian period was that developed by the early-eighteenth-century Neo-Palladians, who saw correct proportions not just as objective rules that expressed a finite beauty but as a manifestation of cosmic, and ultimately spiritual, laws. These early-eighteenth-century theorists – notably Lord Burlington, Colen Campbell and Robert Morris – were pursuing that Renaissance line of thought in which Plato and Pythagoras personified the Greek discovery of the universal laws of beauty.

Robert Morris, the only member of the early-eighteenth-century English Neo-Palladian school to write down its theories on proportion and design, described the origins of classical architecture in his *Essay in Defence of Ancient Architecture* of 1728:

Grecians were the first happy inventors, they extracted the beauteous ideas of it from rude unshapen trees, the products of nature, and embellished it, by degree of perfections, with those necessary ornaments which have been since practised by those of the most sublime genius [and] collected by the indefatigable care and industry of Palladio.

So Andrea Palladio was seen both as the guardian of ancient laws of architectural harmony and as the means by which these laws had been reintroduced. Palladio had achieved this dissemination not so much through his buildings, which few of them knew first hand, but through the publication in 1570 of his *Four Books of Architecture*. In this work he illustrated his seven ideal room proportions, which the Neo-Palladians saw as the key to his architecture and hence to that of the Ancients. They adopted these and also adapted them to create a system of proportionally related ratios; these were used not just to govern the design of rooms, plans and façades but also to relate these elements to one another. As Ware put it: 'there ought to be ... a uniformity of all the parts, first to the whole building, and next to one another'. In this Ware was echoing the words of Palladio himself: 'Beauty will result from the form and correspondence of the whole, with respect to the several parts, of the parts with regard to each other, and of these again to the whole; that the structure may appear an entire and compleat body, wherein each member agrees with the other.'[1]

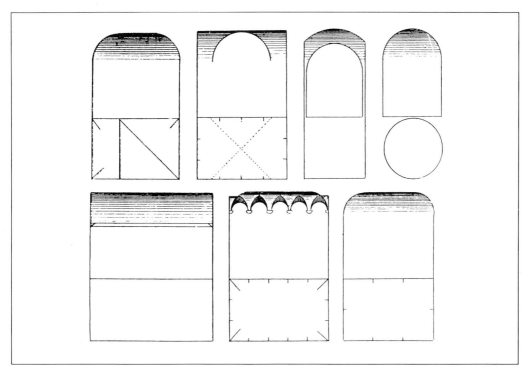

Palladio's seven ideal room proportions as presented by Isaac Ware in his 1738 edition of Palladio's Four Books of Architecture. *Top right to left: circle; square; square and one third; root two. Bottom right to left: square and a half; square and two thirds; double square.*

PROPORTIONS

Palladio's ideal proportions were: a circle or sphere; a cube; a cube and a third; a cube extended by the use of root two (dropping the diagonal of a square by use of a compass); a cube and a half; a cube and two thirds; and a double cube. With the exception of the sphere and the root two rectangle, all these proportions bear a simple relationship to one another, as they are mathematically generated extensions of the square or cube. The sphere and the root two permutation belong to another system of proportions – one that is not developed mathematically but geometrically. The former belongs to a civilization that was literate and where mathematics were used for expressing – and creating – a model of the universe. The latter belongs to a more ancient world, where proportions had to be developed, expressed and applied in practice by use of simple tools: the right angle, the compass, the measuring chain.

Robert Morris, in his *Lectures on Architecture* of 1734 and 1736, made it clear that the English Neo-Palladians rationalized Palladio's seven ideal proportions to exclude the geometrically generated forms. Morris's proportions, also seven in number, were all commensurate with, and very simple extensions of, the cube. They were: a cube; a cube and a half; a double cube; and then four proportions that were, in Morris's words, 'duplicates' of the cube developed on the 'analogous principle'. These were the ratios of 3:2:1 (that is, a proportion three cubes long, two cubes wide and one cube high); 4:3:2; 5:4:3; and 6:4:3.

The fact that Morris chose, like Palladio, seven ideal proportions was a reflection of the well-established connection that classicists saw between

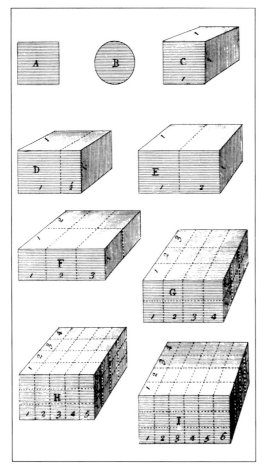

Robert Morris's seven ideal proportions, from his Lectures on Architecture *of 1734. C to E, showing the cube, cube and a half, and double cube are taken from Palladio's system. F to I are Morris's own 'duplicates', with ratios of 3:2:1; 4:3:2; 5:4:3 and 6:4:3.*

musical harmony and visual beauty. In the fifteenth century Leon Battista Alberti had written that 'harmonic ratios inherent in nature are revealed in music'[2] – an observation echoed by Morris in his *Lectures*: 'Nature had taught mankind in Musick certain rules for proportion of sounds, so architecture has its rules dependent on those proportions.' What Morris called the 'diapason' – the cube and a half or 2:3 proportion – contained all his seven proportions and related to the octave of seven notes.

As Morris put it: 'In Musick are only seven distinct notes, in architecture likewise are only seven distinct proportions, which produce all the different buildings in the universe.'

THE PALACE FRONT

This system of proportions was combined with the elevational ideal offered by the Roman temple: a compositional device that suggested the vertical spacing of the windows and the horizontal division of tall façades into Palladian proportioned parts. The architectural livery of the temple was used in full on palatial, uniform terraces embellished with a giant order, cornice, pedestals and pediment such as John Wood's 1728 north side of Queen Square, Bath (see p. 121). In this composition it is apparent that a Georgian façade is a synthesis of Palladian theories of proportion (i.e., the size of the window openings relative to wall areas) and the discipline imposed by the correctly proportioned temple front (the integration of the windows within the inter-columniations of the temple columns).

Even in elevations where the main architectural elements of the temple – columns, pilasters, cornice, pediment – are absent, their presence could be implied by the use of certain details. For example, a cornice – or even a flat string-course – was used to suggest the location of the entablature; a sill-band or string-course at first-floor level could be used to indicate the line of the column base, while another above the ground-floor windows could be used to indicate the junction between column pedestal and temple podium.

The ideal proportion for the façade area of this type of astylar Palladian town house was 2:3 – a square and a half – the façade being one and a half times high as wide. To achieve this the front could be only three storeys high, with the temple composition implied by a string-course at first-floor level: the two storeys above fell within the area of the column shaft, with the ground-floor storey corresponding to the area of the podium (a fourth floor above ground could be accommodated in a garret within the roof space). If the house was three bays wide – the usual width of the common Georgian town house – the elevation occupied by the first- and second-floor windows was roughly square in area,

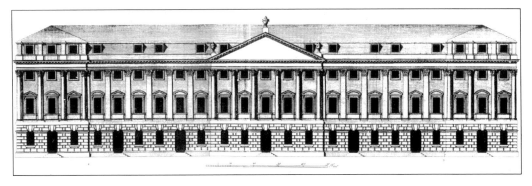

The first realized eighteenth-century example of the Palladian palace-front ideal in which individual houses are arranged behind a uniform and centrally emphasized façade. This drawing of John Wood's Queen Square, Bath, which was begun in 1728, is taken from Wood's Essay towards a Description of Bath *published in 1742.*

while the podium area occupied by the ground-floor windows and door was itself a square and a half in proportion.

CEILING HEIGHTS

The proportions of the window openings and their relationship to the areas of wall around them followed a simple, classical logic that was a reflection of the respective ceiling heights of the various floor levels, which in turn was a reflection of the way in which the house was occupied. As Ware explained when discussing 'the several kinds of windows', 'the height of the rooms enters here into consideration, and as these are lower in the chamber-floor [the second floor] than in that below, the windows should also be lower'.

Ware's observation takes into account the fact that by the mid-eighteenth century it was generally established that the first floor was the main floor – the piano nobile or principal storey – and so had the highest ceilings and tallest windows. In the late-seventeenth century the ground floor had often been treated as the principal storey (as it was again in suburban developments of the late-eighteenth century), while houses of the early-eighteenth century often had ground- and first-floor windows of the same size. This usage was enshrined in the 1667 London Building Act. This Act, in an attempt to ensure sound construction, specified how houses

of certain dimensions ought to be built. So we see that small- and medium-size houses were envisaged as having ground and first floors of the same height (9 ft in small houses and 10 ft in medium-size houses), while the structure of large houses was calculated on the basis of a 10-ft ground floor and a first floor of 10 ft 6 ins. Significantly, by the time of the 1774 London Building Act, it was assumed that the first floor was always the principal storey – a point made very clearly in Peter Nicholson's illustrations, published in his *New and Improved Practical Builder* of 1823, of the four rates of urban domestic buildings specified in that Act (see p. 102).

Typical of grand town houses of the late-eighteenth century are those on the south side of Bedford Square. The July 1776 building contract for these houses states that the 'cellar' must be 10 ft high, 'the ground floor 12 ft 6 ins high, the one pair of stairs floor [the first floor] 14 ft 6 ins high, the two pairs of stairs 10 ft high and the garret floor 7 ft 2 ins high all in the clear'.[3] So by the late-eighteenth century, the ground floor, containing the parlour, would ideally have a ceiling height lower than the first floor and the same as, or slightly higher than, the second floor.

WINDOW SIZES

The height of the windows inserted into the façade could be anything from three quarters high as wide

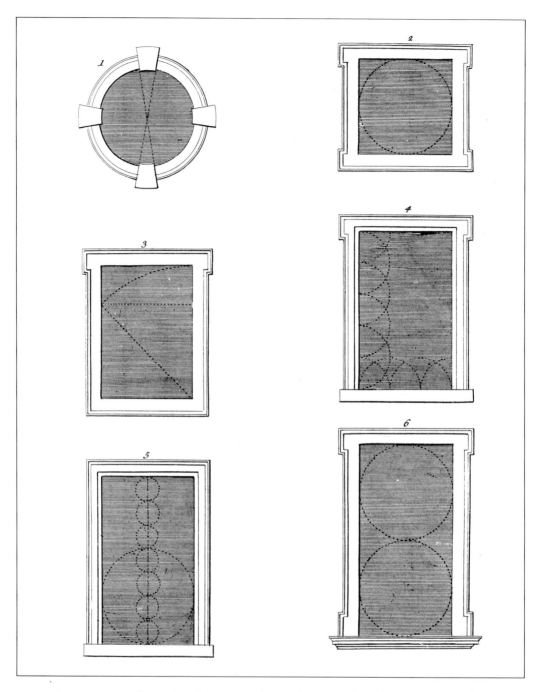

Six window proportions from Edward Hoppus's The Gentleman's and Builder's Repository *of 1737. Nos. 1 and 2 are self-explanatory; No. 3, showing the root two proportion, is described as 'height ... the diagonal of a square'; No. 4 is height square and two thirds; No. 5 is height square and three quarters; No. 6 is double square.*

(a squat proportion recommended by Ware for mezzanine windows) to something over twice as high as wide for windows to principal floors. Edward Hoppus, in his *Gentleman's and Builder's Repository* of 1737, listed what he saw as the five ideal window proportions: 'square; height ... the diagonal of a square [root two]; height the width plus two thirds of the width; height the width plus three quarters of the width; and height twice the width'. William Salmon, in his *Palladio Londinensis* of 1734, indicated how these different sizes related to one another: 'The height of the Windows in the second storey [that is the first floor] be $\frac{11}{12}$ of the first, and the height of the attic, or third storey $\frac{3}{4}$ of the second storey'.

These descriptions of window shapes and placings reflect the basic repertoire and theory behind the early-eighteenth-century three-storey Palladian elevation. The only significant omission is the 2:3 proportion, which Hoppus ignores in favour of the similar root two. In the ideal Palladian early-eighteenth-century elevation the ground- and first-floor windows would be of similar height (perhaps double square for the ground floor, with the first floor being $\frac{11}{12}$ as high as recommended by Salmon), the second floor being lit by square attic windows. Certainly by the mid-eighteenth century, double square windows had become standard for the principal floor – by then the first floor. As Ware explained: 'the height of windows for the principal storey is to be proportioned to their breadth ... the most general proportion in plain windows [is] twice the measure of the aperture in breadth and for its height'. But the designer, pointed out Ware, was 'not to be tied down to this with so much strictness, but ... twice and one sixth may be allowed without violence to true proportion'. Salmon went further and wrote that windows could be 'height double their breadth, with the addition of a quarter, a third or a half part, as shall be found necessary'. These observations appear to anticipate the late-eighteenth-century fashion for elongated first-floor windows – a fashion that emerges in the July 1776 contract for the south side of Bedford Square:

All the windows of every storey of the houses fronting the intended square to be continuous and remain during the continuance of the lease ... in line with each other but liberty to be given to cut down any of the windows so low as the floors of the rooms in

the said houses if the same should be required by the owner thereof.

COMPROMISE OF THE PALLADIAN IDEAL

The pressure to maximize the use of the site by increasing the size and value of the house led to the common practice of creating a fourth floor within the area of the façade above ground. In this way a fifth floor was obtained that had a greater floor area and a higher, more regular ceiling height than could be created within the garret roof space. When this elongation of the façade was undertaken, it was usual to make the second-floor windows one and a half times high as wide – a proportion echoed by the ground floor – with the third-floor windows square. The practice is described by Ware. Speaking of the second-floor windows of a four-storey façade, Ware noted that 'the best measure for these is the diagonal, which is one and a half the breadth; this is what the builders express by the name of a diagonal window'. This description sounds contradictory, for a diagonal window could be taken to be a window proportioned on the diagonal of a square – root two as illustrated by Hoppus – which does not make a shape quite one and a half times high as wide. But perhaps Ware is referring to the fact that in a window one and half times high as wide (the favoured Palladian 2:3 or square to square and a half proportion) a diagonal line can be used to proportion the nine panes of glazing. The third-floor 'attic storey' above this 2:3 proportioned window should, continued Ware, 'have the windows square'.

The discipline of the temple front could be maintained – in this extended elevation – by introducing a cornice or string-course between second and third floors to imply that the square window was housed in the attic of the temple composition.

The width of window openings in modest town houses was almost invariably fixed at between 3 ft 5 ins and 3 ft 6 ins. This same dimension was commonly the width of the piers between the window openings, although very early in the eighteenth century the piers were often considerably narrower than the window openings. This must have been a reflection of north European influence, par-

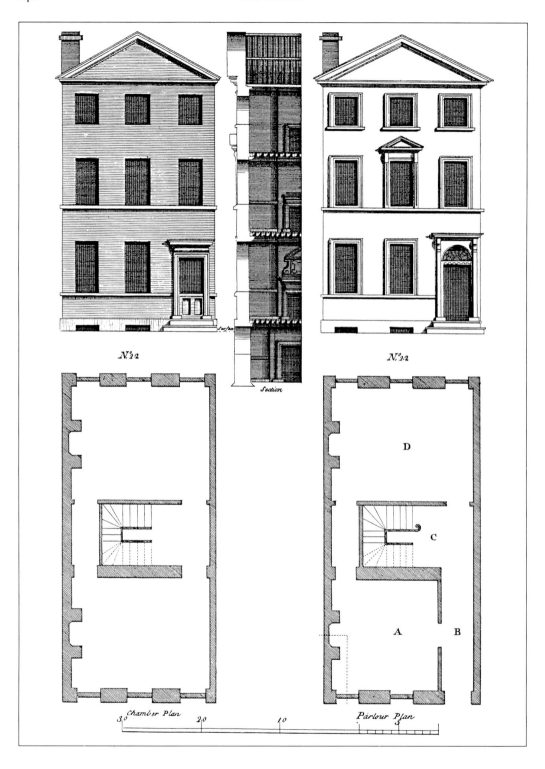

N.º 22

N.º 22

Section

D

C

A   B

Chamber Plan   20   10   Parlour Plan

30

ticularly Dutch, where window voids were wide to capture as much as light as possible. The early Palladians favoured the reverse ratio, with piers considerably wider than the openings; a literal adoption of Italian practice, where the exclusion of the sun and the creation of cool and shady interiors was the pressing concern. This piece of Palladian fancy was soon altered by practical considerations that produced the equal balance between window and pier width.

The horizontal dimensions between windows depended on the grandeur of the house. If the rooms were high, the distance between windowsill and arch soffit could be great – as much as a double square in height between first and second floors to match the double-square-high first-floor windows.

This composition of proportionately related window voids and wall areas could be organized within a larger-scale proportioning system. For example, the elevations of the uniform houses of Bedford Square (begun about 1776) appear to have been composed on the square and a half proportion, while the houses of similar date on the north side of Queen Anne's Gate seem to have elevations apparently organized on the root two proportion. But for most speculative housing built and designed by common builders it is probable that a simple rule-of-thumb proportional system was used.

Robert Morris spoke of analogy in building. He called it a secret of the Ancients 'which hath been preserved from the early days of time'.[4] What Morris meant by this was the proportional relationship of all parts of a building, which he achieved by breaking down his set of ideal proportions into commensurate ratios that could be applied as usefully to a door opening as to a whole elevation or plan.

The jobbing speculator or builder had a clear understanding of this concept but reduced it to its simplest form: the module. Thus a typical late-eighteenth-century façade can by analysed by the application of the module of a 3 ft 5 ins or 3 ft 6 ins square: the basement windows are one module in size; the distance between the arch soffit of the basement window and the sill of the ground-floor windows is one module; the ground-floor windows are a module and a half in area; the first-floor windows are two modules; the second floor a module and a half; the third floor a single module; the distance between windows a module; and so on.

In brick-built cities such as London, another module had to be considered. The geometry that determined the proportions of, and relationship between, the voids and solids of the elevation had to be compatible with the geometry of the individual brick. If this were not achieved, the builder could get into terrible difficulties reconciling the demands of construction (Flemish bond) and the conventions of detailing (window jamb with header and closer over a stretcher) with the proportions of the elevation. Bricks were, in the relationship of their width to their length, of a 1:2 proportion. This was imposed by a statute of 1729 (see p. 238), which required that the stretcher face of a brick measure $8\frac{3}{4}$ ins, while its depth was $4\frac{1}{8}$ ins. This, when two headers were placed over a stretcher, left $\frac{1}{4}$ in for a centre joint with $\frac{1}{8}$ in on each side for joints with adjoining bricks. So a brick, plus its $\frac{1}{4}$ in joints, formed a module 9 ins long and $2\frac{3}{4}$ ins high (bricks were by the same 1729 statute to be $2\frac{1}{2}$ ins high). On this principle four bricks should rise 11 ins if neatly laid, although for common work it was accepted that four bricks would rise one foot (see p. 105).

Opposite: *Elevation, plan and section of a house designed by Robert Morris and published in William and John Halfpenny's* Modern Builder's Assistant *of 1747. In its proportions the plan conforms to Palladian principles. The plot of the house is a double square (20 ft wide and 40 ft deep) with, for example, the ground-floor rear room conforming to Morris's ideal 4:3:2 proportion. In early-eighteenth-century manner, the first floor is slightly lower than the ground floor, which, to judge by the enriched fire surround, is the main floor. In its form the plan is a familiar alternative to the common type in which a dog-leg stair nestles in one of the rear corners. In the plan shown here the central stair would, according to the descriptive text, be lit by a skylight. This arrangement makes it possible for both back and front rooms to run the full width of the house. A central stair also allows for the creation of a regular back elevation – shown here finished with plain windows and a half-glazed door. The parlour and chamber storey of this house (the ground and first floors) are shown, records the text, 'wainscotted chair high for hangings, with plaster cornices enriched'. The cost of this building would, wrote Morris, amount to £480.*

No. 6 Church Row, Wandsworth, 1723. Here the ground- and first-floor windows are of identical size, with the second floor – placed above a string-course/cornice and square in form – treated as an attic. The elevation is divided into a square (measuring from corner to party wall and from ground to string-course) containing the ground and first floors, with the second-floor attic being roughly a quarter the depth of the square. This is clearly a fairly crude piece of artisan proportioning, although the designer clearly had some knowledge of fashionable Palladian principles. The wooden eaves cornice is of the type banned in 1707.

The façade of No. 5 Great James Street, Bloomsbury, built c. 1722, displays a sophisticated proportioning system for its date. Piers and windows are the same width, and window heights are different for each storey (the first floor is a Palladian double square).

No. 3 Henrietta Street, Dublin, built c. 1725, possesses a most austere, though exquisitely proportioned, façade. Ground- and first-floor windows are both double square in size, with their heights matched by the vertical distances between ground-, first- and second-floor windows. The second-floor windows have the 2:3 proportion; the attic windows are square. The distance between second-floor and third-floor attic is the same as the height of the attic window. The broad area of wall between windows reflects the early-eighteenth-century Palladian preference for the Italian practice of small windows and generous piers. Useful for creating shady interiors, it was not entirely suitable for Ireland.

No. 3 Chesterfield Street, Mayfair, built c. 1755. The ground-floor windows are, unusually for this mid-eighteenth-century date, taller than those on the first floor. The division of the tall façade into classically proportioned elements is achieved by the fragments of temple front that are embedded in the façade. The lower, broader string-course marks the bottom of the pedestal on which the proportioning 'column' sits. The sill-course marks the column base, while the block cornice marks the top of the entablature.

Nos. 18–20 Queen Anne's Gate, Westminster, built 1774, possibly to designs supplied by Samuel Wyatt. Here the module system can be seen at work. The windows are 3 ft 6 ins wide, with a square of this size used to determine the elements of the façade and relate all the elements to each other. For example, the first-floor windows on No. 20 (left) are two modules high; the second floor one and a half modules; the third floor a single module. The vertical distance between windows is 3 ft 6 ins, with horizontal distances graded, like the window depth, to reflect hierarchy and interior ceiling heights. The first-floor windows of No. 18 were lowered some time after 1774. Notice the different glazing-bar pattern to second-floor windows of similar sizes on Nos. 18 and 20.

A pair of houses of c. 1776 in Bedford Square, Bloomsbury. The proportions seem to be based on a more sophisticated system than the module. String-course to parapet and party wall to party wall describe one large square, with the ground floor two squares in area (i.e., the height from string-course to ground is half the width of the frontage). The large square comprising the first and second floors divides into six equal squares of 2:3 proportion.

GLAZING BARS

Intimately connected with the proportions of window voids was the proportioning of sash panes. The ideal was that each pane should be the same size and proportion no matter what the size of the window opening – an arrangement that was possible if the windows ranged from square to double square in size, and if it was accepted that windows of different sizes should have a different number of panes. For example, if the double square first-floor window contained twelve panes arranged in two sashes of the same size, the second-floor window a square and a half high could contain only nine panes of the same size and proportion as those in the first-floor window. These would have to be arranged in two sashes of different sizes: a six-pane sash under a three-pane sash.

However, this ideal seems to have been abandoned regularly by designers who felt it preferable to match the number of panes per window rather than to match the size and proportion of panes. Consequently it is fairly common to see square and

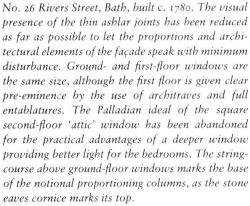

No. 26 Rivers Street, Bath, built c. 1780. The visual presence of the thin ashlar joints has been reduced as far as possible to let the proportions and architectural elements of the façade speak with minimum disturbance. Ground- and first-floor windows are the same size, although the first floor is given clear pre-eminence by the use of architraves and full entablatures. The Palladian ideal of the square second-floor 'attic' window has been abandoned for the practical advantages of a deeper window providing better light for the bedrooms. The string-course above ground-floor windows marks the base of the notional proportioning columns, as the stone eaves cornice marks its top.

No. 46 Fitzroy Street, Fitzrovia, built c. 1792, displays the extreme in first-floor emphasis: the windows are of 1:3 proportion and contain eighteen panes. The second floor is of 2:3 proportion, with the designer opting for a sash with twelve squarish panes rather than a sash with nine panes elongated to match those in the first-floor windows.

Guilford Street, Bloomsbury, built in c. *1800 to the designs of James Burton. The centre houses of the composition are embellished with a correctly proportioned Tuscan colonnade. It is obvious how the vertical window spacing of the Georgian terrace corresponds to the intercolumniation of the temple front.*

a half second-floor windows containing twelve panes of squatter proportion than the twelve panes of the taller windows below. Sash pane proportions could also be distorted by the late-eighteenth-century fashion for first-floor windows elongated beyond the double square proportion. This type of window could be glazed by merely adding another row of panes – of similar proportions to those in a double square window – so as to create a fifteen-pane window. Alternatively, some designers preferred to adhere to the twelve-pane tradition for first-floor windows, so the panes would be of an elongated shape to echo the proportion of the deep window openings but would be very different in

shape to the panes in the 2:3 proportioned second-floor windows above.

INTERIOR PROPORTIONS

The proportions of rooms were subject to the same theories that governed the design of façades – indeed, it was axiomatic to theoreticians such as Morris that insides and outsides should be related through the application of the same system. But, given the nature of the speculative system, which maximized use of land for minimum construction costs, academically correct room proportions were amongst the first aesthetic casualties in the modest town house. However, it is worth recording some of the ideals to which speculative builders could aspire.

Morris observed in his *Lectures* that 'the nearer a room ... is to a square, the more uniform and commodious [it] will be'. It is revealing that nearly a hundred years later Nicholson, in his *New and Improved Practical Builder*, confirmed that little had changed: 'In small houses, the dining- and drawing-rooms may be square, but in larger edifices they may extend even to be a double square' and 'with regard to height, three quarters of the breadth are esteemed good proportions to the other dimensions'.[5]

The proportioning of the parts of the room was, like the proportioning of the room to the rest of the house, to be in harmony. William Pain, in his *Carpenter's and Joiner's Repository*, gave a useful formula for determining the window area that a room of given size should have: 'Let the dimension of the Room be given, viz., the Length, Breadth and Height. Multiply the Length and Breadth of the Room together, and that Product by the Height; the Square root of which is the Quantity of light required.' To illustrate this formula, Pain gives a worked example:

Suppose a Room be 24 ft long, 16 ft broad and 14 ft high [interestingly, a square and a half in plan], how much light will be proper? The Length and Breadth multiplied together is 384 [sq] ft, and the sum multiplied by the Height [14 ft], is 5,376 [square] feet. Whose square root is 73 ft 3 ins [sic], which is the light required; so if you divide the square root 73 ft by three the Quotient will be 24 ft 5 ins; therefore the room will have three windows, each window containing 24 ft 5 ins, each of which will be 7 ft high and 3 ft 6 ins wide.[6]

Pain claimed that 'this rule is universal for all Rooms whatever' and certainly the relationship between window area and room volume that this formula produces is very close to that actually found in even modest town houses.

The size of fireplace openings can also be indicated by another formula – this time drawn up by John Crunden and Thomas Milton and published in *The Chimney Piece Maker's Daily Assistant* of 1766. In a table entitled 'True Size that Chimney Pieces Ought to be, to Rooms from Nine Foot Square, to Thirty Feet Square', the reader is told that, for example, a room 10 ft square should have a fireplace with an opening 2 ft 5 ins wide and 2 ft $11\frac{1}{2}$ ins high and that the chimney-piece should have a cornice 4 ins high. In a room 20 ft square these dimensions are 3 ft $9\frac{1}{2}$ ins, 3 ft $6\frac{1}{2}$ ins and $4\frac{7}{8}$ ins, and in a room 25 ft square these dimensions are 4 ft 5 ins, 3 ft 9 ins and $5\frac{1}{2}$ ins. For rooms that were inconveniently not square in plan, the authors advised 'add one long side and one short side together [and] take that product for the square room'. Getting down to detail, the authors noted that 'architraves to chimney-pieces should be about one sixth or one seventh of the width of the opening. The height of Friezes are various, according to the several ornaments with which they are to be decorated [though] flat friezes should not be less than four fifths of the width of the architrave.' Pain also tabulated the correct chimney sizes for rooms of differing floor areas. His conclusions in *The Carpenter's and Joiner's Repository* are marginally different from those of Crunden and Milton and explained thus: 'For every 6 ins in the Bigness of the Room [add] 1 in to the width of the chimney and $\frac{1}{4}$ in to the Height'. To apply the table to rooms that were not square, Pain instructed: 'add the length and breadth together, and take half that sum for the square of the Room'.

Abraham Swan, in his mid-eighteenth-century publications, revealed how other architectural elements in a room should be related to one another and to the size of the room. He was especially conscious of the ridiculous result that could follow making cornices too large (the room would look low) or the dado rail too high (the room would look small). He advised that if a room were 10 ft high, the dado rail should be 2 ft 5 ins high, and for every foot increase in the height of the room the dado should be raised by $\frac{3}{4}$ in.[7] There was, presumably, a limit to the height that Swan would have a dado rail but he failed to record it. Sebastiano Serlio, in his *Five Books of Architecture*, made it clear that the height of a dado panel (between top of skirting and soffit of dado rail) should be that of a square extended by its diagonal, i.e., root two.[8]

Swan's designs for rooms reveal that for cornice size he followed the rule that a cornice should be one eighteenth the height of the room. William Pain offered another rule-of-thumb method for relating cornice to room size:

give as many half inches to the Height of the cornice as feet in the whole Height ... The Frieze may be of equal Height to the cornice, except required for any particular ornament, then it may be one fourth part more than the cornice ... The Necking mould under the Frieze, may be one fourth part of the Frieze. The Dentil in Front is two thirds of the Height, and the Interval is one Half of the width always.[9]

Nicholson gave the Regency view of the treatment of these elements and, as would be expected, revealed a taste for smaller-scale detailing: 'If a cornice ... is executed, its height may be about one twentieth or one thirtieth part of the height of the room'.[10]

Chapter Three

ELEMENTS OF THE HOUSE

WALL TREATMENT

Ware, in his *Complete Body of Architecture*, identi-fied three types of wall treatment:

first those in which the wall itself is properly finished for elegance [that is to say, moulded plaster walling]; secondly, where the walls are covered with wain-scot; and thirdly where they are hung; this last article comprehending paper, silk, tapestry and every other decoration of this sort.

These treatments, as Ware made clear, existed in parallel, and though their popularity was largely a matter of fashion, each type of wall covering was perceived to possess intrinsic qualities that made it suitable for particular room uses or conditions. So in 1727 Saussure could write that 'hangings are little used in London houses on account of the coal smoke, which would ruin them [while] woodwork is considered to be cleaner and prevents damp on the walls'.[1] Thirty years later Ware wrote: 'a wainscot room, painted the usual way, is the lightest of all . . . a room of the same dimensions, which if wainscoted, will take six candles to light it, will in stucco require eight, and if hung, ten'. This was the case, he argued, because the 'most even surface will reflect most light', but, clearly, this conclusion also suggests that, in the mid-eighteenth century at least, the 'usual' colour for wainscot was white or a very light stone colour (see p. 189). As well as being the lightest-coloured room treatment, wainscot was also, according to Ware, the 'neatest' treatment and the most suitable for parlours (see p. 181); stucco was the 'grandest' and recommended for 'noble halls';

and hangings were the 'most gaudy' and good for 'lady's apartments'.

Stone was very occasionally used as a wall cover-ing, although this practice was confined to areas with a ready supply of good, workable stone. Stone-panelled walls seem to have enjoyed a vogue in Bath in the second decade of the eighteenth century, with the best surviving example being No. 5 Trim Street of about 1720, where the entrance hall is fitted out with stone walls cut and carved to look like con-ventional fielded panelling. The only unusual detail is the dado rail, which takes the form of a bold torus set into, and flush with, the frame of the panelling.

Wainscot

The covering of walls – whether the construction was of stone, brick or timber frame – with wood panelling was an ancient practice inherited by the eighteenth-century builder. It is also worth pointing out that although Richard Neve in 1703 described wainscot as 'The Pannel'd work round [against the walls of] a Room',[2] the word was also occasionally used to mean oak. All the following references to wainscot refer to the process of wood panelling, not to the type of wood.

The particular form taken by eighteenth-century panelling seems to have been established in England very early in the seventeenth century as part of the first Neo-Palladian movement pioneered by Inigo Jones. Characteristically, this panelling was com-posed of a squat panel topped by a tall panel that was divided horizontally by a rail. The squat lower panel was called the dado. The panels were divided vertically by stiles and muntins. They were topped

Ground-floor front room of No. 7 Elder Street, Spitalfields, built 1725. This room, of irregular shape, is lined with simple, square panelling topped by a Doric profile box cornice. The eared ovolo fire surround is partly original, and typical of the date.

by a cornice of more or less elaboration, embellished on the rail dividing the tall and squat panel by a surbase or dado rail, and finished at ground level with a skirting board or base.

As early as 1677 Joseph Moxon, in his *Mechanick Exercises*,[3] described the elevation of a panelled wall: 'For wainscoting rooms there is for the most part but two heights of panels used; unless the Room to be wainscoted be above 10 ft high.' In this case a third, thin horizontal panel, called a 'Friese pannel', was to be introduced immediately below the upper rail supporting the cornice.

Sometimes there is no base or sur-base used, and then the middle and lower rail need not be so broad, for the middle rail need not be above a third part more than the Margent of the rails ... which are commonly about $3\frac{1}{2}$ ins or 4 ins broad ... You may if you wish adorn the outer edges of the Stiles and Rails with a small moulding. And you may .. Bevil away the outer edges of the Pannels and leave a

Table in the middle of the Pannel.

Moxon did not mention the muntin, the non-structural stile that, instead of reaching from floor to ceiling, ran merely from the soffit of the cornice rail to the top of the middle rail and from the soffit of this rail to the top of the base rail. It was used solely for framing the panels that flanked it. In a run of flat panelling two in three vertical members were usually muntins. 'Margent' was the 'flat breadth of the stiles besides mouldings' and 'sur-base' was the usual seventeenth-, eighteenth- and early-nineteenth century term for what is now commonly called the dado or chair rail. Peter Nicholson, in his *New and Improved Practical Builder*, called it 'the cornice of the pedestal of the room, which serves to finish the dado, and secure the plaster against accidents from the backs of chairs and other furniture in the same level'. By 'dado', Nicholson meant the area of squat lower panelling or flush boarding below the surbase.

The composition described by Moxon was

Second-floor front room at No. 14 Fournier Street, Spitalfields, built 1726. The panelling is set in a frame embellished with ovolo moulding and represents the intermediate quality of wall panelling. The marble fire surround is original.

derived from Renaissance observations and interpretations of surviving Roman interiors, where the walls were organized as if to receive, or reflect, an order of columns standing on a continuous pedestal and supporting an entablature. This was understood by Ware, who explained that 'Greece introduced the use of the pedestal and cornice for inside finishing' and first devised the idea of filling the plain areas between cornice and pedestal with 'components correspondent to the ornament of the enriched pedestal'. Thus in eighteenth-century panelling the area from skirting to surbase corresponded to the pedestal; the surbase itself represented the cornice of the 'enriched pedestal'; the area of the tall panels corresponded to the column shaft; and the cornice marked the location of the entablature. In Rome and Renaissance Italy this wall composition was achieved with marble, stone, stucco and paint in either three dimensions or *trompe-l'œil*.

In seventeenth- and eighteenth-century northern Europe it was combined with the traditions for wooden wall panelling; shades of Pompeii and Herculaneum were produced in timber in tens of thousands of modest English homes.

The types of materials used held significance for Ware, who maintained that the system was devised originally by sculptors who 'threw in ornament in the richer apartments [of the house] within the circumference of the pannel'. 'Where less elegance was required,' he wrote, 'the pannels themselves were judged sufficient' and these were 'struck out' by the painter in his 'three colours'. The three colours refer to seventeenth- and eighteenth-century *trompe-l'œil* practice in which the chosen colour is used in conjunction with a lighter and darker shade to produce shadows and highlights (see p. 165). Ware observed that 'all this our people copy without knowing where or why', but, happily, a balance was achieved

Ground-floor rear room at Nos. 4/6 Fournier Street, Spitalfields, built 1726. The panelling is raised and fielded. The fire surround is new although of correct design for the date.

not unlike the ancient prototype, for while 'we decorate the richest apartments with sculpture, we follow the practice [of the Ancients] with panelling'.

The way in which this basic form of timber panelling was embellished changed during the late-seventeenth and eighteenth centuries, as did the timber in which the panelling was wrought. The different ways of embellishing panelling did, to a degree, enjoy vogues, but, like most eighteenth-century fashions in interior decoration (see p. 225), were practised concurrently.

The choice of wood was very limited. Oak had been used for grand interiors in the late-seventeenth century, when it was left unpainted (though often coloured by staining and varnish). But oak was expensive, and very early in the eighteenth century soft wood – pine and fir, referred to as deal – was used almost exclusively and always painted, be it with a plain coat of oil paint or grained (see p. 180).

The different types of decoration for panels, stiles and rails were organized as a firm hierarchy, with certain types of treatment chosen to reflect the expense of construction, the grandness of the house or the importance of the individual room. The grandest treatment was to frame the panels with a bolection mould – that is, a compound, serpentine moulding incorporating concave and convex forms (see p. 172) that raised the panel beyond the plane of the frame. Bolection panelling fell from general use by about 1700. Examples of bolection panelling from the late-seventeenth and early-eighteenth centuries often have a cornice incorporating a large cove below the corona, instead of the ovolo and ogee that became almost standard with all types of panelling during the first half of the eighteenth century (see p. 169).

Raised and fielded panelling – used in all the major rooms of grand houses, in the grandest rooms of medium houses and occasionally for the over-

Detail of raised and fielded staircase panelling of c. 1730 at No. 7 Bachelor's Walk, Dublin. A typical Dublin detail of the 1720s and 1730s was to replace the dado rail with a third shallow panel. When ramped on a staircase, this type of panelling could produce a most curious result.

mantel panel in the main room of a humble house – is of the type described by Moxon in 1677: bevelled-away 'outer edges' and a raised 'table' in the centre of the panel (see p. 151). This bevelling of the edges was called 'fielding', and it is tempting to assume that this way of embellishing the panel was the stylized result of a practical technique. To prevent the glue joint between individual panels splitting as the broad panel dried out, it was essential to make sure that the panel was loose in the frame, so that shrinkage and movement would take place there. To ensure this, the edges of panels were feathered. On flat panels this was done by planing, often rather roughly, the rear face. On fielded panels this was achieved by the very act of embellishing the panel. The frame in which the panel was housed was also decorated – usually with an ovolo moulding though sometimes with an ogee. Further embellishment was added by carving the ovolo with such motifs as egg and tongue or by introducing a second, smaller moulding, usually an ogee, between the ovolo and the panel. In this case the ovolo itself would be furnished with a fillet (see p. 172).

The cornice, dado and skirting to fielded panelling were usually of the types that were standard for most panelling during the first thirty years of the eighteenth century. The cornice, almost invariably of timber and called a box cornice because it was constructed around the 'box' formed by the corona of the cornice, was of an unembellished Doric type. This cornice could, like the panelling, be upgraded by carving or by the addition of a dentil-course beneath the corona. The addition of a dentil-course was the usual way of enriching the cornice of the best room in even humble houses (see p. 219). The surbase was composed around a torus and, although the permutations of the detail of the type were numerous, a vertical section through a stair handrail was characteristic (see p. 170) – a hint that this type of surbase originated as an ornament to panelling accompanying a staircase. The skirting was usually topped with a bold ogee supporting a convex mould-ing but could be simplified to a bead on top of a plain board. Both surbase and skirting could be enriched with carving, but this was done only if the cornice were also carved and the panelling fielded and carved.

The next type of panelling was similar but with the raised and fielded panel replaced by a plain, flat panel framed by ovolo. In this type the mouldings were rarely carved until after about 1735 (this em-bellishment belonging primarily to the raised and fielded family of panelling).

The last type of formal panelling was known as 'square' panelling. Here the frame had no ovolo, being, as the name implies, simply square in section. The cornice was often reduced to merely the top member of the box cornice – a cyma recta supported by a smaller ogee moulding. However, a full box cornice was usual in the best room of a square-panelled house or, at least, over the overmantel of the best room. In these simple panelled rooms the skirting was usually deprived of its moulded top, while the surbase remained much the same as in the other types of panelled rooms.

There were many minor permutations in all these types of panelled rooms. The most common was that mentioned by Moxon, when the surbase was dispensed with and the middle rail narrowed. This pattern was followed for either very low spaces, such as a passage below a stair, or for rooms of excessive modesty where panelling might be used only to form a partition between room and staircase or passage, with the other walls panelled to dado level or merely skirted. Another permutation was the replacement of the surbase rail with a third, shallow horizontal panel. This detail was used with even the finest fielded panelling. It was especially found in Dublin in the 1720s.

Simplified square panelling was not the last word in economy. The panelling hierarchy descended to one type of panelling, really a pre-classical ver-nacular type, where broad, flat rails stretched from floor to ceiling and framed narrow planks of panel-ling. This post-and-panelling type was generally used in attic or garret bedrooms, although, in a well-fronted house of 1727, No. 17 Elder Street, it separated the ground-floor room from the staircase hall. Here a crude attempt was made to disguise the rude panelling by superimposing on its form the painted outline, in three colours, of conventional classical panelling.

These three types of formal panelling dominated the modest interiors of most English cities until the late 1730s. Then the fashion for stucco walls, painted or hung, with dado panelling only became gradually dominant. Panelling lingered on into the early 1760s but usually as a means of decorating one or two rooms – frequently the ground-floor dining-room or dining-parlour. Also the panelling of the

The entrance passage of No. 17 Elder Street, Spitalfields, built 1727. The partition between passage and front room is of the simplest post-and-panel construction. Here the pattern of conventional classical wall panelling has been painted in a crude three-colour trompe-l'œil *manner over the rustic partition. This scheme was discovered during repairs in 1980 and appears to be original. The staircase, with stout balusters, rises on a simple closed string.*

Wall panelling and door at No. 76 Brook Street, Mayfair. Designed in 1726 by Colen Campbell for his own occupation, this house has a fine though modest Palladian façade and advanced internal detailing. Wall panels are of different widths with ovolo mouldings embellished with carving, which was common in the 1740s. The dado rail and skirting are unusual for their date. The restricted site on which this grandeur is displayed is revealed by the cramped placing of the door.

mid-eighteenth century looked distinctly different and occupied a transitional place between the full-panelled room of the 1720s and the post-1760s stucco room with flush-panelled dado and bold, cornice-like surbase. This transitional panelled room was illustrated by Batty Langley in his *Builder's Jewel* of 1741[4] and described very well by Ware:

Best ... practice in the most elegant buildings [is to] Wainscot ... with ovolo and plain pannel with broad margins viz. an ovolo stuck on the framing ... in this sort of work the rails and stiles should be 6 or 7 ins wide ... which are called broad margins.

In this kind of finishing, a regular pedestal of some one of the orders of architecture should go around the room.

Thus the stiles are broad – 6 or 7 ins instead of Moxon's $3\frac{1}{2}$–4 ins – and the panels in their turn were also much broader. The rails and stiles were also thicker, which allowed for the invariable post-1735 practice of adding a fillet to the ovolo that framed the panel.

The composition of this panelling also differed from early-eighteenth-century examples in that it was typical for the broad panels to alternate with

Above: *A fabric-hung interior of the 1760s: Fairfax House, Castlegate, York, restored c. 1986. In this first-floor drawing-room the walls are hung with crimson damask, with the joinery and plaster painted a flatted white. The furniture arrangement is more nineteenth than eighteenth century: the sofa would have stood against the wall.*

Opposite: *The staircase compartment in No. 20 Lower Dominick Street, Dublin, c. 1758: Rococo wall embellishment at its most fanciful. The designer was Robert West. The staircase, with its bulbous column shafts and miniature urns sitting directly on the treads, is typical of Dublin.*

Detail of the first-floor front room at No. 15 Wilkes Street, Spitalfields. This early-nineteenth-century decorative scheme, in which the upper wall areas are framed by painted panels with bold floral corners, was discovered during recent repairs.

This view of the north side of the Strand, drawn by George Scharf in 1824, evokes the bustle and architectural variety of a late-Georgian commercial thoroughfare. A fire is in progress, and an appliance from the Sun fire office is in attendance. The houses are mostly late-seventeenth-century, but the rich variety of shop fronts is Georgian. The road is cobbled, and the substantial and continuous kerb has removed the need for posts, although the new gas lamps, with their solid bases, double as bollards.

A London coffee-house. The drawing is, rather mysteriously, dated 1668, but all the details suggest a time between 1700 and 1710. The arrangement seems to be that coffee-pots are handed out from the fireplace, drinks from the booth and pipes by servants who take them from a chest.

Four gentlemen drinking and smoking in 1723. Judging by the sky, this seems an evening event: could they have retired to this closet after dinner, leaving the ladies to their own devices? The leafy vista suggests a rural setting, but the house could have been on the edge of London – Bloomsbury or Mayfair. The artist was Benjamin Ferrers; the subjects include Sir Thomas Sebright and Sir John Bland.

Taking tea c. 1740. Every detail in this picture rewards study. The mirror with its pair of sconces is a usual arrangement. The strong green is probably an olive green formed with Prussian blue and a little ochre. The door and skirting are painted in imitation of light mahogany. The tea ritual is beautifully recorded: the ladies drink from Chinese teacups; the mistress of the house has her tea caddy at her feet; a servant brings in more hot water. The artist of this painting is unknown.

A fashionable London drawing-room of the 1760s: Sir Lawrence Dundas painted in his Arlington Street house in 1769 by Johann Zoffany. Note the early use of bell pulls each side of the stone fire surround, plain green-blue wallpaper edged with brass fillets, reefed curtain colour matched to the wall, the fitted carpet, the flatted white dado rail and panelling, and chocolate- or mahogany-coloured skirting board.

A London drawing-room of the 1780s. Mrs Congreve and her daughters by Philip Reinagle, c. 1780. The furniture is still formally arranged, with chairs and sofa set back against the dado and off the carpet. The elbow chair has been casually brought forward to the fire. Lighting was by wall sconces, curtains are festooned and skirting boards mahoganized. The walls, cornice and ceiling, painted a uniform drab or stone colour, create a highly restrained background for the family portraits and fine furnishings.

Basement kitchen at No. 14 Francis Street, on the Bedford Estate, Bloomsbury, drawn in 1846 by George Scharf, who depicted the room as it had been in the 1830s. The house had been built in 1772 and seems to have changed little between then and the 1830s. The centre of the carpet, or perhaps the painted canvas floor cloth, appears to be protected by a crumb cloth.

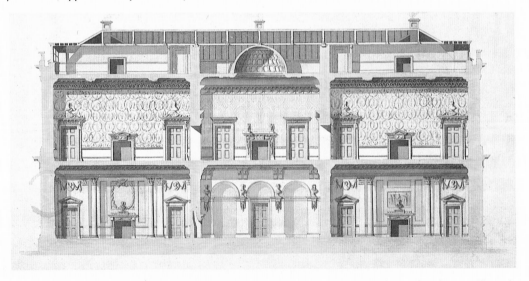

Section through a house, drawn c. 1760–65 by Edward Stevens when in Sir William Chambers's office. The decorative scheme is somewhat typical of its date: first-floor walls are generally hung with fabric or paper, while dados are flatted white and doors are mahogany or mahoganized soft wood. On the ground floor the more robust rooms, such as the hall, are painted stone colour.

The Breakfast Room at Pitshanger Manor, Ealing, designed by Sir John Soane in 1802 and re-created in 1986, contains a rich mix of idiosyncratic Neo-classical motifs and exotic paint finishes. These include pendentive ceiling, abstracted Classical decorative details, painted marble and porphyry, and bronzed caryatids.

Left: Woburn Place – the northern extension of Southampton Row between Russell and Tavistock squares. This group of houses (now demolished) was built in c. 1800 to the design of James Burton and drawn in c. 1815 by a pupil of Sir John Soane for use in Soane's Royal Academy lectures. The paint colours are typical of the early-nineteenth century: green (perhaps bronzed) front doors, dark glazing bars (apparently black) and a stuccoed ground floor painted a very pale grey stone colour to contrast with the pale yellow of the brick walling above.

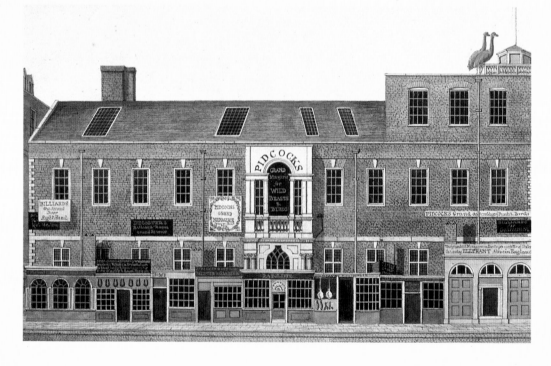

A back garden in Upper Street, Islington.

Opposite: *Exeter Change, Strand, was built in 1676 to house diverse small shops. In 1773 Pidcocks Menagerie moved in. This view is of c. 1810. Note that white was still popular for windows (sash as well as mullioned and transomed windows), and that green and blue appear to be the favourite colours for shop fronts and doors. The brown areas are, presumably, wood graining.*

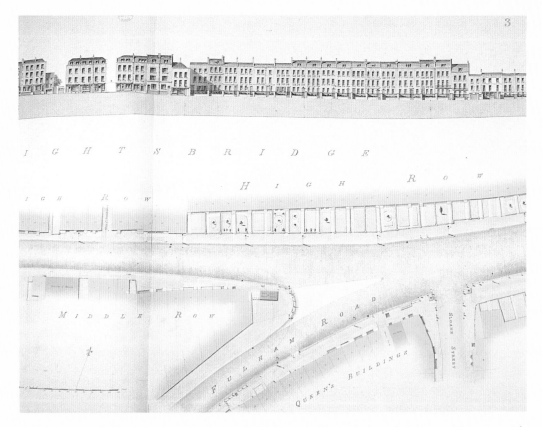

A detail of Joseph Salway's 1811 survey of the Turnpike Road from Hyde Park Corner to Hammersmith. This junction – of Knightsbridge and the Brompton Road – reveals the manner of laying out front gardens, location and regularity of street lighting, and suggests the paint colours used on modest domestic elevations.

Fire surround of 1726 in second-floor front room of No. 14 Fournier Street, Spitalfields. This is a common early-eighteenth-century type. In plainer versions the imposts were occasionally omitted. The hob grate, with its stone cheeks and iron bars, certainly dates from the first half of the eighteenth century and could even be of 1726.

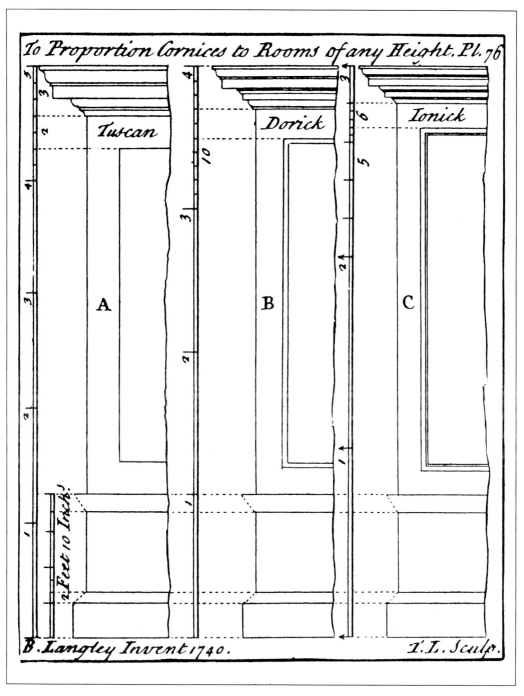

To Proportion Cornices to Rooms of any Height. Pl. 76

Tuscan

Dorick

Ionick

A

B

C

B. Langley Invent 1740.

I. L. Sculp.

Plate from Batty Langley's Builder's Jewel of 1741. This shows the design and proportions of wall panelling that became common after c. 1735. The dado is flush panelled and, with cornice-like dado rail and bold skirting, is envisaged as a classically correct pedestal.

A pedestal as illustrated by William Pain in his Practical House Carpenter *of 1789. Permutations of this type of flat-topped pedestal cornice and of the boldly projecting ogee base became usual for dado rails and skirting from c. 1735 to c. 1770.*

the narrow ones. But perhaps the most striking change was the transformation of the panelling below the surbase into an independent element. It no longer followed the panelling pattern of the wall above but was formed of boards set flush and treated as a classically correct pedestal. In keeping with this new status, the dado had a large, well-moulded skirting and a large, flat-topped cornice-like surbase corresponding exactly with 'one of the orders of architecture'. The cornice was also more than likely

to be dentilled and of plaster. It was but a small change to omit the upper panelling altogether and arrive at the post-1760s room that was characterized by hangings between painted dado and plaster cornice. And it was this basic architectural structure – skirting, dado panelling (or only surbase) and cornice – that was to survive into the post-Georgian period, even though the details of its decoration and the manner of treating the wall area were to be changed by revolutions in late-eighteenth-century architectural taste.

Paper and Hangings

'Paper has, in a great measure, taken the place of sculpture,' wrote Ware in 1756 when discussing the 'decoration of the sides of rooms'. By sculpture he meant the stucco decorations – moulded frame, cartouches, busts – that were favoured by the early Palladians for decorating the walls of really grand rooms, such as those in country house halls and saloons.

The relationships between different types of hangings – paper, silk, damask – and between hangings generally and painted, frescoed or stencilled plaster walls are highly complex. Each enjoyed a vogue, fell from fashion but not completely from use, and then enjoyed a revival. Fabric wall hangings, including tapestry and leather, were popular in the late-seventeenth century[5] and were coming back into fashion in the mid-eighteenth century. Frescoed and stencilled walls, generally regarded as a pre-eighteenth-century fashion, enjoyed a vogue very late in the eighteenth century (see p. 185) and became entwined with the fashion of about 1810–20 for hand-painted wallpaper (often of French manufacture) that showed the sort of architectural, landscape or history scenes that were also being produced in frescos on plaster.

One of the threads that links up this kaleidoscope of revival, survival and reinterpretation is taxation: as in many other spheres of eighteenth-century building activity, it exerted a powerful influence on practice. In 1712 an Act was passed that raised a duty of 1*d.*, and later of 1½*d.*, on every sq. yd of paper 'printed, painted or stained'[6] (paper itself had been taxed since 1694). Thus wallpaper was expensive and presented no significant challenge to the fashion for wood panelling or hangings, although

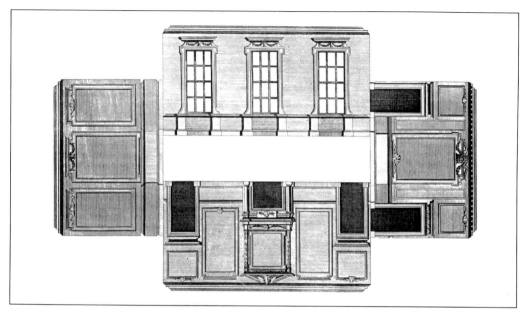

Massively detailed room of modest size from Isaac Ware's A Complete Body of Architecture *of 1756. The panelling could have been executed in plaster, but most likely at this date is a combination of timber and plaster. The bold window architraves, sitting on bases that break forward from the dado panelling, are a detail much favoured in Dublin.*

in about 1690 an Edward Batling (at the sign of the Knave of Clubs, Southwark) advertised paper in imitation of Irish Stitch, flock-work, wainscot, marble, damask and turkey-work.[7] Effectively, Batling was offering paper imitations of fabric hangings for non-panelled rooms or – though there is no evidence surviving to support this – paper that could be pasted on the flat panels between stiles and rails.

If this were the case, then it would echo the way in which hangings were used with panelling. In 1732 Sarah, Duchess of Marlborough, wrote to her granddaughter, who was about to move into No. 51 Grosvenor Street, an early-eighteenth-century house and, no doubt, largely panelled: 'the white painting with so much red damask looks mighty handsome. All the hangings are up in the four rooms above the stairs except some pieces that are to be where the glass don't cover all the Wainscot.'[8] This suggests an arrangement of hangings over wainscot, placed above a white-painted dado and parted for door and window architraves, and by pier glasses. This interpretation is supported by an inventory of 1767 for No. 18 Grosvenor Square, a house of 1728, no

doubt also fully panelled but where panelling, on second-floor bedroom level at least, was covered with hangings. We read of the 'green silk damask bed chamber', the 'printed cotton bed chamber', the 'green harrateen bed chamber' and the 'blue mohair bed chamber'.[9] The description may refer just to matching window and bed curtains, but this seems unlikely.

The 1756 lease for a house in Northumberland Row, Tottenham,[10] suggests how hangings of different colours could be used not only to cover panelling but also to give rooms in a house a sort of colour-coded character. On the second floor were a pair of rooms and closet 'hung with about 25 yds of yellow stuff' and another room 'hung with about 25 yds of blue stuff'. In this room was a 'chimney-piece with Dutch tiles' – no doubt blue and white Delft tiles to match the blue hangings. On the first floor was a back room 'wainscoted yard high and red hangings 20 yds' and a front room 'hung with about 30 ft of green stuff and [another] back room hung with about 30 ft of red stuff'. Reflecting Ware's stricture (see p. 54), the 'Parlour floor' (that is,

Second-floor rear bow room at No. 3 Henrietta Street, Dublin, c. 1725. In typical Dublin manner the eared window architraves are supported on projecting dado panels. This is a very early example of the use of a curved bow.

the ground floor) appears to have been panelled; certainly no hangings were recorded, although one very interesting fitting is mentioned: a 'pair of folding glass sash doors between the rooms'. This reference is particularly intriguing, because 'glass' could mean mirror in eighteenth- century terminology.

Although the presence of full wall panelling does not seem to have greatly hindered the activities of the upholsterer, or upholder (as purveyors of hangings were called during the eighteenth century), it did naturally prevent the wallpaper man from realizing his full potential. But during the 1740s, as full wall panelling gradually fell from fashion, it seems that the wallpaper tax – not repealed until 1836 – was faced up to and wallpaper became a popular challenge to fabric hangings. Characteristically, wallpaper, like the damask hangings mentioned by the Duchess of Marlborough in 1732, would throughout the eighteenth century have occupied that part of the wall between the surbase rail and cornice, with the dado panelling being painted.

By 1770 wallpaper had supplanted fabric hangings in even the most fashionable homes. This is expressed in a letter of May 1770 from Sir William Chambers to his Edinburgh client Gilbert Meason about the decoration of a house in St Andrew's Square, Edinburgh (now No. 26), that Chambers had designed for him: 'I have made choice of some handsome patterns of flock paper ... they will be properest for your Drawing room, as I suppose you have no pictures, unless you chuse to have Indian paper.' The parlour, implied Chambers, may be papered but was best painted. He concluded that the 'common price of most sorts of flock wallpaper [was] 8d. per yard'.[11] E.A. Entwisle, in his *Book of Wallpaper*, recorded accounts of wallpaper costing 11d. per sq. yd in 1740 and 4s. per sq. yd in 1754, and flock wallpaper costing 6½d. per sq. yd in 1756. So even the cheapest of these papers was more expensive than the three coats of a common oil paint: Ware recorded 6d. a sq. yd in 1756 (see p. 181).

Stucco

In the eighteenth century the term 'stucco wall' could refer to a plastered and painted wall or a wall embellished with superimposed plaster decorations. The latter was rarely found in a terrace house below the status of mansion. Ware regretted the passing of 'sculpture' upon stucco walls: 'The hand of the art is banished from a part of the house in which it used to display itself very happily.'

This exaggerated respect for embellished stucco walls was not just due to the fact that they they demanded great skill to make well and were expensive; Ware also saw in them a direct link to the practices of antiquity. Describing the methods of the Greeks (see p. 152), he wrote: 'when they placed in the [wall] compartment pictures of great consequence, they decorated their edges with sculpture along the mouldings, and in the smaller they hung festoons of flowers'. Despite being well aware that this type of heavy wall decoration was falling rapidly into disuse, Ware still argued that if 'we follow the antique practice ... let us follow it strictly'. He then explained how this type of wall treatment permitted furniture to be arranged with dignity: 'Pictures and glasses, our fashionable furniture, may be disposed more happily in these compartments than any other way.'

Plaster walls merely painted seem to have been unusual in the main rooms of even the modest late-eighteenth-century houses, despite Chambers's advice of 1770 (see above). A schedule describing the interior of the newly built No. 11 Queen Anne's Gate in 1773[12] makes it clear that unpapered plaster walls were acceptable only in the entrance hall – where the wall is described as 'stuccoed' and where a robust exterior-like quality was thought desirable – and in the servants' bedrooms on the top floor. The rest of the house was papered (see p. 246).

If painted plastered walls were rare in the eighteenth-century town house interior, stencilled walls were even rarer. Stencilling was a technique of medieval origin – and a very effective and economic way of decorating a room – but it did not enjoy a revival until very late in the eighteenth century, when picturesque taste for the rustic welcomed the peasant-like quality of stencil decoration. If stencilling was used earlier in the eighteenth century, it must have been confined to cottages and humble bedrooms where – applied on paper – it was used as a cheap substitute for printed wallpaper. Significantly, when wallpaper tax was repealed in 1836, wallpaper 'descended the social scale' and stencilling became more exclusive. Wallpaper was then designed to look like stencilling.

Early-nineteenth-century painters' manuals

Pair of panelled rooms from Abraham Swan's A Collection of Designs in Architecture *of 1757. Both are good examples of the prevailing fashion: wide wall panels, with some narrow; flush pedestal-like dado panelling; bold cornice, skirting and cornice-like dado rail.*

included instructions for stencilling, thus confirming that this technique had come back into fashion as a means of embellishing painted walls. Nathaniel Whittock, in his *Decorative Painter's and Glazier's Guide* of 1827, confirmed the role that stencilling played in the early-nineteenth century. It was, he wrote, 'the cheapest and most expeditious method of decorating rooms'. Whittock also described the sort of effects aimed at by the early-nineteenth-century stenciller and explained how to achieve them:

The usual way of proceeding is to procure an elegant pattern, containing about four colours ... The stenciller must be careful to trace upon transparent paper ... all the outlines of the subject that is in middle tint; he will on another piece of tracing paper draw the outline of the first shade, and on a third the darkest shade; and on the fourth the strongest lights. When the tracing of the whole is made, they must be transferred to common thin pasteboard ... then cut with a penknife.

Of the designs produced, Whittock wrote, 'The rosette alone makes a neat ornament for a bedroom, if done in white, shaded with brown, on a pink, salmon, blue, or light green ground.' The work was always carried out 'with distemper colour' and varnished.

MOULDINGS

Mouldings, be they on panelling or stucco walls, on doors, dados or staircase tread ends, or on fire surrounds, can be placed in three distinct groups.

First, there are those mouldings – ornate, often of compound form – that are of the late-seventeenth-century Baroque period. These inventive, licentious mouldings do not figure greatly in the history of the modest Georgian town house interior. Then there are the more orthodox mouldings, derived from the Roman and Renaissance representations of the five orders of architecture. These were promoted initially by the Neo-Palladians after about 1715 and became the basic vocabulary of interior decoration until the early 1760s. After 1740, however, the preference for orthodox Palladian mouldings and details

was complemented by a vogue for more exotic forms – notably Chinese and Gothic. Last are those types of mouldings that appear after about 1760 and that reflect the Neo-classical revolution that overthrew the design dogmas of the previous fifty years. Mouldings of this period include not just the then recently discovered Roman and Greek motifs and variations on the standard Renaissance profiles but also Neo-Gothic (as opposed to the historically inaccurate Rococo Gothic of the 1740s) and other influences such as Hindu and Saracenic.

Mouldings can be most usefully described and explained by reference to their type, their location within the house and their uses (for dado rails, fire surrounds or on door architraves). This type of analysis can be pursued best by reference to illustrations of particular examples, but first there are some general points that need to be made about mouldings of all types and categories.

Although they can look very different and bafflingly complex, all moulded decorations are based upon two simple and complementary forms: the curved convex quadrant called the ovolo (also occasionally called the echinus) and the flat-faced right-angular fillet. The quadrant can also be concave (when it is called the cavetto); it may be of different sizes in the same composition; and its outline can be a perfect quarter of a circle or a quarter of a compact or irregular ellipse. An asymmetrical concave curve is obtained by placing two quadrants of different radii together (this is called a scotia). A serpentine curve is formed by setting a concave quadrant next to a convex one (cyma recta when the concave moulding is above the convex and cyma reversa when the reverse is the case. Both are occasionally called ogees, but generally the term 'ogee' refers to the cyma reversa – the usage followed in this book). A quadrant can be continued to form a semi-circular moulding (astragal if small, torus if large); it can be undercut with a quirk to increase the penetration of its curve and give more shadow, and loaded with more or less decoration. Indeed, the terms 'ovolo' and 'echinus' are derived from the decorations with which the quadrant moulding was traditionally embellished: 'ovolo' is from the Latin for 'egg' and 'echinus' means the shell of a chestnut.

The quadrant, in all its forms and combinations, gives character to the moulded composition, be it cornice, dado rail or skirting, but each curved

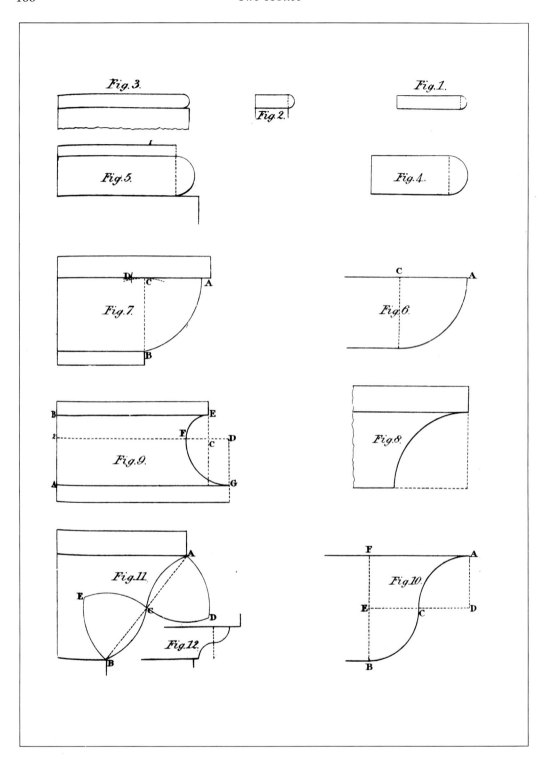

Opposite: The vocabulary of basic mouldings used during the Georgian period, from Peter Nicholson's Mechanical Exercises of 1812. Fig. 1 astragal; fig. 2 cocked bead (bead projected beyond surface to which it is attached); fig. 3 sunk bead; fig. 4 torus (same but greater magnitude than bead); fig. 5 in joinery the torus is always accompanied by a fillet; fig. 6 Roman ovolo or quarter round; fig. 7 geometry for constructing ovolo curve when projection and height are unequal; fig. 8 cavetto (concave quadrant of a circle); fig. 9 scotia (concave moulding formed by curves of two different centres); figs. 10 and 11 cyma recta; fig. 12 cyma reversa.

element is controlled, contained and made legible by punctuation. This punctuation is provided by the flat fillet. The fillet is smaller but proportionately related to the curved mouldings it accompanies. It can project beyond its curved neighbours or be set flush with them. In certain circumstances it can be quite large and the dominant element in the composition. For example, the central element of a cornice is a flat-fronted right-angular element called a 'corona'. Paired fillets, stepped in profile, are called an annulet.

All mouldings are derived from details that were designed initially for external use and that evolved as decorative expressions of the post-and-lintel timber construction of Greek temples. This is well illustrated by the cornice. It was developed to embellish the junction between the shallow pitched roof and the wall, with elements of the roof structure being expressed in its forms – for example, the corona evolved as a boxing out of the rafter ends that, in embellished cornices, are symbolized by square mutules or modillions set below the soffit of the corona. The cornice profile, as well as expressing the structure, is also highly functional in origin. It is designed to throw rain-water off the wall, the various fillets acting as drip moulds, with a large drip mould (in the form of a concave lip) on the outer corner of the corona.

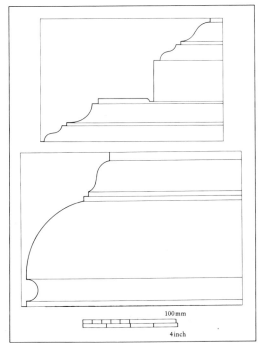

100mm

4 inch

Box cornice, first floor of No. 15 Elder Street, Spital-fields, 1727.

Coved cornice, second floor of Nos. 5–13 Queen Anne's Gate, London, 1770.

Above and overleaf: Collection of representative mouldings from modest town houses of different dates. All are drawn to the same scale.

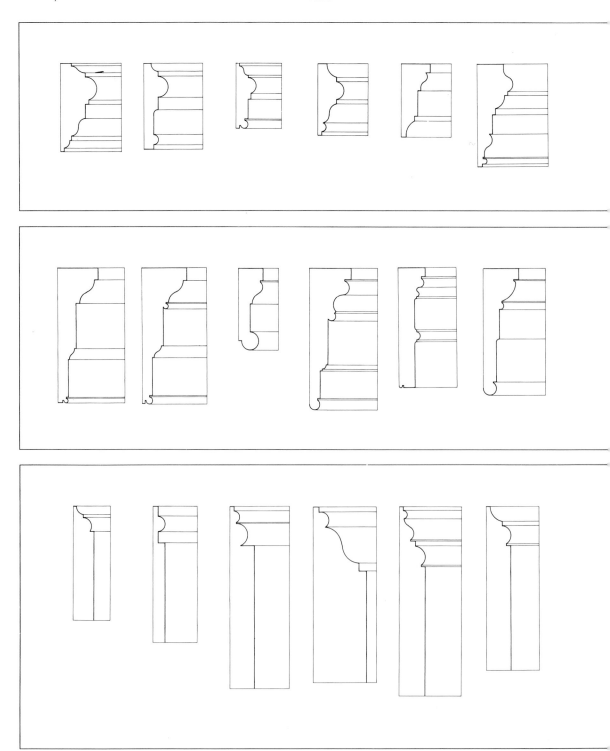

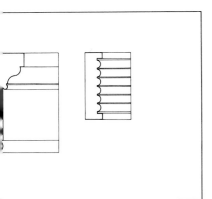

DADOS, left to right:

Dado rail, No. 19 Queen Anne's Gate, c. 1704.

Staircase dado, No. 15 Elder Street, 1727.

Second-floor dado, No. 15 Elder Street, 1727.

First-floor dado, the minister's house, Fournier Street, Spitalfields,
  c. 1726.

Ground-floor dado, Nos. 5–13 Queen Anne's Gate, c. 1770.

First-floor dado, Nos. 5–13 Queen Anne's Gate, c. 1770.

No. 14 Maple Street, Tottenham Court Road, c. 1777.

No. 7 Greenwell Street, Tottenham Court Road, c. 1815.

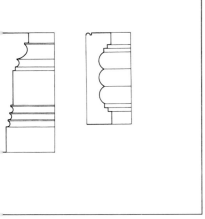

ARCHITRAVES, left to right:

First-floor door architrave, the minister's house, Fournier Street, c.
  1726. This profile, with its large and small ogees and bead mould,
  is typical of the date.

First-floor door architrave, Nos. 5–13 Queen Anne's Gate, 1770.
  The bead added to the ogee is typical of the date.

First-floor window architrave, Nos. 5–13 Queen Anne's Gate, 1770.

Door architrave, Portland Place (by James Adam), c. 1785. The
  undercut, or quirk, on the convex mould of the large ogee is
  typical of advanced work after c. 1770.

Door architrave from vault doors, Chiswell Street, City, perhaps by
  George Dance, c. 1785.

Door architrave from General Office, Cutler Street, City, c. 1795.

Door architrave from Summerhill, Avonmouth Road, Lyme Regis,
  c. 1810.

Door architrave, Whitechapel Road, London, c. 1815.

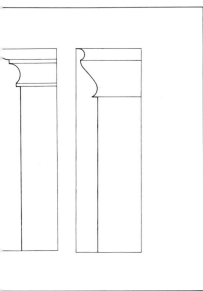

SKIRTINGS, left to right:

Entrance passage and staircase, No. 15 Elder Street, 1727.

Entrance hall, the minister's house, Fournier Street, c. 1727.

Wilson Street, Finsbury, c. 1740.

Stoke Park Mansion, Surrey, c. 1760.

First-floor front room, Nos. 5–13 Queen Anne's Gate, 1770.

Ground floor, Nos. 5–13 Queen Anne's Gate, 1770.

Chiswell Street, City, 1785, perhaps George Dance.

First floor, No. 1 St Chad's Street, King's Cross, 1827.

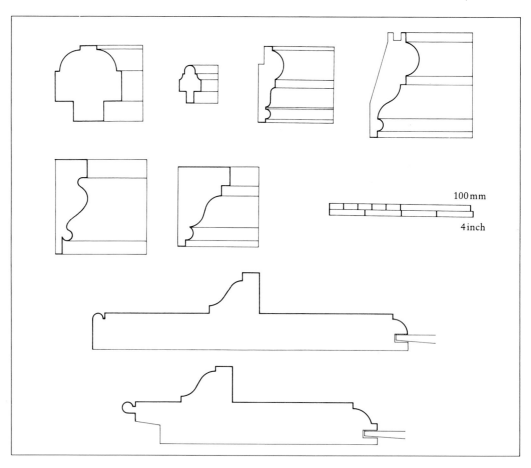

*Mouldings for different elements of the house com-
pared. From top, left to right:*

*Section through glazing bar c. 1726, at the minister's
house, Fournier Street, Spitalfields.*

*Section through glazing bars, c. 1770, at Nos. 5–13
Queen Anne's Gate, London.*

*Bolection moulding, used to connect wall panels to
frame, c. 1690, Dombey Street, Bloomsbury.*

*Bolection moulding, c. 1730, from the minister's
house, Fournier Street.*

Architrave, c. 1825, Canon Street Road, Stepney.

*Capping to half panelling, c. 1726, in the entrance
hall, the minister's house, Fournier Street.*

*Door architrave and portion of panelling frame and
panel, 1727, No. 15 Elder Street, Spitalfields.*

*Window architrave and portion of wall panelling
from No. 27 Fournier Street, 1726. The extra fillet
on the ovolo-moulded panelled frame is a typical
post-1735 detail.*

Opposite, top: *Two cornices illustrated by Batty
Langley in his* City and Country Builder's and Workman's Treasury of Designs *of 1745. The Doric (left)
provided the basic model for the box cornice favoured in the early-eighteenth century. The main
difference is that the scotia bed mould was, in the
box cornice, replaced by a cyma reversa moulding.*

Opposite, bottom: *Four cornices from Abraham
Swan's* A Collection of Designs in Architecture *of
1757. Right: Doric and Tuscan permutations –
typical of their period, they incorporate bead mouldings. Left: An enriched Corinthian cornice with
modillions set below the corona and dentil-moulded
bed course.*

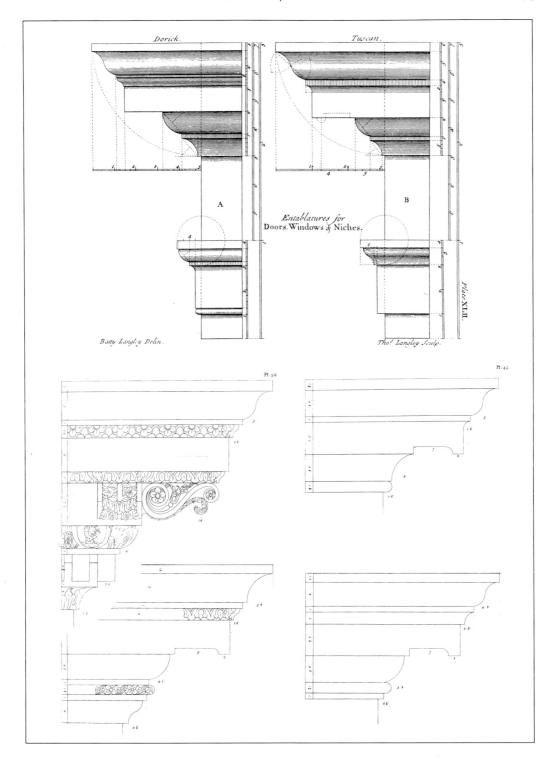

Dorick. Tuscan.

A B

Entablatures for
Doors, Windows & Niches.

Batty Langley Delin. Thos. Langley Sculp.

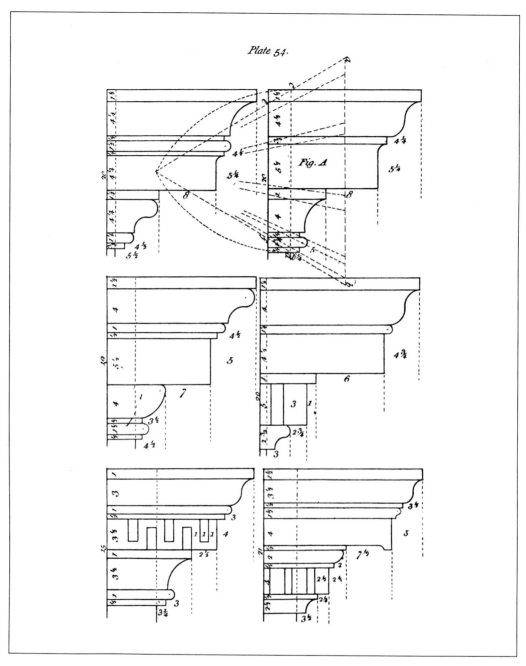

Six cornices from William Pain's Practical House Carpenter *of 1789. The cornice top left is furnished with modest bead moulds and a cyma reversa mould whose top convex curve is cut back. This undercutting, called a quirk, became common after c. 1770 and was one of the innovations introduced by the Greek revival architects of the 1760s. Also particularly Greek is the compressed and quirked ovolo forming the bed mould on the cornice shown centre left.*

Dado rails and matching skirting mouldings from Abraham Swan's A Collection of Designs in Architecture *of 1757. The fret-embellished dados shown were particularly popular in the 1750s and 1760s.*

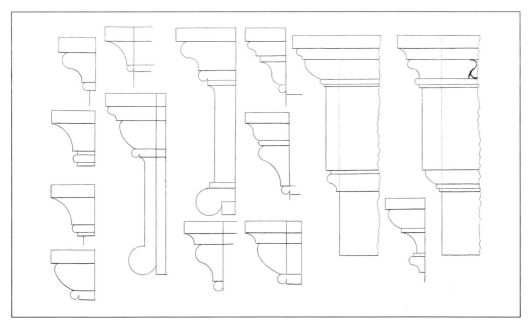

'Architrave mouldings for doors, windows, chimnies, etc.', from William Pain's Carpenter's and Joiner's Repository *of 1778. This collection contains a large number of Greek ovolos and deeply quirked cyma reversas.*

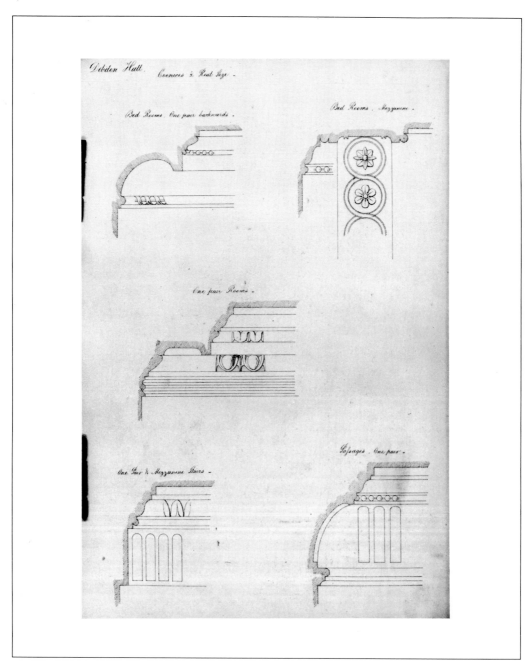

Delicate Neo-classical cornices devised by Henry Holland (or perhaps his cousin Richard) in c. 1795 for Debden Hall, Essex. These designs are most inventive, with Holland using the latest motifs (pea-like beading) and well-established details (flutes, egg and tongue) in an original manner. Top right is the style that was to become universal during the nineteenth century: embellishing the edge of the ceiling rather than the top of the wall at the junction between wall and ceiling.

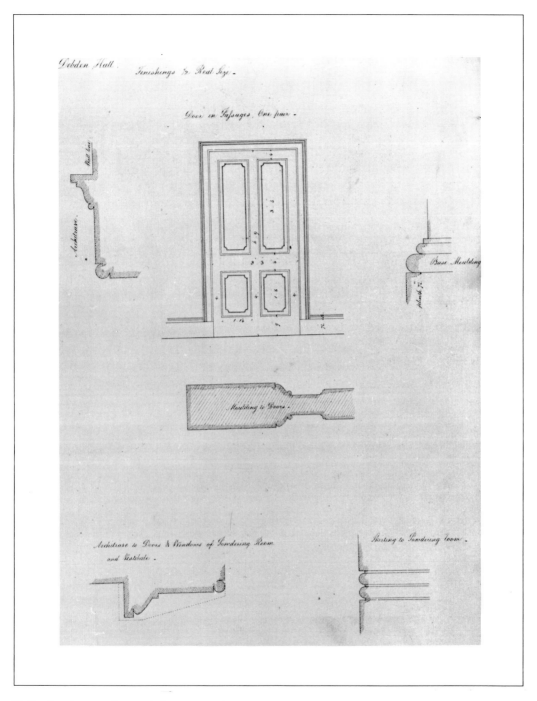

Holland architrave, door and skirting details of c. 1795 for Debden Hall. The flattened ovolos with quirks and beads are Greek-inspired and typical of the period. Particularly interesting is the simple beaded skirting to the 'powdering room' shown bottom right.

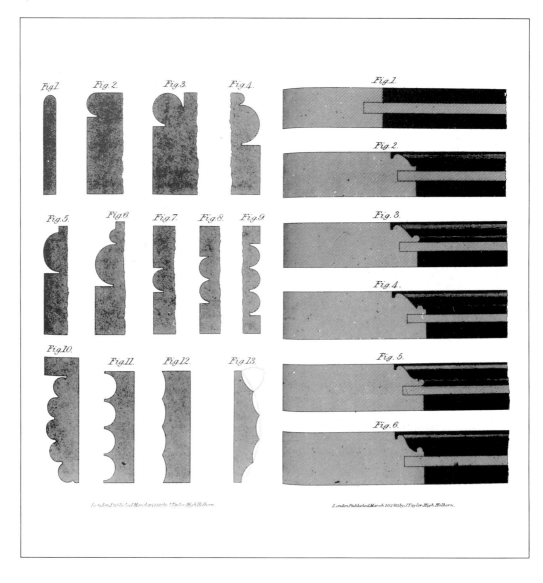

Fig.1. Fig.2. Fig.3. Fig.4. Fig.5. Fig.6. Fig.7. Fig.8. Fig.9. Fig.10. Fig.11. Fig.12. Fig.13.

Fig.1. Fig.2. Fig.3. Fig.4. Fig.5. Fig.6.

London, Published March 26 1811 by J. Taylor, High Holborn.

London, Published March 26 1811 by J. Taylor, High Holborn.

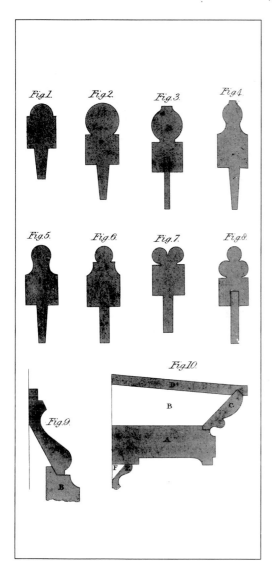

Opposite page, left: *Plate from Peter Nicholson's Mechanical Exercises of 1812 showing moulded compositions favoured in the early-nineteenth century. Fig. 2 is a quirked bead; fig. 3 bead and double quirk; fig. 4 double bead and quirk; fig. 5 single torus; fig. 6 double torus; figs. 7, 8, 9 single, double, triple reeded mouldings; fig. 10 reeds disposed round the convex surface of a cylinder; figs. 11, 12, 13 fluted work.*

Opposite page, right: *Popular early-nineteenth-century door and panel mouldings from Peter Nicholson's Mechanical Exercises. Fig. 1 shows framing without moulding (called 'door square and flat panel on both sides'). Fig. 2 framing has quirked ovolo, and a fillet on one side, but without moulding on the other, and flat panel on both sides (called 'door quirked ovolo, fillet and flat panel with square back'). Note: When the back is said to be square, this means that there is no moulding on the framing, and the panel is straight surface on one side of the door. Fig. 3 differs from fig 2. in having a bead instead of a fillet (therefore called 'quirked ovolo bead and flat panel with square back'). Fig. 4 has additional fillet on the framing to fig. 3 (called 'quirked ovolo bead, fillet and flat panel with square back'). Fig. 5 framing struck with a quirked ogee and quirked bead on one side, and square on the other; the surface of the panel straight on both sides (called 'quirked ogee, quirked bead and flat panel with square back'). Fig. 6 differs from fig. 5 only in having the bead raised above the lower part of the ogee and a fillet (called 'quirked ogee, cocked bead and flat with square back').*

Left: *Mouldings for sashes and cornices from Peter Nicholson's Mechanical Exercises. Fig. 1 simple astragal; fig. 2 quirked astragal; fig. 3 quirked Gothic; fig. 4 Gothic; fig. 5 double ogee bar; fig. 6 quirked astragal and hollow 'bars of this structure have been long in use'; fig. 7 double reeded bar; fig. 8 triple reeded bar; fig. 9 base moulding with part of skirting; fig. 10 cornice. (A) corona formed from a plank; (B) bracket; (C) moulding of the front string; (D) cover board; (E) moulding sprung below the corona; and (F) a bracket.*

PAINT

One of the great problems in reconstructing the eighteenth-century town house interior is that no one bothered either to record detailed instructions for its painting or to fully describe its colouring. Most accounts of interiors refer to paint colour only in passing, and then in very general terms, while documents like inventories or schedules to leases are often silent on paint colours or, at best, extremely vague, perhaps referring to a colour by a name that gives no absolute idea of its appearance. For example, articles of agreement, dated April 1770, for building a house and bakehouse in Fore Street, Limehouse, are exact in all constructional details, but when it comes to 'Painting work' merely instruct the painter 'to paint all the outside and inside wood-work ... three times in oil in any common colour that shall be approved of'.[13]

Pattern-books and various builder's and decorator's manuals help by providing lists of ingredients – and so colours – to match the names mentioned in leases and schedules; these books also, in a general way, reveal what pigments were available at certain times in the eighteenth and early-nineteenth centuries and suggest which colours and colour schemes were fashionable when the book was first published. But, as will become clear, these books create confusions of their own, with the ingredients of a named colour being listed differently in different books.

This evidence will be examined in detail, but first it is worth seeing what general picture emerges from diaries, letters and passing references in pattern-books.

Stone Colours and White Lead

In 1732 the Duchess of Marlborough referred to 'White painting with red damask',[14] implying that the timber dado panelling and architraves were painted white. Ware, in his otherwise highly detailed *A Complete Body of Architecture*, merely wrote that a panelled room painted the 'usual way' is lighter than a 'stucco' walled room or a room with hangings (see p. 150). Again it must be assumed that the panelling is white or a very light creamy stone colour; this is the colour that Ware recommended

as suitable for the parlour of a parsonage and that elsewhere he called 'stone colour in oil'.

What these references seem to be reflecting is Palladian taste, which triumphed in the 1720s and which held the hall of stone-detailed or plaster walls as the ideal room (see p. 165), and so promoted the use of white, pale-grey and Bath stone-coloured paints. These simulated the quality of plaster or stone when applied to panelling, while the doors and skirting could be painted dark brown (or chocolate colour, which would look passably like mahogany) to emphasize both the rhythm of the voids in the plaster/stone wall and its base. This practice supplanted the late-seventeenth-century and early-eighteenth-century taste for more sombre colours, when panelling was 'painted predominantly in oak or walnut colour either plain or grained'.[15] It must be said, however, that white was not entirely excluded from the palette of the late-seventeenth-century room painter. John Smith, in the 1676 edition of *The Art of Painting in Oyl*, wrote that 'divers wainscotting and other carpentry and joinery work are often coloured both for beauty and preservation' with white lead. But a letter of 1736 from a Mrs Purefoy seems to support the use of dark colour. Writing to a tenant of her house in Cursitor Street, Chancery Lane, she revealed that the house had 'never been painted but once since the year 1714 excepting what has been painted for you'.[16] It is hard to believe that a house would be only painted twice in twenty-two years unless it were decorated with dark colours.

The Palladian taste for simple, light colours survived through the century for the joinery in the more modest rooms of a house, while the grander rooms, if not papered or hung with fabric, were painted in a more elaborate fashion. In the late 1730s and 1740s that could take the form of painting panels a slightly different tone or colour to that used on the stiles and rails, as well as picking out mouldings, such as the ovolo surrounding the panels, in white or grey. After 1760 in the grandest houses the Neo-Classical arabesques of Robert Adam and James Wyatt often embellished the walls.

A building agreement of 1769 for Lord Bateman's house in Park Lane shows the survival of Palladian taste.[17] The main rooms were to be left 'Dead White', while the bedrooms and attics were stone-coloured. Sir William Chambers, in a letter of May 1770 to Gilbert Meason, suggested 'stone colour' for 'Parlours if they are for common use', because it 'will last best and is cheapest', but 'if you mean them to be very neat pea green and white, buff colour and white or pearl and what is called Paris gray and white are the handsomest'. The following year, in August 1771, Chambers added a little more detail in another letter, this time to Robert Gregory about his house in Berners Street: 'If you have any particular fancy about the painting [of] your principal rooms be pleased to let me know. My intention is to finish the whole in fine stone colour as us[u]al excepting the Eating Parlour which I propose to finish pea green with white mouldings and ornaments'. A third Chambers letter is worth quoting briefly because he included another finish, one already touched on in the Lord Bateman Park Lane building agreement quoted above. In this letter, dated July 1772 and to John Colecroft for whom Chambers was building a house in Knightsbridge, he mentioned 'our agreement for common stone colouring all over the house' and requested 'if you mean to have ... dead white or party colours in your principal floor please to let me know and I will order it accordingly charging you with the difference'.

These descriptions, if brief and imprecise, do, when analysed and related to other contemporary material, contain more information than is immediately apparent. For example, Ware referred to 'stone colour in oil'. All pigments for use on joinery, both for inside and outside work, were mixed with oil and most contained more or less white lead. White lead was used because of the preservative quality it gave to paint. No outside joinery in soft wood would last long without regular application of lead-based paint, and white lead was used either in its natural white state or coloured with pigments. In 1829 T.H. Vanherman, in *Every Man His Own House Painter*, wrote that white lead was 'the basis of all other colours'. In 1825 Nicholson in his *Mechanic's Companion* had been a little more precise. 'White lead is used in all stone colours; white painting is entirely white lead; lead colours are white lead and lamp black, pinks and all fancy colours have a portion of white lead in their composition, but chocolates, black brown and wainscot have no portion whatsoever'. These non-white lead colours could be made weather resistant by the addition of red lead, for black and wainscots were certainly in extensive use in the early-nineteenth century on both external

metalwork and joinery (see p. 188).

The use of lead was known to have its problems but seemed the only option. Campbell, in his *London Tradesmen* of 1747, described the activities of colourmen. 'There are works at Whitechapel and some other suburbs, for making of white and red lead ... labourers are sure in a few years to become paralytic by the mercurial fumes of the lead; and seldom live a dozen years in the business.' Campbell was habitually cynical in his accounts of the London trades, but the grim picture he painted was undoubtedly based on some truth. The hazardous nature of painting in oil does not seem to have been compensated by particularly high wages. Unlike many trades in the eighteenth century, journeymen painters were generally paid for the job and not on a day rate. So while a journeyman joiner or bricklayer would usually earn 3s. a day (see p. 121), a painter, we are told by Ware in 1756, would expect 6d. for painting a sq. yd 'three times in ... oil paint' – a price confirmed by I. and J. Taylor in the 1787 edition of *The Builder's Price Book*. Although a painter would not face the same danger as a manufacturer of lead paint, it is also clear that the economics of his trade drove him to paint as much as possible, and the more he painted the more his health was at risk.

The process of making the white-lead paint, a most curious affair, is well described in the 1705 edition of John Smith's *The Art of Painting in Oyl*:

Take a sheet of lead, and having cut it into long and narrow strips ... make it up into rowls, yet so as a small distance remains between every spiral revolution, these rowls ... put into earthen pots ... these pots have each of them very sharp vinegar in the bottom, so full as almost to touch the lead ... left for a certain time, in which space the corrosive fumes of the vinegar will reduce the superficies of the lead into a white calx which ... separate by knocking upon it with a hammer.

Smith explained the reason for using white lead: 'you paint with it any kind of timber work or stone, that you would preserve from the weather'. He also pointed out that 'it is best to work it with linseed oyl'.

This was the medium for all paint used on timber, inside as well as out. Smith admitted that 'Linseed oyl within doors will turn yellow' and Whittock in his *Decorative Painter's and Glazier's Guide* was still able to complain in 1827 about the need to use linseed oil as 'its general defect ... is its brown colour, and its tardiness in drying'. The reason linseed remained in use throughout the Georgian period is that there simply was no cheap alternative. William Salmon, a seventeenth-century colourman, recognized the problem of using linseed oil and recommended that 'white lead ... is to be ground with oyl of walnuts'.[18] This oil was colourless, but it was also very expensive, so, whilst an option for the artist, it was not a possibility for the house painter or, as Smith would have it, the 'vulgar' painter.

As well as oil-based paints, there were two other main types. In his letter of 1772 Chambers mentioned 'Dead White' (see p. 181) and made it clear that this finish was more expensive than 'common stone colour'. Dead white was a particular Palladian favourite: a matt paint developed for use on plaster surfaces (though used occasionally on joinery) with the aim of making the plaster look as much like stone as possible. Nicholson said it was made from 'fine old Nottingham lead, and [was] thinned entirely with spirits of turpentine'.[19] Ordinary lead and linseed paint could be given a matt appearance by being flattened with a finishing coat of turpentine. This process is mentioned by Nicholson, who called it 'three times and flat [which] is generally used for new work'.[20] It was described in slightly more detail in his *Architectural Dictionary* of 1819: 'In order to finish the work flatted, or dead, [finish with] one coat of the flatted colour, or colour mixed up with a considerable quantity of turpentine.' In the dictionary Nicholson explained that this matt finish was highly regarded for reasons of both fashion and function. It was, wrote Nicholson, 'the mode much to be preferred for all superior works, not only for its appearance, but also for preserving the colour, and purity of the tint'.

There was also distemper, a water-soluble paint consisting of whiting (made from ground chalk) and size (made from boiled animal skins and horns). Plain white distemper was used for plaster walls and ceilings, except for the grander kind after about 1760, which could be coloured with oil paint or tinted distemper. As well as these opaque paints, there were also translucent finishes such as varnish, which was made from pigments dissolved in linseed oil, oil of turpentine or alcohol, and which was generally used as part of the process of graining, marbling or japanning. There was also a type of varnish treatment called clear coaling (from the French *colle*, meaning glue or size), which Nicholson described in his *New and Improved Practical Builder*: 'Clear cole and finish ... is the cheapest kind of painting ... The whole is ... painted over with a preparation of whiting and size to form the ground. Over this a coat of oil colour, prepared with lead, called the finish, is laid'. This substance ('not much used at present', according to Nicholson in his *Mechanic's Companion* of 1825) had been costed at 3*d.* per sq. yd to 'clear coal and finish' by I. and J. Taylor in 1787.[21] It therefore cost half as much a sq. yd as the standard three coats of 'common painting' – 6*d.* a sq. yd – and half as much again as one coat of oil paint, which the Taylors costed at 2*d.* a sq. yd. If the finish colour was a pigment that became translucent in oil and was used without the addition of white lead or any other opaque pigment, then 'clear coaling' was, in effect, glazing on a white ground.

Lime wash, for use over rendered walls or on plaster, was made from lime putty (see p. 105) with some added water, plus tallow to improve weather resistance, and the required pigment. Green copperas would produce a Bath stone colour, blue copperas, or bice, a dusty blue, Somerset ochre a pink. The usual undercoat or priming material was 'Spanish Brown', described by Smith as 'a dark, dull red, of a horse flesh colour ... generally used as the first or priming colour ... being cheap and plentiful'.[22] A better material was red lead, which was made from lead heated over a hot fire. Red lead could be used in the manner described by Nicholson: 'lay on priming colour ... made from white lead and a little red lead mixed thin with linseed oil'. He suggested that four coats were needed to paint a wall properly and that the proportion of white lead be increased in each coat 'if the work is intended to be finished white', with the third coat being 'white lead mixed with linseed oil and turpentine in equal portions'.

This build-up of glazes was to be completed with a 'finishing coat ... made of good old white lead and thinned with bleached linseed oil and spirits of turpentine, of the portions of one of oil and two of turpentine'. No doubt to give some depth to this flatted colour, Nicholson suggested that 'a very small quantity of blue black may be used in the two last coats'.[23]

Common Colours

In his letter of 1772 Chambers mentioned 'common stone colour' (see p. 181), while the Limehouse building agreement of 1770 (see p. 180) specified 'common colours'. This is a term that recurs throughout eighteenth-century and early-nineteenth-century building documents and pattern-books.

Certain pigments were very expensive during the eighteenth century and were rarely used for house painting. Other pigments, mainly the earth colours, were cheap and so were in common use. So a 'common colour' means a cheap colour, but it also means a colour that was stable and would not fade or rapidly discolour. Clearly there was no advantage in using a cheap paint if it had to be reapplied at frequent intervals. Salmon, in his *Palladio Londinensis* of 1734, published a list of common colours that he described as 'prepared in the best manner, and sold by Alexander Emerton, colourman'. Emerton was one of a dynasty of eighteenth-century wholesalers and retailers of paint who seemed to cater for the do-it-yourself market by selling 'colours, ready prepared'. Broadsheets issued by the company included 'Directions for painting', and Salmon, surely to the mortification of the journeyman painter, wrote: 'since the Advertisement of Alexander Emerton ... several Noblemen and Gentlemen have by themselves and servants painted whole Houses without the assistance or direction of a Painter, which when examined by the best judges could not be distinguished from the work of a professed Painter'.

The Emerton 'Directions for painting' of c. 1744 are very straightforward:

Brush your wainscot very clean, that the dust may not mix with the colour. If the work is oil, brush it over with melted size and when it is thorough dry, stop the holes with putty, and paint it with the colour you would have it. To every six pounds of paint put one quart of oil ... with your brush paint the large pannels upwards and downwards, and be sure to carry the brush the same way with the grain of the wood. If the work is new, cover the knots with size and red lead, and then it must be done three times over. First with primer, then second with primer ... then the next day finish it with the colour you design.[24]

The common colours, listed by Salmon and produced by Emerton, were pearl colour, lead colour, cream colour, stone colour, wainscot or oak colour. All these, ground in oil, cost 4d. or 5d. per lb. Best white lead ground in oil cost 4d. per lb, 'one pound of which,' wrote Salmon, 'with two Pennyworth of oil, will paint 8 sq. yds'. So for a sq. yd of painting in white lead, the material cost $\frac{3}{4}d$. and the labour 4d., for Salmon said 'Painters usually charge 4d. per yd' for common colours. Slightly more expensive colours were chocolate colour, mahogany, cedar and walnut tree. All these, involving the use of more expensive red pigments and ground in oil, cost 6d. per lb. More expensive still, and not included under the heading of common colours, were gold at 8d. per lb and olive, pea and 'fine sky blue mixed with Prussian blue' at 8d. to 12d. per lb. Orange, lemon, pink and blossom, all 'ground in oil', cost 12d. per lb. Fine deep green, ground in oil, cost the staggering sum of 2s. 6d. per lb. Thus it is clear why the modest panelled interior tended to be pale cream or stone colour; as with so many aspects of urban speculative housing, it was purely a question of economics, and this economic argument is reinforced by the fact that, according to Salmon, while common colours cost 4d. per sq. yd to apply, 'extraordinary colours' cost between 8d. and 12d. per sq. yd to apply.

Just over fifty years later I. and J. Taylor also gave a list of 'common colours'. This embraced Salmon's colours at both 4d. and 6d. per lb. 'All common colours, either for outside or inside work, as white lead, or stone colour, lead colour, cream colour, pearl colour, wainscot colour, chocolate colour, etc., cost 6d. per sq. yd for three coats'.[25]

Colour Ingredients

To get some idea of what these colours actually looked like, we need to know more about the pigments from which they were made. Fortunately the ingredients are given in a number of books, notably Smith's *The Art of Painting in Oyl*, which ran through numerous editions from the late-seventeenth century to the early-nineteenth.

Lead Colour

The 1676 edition of *The Art of Painting in Oyl* tells us that indigo and white lead make a lead colour that 'is a pleasant colour to marble white withal, or to shadow it'. By 'shadow' Smith meant *trompe-l'œil* wood grain or panelling. This formula was repeated in the 1705 edition. We know that lead colour was one of the common colours; we also know that indigo (made from a leaf from the Indies) was one of the more expensive pigments in the eighteenth century.[26] Indeed, Smith said as much in 1676 by noting that 'Indico . . . a very dark blew [is] seldom used without a mixture of white [and] is something dear'. A possible solution to this conundrum is that there were two lead colours: a blue-grey version made of indigo and white lead and a grey version. As we have already seen (p. 181), Nicholson in his *Mechanic's Companion* wrote that 'lead colours are white lead and lamp black' – a view supported by William Butcher in his *Smith's Art of House Painting* of 1821. But, as if to highlight the hazard of using these manuals as indicators of paint colour, Nicholson also said, in his *New and Improved Practical Builder*, that 'lead colour is of indigo and white'. 'White lead and lamp black' made something called 'ash colour'.

Lamp black itself needs some explanation. The 1705 edition of Smith's *The Art of Painting in Oyl* described it as made from a 'soot raised from the roseny and fat parts of fir trees'. In the 1738 edition a black made of this material is called 'lam black', while lamp black is described as being made from the 'soot of lamp or candle'. Nicholson mentioned also an 'ivory-black . . . compound of fragments of ivory or bone, burnt to a black coal . . . and then ground very fine'.[27]

Stone Colour

Stone colour, the most ubiquitous of eighteenth-century paints, seems to have fallen victim to its own popularity: virtually no one thought it necessary to describe in detail anything so common.

The 1676 edition of Smith's *The Art of Painting in Oyl* records that 'yellow oaker', was 'much used in vulgar painting'. It seems fair to assume that we are dealing here with one of the ingredients of common stone colour. In the 1687 edition Smith wrote, 'Yellow Oaker is of two sorts, one called Plain-Oaker, and the other Spruce-Oaker, the one is much a lighter colour than the other'. This description of ochres is far from clear, but illumination comes in another statement in the same edition: for a stone colour, wrote Smith, 'mix Spruce-Oaker and white'. So it seems that stone colour, to Smith at least, was a sort of cream or biscuit colour. This supposition is supported by Vanherman in 1829, who wrote, 'white, stained with spruce ochre, umber, etc. . . . will produce what is termed a warm stone colour'.[28] But Nicholson, in his *Architectural Dictionary* of 1819, implied that stone colour could possibly have possessed a grey tint: 'if the work is intended to be of a . . . stone colour . . . the last coat should have a small quantity of ivory black or lamp black added, to reduce its whiteness a little'. But, as in all things, Nicholson's paint descriptions lack consistency, for in his *New Improved Practical Builder* he wrote that 'stone colour [is of] white, with a little stone ochre'. 'Stone ochre' was a name for a superior type of yellow ochre used to produce a Bath-stone colour.

As with lead colour, ambiguity creeps in. In the 1705 edition of *The Art of Painting in Oyl* Smith stated that, far from producing a stone colour, 'yellow oaker' (a generic term that embraces spruce oaker) and white lead made a 'buff colour' – a formula repeated by Nicholson in his *New and Improved Practical Builder*. To add to the confusion Smith's 1738 edition stated that spruce oaker, white lead and a 'little umber' made an excellent 'light timber colour' – a formula again repeated by Nicholson and the *Builder's Dictionary* of 1734, which states that umber and white make a 'Timber colour'. Buff colour was a common eighteenth-century and early-nineteenth-century paint type in its own right and was not synonymous with stone colour. Indeed, in his letter of 1770 (see p. 181) Chambers suggested 'white buff colour' as an alternative to stone colour. Also a description of buff colour given in Butcher's *Smith's Art of House Painting* makes buff seem a very unlikely-looking stone colour: 'white lead mixed with vermilion, orange-lead, rose-pink, or any other rose-colour'.

Despite these ambiguities and seeming contradictions, the weight of evidence suggests that stone colour had a yellow rather than a blue-grey tint – that is, it was rather more like the colour of Bath stone than Portland stone. According to Butcher, even 'Portland stone colour' contained burnt umber, as well as white lead and stone-ochre, all 'mixed by degrees to the colour required'. But the last word on the subject must go to Vanherman, who fielded a decidedly eccentric recipe in *Every Man His Own House Painter*: 'six pounds of ground white lead ... prepared oil or, indeed, linseed oil, half raw, half boiled ... throw in one pound of the road dust ... add more oil to thin it for working. This is a good stone colour.' Vanherman gave road dust the grand name of 'crotia' and defended its inclusion amongst the earth colours: 'Many no doubt will be surprised, and ridicule the idea of admitting filthy road dust as an important part of the composition of paint, but I beg leave to remind such critics, that the umber, ochres, boles, etc., are earth.' His description of crotia gives some idea of the colour of road dust: 'There is little preparation required for this article, as you have only to collect the sweepings of a road which is made up with flints, clinkers, granite, or any other stony substance and, having sifted it through a 45-hole wire sieve, keep it in a firkin or a barrel for use.'

If stone colour did usually have a yellow tint, what is generally thought of as the grey-blue stone colour must be included in those colours listed by Chambers at the end of his 1770 letter (see p. 181) as alternatives to stone colour: 'white or pearl and what is called Paris gray'. Pearl was a light grey made, according to Robert Dossie's *Handmaid to the Arts*, from 'the powder of pearl, or the finer parts of oister shells', and 'Paris gray' was, wrote Butcher, 'white lead and Prussian blue or blue verditer', which 'to make a more beautiful and pleasant colour' a 'small quantity of lake or vermilion' could be added. Nicholson, in his *Architectural Dictionary*, offered another description of the ingredients of grey, as well as of other popular colours:

Grey is made with ceruse [i.e., white lead], Prussian blue, ivory, black and lake ... inferior grey [is] made with blue black, bone black and indigo ... Olive greens [are made] with fine Prussian blue and Oxfordshire ochre ... sage green, pea and sea greens with white, Prussian blue and fine yellows.

Nicholson could also have mentioned 'drab', a popular neutral colour composed of white lead and burnt umber in the ratio 10:1.

Use of Colour

The ways in which these colours were used is indicated by Smith, who listed pairs of colours that were thought to go well together. In the 1705 edition of *The Art of Painting in Oyl* we read that colours that 'set off best one with another' and that 'make each other look most pleasant' are

blue and gold, red and white ... all yellows set off best with blacks, with blues and with reds ... all blues set off best with whites and yellows. Reds set off best with yellows and whites and blacks ... but green and black put together look not so pleasant neither do black and umber.

This list seems to have been regarded as objective rather than as a product of the subjective taste of the late-seventeenth century, because it was repeated faithfully in the eighteenth-century editions of the book. However, the 1705 edition is itself a slight revision of the 1676 edition, which, perhaps significantly, stated that red, rather than going with black, 'set off ... indifferently with blews and blacks'.

As well as these basic colours, there were also those common colours, which were named after, and coloured like, woods and which were grained as well as painted flat. The 1705 edition of Smith's book mentions the then current *trompe-l'œil* practice of 'panelling of wainscot with its proper shadows' and 'imitating olive and walnut wood, marbles and such like'. 'Olive wood', we are told, 'is imitated with oaker, and a little white veined over with burnt umber ... walnut tree is imitated with burnt umber and white veined over with the same colour alone, and in the deepest places with black'. A colour 'resembling new oaken timber is made of umber and white lead' and 'red lead, a little white and yellow oaker make a brick colour'.

Butcher's 1821 version of Smith adds more information on graining techniques – a predictable addition, since graining and marbling had enjoyed a revival in the first two decades of the nineteenth century. This rehabilitation of graining was dramatic, for as late as October 1773 that arbiter of refined taste, Chambers, dismissed the use of scagliola (imitation marble formed with colour pigments and marble chips set in plaster that is then polished) for walls by writing: 'as marble would be a very improper lining for a room ... so its imitation [in scagliola] cannot be very proper'. However, by the first few years of the nineteenth century, marbling and graining were the rage and, according to Whittock in his *The Decorative Painter's and Glazier's Guide* of 1827, this fashion was then at its peak and fuelled by the skill that the decorative painters had developed:

very great improvement ... has been made within the last ten years in the art of imitating the grain and colour of various fancy woods and marbles, and the facility and consequent cheapness of this formerly expensive work, has brought it into general use; and there are few respectable houses erected, where the talent of the decorative painter is not called into action; in graining doors, shutters, wainscot, etc.

Interestingly, Vanherman could write in *Every Man His Own House Painter* two years later that

graining or imitation wood and marble, has for some years formed a considerable part of the decorative system, but is now giving place to the plain and simple. There are two causes assigned for the falling off, namely the additional expense to the painter's bill, and the short lived beauty they exhibit; for being generally executed in water colours, and then varnished, should this covering crack and chip, the work will consequently look shabby, ragged, and mean.[29]

Having sounded this gloomy note of caution, Vanherman, clearly unconvinced by his own argument, proceeded to point out the special quality of graining and explained the manner in which graining and marbling should be disposed in the house:

Judiciously employed, and in a suitable situation, a little and well executed (with just remembrance to nature) adds lustre to an apartment, where the other parts join in unison, and form a complete composition. Graining, like diamonds in a portrait painting, should be sparingly employed, for its scarcity constitutes in a great measure its value.

Or, to be more precise, 'marble graining', wrote Vanherman, 'is only suitable for columns, pilasters, arches, dados, chimney-pieces, and such parts where

the appearance of solidity and coolness is desirable'.

As well as theoretical passages such as this, these painter's guides also contain practical information that gives a good idea of the appearance of these exotic effects and the way in which they were achieved. Clearly this early-nineteenth-century marbling and graining was more sophisticated, life-like and varied than the simulations of the late-seventeenth and early-eighteenth centuries. Butcher, in his 1821 version of Smith, explained how a mahogany colour was produced: 'first coat, white lead; second coat orange (with orange lead); then finished with burnt terra de Sienna, with a flat brush waving and imitating the veins as they run in any fine piece of mahogany'. For wainscot, the 'first colour, white; second coat, half white and half stone-ochre only; and shadowed in imitation of the wood, with terra de Sienna, or burnt umber'. Butcher also said that chocolate colour – a paint that could be used as a cheap way of simulating mahogany – was made from 'lamp black and Spanish brown'.

Whittock, in his *Decorative Painter's and Glazier's Guide*, listed and described popular marble effects that, he advised, could best be obtained by first-hand study and imitation of the real thing. 'Cipolin, or white-veined marble suitable for halls, passages, bars of coffee-houses' would have a 'beautiful effect'. 'Florentine marble ... greyish ... exhibiting designs of a yellowish brown colour' was 'far preferable to any plain distemper colour or stencil work for halls or passages, coffee rooms, etc.' 'Sienna marble ... yellow interspersed with veins of ore of a variety of colours' was 'used with good effect for door posts, halls, passages and in furniture painting'. 'Verde antique and Verde di Corsica ... green, yellow ochre, black ground' were suitable for 'slabs for halls and sideboards'. Whittock also listed Egyptian green, black and gold marble, Porphyry and Lydian and Serpentine marbles.

Vanherman sustained the analogy of house decoration and fine-art painting, and gave an idea of the harmonies attempted by the early-nineteenth-century decorator using these colours and techniques:

An elegantly painted house should be what a good painted picture is – the entrance hall, the foreground, whose parts combine force and strength of colouring, strongly marked and well connected; of a sober and warm hue; the staircase may be of the same tint, but two shades lighter. We now enter the suite of rooms on the first floor, where the skills and taste of the painter must be exerted, and the contents of his pallet consulted, and applied to give due effect without affectation or overloading; but, by a just combination, the eye may be pleasingly surprised, yet not dazzled by too many glaring lights. This being the principal or middle group, should be the most splendid but of a mellow and calm tone; brilliant but not gaudy; magnificent but not heavy. As we advance higher, we should adopt the aerial tint.

Over forty years earlier James Peacock had delivered hints for house painting that make an interesting comparison with the Vanherman passage. 'The distribution of colours in the various parts of the principal rooms' should, said Peacock, reflect a

close study of nature in several select landscapes ... In the ceiling should prevail, the light, cool and delicately softened azure of the sky ... the walls should partake the middle hue, and the floor a deeper die, should be imitative of the carpet of nature ... All strong and vivid tints must be very sparingly used; the glory of the sun is too powerful for mortal sight; though we are delighted with, and rejoice in the reflected beam; hence a sort of delicate tenderness must prevail in the several tints imitative, in some degree of the softened face of the beauties of nature, when viewed in general.[30]

Imprecise as Vanherman and Peacock were in their recipes, they were in essence remarkably similar and represent the epitome of Georgian good taste; colour treatments reflect room use and nature, and colour schemes reinforce the room hierarchy of the house. Nothing is 'gaudy', 'heavy' or lacking in 'delicate tenderness'.

This approach is given substance and related to practice by the descriptions in these books of particular schemes – some of which seem very remarkable. In his *Decorative Painter's and Glazier's Guide* Whittock recommended the decoration of rooms in the Roman manner, with walls divided into panels above a surbase and dado – also described by Vanherman in 1829. 'If the walls are stucco ... it is usual to make one panel only on each side, which is effected by shadowed mouldings ... with ornaments at each corner to relieve the angles.' Given this preference for paint applied as a series of panels, it

seems reasonable to assume that the following scheme by Whittock was envisaged as overlaid with a painted frame of rail and stile (see p. 152). Certainly an entire wall treated in the way described would surely have looked most odd.

One of the fashionable modes of decorating apartments is to let the wall appear in flame-coloured streaks, upon a light ground, and stencil over both. The flame-colour is formed by drawing a long streak of blue, then one of red, next yellow, and lastly green. The whole of the streaks are softened and blended together with a large dusting brush. The flame mixture will run from the top to the bottom of the room in light wavy lines: if a space is to be left between them, it must be marked with chalk lines, and coloured after the flame-colours are dry.

The space referred to is, presumably, the frame of rail and stile. As for the stencilling, Whittock instructed that 'on the white, on a light green ground, a small flower is stencilled in flame-colour – that is, in red, yellow and blue'. The 'white' must refer to that area of wall left uncovered by the flame treatment and so part of the frame. In contrast, 'on the flame-coloured ground the same flower is stencilled in white, middle tint and Vandyke brown ... these separate flowers, or rosettes on a varied ground are much easier executed than the old-fashioned joined festoons; and have a more lively pleasing effect'. This may refer to Palladian stucco festooned walls of the type described in 1756 by Ware (see p. 165) or, more likely, to an earlier-nineteenth-century fashion for a single, large flower-embellished painted frame set above the surbase. Such a panel was recently discovered in the first-floor front room of the late-eighteenth-century No. 15 Wilkes Street, Spitalfields (see p. 160).

Vanherman also offered schemes for rooms: 'Lavender colour ... lake, or rose pink, with a good portion of white (turned into peach blossom colour with the addition of a little Prussian blue) is an elegant tint for a drawing room' (see p. 70), while 'on ceilings it confers elevation from its retiring appearance'. Other ceiling tints recommended by Vanherman were: 'light pink ... light purple, very light French gray ... frequently the same tint as the panels of the wall'. These 'general tints,' he wrote, were replacing 'cloud ceilings' that had 'been in great request, but the rage has of late fallen off'.

But most interesting of Vanherman's rec-
ommendations are those for transforming an early-
eighteenth-century panelled room into a fashionable
apartment of the late 1820s. This was not so difficult
as it might have been thirty years before, because
the panelled wall was, as we have seen, enjoying a
revival in the 1820s. Vanherman wrote:

*If wainscotted and already divided by mouldings,
then the panel may be one colour, and the mouldings
another, e.g., if the panels are a light pink the stiles
may be the same, and the mouldings between a light
reddish purple, of lake, Prussian blue, and white
lead; the upper member of the cornice should be
light pink; the ogee under, light purple, the corona,
light pink, and the ovolo, light purple; and the upper
member of the dado should be light pink, the ogee
light purple, the corona light pink, the ovolo under
the corona light purple, the die or dado light pink,
the torus or top of the plinth, light purple, and the
plinth or skirting light pink.*

Vanherman also offered other colour combinations:
'A light yellowish buff and light plum colour also
form a most pleasing union for wainscot panels, a
lavender and light blueish purple, also a light pink
and light green, light orange and green.' These
colours were also recommended 'for apartments
designed to have each side formed into one panel.
Here, as in the wainscot room, the same system is
to be observed, namely, harmony.'

External Paint Colours

The choice of colours for external use was generally
influenced by the same fashion changes that determined interior colour schemes. This relationship
was made easy by the fact that the same sort of
paint – linseed-oil-based lead paint – was used for
both interiors and external joinery.

The 1676 edition of Smith's *The Art of Painting
in Oyl* states that 'with [white lead] posts, payles,
palissados, gates, doors, windows, divers wainscotting and other carpentry and joynery work are
often coloured both for beauty and preservation'.
The ambiguity of this statement – it is not absolutely
clear whether the white lead is mixed with pigment
or not – is partially resolved by a related description.
'Indico' and white lead – which was known early in

the eighteenth century as lead colour – was, wrote
Smith, 'much used . . . for the last colour of windows,
doors, poles, posts, rails, palissados, or other timber
work'.

The 1705 edition of Smith is more specific, yet
adds a further confusion. 'Poles and posts,' it says,
'are sometimes laid over only with white, which
they call a stone colour.' There is no supporting
evidence anywhere else that white lead paint used
externally was ever called stone colour. But the
relationship between white lead and lead-colour
finish is clarified: 'Window frames are laid in white,
if the building be new, but if not, then they are
generally laid in lead colour, in indico and white,
and the bars with red lead.' With the mention of red
lead this sounds like a formula for undercoating,
but we know from the 1676 description that lead
colour was used as a 'last' coat and that, in any case,
'indico' was, as Smith put it, 'something dear' to use
as an undercoat. This leaves us with the unlikely
image of lead-colour window frames and red-lead
glazing bars – but it must be borne in mind that this
system was thought suitable in 1705 for old work,
which must have meant mullioned and transomed
windows. In this case the red lead would have gone,
most suitably, on the iron frame of the casement
and on the iron bars to which the lead cames were
wired.

Smith went on in this 1705 edition to provide
another fascinating statement. 'Doors and gates, if
painted in pannels' should have 'shadows' of 'umber
and white' if the ground is white. 'Shadows' are the
trompe-l'œil edge of the panel, and the 'ground'
is the background colour in which the illusionary
shadows are painted. 'But,' continued Smith, 'if laid
on a lead colour, then the shadows are lifted with
black.' The *Builder's Dictionary* of 1734 makes it
clear that plain white lead was then the common
colour for all external timber. For 'doors, shop-
windows, window frames . . . and all other Timber
works that are exposed to the weather', the dictionary recommends priming in Spanish brown,
Spanish white and red lead 'and lastly with a fair
white, made of white lead'.

The use of unpigmented white lead for external
joinery, as indicated by Smith and the *Builder's
Dictionary*, is supported by Ware, who stated that
'where there is no stone [externally] there generally
is wood, this being painted white, as is generally the
practice'. Sophie von la Roche, who visited London

in the mid 1780s, observed that the houses had 'big well kept windows whose panes are framed in fine, white painted wood'.[31] But by this time fashions were beginning to change, and the tendency was to use a colour that reduced the visual prominence of the glazing bars and, in the spirit of the picturesque, presented the windows as a void in an exquisite Neoclassical wall. This is well illustrated by Chambers's designs of the 1770s for Somerset House in which, as the surviving elevational drawings show, the glazing bars were painted a dark colour.[32] Pain, in his *Practical House Carpenter* of 1789, provided a useful summary of the then fashionable colours for sashes: 'sash squares dead white ... mahogany grained and varnished ... squares painted black'.

By the early-nineteenth century in London and other cities (notably Edinburgh) dark brown and grained sashes were much in favour. The Crown Estates, under John Nash's guidance, specified in the 1820s that the sashes of the Regent's Park terraces were to be painted every four years in 'imitation of oak'.[33] This choice was explained by Whittock in his *Decorative Painter's and Glazier's Guide*: 'Oak is the wood that is commonly preferred to any other for outside work ... [so] the decorative painter ... who considers propriety, will generally recommend the imitation of oak for street doors, shutters, etc.'

The stucco fronts, which these oak sashes embellished, could themselves be the subject of illusionary paintwork very much in the spirit of contemporary internal decoration. Nicholson, in his *New and Improved Practical Builder*, explained of façades stuccoed in Roman cement that:

they should be frescoed, or coloured, with washes, composed in proportions of five ounces of copperas [sulphate of iron]to every gallon water ... where these sorts of works are executed with judgement, and finished with taste, so as to produce picturesque effect, they are drawn and jointed to imitate well-bonded masonry and the division promiscuously touched with rich tints of umber, and occasionally with vitriol, and, upon these colours mellowing, they will produce the most pleasing and harmonious effect, especially if dashed with judgement, and with the skill of a painter who has profited by watching the playful tints of nature, produced by the effect of time in the mouldering remains of our own ancient buildings.

A little earlier, in his *Practical House Carpenter* of 1789, Pain had implied another method of giving stucco façades – or, indeed, interior stucco walls – a genuine stone feel. In his list of prices, Pain recorded that 'stucco' painted 'three times in oil' cost 8*d*. per yd while 'ditto, and sanded' cost 1*s*. per yd. Presumably sand would have been applied with the last coat, or to the last coat when still wet, to produce a textured finish. Joseph Emerton had been more precise in his directions for painting: 'Use white or writing sand, and lay the Ground-work with White lead, then sift the sand upon it while it is wet and not paint it afterwards.

Items such as shop fronts seem to have been potential subjects for the same sort of illusionary and decorative treatment. Malcolm, in his *Anecdotes* of 1808, recorded that 'the shopkeeper prides himself on the neatness of his shop front; his little portico, and the pilasters and cornices are imitation of Lydian, Serpentine, Porphyry and Verde antique marbles'.

Ironwork – railings and lamps – was generally painted black. Meister, in his *Letters Written during a Residence in England*, noted the English habit of 'placing iron rails against almost every house' and thought 'the sight of a number of heavy black iron bars' rather offensive. 'Perhaps gilding might make them more lively,' he wrote, 'or painting them of a gayer colour.' It seems this had, occasionally at least, been the case in early-eighteenth-century London – when area railings were sometimes painted a steel-blue colour – and in Dublin in the late-eighteenth century, where area railings were occasionally painted white. In London too, at roughly the same time as Meister was writing, a modest change in taste was occurring. Ironwork was being painted blue again – this time a rich royal blue of the sort shown in Chambers's 1770s elevation of Somerset House.[34] By the early-nineteenth century a light-green bronze colour was enjoying a vogue and, indeed, was specified in the 1820s for the Regent's Park terraces. This colour was almost certainly applied to façade features other than area ironwork. Iron balconies shown in Joseph Salway's 1811 survey of Kensington High Street are all painted green,[35] while David Laing, in his *Hints for Dwellings* of 1800, recorded that a 'trellis work' porch should be painted green. To judge from late-eighteenth and early-nineteenth century watercolours, green was the most popular colour for front doors.

Chapter Four

TOWN GARDENS

There have been gardens in towns for centuries, but the ordinary town house garden is a product of the eighteenth century. In 1700 few small town houses had anything but paved yards, but by 1800 back gardens with flowers and shrubs were commonplace. London's gardens in 1700 were mostly to be found in the corridor linking the City with Westminster, where there was a concentration of aristocratic mansions like Bedford, Somerset and Arundel Houses, besides the Inns of Court.

Wenceslaus Hollar's *London Panorama* of 1658 shows several of these houses and their gardens, all of which were formally laid out with straight avenues and well-disciplined trees. Such formality was the norm in the seventeenth century, but it is remarkable that the gardens of large town houses remained formal till the very end of the eighteenth century. The new Bedford House on the north side of Bloomsbury Square was built by the Earl of Southampton in the early 1660s. When John Evelyn dined there in 1665, he observed 'a naked garden to the north',[1] bordered by a row of trees on either side and extending from the mansion to an old Civil War bastion. Comparison between a late-seventeenth-century plan of the garden, a similar plan of 1751 still in the estate archives, Thomas Sandby's painted view of *c.* 1770 and Richard Horwood's 1792–9 'Plan of the Cities of London and Westminster, the Borough of Southwark and Parts Adjoining' shows that the simple lay-out of this garden remained unchanged for almost 150 years.

Later grand houses in London, built when the formal lay-out of country parks had given way to more naturalistic arrangements, mostly had very simple gardens consisting of open turf surrounded by a border of trees. This was the arrangement at Grosvenor House in Park Lane and at Robert Adam's Lansdowne House of 1768, off Berkeley Square. It does not appear that any of the famous Georgian landscape gardeners like Charles Bridgeman, William Kent or Capability Brown ever turned their attention to the town houses of their country clients. Most of the work of laying out and planting large town gardens was probably carried out by nurserymen and jobbing gardeners, in consultation with the owners. This seems to be the implication in the only mention made by the garden enthusiast Lord Chesterfield concerning the making of a garden in the unusually spacious grounds to the rear of his new house off Park Lane (designed by Ware in the 1740s). In March 1749 he wrote, 'I am got into my new house ... my garden is now turfed, planted and sown and will in two months more make a scene of verdure and flowers not common in London.'[2] At Aubrey House in Kensington, only two and a half miles from town, Lady Mary Coke was certainly the prime mover in her garden, aided by the nurseryman Mr Lee of Hammersmith. She also drew much on town seedsmen and in June 1768 recorded that 'I continue buying flowers at Covent Garden to replace those that go out of bloom.'[3]

Lady Mary's casual remark draws attention to the crucial fact that a wide variety of seeds and plants was readily available to the inhabitants of Georgian London. For most of the eighteenth century the horticulture trade was centred in the capital. In 1700 there were about fifteen important seedsmen, all in London; by 1730 the total had risen to about thirty, still mostly in London; and by 1760 there were at least thirty nurserymen and ten seedsmen in London and as many again scattered throughout the rest of England.[4] Many of these

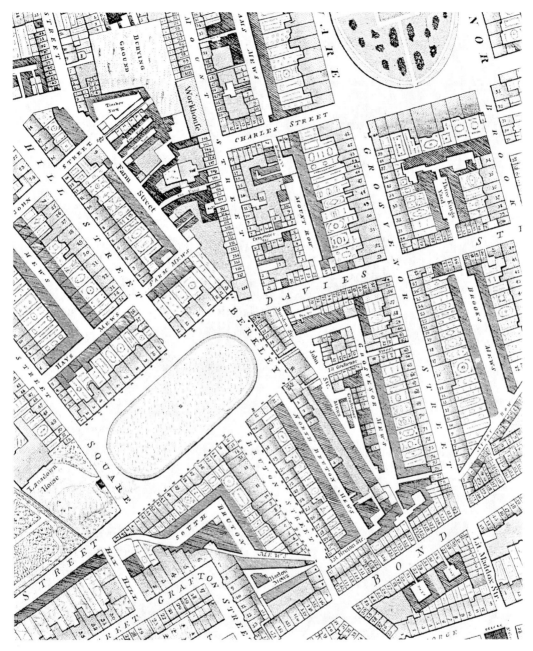

Richard Horwood's large-scale map of London, first published in 1792–9 with another revised edition in 1819. Horwood covered a much wider area in detail than any previous map, and shows a very large number of town gardens. As yet it is not clear whether Horwood depicted the true lay-outs or drew on a very extensive repertoire of standard patterns, but the formal and geometrical character of many of these layouts suggests that a large number of London gardens were still being maintained in a mid-eighteenth-century style.

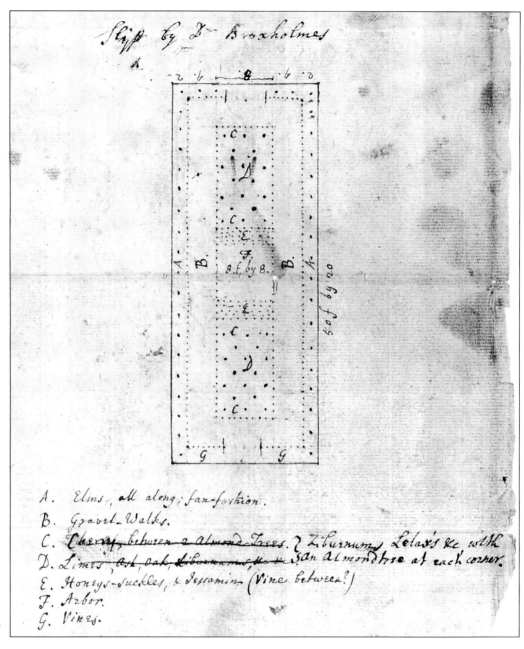

A design for 'a London slip' 20 × 50 ft drawn by the amateur garden designer Thomas Spence of Byfleet.
The slip in question was in Bond Street and the design was made in 1743. The arrangement is simple: an
elm hedge round three sides, with vines on the fourth (and presumably south-facing) side, gravel walks 4
ft wide, and two central beds divided by an arbour 8 ft square. It is notable that both here and in the Twiss
design of fifty years later the central beds were to be planted with flowering shrubs, including laburnums,
lilacs and almond trees.

A primitive mid-eighteenth-century drawing of some suburban houses in Kew. The back gardens are divided by wooden fencing of the kind that was widespread even in the centre of town. The formal patterns are presumably meant to represent borders and beds but look a little unconvincing.

nurseries were concentrated in inner suburban areas, like Hoxton and Hammersmith, but plants were readily available in the centre of town. Covent Garden Market offered all kinds of shrubs, pot-plants, annuals and seeds for immediate purchase.

Plant buyers were of all sorts and classes, from Lady Mary Coke with her garden of several acres to garret dwellers with only a windowsill. Pehr Kalm, a Swedish visitor to London in 1748, was struck by the number of flowers in the city, commenting that 'At nearly every house in the town there was . . . a little yard. They had commonly planted in these yards and round about them, partly in the ground itself, partly in little pots and boxes, several of the trees plants and flowers which could stand the coal smoke of London.'[5] It is these smaller gardens, belonging to terrace houses and tenements, that are the most interesting and at the same time the most elusive. Until the early-eighteenth century the centres of most of the larger towns were tightly packed; space was at a premium, and small back-yards were the only private open space. There were exceptions, like Oxford where many of the houses stood on very long thin plots that stretched back from the street frontage, but even in Oxford the

most modest dwellings had to be content with a backyard.

Town yards could be very small: the three-storey houses newly built in Meard Street in London's Soho in 1722 and 1733 had yards only 13 ft long. They must also have been smelly, because their main function for the whole of the eighteenth century was to contain the privy. In his *A Complete Body of Architecture* Ware noted:

The houses in London are all built one way, and that so familiar that it will need little instruction. The general custom is to make two rooms and a light closet on a floor, and if there be any little opening behind, to pave it. Some attempt to make flower gardens of these little plots, but this is very idle: plants require a purer air than animals, and however we breathe in London, they cannot live where there is so much smoake and confinement: nor will even gravel continue many days from the turning. In this respect, therefore, instead of borders under the walls, the best method is to lay the whole with good sound stone pavement, and at the farther part to build the needful edifice that cannot in London be removed farther off, and something of a similar shape and service opposite. An alcove with a seat is a common contrivance in the space between, but it is a strange place to sit for pleasure.

Forty years later these small backyards were still very common in the capital. According to J.L. Ferri de St Constant, who visited London in 1804, 'the entrance of the houses gives onto a corridor 6–8 ft wide, which usually ends in a small paved court-yard'.[6]

The smoke mentioned by Ware was certainly a problem for town gardeners, especially those in London, and it seems likely that in the first decades after 1700 the majority of them did not attempt proper flower-beds, but preferred to keep their plants in pots, which could be moved about and replaced to provide a permanent display. Pot-plants

could also be moved inside the house, and there is plenty of evidence in paintings and other sources that house-plants enjoyed widespread popularity in the first half of the eighteenth century. Thomas Fairchild put it most explicitly in his *City Gardener* of 1722: 'One may guess at the general love my Fellow citizens have for gardening ... by observing how much use they make of any favourable glance of the sun to come abroad, and of their furnishing their rooms and chambers with basons of flowers and bough-pots, rather than not have something of a garden before them.' Even later in the century, when many of the wealthier town dwellers were able to enjoy somewhat larger gardens with proper flower-beds, plants in pots remained an important element, often placed at intervals along garden paths, or clustered on green-painted plant stands.

A view from the back of Admiral Nugent's house, No. 14 Wigmore Street, in July 1810. The artist, John Claude Nattes, seems to have concentrated on the back garden of the house next door. He shows the flat lead roof extending over what was probably the servants' quarters, and providing a convenient terrace. Beyond the terrace to the right can be seen the door of the privy in one of the customary positions immediately next to the rear of the house. The garden itself has a wide border with shrubs and a broad area of what by this date was probably grass.

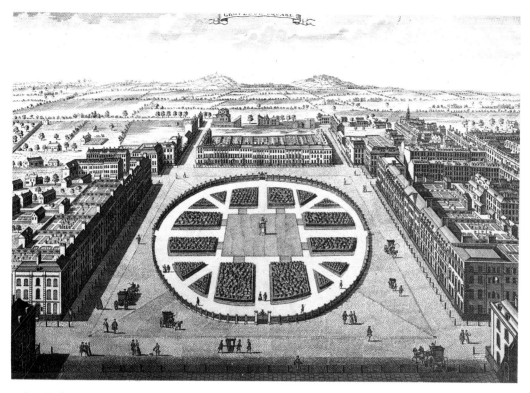

A detail of Sutton Nicholls's view of Grosvenor Square, published in 1754 but probably drawn somewhat earlier. All the houses in the square had substantial back gardens divided from each other by brick walls. In almost every garden shown here the ground is laid out with small plots of grass or flowers between broad paths that were probably gravelled. In one instance the centre of the garden is formally arranged with round pools and topiary. The walls were used for espaliered fruit trees. Several of the gardens are terminated by handsome stable blocks, which provided a focus for the prospect from the rear windows of the main house. Views by Nicholls of other London squares show similar garden lay-outs.

Poorer people, or upper-floor tenants with no yard or garden, arranged their pots on windowsills and also on roof parapets, which made a cheerful appearance in the streets, but must sometimes have been precarious for those walking past below (see p. 19). Fairchild even recommended miniature window-box water gardens, which sound extraordinary:

as water in London may be generally brought as high as a balcony, it might be ordered so as to play now and again in a little stream or jet from some figure or piece of rockwork, proportionate to the bigness of the balcony or leads where we have our garden. There has been a long time a fountain in

the manner I speak of at a plummers at the upper end of the Haymarket, near Piccadilly.

The town garden as we understand it, that is to say, the back garden of a terraced house, was an upper-class innovation that probably first appeared in central London around 1720 or perhaps a little earlier. One of its first manifestations was on the Grosvenor Estate in Mayfair, behind the fashionable houses in the streets surrounding Grosvenor Square that were built in the 1720s and 1730s. These houses were intended for the kind of people who would also have a country estate and they were generally larger than the usual terrace house of the time, with a good width of garden ground. John Strype's 1720

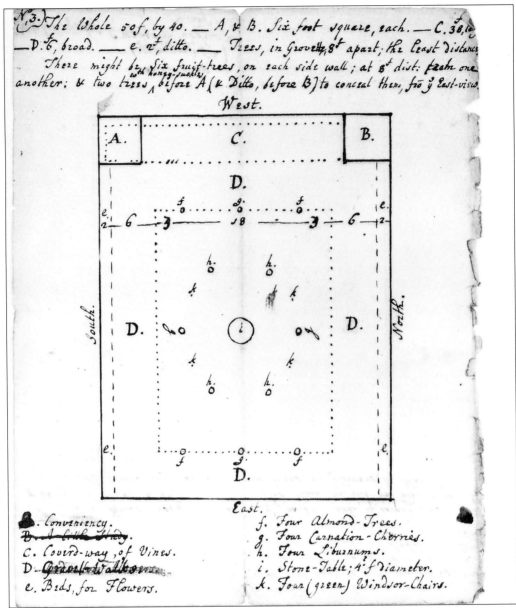

A design made by Spence in 1744 for a London garden belonging to Lady Falmouth. The garden was 50 × 40 ft, with narrow flower-beds under the walls and the usual square of gravel walk. Spence took advantage of the greater width to introduce a formal central feature consisting of a circular stone table surrounded by ornamental trees, alternating with green-painted Windsor chairs. He proposed a similarly artificial treatment of the house end: 'The house itself would add to ye garden-look if covered with creepers filleray or vines: and before ye iron rails there might be (blew and gold) flower-pots; (with myrtles and orange trees, or flowers in them).' The far end of the garden was laid out in just the fashion described by Isaac Ware, with a 'conveniency' in one corner with a little study opposite.

edition of John Stow's *Survey of London* says explicitly that 'every house [in Grosvenor Square] has a garden behind it, and many of them stables and coach houses adjoining'. Sutton Nicholls's engraved view of the square confirms this and shows a considerable number of gardens, all formally laid out and with handsome architectural features, which presumably contained the stables, at the end furthest from the house.

Thanks to their size, these could be proper gardens. As the garrulous Mrs Delany wrote to her sister in 1734 from her house at No. 48 Upper Brook Street in Mayfair: 'You think madam that I have no garden perhaps, but thats a mistake. I have one as big as your parlour in Gloucester and in it groweth damask roses, stocks variegated and plain, some purple, some red, pinks, philaria, some dead and some alive, and honeysuckles that never blow.'[7] And in 1748 Mrs Edward Boscawen of No. 14 South Audley Street, Mayfair, was boasting that 'My garden is in the best order imaginable, and planted with a hundred shrubs and flowers.'[8] Fifty years later she mentioned laburnum and lilac growing in the same garden, and praised their efficiency as a screen against her neighbours.

The idea of a garden in town quickly spread to other fashionable parts of London and beyond. At Bath, which was just emerging as an upper-class spa, it is interesting to observe the permeation of the idea. The large houses in Queen Square, laid out by John Wood in 1728 as the first stage of his grand idea for the development of the city, had no gardens to speak of, but later houses in Gay Street (laid out in the 1740s), the Circus (1750s), Brock Street and the Royal Crescent (1760s) all had proper gardens from the start.

The arrangement of these town gardens is still obscure, and obviously there was a great deal of individual variation. One might expect some examples of the commonest modern arrangement, with two long flower-beds under the walls and a central lawn. Ware mentioned 'borders under the walls', but these were by no means universal. An archaeological examination of the ground behind No. 4 The Circus, Bath, has revealed a different, wholly formal lay-out, with gravel walks, circular beds and lines of small trees. In the Nicholls view of Grosvenor Square all the garden grounds are divided into small rectangular plots separated by narrow walks, with broader walks along each side.

Some of the gardens have small standard shrubs or trees arranged round the edge of a bed or along a walk. These paths or walks were evidently much more important in the eighteenth century than they are today, and it is interesting to find that the most thorough book on gardening available at the time, Jean de la Quintinie's *Compleat Gard'ner*, recommends that even the smallest garden should have one broad walk at least 8 ft wide.[9] Multiple division into many small plots seems to have remained a feature of smaller Georgian gardens well into the second half of the eighteenth century. Vivid confirmation is provided by a splendid Admiralty model now in the National Maritime Museum that shows the buildings of Chatham Dockyard in 1773, including a row of early-eighteenth-century officers' houses with gardens laid out in this fashion.

Another frequent component of the better-class town garden was an architectural feature terminating the vista from the back windows of the house. Very often this was a pedimented arch or something similar, formed on the blind wall at the back of the stable and coach-house that faced on to a back lane or mews, and serving to obscure the proximity of this necessary building. A surprising number of these features survive, though often they are obscured or completely hidden by later additions made to the main house. One example is the elaborate obelisk that can be found behind No. 71 South Audley Street in Mayfair.

Servicing could influence the appearance of town gardens. Many larger late-eighteenth-century houses had such an extensive array of kitchens, pantries and servants' quarters that the basement storey had to be extended over the whole space behind the house. These rooms were covered with lead and perhaps paving as well to produce a wide terrace for the use of the house-owner. With such terraces, proper planting was out of the question and pot-plants or architectural ornament the rule. One particularly fine example of the latter was designed by Robert Adam for Sir Watkin Williams Wynn's house in St James's Square, begun in 1772. Adam's scheme, which was illustrated in his *Works in Architecture*, entailed transforming one of the long side walls of the enclosure behind the house into a richly decorated triple-arched screen.

There was clearly a lot more hard surface in the Georgian garden than one would expect to find nowadays. Stone paving was used extensively by the

The immensely detailed Admiralty model of Chatham Dockyard that was made in the 1770s shows the lay-out of the gardens belonging to the houses of the Dockyard officers. The gardens, which still survive, are at a higher level than the houses and separated from them by a service road. Covered flights of steps lead up from road level. The original garden lay-outs shown on the model are very like those in the Nicholls view of Grosvenor Square, with broad gravel walks, rectangular beds planted with trees, shrubs and flowers, and also some beds in geometrical patterns. Grass played a very small part in such gardens.

wealthy, but it was relatively costly and much the most common surface material was gravel; in fact, gravel seems to have been used where one now finds grass, both for paths and for larger expanses. Besides its cheapness, gravel had the advantage that it could be raked over when the top surface had become discoloured by sooty town rain. In most cases town gardens and the gardens of smaller houses in less urban areas were enclosed by palissados, or fences made of wooden boards. There are several eighteenth-century views that show this kind of fencing in use, and, allowing for the distortions of early perspective, it looks as though these fences were about 5 ft high. There are certainly many examples of brick garden walls dating from the eighteenth century and before, but in general these walls were built to enclose the gardens of larger and more important buildings, and they were constructed in a very substantial manner that would have been too expensive for the ordinary householder. The standard one-brick-thick garden wall was a nineteenth-century introduction.

For the plants themselves the best and fullest source of information is Thomas Fairchild's *City Gardener* of 1722. Fairchild ran a successful nursery business at Hoxton, on the edge of London, and brought out his helpful little book because, as he put it, 'I find that everything will not prosper in London, either because of the smoke, or else because those people who have little gardens in London do not know how to manage their plants when they have got them.' Although, sadly, Fairchild gave no information about the best way to lay out private gardens, he offered advice on the planting of public squares and named those plants that could flourish in London, often giving examples of where they could be seen in the ground. There is also a section describing the plants that could be used in 'courtyards and close places in the city'. Many of his plants are still the mainstay of modern town gardens. His list of evergreen shrubs included privet, box, holly, ivy and bay. Of Virginia creeper he noted, 'This plant is excellent for the ornament of balconies and windows and will grow so well in pots and cases that it will soon cover the walls and shade the windows if they lie exposed to the sun ... there is hardly a street, court or alley in London without some example of what I relate of it.' Lilac, laburnum, broom and jessamin were named as easy flowering, along with syringa and honeysuckle (but

A mid-eighteenth-century gardener in his domain. Although the garden is clearly a large one, with a handsome classical orangery and an ornamental fountain in the pond, the plants are set in the same small rectangular plots shown in representations of town gardens.

only the Russian variety). Smaller perennial flowering plants on Fairchild's list included thrift ('which does best of all'), the white lily, perennial sunflower, sweet-william, primrose tree, aster, campanula, dwarf flag iris, monkshood (to be seen 'in a close place at the back of the Guildhall'), everlasting sweet pea and the double rose. Among the annuals were poppy, lupin, nigella, sweet pea, stock, viola, candytuft and marigold, together with the great convolvulus and scarlet bean as ornamental climbers.

Scattered among these ornamental specimens were many varieties of fruit-bearing plants, and it

seems clear that gardeners in the eighteenth century mixed fruit, flowers and perhaps even vegetables indiscriminately. The French royal gardener De la Quintinie felt that the smallest gardens should be devoted wholly to fruits and vegetables, although he did not condemn 'those who, having but a very small garden, affect flowers, their inclination leading them to it preferable to any other plants'. Fairchild was evidently a fruit enthusiast and his list included the apple, pear ('they will bear very good fruit, as may be observed in confined places about Barbican, Aldersgate Street and Bishopsgate Street'), vine ('in many close places such as tavern yards there are vines growing in good perfection, and even bear fruit'), morello cherry, fig ('in some close places near Bridewell') and mulberry ('There are now two large mulberry trees growing in a little yard about 16 ft sq. at Sam's Coffee House in Ludgate'). A century later the same kind of enthusiasm for fruit growing was still shown by some London gardeners. Smith, in *Nollekens and His Times*, remarked that 'Upper Gower Street was until lately so free of smoke that at No. 33 Col. Sutherland ripened grapes by the sun in the open air at the back parlour window.' He also noted that 'As late as the year 1800, William Bentham Esq. of No. 6 Upper Gower Street ... had nearly twenty-five dozen of the finest looking and most delicate nectarines, all fit for the table, gathered from three completely exposed trees.'

Fairchild's book is particularly unusual and valuable for two reasons: he is the only Georgian garden writer who dealt directly with the subject of town gardens, and he was also the only one to address the amateur. Other gardening books published in the eighteenth century were intended exclusively for professionals, and usually comprised only a more or less elaborate calendar of the jobs that had to be done in each month. Such are William Thompson's *New Gardener's Calendar*, Mawe's *Every Man His Own Gardener* of 1767 and Gilbert Brookes's *The Complete British Gardener* of 1779. These three, gardeners respectively to the Dukes of Cumberland, Ancaster and Leeds, concerned themselves with

large establishments and made no specific mention of the peculiar problems of town gardens. The massive two-volume *Flora Londinensis* by William Curtis, which appeared in 1777 and 1798, is a detailed illustrated study of the wild plants to be found in and around London and does not concern itself at all with gardens. Even as late as 1833 William Cobbett's *The English Gardener* concentrated wholly on the best methods of growing fruit and vegetables in large country gardens, though by this time John Claudius Loudon had begun to write about town gardens in his *Gardener's Magazine*.

From the evidence of maps and drawings it seems clear that the last quarter of the eighteenth century saw a shift from formality in the lay-out of many town gardens towards a freer and more natural appearance. This is most easily seen in the lay-out of London's squares. All the early squares were rigidly formal. St James's Square was first laid out in the 1660s and in 1726 was surfaced entirely with gravel, although in this year a great water basin was constructed in the centre as part of the local water-supply arrangements. In the same period Soho Square was laid out with four small symmetrical grass plots and some lollipop trees in a sea of gravel. Fairchild bewailed their aridity: 'The plain way of laying out squares in grass platts and gravel walks does not sufficiently give our thoughts an appetite of country amusements: I think some sort of wilderness work will do much better.'

It was not until the 1760s that residents began to obtain private Acts of Parliament to ensure that the view from their front windows consisted of more than scuffed gravel. The act relating to Berkeley Square was passed in 1766, that for Grosvenor Square in 1774. Both of them provided for the fencing off, planting and up-keep of the ground with money raised by a local rate. The new planting was invariably denser than the old, with shrubs and trees screening off the surrounding streets. The continuing popularity of garden squares as a component of late-Georgian planned development is a measure

Opposite: *The terminal feature of the garden of No. 71 South Audley Street, Westminster. The main house was built in 1736 on a restricted corner site that allowed for only a small garden or back area. The kitchen quarters extended the full depth of the site, covered by a flat lead roof. Despite these restrictions this handsome Palladian façade was built to give consequence to the little space. The blunt obelisk rising above the central pediment is in fact the kitchen chimney.*

One of a series of watercolours of c. 1800 that shows the back garden of a house belonging to the Pole family in King Square, Bristol. This view shows the bottom of the garden, with a door leading out into the back lane. The door itself is camouflaged by a pergola, which forms a decorative focal point at the end of the broad gravelled walk that runs the whole length of the garden from the back of the house. The walk is flanked by rather narrow flower-beds, and the enclosing walls are completely covered with creeper.

of their importance to town dwellers, and certainly most of the foreign travellers to England (who, like modern tourists, spent much of their time tramping the streets) found the greenery of these gardens very welcome. The Dane Andreas A. Feldborg wrote in 1809 that 'the shrubbery walks and grass plots in the squares afforded very seasonable relief: the eye being wearied of the sameness of colossal piles of bricks and mortar'.[10]

Evidence of the appearance of private town gardens in the twenty years either side of 1800 is hard to come by, although large-scale, late-eighteenth-century maps like Horwood's 1792–9 'Plan of the Cities of London and Westminster' show a wide variety of garden lay-outs, some still with geo-metrical beds, some with borders under the walls, and some with serpentine paths. Like most carto-graphers, Horwood almost certainly used stan-dard conventions when representing gardens; it has been calculated that there are eight dozen of them in his survey. Nevertheless, we can probably assume that these conventions are based on actual garden lay-outs and give a fair indication of what could be expected behind late-Georgian houses. Such con-temporary documents as are known are not always helpful with information about ordinary gardens. The splendid plan preserved in the Bodleian Library showing an intended back garden behind Francis Douce's house at No. 13 Gower Street is hardly representative.[11] Douce was an antiquary and bot-

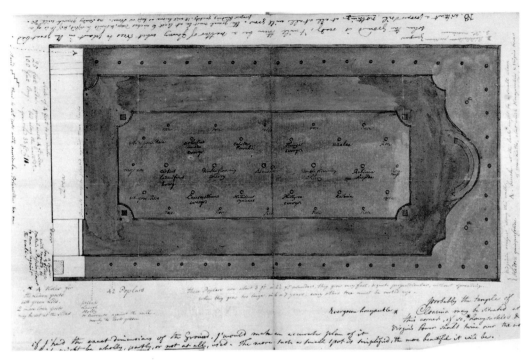

A plan for an intended garden at No. 13 Gower Street, drawn in 1791 for the antiquary and botanist Francis Douce by his friend Richard Twiss. The space measures 25 × 100 ft and the lay-out is simple. Indeed, Twiss wrote in the margin of his design 'the more such a small spot is simplified, the more beautiful it is'. A single great bed is surrounded by a gravel walk, and the whole is enclosed by a wall and a hedge made of poplar trees. It is a botanist's garden, and the centre bed contains specimen bushes, all enclosed by a rose border. On a more humdrum level, sockets for poles to support a washing line were sited at each corner of the bed, to be capped with green lids when not in use. As for the outside lavatory, Twiss noted by the far corner of his plan, 'probably the temple of Cloacina may be situated at this corner, if so, honeysuckles and virgin's bower should twine over the entrance'.

anist. When he moved into his house in 1797, he obtained a garden plan from his friend and botanical mentor Richard Twiss, who proposed a single great bed planted with flowering shrubs like moss rose and hibiscus, edged with box and surrounded by a gravel walk. Both the flank walls were to be screened by thick poplar hedges, straddling herbaceous borders. There is no grass at all in the proposed lay-out. It is interesting to see Twiss assuming that the privy (or rather the 'temple of Cloacina', goddess of sewers) would be sited at the far end of the garden, and proposing that it should be discreetly hidden under a covering of evergreen, honeysuckle and virgin's bower. It is unclear whether Douce ever carried this elaborate plan into effect; if he had, his garden

would have been conspicuously different from those of his neighbours. The few surviving views of ordinary gardens of the time show simpler arrangements, still with plenty of gravel, straight beds and large numbers of potted flowers, but also with creeper-covered walls and shrubs that were allowed to grow fairly freely.

Towards the end of the eighteenth century there was a major new development in town gardening, marked by the wholesale emergence of front gardens. Such gardens or yards were not wholly new and much earlier examples can be found, for instance in the amateur architect Roger North's late-seventeenth-century drawing for 'a city howse lying backwards'.[12] This shows a medium-sized house

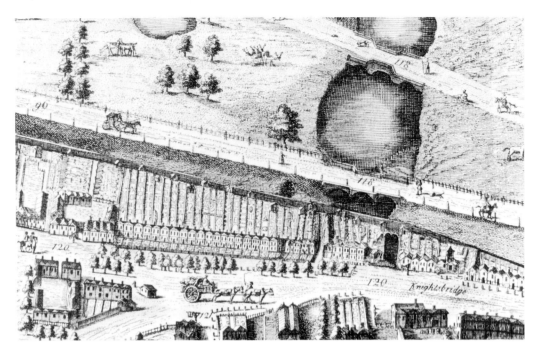

A section of Rhodes's 1766 map of Kensington, which shows the lay-out of town house gardens. These are often dismissed as merely conventional, but even if they were not based on the actual lay-outs, it is becoming clear that town gardens in the eighteenth century were laid out in very much this style.

built towards the rear of a long plot and separated from the building on the street front by a rectangular garden (containing a three-hole privy). In smaller towns it is not very difficult to find surviving examples of eighteenth-century houses set back from the roadway to give a small *cour d'honneur*. Geijer observed of Great Yarmouth in 1809: 'should there be a couple of square yards unoccupied between the house and the road one is sure to see there as many flowers and as many neat little paths among these flower-beds as can be put there. Many houses are embellished on the outside with ivy and other plants.'[13]

In London and the other large towns of Georgian England, street frontage in the central districts was too valuable to waste. It was a different matter in the wide streets of new suburban districts, where land was cheap and the occupants of the houses would be sensible of the value of a picturesque barrier between their living-rooms and the road. Late-Georgian suburbs like London's Kennington, Islington, Clapham and Kensington were all laid out

with front gardens. Single-storey shops have been built over these gardens, or they have been submerged under concrete or tarmac for the benefit of the motor-car, but they can still be found. A very good idea of their usual lay-out can be gleaned from Joseph Salway's 1811 survey of Kensington, which shows both the plans of these gardens and their appearance from the street. Most are given over almost completely to grass, with or without a walk round the edge, but there is a fair sprinkling of more picturesque lay-outs with serpentine paths and rough planting, as well as a few reactionary arrangements, laid down entirely to gravel with geometrical beds. Solway's map documents the arrival of grass as a common ground-cover, a development that must have had a remarkable effect on the appearance of Georgian towns. It also makes clear that the universal way of enclosing front gardens in the Regency period was with a dwarf wall topped by an iron railing.

In the early-nineteenth century the sharp distinction between town and country was beginning to blur, especially along the feeder roads. When one observer rode from Battersea to Clapham in 1814, he saw 'a row of elegant houses with the neatest gardens in front of them; where round the chequered parterres of flowers your eye is pleased to behold the laurel, the myrtle, the woodbine and charming little thuias'. Closer to the centre, 'in the suburb of Vauxhall there are yet some rural features . . . pretty flower gardens adorn the fronts of the houses as far as the turnpike'.[14]

Between and beyond the suburban boulevards, small middle-class villas were springing up, occupied by commuters and the kind of people who would hitherto have lived in town. Each of them was surrounded by gardens and shrubberies to give as much of a rural aspect as possible. These villa gardens were seen as an extension of the home, an attitude made possible by the arrival of glass doors or french windows in the 1780s or 1790s. French windows were widely installed at the back of terrace houses, while at the front the first-floor windows were enlarged by cutting them down to floor level, very often to allow easy access to a narrow iron veranda. The desire to unite interior and exterior also found expression in the glass conservatories, that became very popular in the early-nineteenth century. Improvements in cast-iron and the manufacture of glass brought such luxuries within the reach of the urban middle classes, so much so that John Claudius Loudon, in his *Greenhouse Companion* of 1829, could express the hope that greenhouses 'would be an appendage to every villa, and to many town residences, a mark of elegance and refined enjoyment'.

Late-Georgian town gardening is best epitomized in the works of John Nash, a designer who was very much alive to both townscape and landscape, and in the writings of Loudon. Nash's Regent's Park development is an immensely successful synthesis of town and country. Individual gardens behind the stucco terraces were extensively planted with clumps of shrubs and a large amount of lawn, but what few people appreciate is that several of these splendid terraces did not have any private gardens of their own. For example, the houses in Hanover Terrace had back gardens, but those in the adjoining Kent Terrace had none. Instead there was something like a private square in front, between the main carriage drive and the Inner Circle. This luxuriantly planted enclosure formed a buffer between the

houses and the road, and also afforded a generous outdoor space for the use of the residents. The first-floor principal rooms of the Regent's Park houses – many of which had generous balconies – looked out across the private enclosure and into the park. By this means Nash managed to combine the English landscape tradition with the London terrace house in a way that satisfied both the individual occupant and the casual observer.

Loudon began publishing the *Gardeners' Magazine* in 1825. The following year there was a letter from 'R.A.M.', asking for guidance in the planting of town gardens. It is significant that Loudon felt constrained to reply, 'Till some correspondent replies to R.A.M. he may look into *Le Jardinier des fenêtres des appartements et des petits jardins*, Paris, 1823'. Evidently there was no satisfactory book on the subject in English. French town gardens, at least those of the larger houses, were certainly more elaborate and sophisticated than their English counterparts. Many of them were influenced by the idea of 'le jardin anglais', which was a pocket version of the English landscaped garden, with serpentine walks, woods, hills and a variety of garden buildings all condensed into a small compass. It is possible that a reverse influence was exerted by Paris on the English town garden. In 1828 the magazine published a short piece with hints for improvements to town gardens, proposing an informal lay-out as if it were a novelty, and suggesting the sowing of front gardens with mignonette, larkspur, snowdrops, crocuses and aconites. After this there was nothing more about town gardens in general until 1835, when there appeared a very opinionated article on the subject by Thomas Rutger. He illustrated his article with plans of elaborate gardens with complicated paved walks, of which he remarked, 'I should prefer them to be surrounded with grass rather than gravel, for I consider the latter to be in bad taste, though it is frequently employed in the vicinity of the Metropolis.'

In 1836 there was a sudden flood of articles on the subject of suburban gardening, which doubtless found their way into Loudon's *Suburban Gardener* of 1838, which is the fullest and most useful statement of his views. But the town gardens described in this work are really Victorian gardens, with grass and shrubberies not at all Georgian, and whose paths were contrived to give protection to the gas and water mains coming in from the street.

PART FOUR

———◆———

APPENDIXES

East side of Elder Street, Spitalfields, looking north. All these houses were built as pairs between 1725 and 1727 by Thomas Bunce and Thomas Brown on building leases granted by the Isaac Tillard Estate. From left to right are Nos. 5 and 7, 9/11 and 13, and 15 and 17.

Appendix One

Case Study – No. 15 Elder Street and No. 2 Fournier Street, Spitalfields

The building of early-eighteenth-century Spitalfields was mostly undertaken by modest members of the building trades (carpenters, plasterers, paviors, smiths) who could generally manage to finance only the construction of one or two houses at a time.

A typical product of the Spitalfields speculative system is No. 15 Elder Street, while No. 2 Fournier Street is a very far from typical product. No. 15 Elder Street was built on a 61–year building lease dated July 1727, and an analysis of it reveals not just how much a speculative house cost to build in early-eighteenth-century London but also how the house was occupied and by what manner of people. No. 2 Fournier Street is exceptional in every way. It was designed between July 1725 and May 1726 not by a builder but by one of the eighteenth century's leading architects, Nicholas Hawksmoor, and was intended as (and remains) the minister's house for Hawksmoor's adjacent Christ Church. As it was built for the Church Commissioners and, therefore, built to last beyond the duration of a relatively short lease, the house is far more substantial than the majority of other houses in the area. But despite its authorship and expense, the building is still a terrace house, no larger than some of the other houses in the street. What makes its study so interesting is that its building history is meticulously detailed. Viewed together, these two houses present a very vivid and rounded view of the making of early-eighteenth-century domestic urban architecture.

NO. 15 ELDER STREET

The story of No. 15 Elder Street begins in 1724, when a document drawn up between Thomas Bunce and the Isaac Tillard Estate refers to a 'street intended to be called Elder Street' that was to be built in the ancient Liberty of Norton Folgate on what was then (May 1724) called 'waste land'.[1] This document refers to a 61-year lease being granted to Bunce at a yearly rent of £5 17s. The land that was finally leased to Bunce, a plasterer, and his associate Thomas Brown, a pavior, seems to have been a plot making up most of the east side of Elder Street, with a 180-ft frontage to the street and running back approximately 40 ft. On this basis Bunce and Brown were paying the Tillard Estate nearly 8d. per ft frontage in ground rent (it was usual in the eighteenth century to calculate a ground rent for a development site by the width of its main frontage; see p. 124). The Elder Street plot was duly parcelled into lots. Bunce and Brown started operations in 1725 at the north-east end and by mid 1727 had completed or begun three pairs of houses of different sizes and designs and arrived at the southern end of the plot: the sites of No. 15 and its pair, No. 17.

The land on which these two houses now stands is referred to in a lease assignment dated 28 June 1727[2] between 'Thomas Bunce of Spitalfields ... plaisterer' and the Tillard Estate. This document, it seems, refers mainly to No. 17, but, because the houses were to be built as a uniform pair with a continuous brick façade, it is undoubtedly the case that the description and specification imposed on Bunce for No. 17 applied equally to No. 15, which was leased in the name of Bunce's associate, Thomas Brown. In this document we learn that 'all the piece or parcell of waste ground situate, lying and being on the east side of Elder Street ... from north to south 18 ft in size ... from east to west ... 40 ft abutting ... north upon the waste before intended to be leased to Thomas Brown, paviour' (i.e., the site of No. 15) was to be leased to Bunce 'for the term of sixty-one years ... at the yearly rent of 18s. ... for the last sixty years'. The ground rent had now increased to 1s. per ft, while this final provision suggests that the lease included a year's peppercorn period.

We do not know how Bunce and Brown financed the construction of Nos. 15 and 17 Elder Street. However, we do know a little more about their methods in the case of building Nos. 5–13 Elder Street and, no doubt, they would have resorted to similar financial manipulations to complete Nos. 15 and 17.

The site of Nos. 5 and 7 was granted to Bunce on a 61-year building lease in July 1725 and both houses – with façades of shared construction and design, like Nos. 15 and 17 – were complete by March 1726/7.[3]

The source of finance for construction is suggested by two documents.[4] The first, dated February 1725/6, reveals that Bunce assigned a 36-ft frontage of ground he had leased from the Tillard Estate to a Francis Martell, weaver, for £250. This sum was, quite feasibly, enough to complete the shell of this pair of modest houses, with Martell providing a further £337 10s. in February 1727/8 – that is, about a year after the houses were said to be complete. It seems likely that in this operation Bunce sold the pair of houses before he had constructed them to a prosperous local weaver (Martell was said to be of St Leonard's, Shoreditch), with the initial instalment paying for construction of the shell. The second sum was probably paid by Martell after he had either moved into one of the houses (both were purpose-built for weaving, with two storeys of weaving garrets) or after he had sold them both on. If this were the case, then it would suggest that Martell had bought the speculation from Bunce, with its inherent risk and potential profit, having, perhaps, retained Bunce as builder.

In the case of Nos. 9/11 and 13 Elder Street (No. 9/11 had been built as one house), the land was leased from the estate for sixty-one years in March 1726–7 in Brown's name.[5] The ground rent was £3 10s. (again calculated at the rate of 1s. per ft frontage) with a peppercorn 'for the first year of the said term'. By July 1727 'two brick messuages or tenements' had been built and Brown mortgaged these buildings and the remainder of the lease for £200 to Henry Williams of Hoxton, a cooper.[6] This seems a small sum for two large new houses (though they may well not have been completed), but it was probably not meant to reflect the value of the houses. It may well have been a loan secured on the houses, for the agreement concludes with a 'proviso that the same [agreement] shall be void on payment [by Brown] of the sum of £210 on 22 July 1728'. This short-term loan at 5 per cent interest may have been used to complete the construction or fitting out of these two houses, thus making it possible to sell on their leases; or the money may have been used by Bunce and Brown to begin work on their next venture: Nos. 15 and 17 Elder Street on the adjoining site.

Eighteenth-century pattern-books and building manuals, read in conjunction with the detailed building accounts for No. 2 Fournier Street and for other ministers' houses, give a very good idea of how much No. 15 Elder Street would have cost to build. But the first step in the analysis is to discover how the house was constructed and with what quantity and quality of materials.

The building lease records that the plot on which No. 15 stands measured 18 × 40 ft. The house itself occupied roughly half this area, with an 18-ft front to the street being square in plan and only one room deep. Its height above ground is 40 ft and incorporates four storeys. At some point after, or even during, construction of the brick shell it was decided to extend the house by 12 ft into the yard. This extension, stretching the full width of the house, was carried out in timber – a soft-wood frame clad in clapboard. This use of timber suggests that the extension may have been constructed by the joiners and carpenters employed on fitting out the front, brick-built part of the house, as does the fact that the panelling and detail within the extension match exactly – in style, construction and patina of age – that surviving in the front part of the house. This extension would have involved only one major

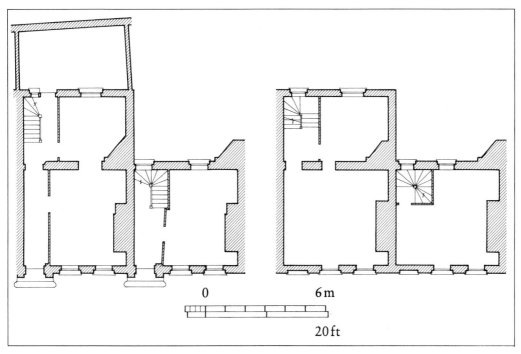

Ground- and first-floor plans of Nos. 15 and 17 Elder Street, built 1727. No. 15 was extended (probably during initial fitting out) with a rear timber-frame addition containing the staircase.

piece of remodelling (as well as cutting rear windows into door): the removal of the staircase from the north-east corner of the shell and the creation of a more generous staircase in the north-east corner of the extension.

If the quality of the fittings within the timber frame extension suggests that it is contemporary with the brick shell, then the structure within the brick shell makes it clear that the shell was floored and roofed before the extension was decided upon – confirming that the extension was the work of the first occupier of the house rather than Bunce or Brown. The main beams, running between party walls, in the shell were placed off centre as if to accommodate trimmers for a staircase well, while the roof of the extension is merely a shallow, mono-pitch continuation of the rear pitch of the struc-turally self-contained roof over the shell.

The original plan of No. 15, especially the location of the staircase, is suggested very strongly by No. 17, which is still only one room deep with a cramped newel stair in its north-east corner creating a series of L-shaped rooms on the upper floors. At the higher levels these are divided by a partition set along the line of the exposed main beam running from party wall to party wall. When this partition is in place, the awkward, off-centre placing of the fireplaces in the front rooms of both Nos. 15 and 17 makes sense. Clearly they were positioned to be central in a room defined by the front wall and by a partition set beneath the main beam.

Since the extension to No. 15 was almost certainly carried out by the first occupant and not by Bunce and Brown, it will not be part of the following analysis of the building costs of No. 15.

In its original form the house was a brick box of roughly double cube proportions – that is, 18 ft square in plan and rising 40 ft in height. This meant a brick wall area, after deductions for door and window openings (10 in front, 5 behind) and after addition of the brickwork of a 6-ft deep basement, of around 2,922 sq. ft. To this must be added the 225 sq. ft of brickwork of chimney-breasts and flues and the 175 sq. ft of brickwork in the stack. This makes a total superficial area of brickwork of 3,322 sq. ft.

This quantity of brick wall was made up of different types of brick laid in different thicknesses. There were basically three types. The facing brickwork of the front façade consists of the most expensive and best-laid bricks but is, typically, a sham. The good bricks are only a 4-in skin casing, but not bonding into, piers of cheaper, poorer-laid bricks. The rear elevation is of cheaper bricks – perhaps second stocks or picked place bricks – neatly laid but with simpler detailing than the front façade. Last are those walls, concealed from the weather and the eye, in which the cheapest bricks are used, often laid rapidly and poorly. The tragedy was that it is precisely these walls – party walls and piers behind well-covered façades – that do most of the structural work.

Of the total superficial area of brickwork, approximately 1,881 sq. ft is of the cheaper, unadorned place brick variety. Place bricks were the cheapest of bricks, often containing more dirt than clay, underfired, ill shaped and flawed. Most of these bricks would have been used in the construction of the structurally vital party walls that were of two types in No. 15. That to the north would have been built over hand to abut the existing party wall of No. 13, while the other would have been built as a shared party wall with No. 17. In both cases the party walls need not be more than a brick and a half in thickness and are probably only a brick in thickness at second- and third-floor level.

Throughout the Georgian period the unit for measuring the time and cost of brick construction was the rod, which was a $16\frac{1}{2}$-ft square of brickwork (that is, $272\frac{1}{4}$ sq. ft) of brick and a half thickness. By tradition it was agreed that, on average, a rod contained 4,500 bricks (although in practice this could vary quite significantly depending on type of brick, bond and thickness of mortar joint), and that a bricklayer and his labourer could lay 1,000 bricks a day, so taking four and a half days to complete a rod of brickwork. For example, Salmon, in his *Palladio Londinensis* of 1734, stated categorically that 'the materials required in a Rod of Brick-work ... are 4,500 Bricks, 1 Hundred and a quarter of Lime, and 2 loads and a half of Sand' and that 'a Bricklayer will lay a thousand Bricks a day'.

However, Batty Langley, in his *London Prices of Bricklayer's Materials* of 1748 gave a more realistic and accurate breakdown of likely costs for the different types of brickwork found in the speculatively built terrace house.

Place bricks, wrote Langley, are sold prime cost at 11s. per 1,000 if bought at the kiln but 'delivered to Westminster or London cost 14s. per 1,000'. Ware gave the same price in his *A Complete Body of Architecture* of 1756, while I. and J. Taylor in the 1776 edition of their *Builder's Price Book* quoted the price of place bricks as £1 5s. per 1,000. This price is particularly interesting, for the building accounts of No. 2 Fournier Street – exactly contemporary with No. 15 Elder Street – show that the Church Commissioners were paying this relatively high price of £1 5s. for place bricks. The place bricks used at No. 15 Elder Street were, no doubt, of the 14s. a 1,000 variety.

Langley confirms that, even by practical computation, 4,500 place bricks would be needed to construct a rod of brickwork, for, although only 4,352 were needed in theory (at four bricks to the ft), wastage would quite realistically raise the total of bricks needed to 4,500. However, as regards speed of construction, the rule-of-thumb formula was, according to Langley, quite wrong. Langley was of the opinion that, for 'common, rough, unpointed place brick walls', such as used for 'party walls, behind wainscot ... Bricklayers and labourers can lay 1,500 bricks per day (and not over heat themselves)'. At this rate, observed Langley, a rod of this brickwork could be laid in three days.

Langley gives a detailed breakdown of the cost of one rod of this type of brickwork: 4,500 place bricks he costed at the rate of 14s. per 1,000, so the total cost of bricks was £3 3s. Twenty-five heaped bushels of unslaked lime cost 10s. 10d. and twenty-five bushels of sand cost 3s. $1\frac{1}{2}d$., so the cost of mortar was 13s. $11\frac{1}{2}d$. One labourer would need to be employed for three quarters of a day to 'slack and skreen the lime and to turn up and chaff the Mortar'. At the rate of 2s. a day, this work would cost 1s. 6d. Finally, three days of a bricklayer's time at 3s. per day cost 9s. and three days of a labourer's time in assisting the bricklayer at 2s. a day cost 6s. So the

Opposite: Detail of the staircase from ground floor to the first half-landing: on the next flight the balusters are plain shafted, while on the upper flight they rise on a simpler closed string.

total for a rod of place bricks was, according to Langley, £4 13s. 5½d., which breaks down into £3 16s. 9½d. per rod for materials and 16s. 6d. for labour.

By comparison, Salmon recorded in 1734 that a rod cost 16s. for 'workmanship' and for 'work and all materials £5 10s. or £6 per rod'. But Salmon did not indicate the type of brick this costing was based on. In 1776 I. and J. Taylor wrote that place bricks cost £6 6s. per rod, while at No. 2 Fournier Street the master bricklayer, Thomas Lucas, charged £5 15s. per rod in 1726 as a general figure to cover all the types of brickwork used.

To discover how many rods of brickwork are contained within the 1,881 sq. ft superficial area of place brickwork in No. 15 Elder Street, another eighteenth-century bricklayer's formula has to be used. This is described very clearly by Salmon and Langley. A rod is deemed to be one and a half bricks thick; therefore, a wall thicker than this would naturally contain more rods than a thinner wall, even if both are of the same superficial area. To discover the number of rods contained in a wall of any thickness, it was merely necessary, as Langley explained, to 'multiply the superficial content by the number of half bricks contained in the thickness of the wall'. The result of this is then 'divided by three [the number of half bricks in the standard thickness]'. This gives the area of the wall into which 272 (the number of whole sq. ft contained in a $16\frac{1}{2} \times 16\frac{1}{2}$ ft rod) is divided to discover the number of rods contained in the wall.

In the case of No. 15 Elder Street it is reasonable to assume that the whole of both party walls are one and a half bricks thick, for, if the basement party walls are two or two and a half bricks thick, this is offset by the taller third-floor party wall, which is probably only one brick thick. On this basis the 1,881 sq. ft of place brickwork in the party wall and chimney-breasts contain nearly seven rods of brickwork, which, at Langley's figure of £4 13s. 5½d. per rod, makes a total cost of £32 14s. 2½d. Of this, £5 15s. 6d. was for labour, and the work would have taken a team of bricklayer and labourer twenty-one days to complete.

The front façade of No. 15 Elder Street contains, basement brickwork included, 585½ sq. ft of brickwork and, like the party wall, can be assessed on the basis of being a uniform one and a half bricks thick; the two to two and a half brick basement

again offsets the one-brick-thick third floor and parapet. This minimal wall thickness puts the house in default of legislation that, theoretically, governed house building in London.

Being of five storeys, No. 15 Elder Street was of the 'second sort' of house listed in the 1667 Building Act. Houses of this sort should, according to the Act, have ground and first floors of 10 ft (they are only 8 ft to 8 ft 6 ins at No. 15), with façades being two and a half bricks thick at basement level, two bricks thick to second floor and one and a half at third floor. The party wall thickness for this grade of house was also specified: two bricks thick to first floor and then one and a half to garret.

It should not be surprising that this deviation from legislation was possible, for much more visible lapses were also tolerated. An amendment to the 1667 Act, passed in 1709, stated that box-sashes should be recessed 4 ins behind the face of the façade. This was to prevent the spread of fire, but the builder of No. 15 Elder Street, in common with most of his fellow speculative builders in London, ignored the legislation and set his box-sashes flush with the façade in the established manner.

This practice probably continued for a very practical reason. Windows were usually about 3 ft 6 ins wide, so that internal shutters, which were folded in boxes set at right angles to the window, had to have reveals of at least 10½–11 ins in depth. If the façade was (as at No. 15 Elder Street) only one and a half bricks thick, then there was only just enough space for the reveals when the box-sashes were set flush with the façade. If the box-sashes were recessed 4 ins as specified, then the shutter boxes would either have to project into the room (as occasionally does happen) or the panelled wall would have to be set some way back from the brick wall to accommodate the shutters. This would be a waste of floor space as well as a structurally unsatisfactory solution.

However, if this demand for recessed sashes was universally ignored, the major requirement of the 1707 amendment was generally, and rapidly, followed. This Act required that wooden eaves cornices were to be dispensed with, as they were fire risks, and replaced by parapets 18 ins high of the sort that tops the façade of No. 15 Elder Street. This Act also required this parapet to be continued above the party wall to separate the roofs of each house as a means of preventing the easy spread of fire. This sensible legislation was ignored by the

First-floor front room: the panelling is fixed in an ovolo-moulded frame and topped with a full box cornice. This room cost an estimated £20 to panel, floor and plaster in 1727. The fire surround, though from Spitalfields and of the 1720s, is not original to the room.

builder of Nos. 15 and 17, which share a common roof.

The façade of No. 15 is faced with grey stock bricks of a rather reddish colour and inferior quality that were laid with indifferent skill. They appear to be laid in Flemish bond but are, typically, merely a 4-in casing over 9-in piers of place bricks. Internal recesses below the windows mean that here the façade is no thicker than the 4-in facing skin. Floor joists that run into this façade are housed into a soft wood bressummer or wall plate that spans along the piers from party wall to party wall and that acts as a lintel above the windows. The rubbed and gauged brick arches cover the timber lintel in a handsome manner but, like the façade, are only a decorative veneer contributing virtually nothing to the structural stability of the house.

The reason behind this type of mock construction was simply one of economics, as will be revealed when the cost of building this façade is discussed.

We have seen that place bricks cost 14s. per 1,000; grey stocks, wrote Langley, could cost from 18s. per 1,000 from the kiln up to £2 7s. if delivered and of picked quality and colour matched. Ware in 1756 priced grey stocks at £1 per 1,000, while the building account of No. 2 Fournier Street priced red stocks (superior to grey stocks) at £1 15s. per 1,000, and the 1727 accounts for the minister's house at Bloomsbury priced grey stocks at £1 10s. per 1,000.

Langley gave a cost for a rod of brickwork that contains 2,000 grey stocks and 2,500 place bricks and recommended a method of bonding so that the two types of brick could be fully and regularly bonded. This method would consume more expensive grey stocks than the double-skin method (the ratio of grey stock brick to place brick is one to two in Elder Street but four to five in the Langley method) and assumes that the place bricks used are of high quality, being of regular shape and the same size as stock bricks. With cheap place bricks – that

Second-floor front room: here the panelling is of the simple square-framed sort and the cornice has been reduced to a cyma recta and cyma reversa only.

is the sort used by most speculative builders – this co-ordination could not easily be achieved. The materials of which place bricks were made and the way in which they were fired tended to make them odd sizes and shapes, while statutes controlling brick sizes even specified that place bricks and stock bricks should be of different dimensions. The relevant statute for No. 15 Elder Street, passed in 1725, specified that stock bricks were to measure $9 \times 4\frac{1}{2} \times 2\frac{1}{8}$ ins, while place bricks were to measure $9 \times 4\frac{1}{2} \times 2\frac{1}{2}$ ins (in 1729 dimensions changed and applied to all bricks made within fifteen miles of London, which were to measure $8\frac{3}{4} \times 4\frac{1}{8} \times 2\frac{1}{2}$ ins).

Langley's price for the construction of a brick wall $13\frac{1}{2}$ ins thick in true Flemish bond in which grey stocks and place bricks were properly integrated was £5 12s. $\frac{3}{4}d.$ per rod. This total was broken down into £1 15s. for 2,500 place bricks at 14s. per 1,000; £1 16s. for 2,000 grey stocks at 18s. per 1,000; 15s. for lime and 2s. $\frac{3}{4}d.$ for sand, making 17s. $\frac{3}{4}d.$ for mortar. 'Slacking, screening, etc.', of the lime and sand cost 1s. 6d. in labourer's time, while the labour of laying the bricks cost £1 2s. 6d. Langley pointed out that this total of £5 12s. $\frac{3}{4}d.$ was a prime cost sum and, with profits added for materials and labour, could rise to £6 7s. 2d. per rod. But, since Bunce and Brown were operating as their own builders and had probably developed special relationships with suppliers, it is reasonable to assume that a rod of facing brickwork at No. 15 Elder Street cost the lowest of the prices, especially since a rod here contained fewer expensive grey stocks than in Langley's equation. It is, therefore, likely that the cost of a rod would have been somewhere around Salmon's £5 10s.

But we shall take Langley's figure for the sake of analysis. First of all, it shows us that laying grey stocks well and bonding them with place bricks took a lot more trouble than building place brick party walls. The £1 2s. 6d. for workmanship, when broken down into 3s. a day for a bricklayer and 2s. for his labourer, reveals that the rod took four and a half days to lay at the standard rate of 1,000 bricks per day. Second, we see from the relationship between total labour costs (£1 4s.) to material costs that materials are nearly three and a half times more valuable than labour.

This differential between labour and material costs explains the economic basis behind the mock Flemish bond wall and many other eighteenth-century building practices. Clearly it paid the builder to employ a labourer to cut bricks in half if, by doing this, he could save on the number of expensive facing bricks used. The high value of materials (all of which, whether sawn timber or hand-moulded bricks, reflected a lot of hard toil and man hours in manufacture) also explains why it was common practice to pack all manner of odd bricks and parts of bricks into the construction of a house even when, to modern eyes, it would seem to have been easier, as well as better, to use whole items.

The economic background to this practice was acknowledged – and condemned – by Langley:

For the sake of saving about 400 grey-stocks in a rod of work, whose value is not half a crown, Bricklayers will often carry up the face of a building of a brick breadth only, for eight, ten, nay even twelve courses together before they bond in upon the place-bricks: so that, in fact, the whole wall, though of a brick and a half in thickness, is very little stronger than a one brick wall; because, between the grey-stock and the place-bricks, there is an almost continuous upright joint. Which is not only a very great deceit, but, in lofty buildings, is dangerous.[7]

As Langley suggested, a vertical section through one of these two-skinned façades would show that a grey stock header bonded back into the place brick pier at about every eighth course.

This rhythm suggests the manner in which the façade was built. The bricklayer and his labourer would have had three piles of bricks on the scaffold: grey stocks, grey stocks snapped in half and place bricks. There may also, on occasion, have been two types of mortar: lime rich for the stock and extra sandy for the place bricks. Presumably, the place brick wall (9 ins thick in the case of No. 15 Elder Street) would rise, in sections, eight courses at a time – incorporating soft-wood bond timber to keep it stable while the slow setting lime mortar hardened.

After these eight courses had been raised, a 4-in skin of well-laid grey stocks would be run up in front of it – with the top, eighth course of this now being kept steady by being occasionally bonded into the place bricks behind. Also, if the grey stocks were run in a continuous band across the full width of the façade (which would be preferable, creating a more regular-looking end result), then, perhaps, a few headers were incorporated and left protruding to be absorbed by the flexible coursing of the place brick wall built behind. The two skins should butt together, but settlement of the load-bearing place brick piers, which were supported on the shallowest of corbelled foundations, decay of the soft-wood bond timbers, and resultant bowing movement of the 4-in façade, must have meant that the two skins were soon separated – a separation that snapped the few bond bricks that spanned the two skins. Certainly the $14\frac{3}{4}$-in width of the Elder Street façade at ground level suggests a possible $1\frac{1}{2}$-in gap between facing skin and pier.

The cost of constructing the façade of No. 15 Elder Street, which contains just over two rods of brickwork, would have been, at £5 10s. a rod, about £11 and would have taken about nine to ten days to complete – although it must be said here that the eighteenth-century working day was ten hours, from six until six, with an hour off for breakfast and dinner.

To this sum of £11 must be added the cost of a little stone work (the Portland stone coping), the pointing of the bricks and the cost of the brick arches. The accounts for No. 2 Fournier Street price arches at 1s. 3d. per ft. The No. 15 arches are simpler than those on the minister's house, but, at this rate, the eleven arches in the front elevation, each 3 ft 5 ins wide, would have cost around £2 7s. 1d. Although the cost of the facing brickwork should be a little less because it would have been reduced by around 40 sq. ft of arch work, it is reasonable to let the £11 total stand to represent the cost of the stone coping.

Pointing at No. 15 would probably have been of the usual flush pennystruck type in lime mortar, although a little tuck pointing does survive on the façade of No. 17. Tuck pointing – where a false thin join made of putty mortar (slaked lime and water with no sand) is placed on top of a camouflaged real joint – was much used in the eighteenth century to improve the appearance of relatively rough brickwork (see p. 105). Flush pointing in lime mortar could not have cost more than about 4d. a sq. ft, making the total cost of constructing the front façade of No. 15 about £20.

The rear façade of No. 15 seems to have been one and a half bricks thick and, to judge by the rear of No. 17, was of place bricks regularly, if somewhat randomly, laid. This façade, possessing fewer windows, had a surface area of around 681 sq. ft, which is about two and a half rods of brickwork. Langley's suggested price per rod of 'common jointed place-brick walling for carcasses of ordinary houses' was £5 4s. $\frac{1}{4}d.$ per rod, with the bricklayer and his labourer laying 1,000 bricks per day. The back elevation would, therefore, have cost around £12 10s. 1d. and taken about eleven and a half days to build.

The subtotals can now be combined to give a total for the construction of the brick shell: £12 10s. 1d. for the rear elevation; £20 for the front elevation; and £32 14s. $2\frac{1}{2}d.$ for the party walls and flues, although half the cost of one party wall must be shared with No. 17 so this subtotal is reduced to £26 17s. $8\frac{1}{2}d.$ Last, there is the cost of building a chimney-stack that, containing roughly two thirds of a rod of jointed place brickwork, would have come to about £3 10s. So the final total cost of the shell is £62 17s. $9\frac{1}{2}d.$, taking one team of bricklayer and labourer forty-four to forty-five days to complete.

Although the London terrace house of the 1720s appears to be a brick building, it does contain a great deal of structural and decorative timber. Not only are the roof, floor structure and covering, staircase and room partitioning of timber, but there is also a large amount built into the brickwork. Here there are bond timbers, laid to hold the wall firm while the lime mortar set and to provide fixings for panelling, lintels, wall plates and bressummers. The large amount of timber used meant that, for materials and workmanship, the joiners and carpenters' bill was at least as much as the bricklayers', with the final cost of the house – with bills from other trades such as plasterers, glaziers and plumbers added – probably being twice again the bricklayers' bill. This is the case with No. 2 Fournier Street, where the bricklayers and masons' bills represent roughly a third of the total building cost. This house is, indeed, not typical, being better built than its speculative contemporaries, but the extra quantity of brickwork (the house possesses a brick spine wall as well as stout stud partitions) is balanced by the unusual quality of the timber work. If this ratio of cost is correct, then the final cost of building and fitting out No. 15 Elder Street would have been in the region of £180.

To give an indication of the expense of internal joinery and finishing compared with bricklaying costs, it is only necessary to analyse the first-floor front room at No. 15 Elder Street. This room, the largest in the house, measures 15 ft 6 ins × 16 ft 2 ins and is 8 ft high. It is lit by two windows, has two doors, two cupboards in a panelled wall set flush with the chimney-breast (hence the room is 15 ft 6 ins wide compared with the 18-ft width of the plot) and possesses a large fireplace opening. The panelling, of pine, with ovolo (quarter round) moulding at the junction of panel and frame, was priced by Salmon in his *Palladio Londinensis* at 3s. 6d. per sq. yd, of which sum two thirds was for materials and one third (1s. 2d.) for workmanship. The room contains 45 sq. yds of panelling after deduction for the door and window openings, which, at 3s. 6d. per sq. yd, makes a cost of £7 17s. 6d. The doors and window shutters, because worked both sides, were costed at work and a half, making a total of £2 17s. 9d. The panelling was finished off with a full box-cornice that Salmon implied could cost from 1s. to 1s. 6d. per ft for work and materials (or 6d. to 9d. for workmanship alone). So taking the lowest figure, the cornice would have cost £3 3s. Add to this the cost of other moulded timbers – ogee door architraves, dado and skirting – and the total cost of the joinery in the room was in the region of £15. To complete the room, another £3 15s. would be spent on boarding the floor at the rate, recorded by Salmon, of £1 10s. per square. A square was 100 sq. ft and the Elder Street floor needed two and a half squares. Last, the plastering of the ceiling would have cost, according to Salmon, from 18s. to £1 11s. 6d. at the rate of somewhere between 8d. and 1s. 2d. per sq. yd. The final cost for panelling, floor and plaster would have been around £20.

All the wood used in No. 15 Elder Street is pine and all exposed surfaces were painted. The usual medium in the 1720s – indeed, throughout the eighteenth century – was white lead ground and mixed with linseed oil. The colours used in No. 15 were probably those typical of their time: a stone colour created by mixing yellow ochre with the white lead and a blue-grey lead colour created from indigo leaf, black and white lead.

Little evidence survives to reveal how No. 15 was occupied when first built. All that is clear is that the basement front room contained the kitchen – where a fine contemporary dresser survives – and that the ground floor, not the first floor, was the piano nobile. The ceiling height here is a few inches taller

than in the upper floors, and both ground-floor rooms contain panelling with ovolo moulded frames, while the box cornice in the front room is further embellished with a dentil-course. This hierarchy is confirmed by the staircase. From ground to the first half landing it possesses balusters with twisted shafts; from this half landing to second floor the plain balusters rise on an open string, and from second floor up they are housed in a more archaic closed string. The second floor panelling, like the first-floor back room, is simple square panelling, while the third floor possesses no panelling but a very simple post-and-panel partition dividing the stair and landing from the back room.

The type of person that would have lived in the house is revealed by its cost of construction and the 'rent' it was worth. Throughout the eighteenth century the rates each householder needed to pay the parish were calculated on the value of the house, and this value was expressed in terms of the notional rent that the house could command. Ware, in his *A Complete Body of Architecture*, suggests the formula by which house values and rents were related. He wrote that builders were generally ready to sell their speculation 'for fourteen years purchase exclusive of ground rent'. Inverting this, if we divide fourteen into the value of No. 15 Elder Street – £180 – we arrive at an annual rentable value of around £12 15s. But in reality No. 15 Elder Street was soon enlarged by the addition of a set of five rear rooms and so its cost, and value, were greatly enhanced. If its value after this addition was in the region of £250, the annual rentable value was around £18.

The first occupier, if he bought the remainder of the lease of No. 15 for cash, would have needed £100 or so to buy the roofed and floored brick shell and another £150 or so to complete the house as it stands today. If he merely rented the completed house (seemingly unlikely, given the building's individual finish), then he would have had to be able to pay an annual rent of about £18.

Surviving eighteenth-century budgets suggest that, on average, about one eighth of a working man's annual income went on rent.[8] This means that the occupier of No. 15 Elder Street would have to have been worth (after taxes) about £145 per annum. To put this figure in context it needs only to be stated that the average London working man – the sort of man that built No. 15, the journeyman carpenter, bricklayer or mason – could, at the rate of 3s. per day, have earned £40 per year at most and, with regular and unavoidable periods of unemployment, very much less. Quite clearly, even a relatively modest house like No. 15 would have been occupied by a member of the rich merchant class and was well beyond the reach of the average working Londoner able to pay only around £5 a year in rent.

NO. 2 FOURNIER STREET

In contrast to No. 15 Elder Street, very little has to be deduced about the means of construction and cost of building No. 2 Fournier Street. The detailed building accounts, lodged at Lambeth Palace, stretch from late 1726 to early 1731 and record who did what, how much they were paid, and how much materials and details cost. From these records it is easy to calculate that the final cost of constructing the house, after five years of intermittent work, was £1461 15s. – a colossal sum when compared with the cost of No. 15 Elder Street.

The story begins in the minute book spanning April 1718 to May 1728, which records the transactions of the commissioners charged with the task of fulfilling the 1711 Act for building fifty new churches in London. Christ Church, Spitalfields, begun in 1714, was one of the dozen churches finally completed.

Item 9 in the 12 July 1725 minutes 'ordered that ye surveyors do bring in a plan of a house for the minister of [Christ Church] together with the expense of building the said house'. The surveyors, Nicholas Hawksmoor and John James, acted very quickly, for, on the same day, they produced a rough estimate that, bearing their signatures, states, 'The minister house – £800'.[9] In item 6 of the same meeting it was noted that the tower and spire of the church were nearly finished. This underlines the fact that the church was nearing completion when the minister's house was commissioned and suggests that the house had not been regarded by Hawksmoor as integral to the setting of his church.

In November 1711, for another site in Spitalfields (in the corner of Brick Lane and Cheshire Street), Hawksmoor had designed an elaborate demonstration project. Entitled a 'Basilica for the Primitive Christians', this showed the church at the centre of an ecclesiastical complex that made a powerful urban composition. The church was surrounded by a wall. At the four corners of the wall were houses, and beyond the wall were small squares and a walled churchyard. One of the four corner houses was to be for the minister.

The reality fell far short of this ideal. The commission to design the house not only came more than ten years after the church was begun, but the site was merely the end plot of a terrace of speculative houses of varied design that were springing up in the shadow of the church. But, despite this unpromising site, Hawksmoor was able to create a building that bore a visual relationship to his monumental church while also fitting happily within the somewhat humdrum terrace.

Above: *Elevation, probably by Nicholas Hawksmoor and dating from July 1725, for the minister's house, Christ Church, Spitalfields. This design, very different to the building eventually constructed, seems to have been conceived for a freestanding site.*

Opposite: *The minister's house, as built between 1726 and 1731, next to Christ Church. The façade is of conventional 1720s design – segmental window arches and red brick window jambs – but of unusually substantial construction. The stone cornice on the house is a smaller version of that on the church.*

The design for the minister's house had been produced by 23 May 1726 when item 1 in the minutes ordered 'a minister's house for the Parish of Spittlefields according to the plan laid before the board by Mr Hawksmoor be built for a sum not exceeding one thousand pounds'. The design then 'laid before' the board was probably the version that was finally built, but this was certainly not the first, or only, design to be produced. Salted away amongst the palace archives is a rare thing: an early-eighteenth-century sketch of the elevation of a relatively modest town house.[10] The sketch is inscribed, in a contemporary hand, 'houses' and below 'Spittlefields'. It is a strange design – far more unusual than the elevation as built – and worthy of the hand of Hawksmoor. The design most likely dates from the time of the £800 estimate in July 1725 and was quickly superseded for various reasons, including, probably, the changing character of the site and the increase of costs. Certainly a commissioners' order of 29 April 1726 for Hawksmoor and John James to make plans for four ministers' houses, including Spitalfields, suggests a date by when this design had been abandoned.

The proposed elevation is free of the motifs that characterize the standard London terrace house of the 1720s – notably segment-headed windows and a plain flat-fronted elevation. Instead it has a striking, if miniature, monumentality in which Palladian and Baroque influences combine. Monumentality is given by the bold Tuscan torus-moulded base that ties the house to the ground and by the broad string- and sill-bands that imply a cornice level below the second-floor windows and that are used purely decoratively on the parapet. The Palladian presence is most notable on the square second floor, which reads as an attic above the implied cornice.

The clue to the reason for abandoning this design may lie in the breaking back of the chimney-stacks that flank the three-bay façade. It seems probable that this design was made when the minister's house was conceived as a free-standing building (as they were to be built at other new churches, notably St George-in-the-East and St John Horsleydown), rather than joined on to the end of a terrace. The terrace was not in existence when the design was most probably produced, for the building leases for the houses forming the rest of the terrace were not granted until 26 July 1726[11] – two months after the final Hawksmoor design had been approved.

It is now impossible to determine if it was the imminent arrival of this terrace that persuaded Hawksmoor to design a more conventional elevation or whether some other factor came into play. What seems certain, however, is that the design of the elevation as built is by Hawksmoor. Although it is a conventional 1720s design, complete with segment-headed windows and red brick dressings to window jambs, the elevation does possess a sense of monumentality and substance lacking in most of its neighbours, not least because the piers between the windows are as wide as the windows themselves. This was an Italian classical convention introduced into England by the Palladian movement; it replaced the old northern European classical tradition, seen in most of the Spitalfields terrace houses, where windows were considerably wider than the brick piers as a means of getting as much light as possible into the house. Much of this feeling of extra solidity comes from the fact that, in accordance with the 1709 Building Act, the sashes are set back from the façade. In fact, Hawksmoor had gone beyond what was required and set the sashes back by almost one full brick – nearly 8 ins. Apart from creating a strong visual impression of solidity in the wall, this detail reveals that the wall must be of truly unusual thickness. As shown by the analysis of No. 15 Elder Street, the wall of the average speculative terrace house was one and a half to two bricks in thickness (13–18 ins) at ground and first floor. The front wall of the minister's house must – with deep window reveals internally as well as externally – be two and a half bricks thick at ground and first floor.

The impression of monumentality is heightened by Hawksmoor's use of stone, unusual for the date, for both door surround and cornice. The door surround is a handsome Tuscan design of a Palladian sobriety and correctness. The cornice is strange. Its top member, a bold cyma recta directly over a corona, is a larger-scale version of the top member of the door surround cornice. But beneath the corona is a dentil-course – an Ionic detail – and below this there is a simple fascia finished with a bead mould, rather than the conventional frieze and architrave. If this eccentric cornice seems familiar, this is because it is a smaller-scale version of the cornice used on the church. By this simple repetition of motifs, Hawksmoor united, in the subtlest of ways, his minister's house with his church.

Within the house the same subtle balance is main-

Rear elevation of the minister's house: the pair of full-height canted bays are original.

Detail of the stone Tuscan doorcase. The door, typically for its date, is full height with no fanlight. The glazing bars to the right are late-eighteenth century and the area ironwork nineteenth century.

tained between originality of detail – an originality inspired by the particular circumstances of the site and use – and convention. This is revealed immediately upon passing through the front door. The entrance hall, within which the bold and beautiful stair rises, has walls that are panelled to three quarters height only. Above the panelling is an area of plaster and then a cornice that is another essay upon the cornice design of the church. Hawksmoor, in the manner of both Baroque and Palladian country house designers of the early-eighteenth century, conceived the hall as transitional spaces, as indeed he did the staircase landings above. They have half-panelling, simple bold details and exposed plaster. The effect created is of a semi-outdoor space, a space that mediates between the public realm of street and the private world of the room; not, perhaps, an inappropriate arrangement for a minister's house that must have been much visited by public and vestrymen on business.

It is instantly clear from the entrance hall that Hawksmoor did not use panelling here as a cheap form of room partitioning, as was the case in most contemporary Spitalfields houses. As the treatment of the hall reveals, panelling is used as an ornament, applied over timber stud or brick walls, with each room conceived as a panelled compartment fitted out in a fashion appropriate to its status or use. A couple of room descriptions confirm the point. The panelling throughout the ground and first floors is, with the notable exception of one room, raised and fielded. The panelling arrangement within the rooms is conventional, with ovolo mouldings set between frame and raised panel, but the cornices are more original. Rather than specifying the usual Doric box cornice, Hawksmoor decided on something bolder: he took just the top member of the Doric box cornice – the cyma recta over a small ogee or cyma reversa – enlarged the scale slightly, and finished his rooms with cornice detail that is free of association with any of the orders – an uncanonical cornice.

The original fireplaces that survive are in this same spirit of stripped-down astylar utilitarian classicism that characterizes one aspect of the early-eighteenth-century English Baroque school. This approach is best shown in the military buildings produced by the Board of Works when under Vanbrugh's control. At Spitalfields this spirit produced the fire surround that survives in the ground-floor rear room in the south-west corner. This was clearly an important room but the fire surround is remarkably simple – plain stone, with moulded edges to the slabs and radial corners linking the stone lintel with the stone uprights. The stone fire surround in the room above – also simple – is a more common early-eighteenth-century design. Here the lintel and uprights are panelled and separated by impost blocks from which spring the radial corners of the lintel.

The notable exception to the raised and fielded rooms is the second-floor back room that occupies the south-east corner of the building. Despite art-historical improbability, this room is fitted out with bolection moulding of the style that was meant to be extinct by 1700. As the account books reveal, this panelling is made from deal, not oak, and so was undoubtedly painted, although it could have been stained and grained rather than painted with the stone colour that probably covered most of the other panelling in the house. The treatment of this room must relate directly to its original use. It was not uncommon in the early-eighteenth century to locate the dining-room on the first floor, and it was also not uncommon to strike a note of ancient pedigree and masculine disdain for transient fashion in the decor of the dining-room. But, in this case, this room was probably not for dining but for parish use, and Hawksmoor thought it appropriate to invoke a gravity and an architectural quality that he must have known from late-seventeenth-century City vestry rooms and ministers' houses.

The plan of the house is, like many of its details, uncommon for speculative houses of the date, but not unknown in the early-eighteenth-century Baroque circle of which Hawksmoor was part. Most notable are the pair of canted bays that enlarge the back rooms and that form the faceted rear elevation. Bays, both curved and canted (half-hexagonal), were rare in the early-eighteenth century but were used fairly regularly by Vanbrugh (Blenheim, 1705–23;

Castle Howard, *c.* 1700–1726; Old Board of Ordnance, Woolwich, 1718) and by Thomas Archer (Chettle House, Dorset, *c.* 1720). The plan form is roughly a 30-ft square (excluding the bays) and divided into four quarters. The two rooms in the eastern half of the house are well balanced; both roughly 14 ft square (if the canted bay is excluded) and 10 ft high on ground and first floor, which makes them a permutation upon the favoured Neo-Palladian proportions of 2:3 or cube and a half.[12]

Also remarkable is the staircase. It occupies roughly a quarter of the plan area and, unique in Fournier Street, it rises against the front façade, leaving the rear of the house free for rooms to enjoy the tranquillity of the garden. This location brought with it problems as well as advantages. Most notable is the loss of the option, available on loosely symmetrical rear elevations, to arrange windows to suit the convenience of staircase landings. On the front elevation the uniform arrangement of the windows is paramount, so stair landings have, rather awkwardly, to cut in front of windows. This problem provoked Hawksmoor (or Samuel Worrall, the carpenter who built the staircase) to design an ingenious detail. Balustrades run across the window to prevent mischief, but these are hung on brass pins in sockets and can be unhooked to allow access to the glass and sashes for cleaning and maintenance.

In many other ways this staircase is a remarkable and revealing piece of work. It rises around an open well and is designed in three distinct stages that indicate the house's original hierarchy of occupation. From ground to first floor the stairs rise on an open string, with three balusters to the tread. The tread ends are carved. The balusters are of the common Doric column-over-urn type and are arranged so that a pair of balusters with twisted column shafts alternates with a single baluster with a straight column shaft. From first floor to second floor the design is a little simpler: the balusters rise on a deep closed string with twisted balusters alternating with plain shafted balusters. From second floor to third floor the balusters are all plain shafted. Clearly the ground floor was regarded as the floor of prime importance, with the first floor coming a close second. Although the means of ascending from ground to first floor was grand and implies that the progress was of importance and deserving of maximum pomp and circumstance, it must be remembered that, when at first-floor level,

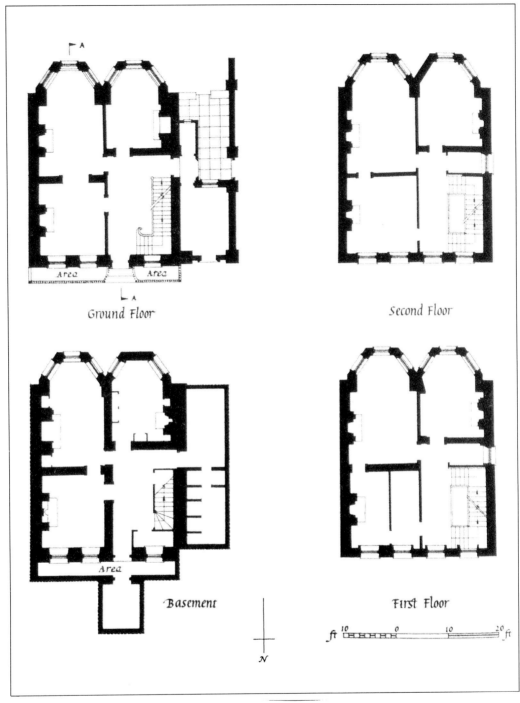

Plans of the minister's house, taken from The Survey of London. *The partition in the left-hand front room on the first floor is modern.*

the more modest work of the second flight was visible. The importance of a storey was not just revealed, and symbolized, by the grandeur of the stair leading to it but also by the less imposing appearance of the stairs ascending from it.

Enough evidence survives within the house and grounds to suggest the manner in which it was serviced. A vault beneath the pavement, reached via the area, was, no doubt, for the storage of coal. It is now impossible to be sure how these coals reached the vault. Coal holes in the pavement seem to have been a later-eighteenth-century development and the existing area ironwork dates from the nineteenth century, so it is now not possible to be sure if the area possessed a staircase. Area staircases were not universal in London until after about 1770 – presumably because their presence compromised the security provided by the moat-like area. If there was a stair, then it not only served the coalman but also those bringing other goods to the house, as well as those removing all manner of household waste and rubbish.

The main kitchen seems to have been in the back basement room in the south-east corner – certainly this possesses a large key-stoned fire surround within which would have been housed the cooking range. The other basement rooms fulfilled the function of living quarters for domestics, scullery and storage. A range of wine bins survives in the vault beneath the single-storey office attached to the western wall of the main house.

The walls of a bog house survive in the south-west corner of the garden – a usual location for such a building. It probably connected with a cesspit that, in turn, drained its liquid waste into the main sewer below the street with the residual solid waste being cleared from time to time by nightsoil men.

Locations for close stools within the house are suggested by the small closets fitted beside the staircase at first and second floor. These closets, each lit by an original window placed in the flank wall of the house, may not be contemporary with the building of the house. They are formed by simple square panel partitions set behind balustrading but with door architraves and furniture that appears to be of the 1720s. The space these occupy may simply have been generous landings whose form echoed the ground-floor plan where the northern wall of the south-west back room was set back to permit the creation of a door in the blank wall leading to

the church. This ground-floor plan reverberated, somewhat uselessly, to the upper levels, because the partition between the stair hall and the south-west rear room is built of masonry and so has to follow a perpendicular line through the full height of the house. If these closets were original, or even if they were later additions, they could have been used not just for close stools, but also for useful things such as dressing-rooms, powdering-rooms or even servants' bedrooms.

The Account Books

The account books not only show who was involved with building the house, what they were paid and what materials cost, but also reveal the sequence and peculiarities of construction.

The first accounts appear in the book of works dated from 25 March 1725 to 31 December 1726. These show that works must have started very soon after 23 May 1726, for by the end of the year (seven months later) the shell of the house had been completed, the timber of the roof constructed, the windows glazed, rain-water goods and cisterns installed and iron chimney bars fitted.

The total spent by 31 December 1726 was, according to the account book, £638 18s. 10d., although if the subtotals for the different trades are added up, the total is £639 15s. (I should note here that, on a couple of items, my readings of the account books differ from those of the *Survey of London: Vol. 27* and that the book of works records a total cost of £1,460 18s. 10d., while addition of the figures totals £1,461 15s.) Of this £639 15s. the largest amount went to Thomas Lucas, the bricklayer, who received £289 9s. 4d. for his work. This was completed by the end of 1726, for his name does not appear again in the accounts. He charged £5 15s. per rod and asked a total of £222 1s. 5d. for brickwork. The price per rod included an 'extra charge ... caused by the late Act of Parliament', which increased his price per rod by 8s., up to the £5 15s. charged. This must refer to the 1725 statute that not only fixed the size for place and stock bricks (see p. 141) but also ordered that brick earth should no longer be mixed with 'Spanish' (i.e., ground coal ashes). This ban, which made bricks sounder but more expensive, was lifted in 1729. The total for brickwork of £222 1s. 5d. suggests that the house contains around thirty-

The staircase at ground-floor level. The elaborate open-well stair, rising three storeys within a generous compartment, cost around £41 to construct.

eight and a half rods of brickwork or, at the rate of 4,500 bricks per rod, 173,250 bricks of various types. At the rate of 1,000 bricks laid a day, the brickwork of the house would have taken one team of brick-layer and labourer just over six months to complete.

We also learn from the accounts that 'Rubbed and gauged arches' to windows cost (at 1s. 3d. per ft) £11 4s. 6d. and that rubbed returns to window jambs cost (at 6d. per ft) £18 7s. 6d. The solidity of the structure is hinted at by the fact that 'inside arches' are mentioned at the cost of 2d. per ft. This implies that the place brick piers behind the facing bricks are connected by proper arches set behind the rubbed and gauged facing arches and not – as in most speculative houses – merely spanned by timber lintels or wall plates. That the house was roofed by the end of 1726 is made clear by Lucas's charge of £13 4s. for 'plain tyling'. Salmon, in his *Palladio Londinensis*, prices tiling at £1 12s. per square (i.e., 100 sq. ft). The roof area covers over nine squares on plan, so the price of £13 4s. suggests that this is the cost for covering all of the main roof of the house.

The Portland stone cornice, coping and door sur-rounds were complete by December 1726 and cost the commissioners £86 9s. 11d. for materials and labour. The mason, Thomas Dunn, had by 31 December 1726 yet to begin internal and external paving operations or work on the stone fire surrounds. The smith, John Roben, charged £7 10s. 6d., virtually all of which was for 'chimney bars'. Before cast-iron hob grates were mass-produced in the late-eighteenth century coal-burning fires were generally equipped either with movable basket grates or with bars set in decorative stone cheeks fixed into the fire surround. Such a fireplace survives in the second-floor front room of No. 14 Fournier Street (see colour plate).

The plumber, George Deval, charged twenty days' work at 3s. per day that, with materials, totalled £84 4s. 6d. For this he installed lead rain-water pipes, hopper heads and cisterns.

Samuel Worrall, the carpenter, charged £142 18s. 10d., for which he provided fir flooring and the roof structure, including four sashed dormers with 'ploughed and tongued cheeks to windows'. He also installed the stud partitioning on which internal panelling would be fixed. This account shows that a carpenter's rate was 3s. per day. The last sum was £19 1s. 1d. to Jos. Goodchild, the glazier. He supplied 'crown glass in putty for the windows', but this seems to have been an over-optimistic move, for he had to be recalled four years later and paid a further £2 15s. 9d. to reglaze thirty-eight sash squares at 11d. per ft and clean the lot at 4½d. a dozen panes.

An item in Worrall's account in the book of works (dated 1 January 1726/7 to 25 March 1728) and one in an account by Thomas Dunn (dated 25 June 1729 to 25 March 1731) confirm that completed work was being damaged by accident and had to be secured against theft and vandalism. During this period Worrall charged £16 9s. 3d. (at the rate of 3s. a day for a carpenter and 2s. for a labourer) for 'mending the fences, gates, windows, shutters and doors to the house' and 'making good the damage done to ye house in building a wall'. Dunn's charge was for 'mending the tiling for the roof'. In the later stages the value of the completed work, or the threat of theft, prompted the commissioners to hire a watch-man, one Stephen Hall, for 'one hundred days watching from 25 June 1729 to ye 18 October fol-lowing' for £5.

The slow rate of progress to completion and occu-pation reflected not only that the house was being built by the same complement of men working on the church, who, presumably, only worked on the house when church commitments permitted, but also that the house was simply not needed until the church was complete.

The 25 March 1725 to 31 December 1726 set of accounts offers one more piece of information. They were signed and approved by Hawksmoor and John James but not until August 1727, suggesting that the craftsmen had to wait at least eight months – or as much as two years – to get paid for the work they had undertaken.

The next book of works dates from 1 January 1726/7 to 25 March 1728. During this period Thomas Dunn charged £186 4s. 9d. for the 'chimney pieces in the house' and for 'paving in the cellars, the steps to the front door, and curbs under iron work there'. Going into more detail, Dunn is recorded as supplying 'Portland chimney pieces 3 ins thick at per ft 2s.'. The total for this work was £18 6s., suggesting that he provided 183 ft of stone fire surround. The two surviving upper-floor fire surrounds contain about 12 ft of stone, suggesting each cost as little as £1 4s. to make. The house contained twelve fireplaces, so that this total of 183

sq. ft of stonework sounds appropriate given the large width of the basement surrounds, the surviving one of which is over 8 ft wide. Dunn also provided 'white and veined marble squares for foot paces [hearth stones]' to the grander rooms, 'rigate [Reigate stone] hearths' for the more modest ones and 8 18 ft 6 ins of common Purbeck at $7\frac{1}{2}d.$ per ft – no doubt for the basement. Dunn also provided 277 ft 9 ins of Purbeck laid in terrace at $8\frac{1}{2}d.$ per foot. Terrace probably refers to terrace mortar, which was for use in particularly damp areas – no doubt the wine bins under the single-storey western extension. Dunn referred to 18 sq. ft of Purbeck step at 2s. per ft – this may refer to area steps, although the length of flight sounds unlikely for this location.

As well as other stone details (such as 'work on three sink stones' at 1s. each) Dunn catalogues a good deal of brickwork, which suggests that bricklayer's and mason's work was interchangeable to a degree, although it must be pointed out that all the brickwork mentioned by Dunn is of a pretty rough type, while all the face and decorative brickwork was undertaken by Lucas. For example, Dunn refers to 'turning trimmer arches to all chimneys in the house' – this, presumably, refers to the brick covings to take the hearth stones; he charges for 'the brickwork in the vault, bog house, area walls, and under ye window curbs in the back front and wall west side of the house'. He also undertook paving with red stock bricks at 1s. 8d. per yd and 'common flat bricks' at 1s. 4d. per yd. The small totals for these, 5s. 10d. and £1 13s. 4d. respectively, suggest that this $25\frac{1}{2}$ yds of paving refers to the garden path to the bog house and the area between the western flank door to the church and the garden wall.

It is in these accounts that we learn the cost of bricklayer's materials: £1 5s. for 1,000 place bricks, £1 15s. for 1,000 red stocks and £1 10s. for 1,000 plain tiles. We also find that a mason was paid 3s. a day and his labourer between 1s. 8d. and 2s. per day.

The mason's role in this particular job was very far ranging. As well as taking on bricklaying and paving, Dunn also cleared 'the rubbish out of the cellars' and made 'drains to carry the water out of the same, claying the crowns of the vaults and levelling the ground for ye masons to lay their paving ... raising and levelling the ground in the kitchen area, vaults and yard for the masons to lay their paving'.

This description raises a couple of particularly interesting points. First, what was the 'rubbish' that had to be cleared out of the cellars? This could mean waste material that had fallen in during construction or soil that needed still to be excavated to gain full depth for the basement rooms. It could, on the other hand, have meant rubbish pure and simple. A reference in the same book of works to the construction of the minister's house at Smith Square, Westminster, includes a charge by bricklayer William Tufnell for 'carrying in rubbish to raise the ground in ye cellars'. At 14s. 6d. the 'rubbish' seems to have been a fairly expensive material.

Recent excavations of Spitalfields basements (an inevitable part of conservation and the recent high number of house repairs) reveal that all are built on a bed of domestic rubbish. The district could have been thickly strewn with broken Delft tiles and plates, slipware, bags of ox bones and clay pipes left by city refuse dumpers before the houses were built, but more likely the rubbish was, as at Smith Square, part of the building process. In this case Dunn was probably charging for removing part of the rubbish fill that had been used either to level the site and act as a sort of hard-core 'gravel' layer to help drainage, or as packing to help provide a firm footing for the foundations. It is probably significant that Tufnell, in the same passage in which he mentions raising the cellar level with rubbish, referred to 'wheeling and laying ground round the house to keep the water from soaking into the foundations'.

The second point is drainage. Dunn recorded 'making drains to carry the water out' of the cellars, but it was not until some time between 25 March 1728 and 24 June 1729 that one William Tayler made a sewer '2 ft 6 ins wide, 5 ft high, $1\frac{1}{2}$ brick walls, 1 brick arch, paved at the bottom' for Dunn's drains to flow into. The account books record a

Opposite: The stair at first-floor landing level. The hierarchy of the house's occupation is revealed in the staircase design. From ground floor to first floor the stair is at its most elaborate, with alternating twisted and plain balusters set on an open string embellished with carved tread ends. From first floor the alternating balusters are set on a simpler closed string. On the higher level the balusters are all plain. The balustrade across the window unclips for cleaning.

payment of £17 to Tayler, who, presumably, obtained payment from other occupants of the street for the use of his sewer. The residents of Fournier Street would have had to contribute to the construction of the sewer, as well as pay a regular rate for its use. This rate paid to the Commissioners of Sewers was only one of several rates or taxes that the inhabitants of both Fournier Street and Elder Street would have paid to the government (window tax, land tax) and to the parish (lighting, cleaning and watching). A rate book of 1743 for the parish of Christ Church, Spitalfields, includes a little about the Spitalfields sewer.[13] The sewer had 'its current from Frying Pan Alley, Petty Coat Lane, through Spitalfields division to Limehouse dock, Limehouse', and the eleven 'justices and commissioners' were empowered to raise £493 17s. 3d. a year from the users of the sewer for 'defraying the charge of casting, cleansing, reforming and amending the common sewers'. On average the inhabitants of Fournier Street paid a rate of 11s. 6d. each per annum, a rate that was assessed on the size and value of their houses. The inhabitants of nearby Wilkes Street paid on average 10s. each per annum, because their houses were generally smaller than those in Fournier Street.

Having carried out the main structural timber work by December 1726, Samuel Worrall completed the carpenter's contribution to the house at the cost of £251 15s. 7d. during the next fifteen months. He clad the floors with deal boards: those in the best rooms were dowelled together for a close fit. The common boarding cost £2 10d. per square and came to a total of £38 8s. while the dowelled boarding cost £5 per square and made a total of £17 15s. He also undertook to provide some of the interior panelling, trespassing, it seems, on the realm of the joiner. Worrall charged £22 1s. 3d. for 176½ yds of 'deal square work' at 2s. 6d. per yd, which is exactly the same price given by Salmon in 1734 for 'plain square Wainscoting with Deal'.

This, the simplest of panelling, was probably for dado panelling in upper rooms and for the basement rooms and kitchen (which gets a specific mention with a charge for a 17 ft 'Double deal dresser with three turn'd bearers 3½ ins square, two ft high at per ft 1s. = 17s. total'. The account book relates also that Worrall charged for 67 ft 6 ins of 'double deal doors, bead raised ... at 1s. per ft', 36⅓ yds of ¾-in deal skirting board at 2s. 3d. per yd, £4 9s. 4d. for

an oak doorcase and £54 18s. 9d. for 'window sashes and frames sliding double at per foot 1s. 6d.'. But it is the costs related to the staircase that are most interesting, because it is possible to relate these to staircases in other houses and to see exactly what the commissioners got for their money. Twenty-three deal steps, '3 ft 10 ins going on 11 ins treads, 7 ins risers with moulded nosing', cost, at 10s. each, £11 10s. This refers to the steps of the grandest flight leading to the first floor. Then a 'four ft run of [circular?] steps at 4s. per ft'. This must refer to winders that connect straight flights and landings. Finally, '33½ deal steps ... 3 ft 10 ins going on 11 ins by 6 ins', each at 7s., totalling £11 14s. 6d.

So much for the treads. There is a charge of £9 12s. for a '48 ft 6 ins run of deal rail and ballusters 3 ft high ... half turned and half twisted at per ft 4s.'; £1 4s. for a '3 ft run of the same ramp't and twist at per ft 8s. 10d.' and '£3 for a 10 ft run of ditto ramp't only at per ft 6s.'. Finally, Worrall charged £2 14s. for an 108-ft run of 6-in deal architrave at 6d. per ft. This, presumably, was used for embellishing the closed strings of the upper flights.

Thus the carpenter's bill for this stair, including materials and labour, was £40 10s. 6d. But more has yet to be added, for the wood carvers' (Thomas Darby and Gervas Smith) only contribution to this house was to provide sixteen 'brackets to end of steps, carved, 9 × 4 ins each at 1s. 6d.', making a total cost of £41 14s. 6d. for the staircase.

Salmon, in his *Palladio Londinensis*, broke down carpentry and joinery costs into materials and labour, and suggested that about one third of the total was for labour (although for more detailed work like balusters the ratio is nearer 1:1). On this basis we can calculate that, of the £41 14s. 6d. total for the staircase, about £14 was for labour. Since we know from the account books that a carpenter was paid 3s. per day and a labourer between 1s. 8d. and 2s. a day, it would have taken a single carpenter about ninety-four days to construct the staircase or a carpenter and labourer team about fifty-six days.

It was during 1 January 1726/7 to 25 March 1728 that the joiner, plasterer, painter and wood carver made their contribution to the construction of the house. By comparison with the carpenter, the joiner, Gabriel Appleby, played a minor role. He charged only one sum, £93 19s. 1d., which included £78 1s. 8d. for providing 468½ sq. yds of 'Deal Beadwork ... pannels raised square'. This refers to the fielded

One of the carved tread ends on the ground-floor flight. This cost 1s. 6d. to carve in 1727 or 1728.

panelling with ovolo moulded frame that fits out most of the ground and first floor and that was priced at 3s. 4d. per yd. Appleby also supplied 'fir door cases' – presumably the architrave door surrounds – at 7d. per ft and 'double deal doors' with 'a bead on one side raised square' at 1s. per yd.

The plasterer, Isaac Mansfield, charged £34 3d. for lathing and plastering at 1s. per yd, rendering at 4d. per yd and whiting at 1d. per yd. Whiting – painting plastered surfaces with a mixture of ground chalk and size – was the only painting that fell on the plasterer's side of the division of responsibilities between plasterer and painter.

The painter was James Preedy, who charged a total of £43 12s. 8d., most of which (£37 4s. 2d.) was for painting 893 yds 'four times ... on wood at per yd 10d.'. He also charged for painting ironwork at 1s. 4d. per yd and £1 16s. for painting the thirty-six sash frames and 2d. each for painting the 'sash lights'. Unfortunately, no indication is given of colours used. It is somewhat puzzling that this house now contains thirty-eight sashes (excluding the

dormers), with two being on the flank elevation lighting the closets behind the stairs. The detailing of these two flank windows looks original but the painter's account suggests that they may be later alterations.

George Deval, the plumber, charged a further £49 1s. 7d. for work and materials including a 'pump with iron work, bucket and sucker' for £3 and £20 6s. for lead sash weights. Deval in this account confirms that a plumber charged 3s. per day.

John Roberts, the smith, also charged a further £25 6s., mostly prime cost sums, for items such as 'two 12 in home-made iron rim'd locks to ye outer doors at £1 each ... H hinges ... rising side hinges for shutters at per pair 2s. 6d. and various types of nails and screws'. Another smith, John Cleave, now appeared on the scene. He may have been more of a locksmith than Roberts, for his bill (£42 13s. 5d.) is mostly for locks: 'two large iron rim'd locks for outer doors each at 15s. ... a new stock lock to a door 2s. ... a pair of large round bolts and plates for outer doors, 15s. ... H hinges for doors at per

The bolection-moulded pine panelling in the first-floor back room on the east. The dado panels, hidden by the radiators, are raised and fielded. Instead of the usual box cornice, Hawksmoor used a bold cyma recta and cyma reversa profile.

16s. 11d., an iron rim'd lock and key for an iron gate 7s. 6d.'. This last item relates to the 'iron gates and railings' that cost £31 7s. 9d. These must be the area railings, and the gate and lock suggest the presence of an area stair, although it was common practice in the late-eighteenth century (and probably in the early-eighteenth century as well) to provide gates in area railings even when stairs were not constructed. These gates provided easy access into the area, and so into the basement, for heavy goods such as casks, which would be lowered down by block and tackle (see p. 87).

The works undertaken between 1 January 1726 and 25 March 1728 cost £727 17s. 4d. and left the house virtually complete, although it was to be another three years before final completion. These accounts were 'measured, weighed and costed up by John James', with all tradesmen being paid by 4 December 1728 – a great improvement over the previous tardy payments.

Accounts appear in two more books of works, but they record very little activity. In the books recording works from 25 March 1728 to 24 June 1729 there are only two references to the minister's house. One records the payment of £17 already mentioned to William Tayler for a sewer; the other records a further payment of £24 8s. 5d. to the plumber, George Deval. This time these sums were approved by Hawksmoor as well as James.

The book of works from 25 June 1729 to 25 March 1731 records the final stages of the house's construction. As we have seen, the glazier was brought back during this period to repair thirty-eight panes of glass, but Worrall was also to claim another £20 1s. He not only charged £3 for 'new hanging thirty windows with some new lines and lead weights' (this must represent repair of damage, for it was Worrall who had installed the sashes initially so he could hardly charge for putting right faulty workmanship or for dealing with sticking or warped sashes) but also for making and fitting '26 yards of Deal bolexion panelling at per yd 4s.'. The

Detail of the cornice in the ground-floor back eastern room. This profile, at a smaller scale, was generally used at bedroom level or in main rooms in very humble houses. Hawksmoor used it at a large scale to achieve a bold simplicity.

installation of this panelling, which cost £5 4s. – along with a 'fir doorcase, 6 ft 10 ins × 3 ft 6 ins, for 10s. and 17 ft of 5 ins wainscot moulding at 1s. ½d. per ft' – completed the interior of the house. Thomas

Dunn, the mason, carried out a few repairs (mending the tiling of the roof as already noted), laid a few more flat paving bricks and 'filled in a drain and levelled the ground', all for £24 17s. 6d. With this the house was ready for occupation. This last account, for £52 14s. 3d., was approved by Hawksmoor and James, and all the tradesmen were paid on 6 October 1731.

A breakdown of these costs is revealing. The mason was paid a total of £297 12s. 2d. and the bricklayer was paid £289 9s. 4d. Since the mason was also involved in a certain amount of structural bricklaying, it is reasonable to add the two sums together to discover the cost of building the brick shell and of embellishing it with stone trim. This total of £587 1s. 6d. reveals that just over a third of the total cost of £1,461 15s. was paid to the bricklayer and the mason. It also suggests a neat formula for assessing the cost of constructing an eighteenth-century London house. When this £587 1s. 6d. is set against the total cost of carpentry and joinery, £508 14s. 6d., it is possible to say that, roughly, masonry costs balance timber costs and that together these represent roughly two thirds of the building cost, with the remaining third being accounted for by the operations of the other trades.

This theory can be tested against the costs specified in 1756 by Ware in *A Complete Body of Architecture* for the construction of the 'common' London house. Of four storeys and a garret, with three rooms on all the main floors and three bays wide, this house could, said Ware, be built for between £600 and £700. It would consume '32 rods 39 ft of 1½ brickwork ... at £5 15s. per rod', making a bricklayer's bill of £184 16s. 6d., or just under a third of the £600 total cost.

Nos. 5–13 Queen Anne's Gate, built between January 1770 and May 1771, are a product of the pattern-book, the Building Acts and late-Palladian urban convention. The designer was probably Emanuel Crouch. The house on the right was built c. 1704 and displays those details (wooden eaves cornice and box-sashes set flush with the façade) that were outlawed in 1707 and 1709.

Appendix Two

Case Study – Nos. 5–13 Queen Anne's Gate, Westminster

On 30 November 1769 the Court of Christ's Hospital considered a report by its committee of rentors. This report, dated 23 November 1769, stated that 'it is the opinion of this Committee that part of the hospital freehold estate in Carteret Street and Park Street West, being in a ruinous condition, and past repairing, be pulled down and rebuilt at the charge of the hospital'. The Court 'by Vote approved and confirmed the same'.[1]

The 'ruinous' buildings referred to were those built on the hospital's Westminster Estate in the late 1680s and that as early as 1726 were suffering from lack of maintenance and showing the signs of shoddy construction.[2] The five houses that were built following the decision of 1769 were known initially as Nos. 9–12 Park Street (with the corner house entered from, and numbered as, part of Carteret Street[3]). They were renumbered 13–17 Park Street, which, after 1847, changed to Nos. 14–18 Park Street. After the union of Park Street with the adjacent Queen Square to form Queen Anne's Gate in the late-nineteenth century, the houses were numbered 5–13 Queen Anne's Gate.

CONSTRUCTION

A subcommittee was appointed by Christ's Hospital for rebuilding the estate in Park and Carteret Streets and on 10 January 1770 recorded that 'Thomas Clark, bricklayer, proposed and agreed to take down several houses in Park Street, Carteret Street, Westminster, intended to be rebuilt under the direc-

tion of the Hospital Surveyor. To allow 10s. per square for the old tyling and 30s. per rod for the old brickwork.'[4]

This information is particularly interesting because it suggests that it was the habit to salvage and reuse building materials – a practice implied in eighteenth-century pattern-books[5] and to which reference is made in other surviving eighteenth-century building agreements and inventories.[6]

Having agreed that Thomas Clark should be 'allowed' the salvaged tiles and bricks, the document states that Clark agreed

to build five new houses, vaults, walls, etc., as shall be directed with hard well burned Grey Stock bricks. The fronts next the street to be cased with the best Malme Stocks and pointed in the best manner and the whole to be laid in good sound mortar with not less than 200 of lime to one rod of brickwork at £7 10s. per rod and 4d. per ft for the pointing, and 18d. per foot for the gauged arches over the windows. To lath the roof to a 7-in gauge with new double heart oak laths worth 3s. 6d. per bundle and plain tyle the whole in the very best manner with well burned sound tyles for 30s. per square providing all materials, carriage, scaffolding and labour and to carry away all the rubbish occasioned by the above mentioned works. The whole to be done in the most workman-like manner under the inspection and to the satisfaction of the Hospital Surveyor. The whole to be completed on or before Michaelmas day next.

The subcommittee also 'ordered that John Wilkinson Long, journeyman carpenter to this hospital, superintend the carpentry work and workmen in

rebuilding the said houses under the direction of the Hospital Surveyor'.

These specifications provide enough information to assess the cost of constructing each of these houses and reveal the way in which a late-eighteenth-century London terrace house was designed and built, although it must be emphasized that Nos. 5–13 Queen Anne's Gate are not typical. Unlike most of the domestic architecture of Georgian London, they were not built as speculations on a building lease from the ground landlord (see p. 111) but were financed directly by the landlord. Consequently we can expect the construction to be more substantial than the usual speculatively built London house, for Nos. 5–13 Queen Anne's Gate were not built shoddily to last the length of a 61- or 99-year lease (with the aim of making a quick return) but as a long-term investment. This development strategy also meant that the houses were fully finished internally (see p. 115), for, initially at least, the aim of the hospital was to let them on short leases with a rack rent (see p. 111) rather than follow the usual pattern of letting them on long leases as carcases to be fitted up by the first occupier, who would pay only a ground rent.

Why the hospital chose this relatively unusual course of action is not now clear. In 1759 the hospital viewing subcommittee had suggested that this site on the south side of Park Street be developed in the conventional way and 'let on a building lease'.[7] This course was pursued in 1774, when the hospital let the north side of Park Street on a 61-year building lease.[8] It can only be supposed that the 1769 decision to retain control of the rebuilding of the south side of Park Street must have had something to do with the fact that the speculatively built late-seventeenth-century houses on the site had decayed so quickly as a result of poor construction.

The description of the construction of these houses does, however, suggest that, like the average speculative house, they have a two-skin façade in which piers of inferior bricks are faced with a 4-in skin of more expensive bricks (see p. 106). Grey stock bricks took the place of cheaper, softer place bricks normally used for concealed, though structurally important, brickwork, with Malmes being used for the outer skin. This upgrading of the specification reflects the superior construction of these buildings. This supposition is supported by the fact that '200 of lime' for the mortar per rod of brickwork was specified. A common specification was a hundred and a quarter to a hundred and a half of lime per rod.[9]

Also the bricks – which measured $8\frac{1}{2} \times 4 \times 2\frac{1}{2}$ ins in accordance with the 1770 statute controlling brick size within fifteen miles of London[10] – were laid in a relatively generous manner. Four courses rise 11 ins, which ensured a finer joint than that produced by the usual four courses to 12 ins, but this meant more bricks to the rod – 4,875 said Batty Langley, as opposed to the conventional 4,500.[11] The use of Malmes is in itself interesting. They had a distinctly yellow cast and did not generally supersede grey stock as facing bricks in London until very late in the eighteenth century, although Robert Adam had used a very pale Malme at Kenwood House, Hampstead, as early as 1767.[12]

Significantly, perhaps, I. and J. Taylor did not include Malmes in the 1776 edition of their *Builder's Price Book*, but they did in the 1787 edition, under the name of Marls. They were very expensive. Best Marls cost £4 per 1,000 and common Marls £2 2s. 6d. per 1,000 when, by comparison, grey stocks cost only £1 15s. per 1,000.

The charge of £7 10s. per rod provides a good clue for assessing the construction costs of these houses. A rod is a $16\frac{1}{2}$-ft square of brickwork containing $272\frac{1}{4}$ sq. ft, and its price is calculated on the assumption that the $16\frac{1}{2}$-ft squares are one and a half bricks thick.[13] If the walls were thicker, then a simple formula (see p. 214) calculated the cost per rod according to the extra half brick beyond the standard brick and a half thickness.[14] In No. 11 Queen Anne's Gate, for example, the back and front elevations, including the basement, contain 2,352 sq. ft of brickwork that, after deduction of 512 sq. ft for doors and windows, leaves 1,840 sq. ft of superficial brickwork. The third floor is a brick and a half

Opposite: *Façade detail of Nos. 9 and 11: window width equals pier width; first-floor windows are double square in area; second-floor square and a half (or 3:2) with ground-floor something between the two. The window jambs and arches were painted red in the 1950s.*

thick, while the basement is two and a half thick. Allowing that these cancel each other out, both façades can be calculated at two bricks' thickness, which is the thickness of the wall between third-floor and basement levels. Applying Langley's formula (see p. 106), this 1,840 sq. ft of two-brick-thick walling reduces to nine rods. To this must be added the party walls, which contain 2,296 sq. ft of two-brick-thick ($2\frac{1}{2}$ bricks thick at basement level) brickwork, which reduces to roughly twelve rods – half the cost of which must be shared with the neighbouring houses (which, of course, enjoy the same party walls). In this agreement Thomas Clark did not differentiate between the types and cost of brickwork used. As Langley made clear in his *London Prices of Bricklayer's Materials*, the cost in time and money of constructing rods of 'common rough unjointed place brick walling' suitable for 'party walls' was very different from the cost of constructing facework in grey stocks (see p. 105).

Presumably Clark's £7 10s. a rod is an averaging out. This would explain the relatively modest charge when compared with the Taylors' figure of £8 5s. for a rod of mixed place and grey stock with an extra £3 per 1,000 bricks if the wall were 'faced with best Marl Stock'[15] and William Pain's £12 a rod in 1786 for 'new fronts faced with best Malme stocks, inside Grey Stocks'.[16] This charge per rod could also mean that Clark acquired his bricks at prime cost, directly from the kiln, and so avoided paying a retailer's profit – a system recommended by Langley.[17]

In addition to the bricks of the party walls this calculation must include the brickwork of the pair of internal walls that enclose the central staircase. These, ranging from a brick to half a brick thick, represent – roughly – a further four rods to make a total of twenty-five rods of brickwork in the carcase and internal partitioning of one of the Queen Anne's Gate houses. In working out this total the cost of the twelve rods of the party wall must be reduced by 50 per cent to reflect the shared cost with neighbouring houses (which brings the number of rods per house down to nineteen), and the resulting total must be rounded up to take into account the extra bricks used in the chimney-breasts, stacks and hearths. On this basis it seems reasonable to conclude that the total cost for brickwork – all materials, labour and scaffolding included – was around £150 per house. Also, it is possible to

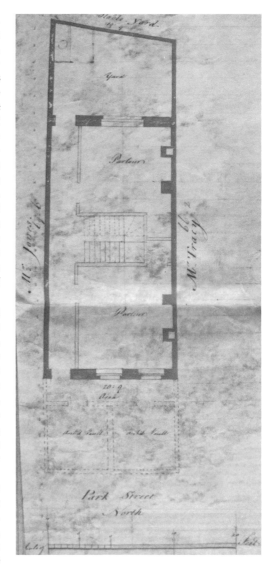

Above: *Ground-floor plan of No. 11 Queen Anne's Gate from the first lease, dated 3 September 1773. The family lavatory can be seen in the rear yard. On the first floor the back and front rooms stretch the full width of the house.*

Opposite: *Staircase in No. 11 at first-floor level looking towards a closet door on the half-landing. The dramatic ramp of the handrail, with an elongated baluster, is a notable detail. The design of the newel and baluster is decidedly old-fashioned for the date.*

First-floor front room in No. 11: the dado is composed of flush panelling set an inch or so forward of the wall surface above.

extrapolate from this total of nineteen rods per house that, at an average of 4,500 bricks per rod (the eighteenth-century rule-of-thumb number of bricks per rod[18]), each house contained around 85,500 bricks, which represents $85\frac{1}{2}$ man-days' labour for a bricklayer and labourer team on the basis that they would lay on average 1,000 bricks a day (see p. 213).[19]

Applying the basic rule that only 20 per cent of any brickwork bill is for labour (see p. 214), then the wage paid for this work was around £21 in total or about £1 1s. 4d. per rod – a figure that compares well with the Taylors' 'labour only to brickwork £1 6s. per rod'[20] and with the '20s. to 30s. per rod for labour [and] scaffold' that Chambers recorded in May 1771.[21] This rough total for labour is confirmed by the fact that, as the Taylors' *The Builder's Price Book* of 1776 tells us, bricklayers were paid about 3s. a day and labourers 2s. (see p. 121), so $85\frac{1}{2}$ days × 5s. = £21 7s. 6d.

In addition to this £150 there were also the brick-work charges related to the construction of the gauged brick arches, pointing and the tile roofing.

Each house possesses twenty-one gauged brick arches that, with windows at 3 ft 5 in wide and arches charged at 1s. 6d. per ft, totals £5 8s. The 4d. per ft for pointing was per sq. ft and reveals that pointing was a very expensive business. The front façades of Nos. 5–13 Queen Anne's Gate each contained about 196 sq. ft of brickwork (minus areas of gauged brick arches) to be pointed (196 × 4d. = £3 5s. 3d.). So pointing a façade of relatively modest size was roughly as expensive as buying and laying 2,000 bricks.

What kind of pointing consumed so much time? In the Taylors' 1776 edition of *The Builder's Price Book* 'tuck-and-pat' pointing (see p. 105) cost 5d. a ft on new brickwork, while in their 1787 edition it cost 4d. per ft. The evidence that the pointing was originally tuck and pat is further strengthened by a building agreement of April 1770 for the con-struction of a dwelling house and bakehouse in Fore Street, Limehouse.[22] In this agreement it is specified that the builder of the three-storey pair on a roughly 38-ft frontage 'will point down the front of the buildings with tuck point in a good and workmanlike manner for the sum of £5 5s.' – a figure that corresponds well with the £3 5s. 3d. cost for pointing the slightly smaller Queen Anne's Gate frontage of 20 × 43 ft that, to this

day, retains substantial remains of tuck pointing.

Further light is thrown on the costs and appli-cation of tuck-and-pat pointing by Langley who, in his *London Prices*, said that bricklayers were generally paid 6d. to 9d. per ft superficial for tuck-and-pat pointing, which 'takes up a great deal of time' and which could double the price of a rod of brickwork (see p. 105). This extravagance seemed to baffle Langley, who felt that 'nothing can come up to this monstrous imposition' and 'no person ... (unless mad) will go to such an expense'. In any case, it had but an 'ill effect'.

The roofs, consisting of three pitches with their ridges running parallel to the façade and with lead flats in between, were covered with tile, except for a large portion of the centre pitch that was glazed and top lit the central staircase. It is interesting, however, that even for high-quality houses like these, 'well burned tiles' rather than slates were still being specified as late as 1770.

Each roof contains about $7\frac{1}{2}$ squares of tile area (a 'square' being 100 sq. ft) that, at 30s. a square, totals £11 5s. To this must be added the cost of the 'double heart oak laths', costing 3s. 6d. per bundle. According to Langley, a 'bundle' would contain 480–500 ft, according to the length of the laths, and one bundle would be needed per square. The cost of laths per roof was therefore roughly £1 6s. 3d. Langley also wrote that '654 $\frac{6}{11}$ tiles are needed to cover a square at a 7-in gauge', which means that each roof comprised about 4,908 tiles. The Taylors recorded, in their 1776 edition of *The Builder's Price Book*, that plain tiles cost £1 10s. per 1,000. So tiles alone cost £6 7s., with the remaining £4 18s. for labour, mortar and scaffold. If subtotals of £150 for the carcase and internal walls, £5 8s. for the gauged brick arches, £3 5s. 3d. for the pointing, and £12 11s. 3d. for the roofing are put together, the total is £171 4s. 6d. for workmanship and materials for the shell and internal brick partitioning of a Queen Anne's Gate house. To this total must be added other costs: carpentry for floors, room partitions and stairs; joinery work for doors, architraves, dados, skirtings, windows, balusters, chimney-pieces and doorcases; plastering work for walls, ceilings and cornices; masonry work for paving, sills and fire surrounds; plumbers' work for lead to the roof, cistern and pipes; smiths' work for railings and bars; glaziers' charges; painters for inside and outside work in oil paint; and upholsterers' work for papering the various rooms. The final total would be a little more than the usual ratio (see p. 235), in which total cost divides into one third bricklayers' bill and two thirds other work. This would suggest that the final cost per house was somewhere between £550 and £650, which relates very closely to Ware's statement in *A Complete Body of Architecture* that a 'common house in London' (three rooms per floor, five floors high, three windows wide) can 'be built for between £600 and £700' (see p. 119). Ware gave further support to this estimate when he said that builders were generally ready to sell their speculation 'for fourteen years purchase, exclusive of ground rent' (see p. 219). The rack rent that was established for each of the Queen Anne's Gate houses in 1773 was £50 per annum (see p. 245), which, multiplied by fourteen, gave the house a value of £700 on the market.

The responsibility for the design and the supervision of the construction of the houses is made clear by the roles occupied by the three men mentioned, two by name and one by title, in the building agreement. Thomas Clark, bricklayer, is clearly the contractor whose 'proposal', or tender, on a Christ's Hospital building specification had been accepted. John Wilkinson Long is a more curious appointment. He was a journeyman – so a salaried carpenter, not a master – employed by Christ's Hospital, presumably on a regular basis, to supervise or carry out maintenance works on their many properties. He was the clerk of works, superintending 'the carpentry work and workmen' and protecting the interests of the client. The designer of the building must have been the Hospital Surveyor, who is cited as having 'direction' of the works that had to be completed 'to his satisfaction'. In the eighteenth century the term 'surveyor' was synonymous with architect[23] and the Surveyor to the Hospital in July 1770,[24] when these houses were being built, was Emanuel Crouch. He was still Surveyor in November 1771 when the houses were completed.[25]

Another piece of information revealed by this building agreement is the length of time it took to construct the five houses. If work began soon after the building agreement was approved on 10 January 1770 and completed on schedule ('Michaelmas day next') then these houses took about eight and a half months to build – a not unusual rate of construction (see p. 131),[26] with five teams of bricklayers and labourers being able to complete the shells in about

eight and a half months (see p. 218). Much of the internal detailing would have been prefabricated during the same period by carpenters, joiners and masons.

Certainly by May 1771 the houses were complete, for on 20 May they were inspected by the hospital viewing subcommittee, which reported that 'nothing beneficial can be done with these new buildings till the high wall parting this street [Park Street] from Queen's Square is either taken down or lowered and iron rails placed thereon, or an opening made through the same. We are also of the opinion that the pavement in this street be properly raised.' For reasons now difficult to explain, these new houses were not immediately offered for letting – perhaps the hospital aspired to higher rents than the blighting presence of the wall and the ruinous houses and rowdy cockpit opposite made it possible to achieve.

A year later the viewing subcommittee returned to the street: 'we examined the five new houses and are of the opinion when painting and papering is finished they will be worth £60 a year each, the Hospital allowing the land tax, and as it must be for the interest of the Hospital to have them occupied as soon as possible therefore recommend they may be immediately advertised to be let for seven years only'. The new development also contained, behind the houses, 'nine coach houses, six rooms over ditto, and eighteen stalls for horses new built'. These, the viewing subcommittee recommended, should be let on the basis of 'horsestalls £3 a year each, coach houses £5 and six apartments at £1 10s. each'. This could make the hospital 'one hundred guineas a year with the Hospital paying all the taxes'. On 16 December 1772 the committee of rentors finally 'agreed that the new houses on the south side of Park Street West be advertised to be lett for seven years from Lady Day [25 March] 1773'. This obviously proved a success, as all five houses were occupied by the end of 1773.[27]

The short lease confirms just how different this development was from the generality of London building operations. Not only did the hospital not follow the usual practice of leasing the land to a speculator on a building lease (see p. 111), but, when it had built the houses at great expense, it decided to let them on seven-year leases rather than the usual 61- or 99-year leases. This arrangement allowed for frequent review of the rack rent of £50, but was possible only for a relatively rich organization like Christ's Hospital, which could afford to have capital tied up in buildings from which it got a small but steady return. Only the most successful of speculating builders could afford to forgo the quick return of capital (enhanced with as much profit as possible) by selling on the completed shell and, instead, enjoy the benefit of a regular income in the form of rack rents from sublessees.[28]

INTERIORS

The decision by the hospital to let on short leases obliged them to decorate the houses and fit them out (even providing such details as internal door locks). An entry of 17 June 1773 in the Christ's Hospital committee minute book[29] records that plot No. 3 (plot No. 3 is now No. 9 Queen Anne's Gate) was to be let for £50 per annum clear of taxes (a £10 drop on the rent proposed by the viewing subcommittee in 1772) and that the house was 'to be completed painted, paper'd, proper locks put upon all the doors, the sashes and shutters properly hung with good fastenings to them and a leaden cistern to be erected with the hospital's arms thereon at the expence of the Hospital'. A cistern still survives at No. 9 Queen Anne's Gate (now in the yard), bearing the arms and initials of the hospital and dated 1774 – which suggests that its installation did not follow immediately upon this decision.

More detailed information is given in a lease dated 3 September 1773.[30] This lease between Christ's Hospital and Thomas Watson-Ward relates to plot No. 4 (now No. 11 Queen Anne's Gate) and was for a seven-year period, beginning midsummer 1773 and worth a yearly rent of £50, 'payable quarterly clear of all taxes'. An unusual omission on this lease

Front kitchen at No. 11: the fire surround and panelling are original, although early-eighteenth century in style: for functional parts of the house the Georgian builder had a tendency to revert to tradition, saving up-to-date fashion for the showier parts. The hob grate is a later insertion.

is that no restrictions are put on the activities that could be carried on in the house. This had been common practice from at least the early-eighteenth century and was standard on the Cavendish-Harley Estate,[31] the Grosvenor Estate[32] and the Bedford Estate[33] (butchers, tallow chandlers, soap-makers, tobacco-pipe burners and dyers were all prohibited). This omission was corrected in later leases for Queen Anne's Gate when the full range of uses mentioned above, plus a few others such as 'common brewers, distillers and pewterers' were prohibited from carrying on business in the houses.[34]

Attached to the lease of 3 September 1773 are a ground-floor plan and schedule that reveal how the house was decorated and fitted out, and suggest how it was occupied. This schedule was intended as a check-list of fittings that both parties agreed were in the house when the lease commenced and that should remain in it when the lease terminated or when the house was handed back to the landlord.[35] Consequently the schedule takes the form of a room-by-room description of the house as it stood ready for its first occupant in 1773.

We learn that the 'three pair of stairs' floor (the third floor) was divided into three rooms. The initial description of these rooms being fitted with 'brass knob locks and keys' and 'paper'd' was crossed out and replaced with the description that they were fitted with latches, were painted and skirted (with no reference to dado or cornice) and had simple 'single architraves' to the door. These rooms – a mere 7 ft high – were intended for servants or children (see p. 58), or to be used as dressing-rooms. Indeed, the small front room on the east side (one window, no fireplace) was fitted with a 'row of cloak pins', suggesting its use as a spacious clothes cupboard or a dressing-room sited conveniently near the bedroom floor below. The 'two pair of stairs front room', 8 ft 8 ins high, $15\frac{1}{2}$ ft deep and 19 ft wide, was 'dadoed and papered' with 'a plaister cornice on the top'. The shutters to the sash windows had 'six brass rings'. The chimney-piece was of 'veined marble' with slate slips and nosings; there was a 'fire stone hearth and covings and a wood shelf' (fire stone was a common name for Reigate stone[36]).

The room contained 'a closet with three shelves', presumably a reference to the dark closet (see p. 59) placed between the staircase and party wall, and serving both back and front rooms. This room

was also provided with 'one lock and key', probably for the closet, and 'a brass handle lock and key to the room door'. The second-floor back room was also 'dadoed and papered' with a 'plaister cornice on top ... brass rings to the shutters' and a 'closet with three shelves'. But here the chimney-piece was of 'Portland stone' – a notch down from the 'veined marble' of the front room. It is likely this was the second-best bedroom. Like all the back rooms, this was slightly smaller (12 ft 10 ins deep and 19 ft wide) than the front bedroom, possessing only two windows instead of three, and its view over the stable yard and coach-houses was no doubt thought less fortunate, despite its south orientation, than the view on to the street. The 'landing' was also 'dadoed and papered' with 'a plaister cornice on the top' with 'double architraves on each side of the door ways'. 'Double architraves' are full architraves rather than the mere ogee moulding planted around the doors on the third floor and called 'single architraves'.

The next room referred to is the 'Dining room'. From the previous, and the following, descriptions it is quite clear that this was the first-floor front room – an unusual though by no means unknown location for the dining-room in the late-eighteenth-century terrace house (see p. 54). This room was 'dadoed and papered', but now the plaster cornice is described as 'enriched', the door possesses more expensive 'mortice lock and key ... and brass furniture' and no mention is made of a closet. It can be assumed that a deep, dark closet was a utilitarian arrangement beneath the dignity of this formal piano nobile dining-room. The closet space was, it seems, reached by a door off the half landing between first and second floors or by the door in the rear room. The chimney-piece in the dining-room was of marble, with 'veined slab and statuary jambs, astragal slips and plinth, black marble nosings; fire stone hearth and covings, and an ornamented wood shelf and fluted terms'.

One of the minor mysteries about this schedule when compared with the interior as it survives is that few of the chimney-piece descriptions – vague as they are – fit convincingly with the chimney-pieces that exist. Most of the chimney-pieces appear to be, broadly, of the types described, and with the right patina of age, but seem to have been altered or moved around the house. The last theory is supported by the fact that the chimney-piece now in the

Fire surround and hob grate in ground-floor front room of No. 7: the surround has the tapering 'fluted terms' referred to in the schedule for No. 11.

ground-floor front room has 'fluted terms' unlike the ground-floor front fireplace described in the schedule but like the design ascribed in the schedule to the first-floor front room.

The back room on the first floor was similarly 'dadoed and papered' with an 'enriched plaister cornice'. It was also fitted with 'mortice lock and brass furniture' to its door and had a 'veined marble chimney piece with slate slips and nosings . . . and a wood shelf'. The shutters had 'iron bars and brass turns', suggesting that good security even at first-floor level was considered prudent. The closet space was accessible from this room, this time with four shelves, and perhaps stretching the full length of the staircase up to the front room.

The landing at this level was 'dadoed and papered' with a 'plaister cornice' and 'double archi-

traves to each side of the door'. The ground floor possessed a 'front parlour' (see p. 54) that was 'dadoed and papered' with 'a plaister cornice on top'; the shutters also had 'iron bars with brass turns'; the chimney-piece was a 'veined marble slab' with 'statuary jambs, plymouth plynths, black marble nosings, fire stone hearth and covings and an ornamental wood shelf to the chimney'. The door had a 'mortice lock with brass furniture' and was surrounded by a 'double architrave'. The 'Back parlour' was fitted out in a very similar manner but with a slightly simpler sounding chimney-piece and, as with the arrangement on the first floor, the closet behind the staircase was reached only from this rear room.

The 'Passage' from the front door to the staircase was 'dadoed' but 'stuccoed' rather than papered. It

Detail of fire surround in ground-floor rear room in No. 11. The eared architrave surround is undoubtedly original, although it is hard to believe that the 1770s-looking mantel shelf is in its original position.

was a common eighteenth-century decorative device, favoured by both Baroque and Palladian designers, to treat the entrance hall/passage as a transitional space bringing exterior qualities – such as simulated stone in the manner of stucco – into the interior of the house. The stairwell above the 'stuccoed' ground-floor level was 'dadoed and papered' and lit by a 'skylight on the top'. Off the stairs to the basement kitchen was a 'closet with two shelves and a lock and key'. Under the kitchen stairs was an 'enclosed chip hole'. This mysterious sounding object may have been a sump or a drain connected to the sewer for the disposal of liquid kitchen waste.[37]

The front door was fitted with lock and key, 'chain and worm ... and a fan light and gard iron over it'. The 'back sash door' had a 'brass knob

latch, two bolts and an iron bar ... and outside shutters and screws, a fan light [with] iron bars over'. Security was obviously important – a 'worm' is a spiral of metal fixed to the door frame used to secure the chain, which, riveted to the other side of the frame, would be stretched across the door. But more interesting is the fact that the back door was glazed to provide a good focus of light at the end of the tunnel-like passage from the front door, and that this potential security hazard was dealt with by outside shutters. Also interesting is the fact that both front and rear fanlights were viewed as possible entry points for housebreakers and were secured by iron bars. These unsightly but once essential fanlight 'gards' rarely survive, having been removed as soon as times became more secure.

The 'kitchen' – the front basement room – was 'paved with stone and wainscotted almost to the top' with a 'stone chimney piece and wood shelf fix't complete, two dressers with four shelves, eight Dutch rings, five shelves, one closet with four shelves'. The 'wash house' was the rear basement room. This room, 'paved with stone and skirted with deal' (not panelled), contained a 'stone chimney piece and wood shelf, a lead cistern with one ball and one common cock to the lead pipe and a wood cover, enclosed wood sink lined with lead, one dresser with two shelves, a pantry, an arched vault and three wine bins, a lock and key to the door, a latch to the wash room door'.

This is a fine and complete description of a late-eighteenth-century kitchen. The 'pantry' seems to refer to a barrel-vaulted room located beneath the staircase and the 'vault' to a small room beneath the backyard. The water supply was provided by the Chelsea Water Works Company, which began operations in 1726 and which probably included Park Street in its network in about 1740.[38] The supply was intermittent, delivered in elm pipes (see p. 87), and reached Park Street from the Tothill Street main via Carteret Street. The connection from the elm pipe to the cistern was by lead pipe – a most leaky arrangement – but then the entire system was far from watertight. For this service the tenant paid, in 1773, about a £1 a year.[39]

Security to the basement rooms was important – 'inside shutters, wood bars' to the kitchen window, '23 bars to wash house window' and 'a lock, key, latch, and two bolts' to the area door – despite the fact that, according to the schedule, there was no

Detail of Corinthian plaster cornice that embellishes all the first-floor front rooms in these houses. Each house possesses five different types of cornice design that reveal very clearly the original hierarchy of occupation. This is the richest; the first-floor back room is similar but without the dentil-course; the ground-floor cornices have modillions but no enrichment; and the second floor has plainer coved cornices (see p. 169). The fifth type is found in the ground-floor entrance passage and is decorated with scrolls instead of modillions.

stair from front area to the street (see p. 84). The absence of this useful device meant that all goods entering the house, such as food and milk, had to come via the front door, and all waste – nightsoil, dust, garbage – had to leave by it. All areas (with the exception of that to No. 11) now possess gates (all of different design) and stairs (clearly of post-eighteenth-century construction), suggesting that this inconvenient omission was soon rectified by the respective tenants.

SERVICES

Although the area did not possess a stair linking kitchen directly to street, it did contribute to the servicing of the house. Off it were located 'two enclosed arch'd vaults' – one containing a privy and both supplied with coal holes and so providing fuel storage. Surviving evidence in the areas of Nos. 7 and 13 Queen Anne's Gate suggests that this privy, no doubt intended for the servants (see p. 56),[40] was accommodated within a brick cell formed within one of the vaults. This arrangement, with the cell entered by a separate door, allowed the rest of the vault to be used for storage. Indeed, this arrangement at No. 7 is very handsome, with the pair of doors grouped within a Diocletian arch.

The area also, records the schedule, contained a 'lead pipe', which undoubtedly brought in the Chelsea water. The rear yard was 'paved with stone' – no mention of plants or tubs – and contained an 'enclosed privy lined with deal' with 'three squares of glass on the west side [that is, looking

Water cistern in yard at No. 9. Dated 1774 and bearing Christ's Hospital's initials, this was originally in the back basement room.

over the yard, not towards the house] and a flap to the seat, and a brass knobbed latch to the door'. This, clearly, was the family privy.

Unfortunately the schedule does not reveal where the waste from this, or the front area privy, went. Park Street had been provided with a sewer as part of the late-seventeenth-century development of the estate. In 1690 the commissioners for sewers in the London area obtained the power to make sewers, and in this year 'the proprietors and inhabitants of messuages or tenements in Park Street and Cartwright Street [that is Carteret Street] prayed an order to impower them to carry a new sewer made by them for the said buildings into the old sewer in Liquorish Gardens thereto adjacent'.[41]

The sewer beneath Park Street was built by a bricklayer, Henry Dagley, who had built several of the late-seventeenth-century houses in Park Street. The sewer was begun late in 1690,[42] was 220 ft long, measured 4 × 3 ft and connected with another smaller sewer, also built by Dagley, beneath Carteret Street. The Park Street sewer was not altogether satisfactory, and in 1752 it was reported[43] that 'there is an annual rent of £4 a house for a man to live in on ye spot, to pump att a pump in ye street to keep ye kitchens dry'.

As well as revealing the unsatisfactory design of the street's drainage system, this report also suggests the main purpose of sewers in the seventeenth and eighteenth centuries. They were not intended for carrying away solid waste from the houses they adjoined – indeed, connecting the privy directly to the sewer was illegal, if not unknown (see p. 91) – but rather were intended to carry away rainwater and liquid wastes. So in 1773 the practice in the Park Street houses would have been, in theory at least, to discharge liquid directly into the sewer and solid into a cesspit located, probably, immediately beneath the backyard privy, which would demand regular, if not frequent, emptying by the nightsoil man. However, it is hard to believe that the builder could have resisted the temptation to connect the front area privy directly into the nearby sewer.

ELEVATION AND PATTERN-BOOKS

The schedule also gives a brief description of the two elevations. The 'back front' supported a 'party stack of lead rain pipes and a wood trunk' and was embellished with 'a wood frontispiece covered with lead' that was reached via three stone steps. This description refers to the rear doorcase and highlights one of the unusual features of this terrace: its rear façade is as regular and as well and expensively built (though not tuck-and-pat pointed) as its front façade, and, like the front, was fitted out with door-cases. This regularity was possible because the centrally placed staircase did not disrupt the rear fenestration, as generally happened when a staircase rose against the rear elevation.

The front elevation had a 'lead cistern head and party stack of pipes and a wood trunk ... a Doric frontispiece covered with lead [and] iron work to the area'. There were also 'Four stone steps to the door' – an arrangement that suggests that the yard, with only three stone steps to the door, was a little higher than the street level. This indicates, perhaps, that it had been fully excavated to provide not only the vault containing 'wine bins' but also a commodious cesspit.

Written in but crossed out is the description that beside the 'frontispiece' was an 'iron screen and lamp from it'. It was common practice throughout the eighteenth century to light streets with a combination of lights suspended over, or beside, front doors or supported on area ironwork, and parish

lamps on posts and brackets (see p. 5). The occupier, if he provided this service according to parish regulations, could be excused payment of the parish lighting rate.[44] Why the item is scratched out is not clear, but this schedule is, presumably, something of a standard list applicable to all five houses, and this particular house did not have a lamp outside its door, whereas its neighbours may have done. There is, however, now no evidence that any of the houses had lamps rising from their area ironwork.

What the schedule does not tell us, unfortunately, is the colour that the joinery was painted or the type or pattern of the wallpaper that was used so prodigiously throughout the house. Nor does it say anything about the design of the plasterwork or joinery details, but, since these generally survive, this omission is not so serious. The colour and paper would probably have been similar to those mentioned by Chambers in letters he wrote in May 1770 and in July 1771[45] (see p. 181).

The schedule also fails to mention what type of grate the chimney-pieces surrounded. Again, Chambers is of assistance. In a letter of November 1771 to Henry Errington, Chambers recommended for a house under construction beside Green Park 'iron bath stoves', which 'may be had for about 36s. or two guineas a piece'. Bath stoves were a type of hob grate and had been illustrated in William and John Welldon's *The Smith's Right Hand* of 1765. This is probably the type of grate that would have been fitted in most of the rooms in the Queen Anne's Gate houses, with the possible exception of the piano nobile front room, where freestanding grates may have been installed. These houses still possess a good collection of late-eighteenth-century hob grates that could well be those originally fitted.

The design of the elevation and of the internal detailing, and the type of plan form chosen, underline the fact that the 1770s was a decade when architectural taste underwent great changes. When these houses were designed, probably in late 1769 or very early 1770, early-eighteenth-century Palladian theories still governed the design of street elevations, and the Building Acts of 1667, 1707 and 1709 were the current legislation for regulating methods of construction and materials used and for assuring that room dimensions related to the scale of the house and that the size of house related to its site and location (see p. xiii). The elevations do not follow the Palladian urban ideal, which would have had them united in a single palace-like composition with a pediment over the central house, but the individual elevations are uniform and conventional Palladian essays with a fine piano nobile (rooms 12 ft high and windows 7 ft high) terminated by square 'attic' windows to the third floor (see p. 139). The subtlest of allusions to the fully embellished temple front, whose proportions were the basis of the Georgian terrace house (see p. 136), is achieved by the string-course, which, running between second and third floors, both marks the point where the façade thickness diminishes from two bricks to one and a half bricks and implies an entablature, thus breaking the tall elevation down into two happily, and classically, proportioned sections. From ground floor to the string-course is the area in which the columns on their pedestals or basement would stand; from string-course to parapet is the attic (see p. 136).

This manner of proportioning street elevations was continued by even the most revolutionary of the Neo-classical architects (such as Robert Adam or James Wyatt) who came to maturity during the 1770s, so it is not by their façade proportions that these houses differ from later products of the same decade. It is their details that reveal their designer was not a man of fashion. The hint is given externally by the design of the matching Doric doorcases (No. 13 being a nineteenth-century alteration), which are of a type popular in the 1750s. But, once inside, it is instantly clear that the spirit of Neo-classicism, which had been transforming taste since the early 1760s, is almost entirely absent in Nos. 5–13 Queen Anne's Gate. The plaster cornices, dados, skirting and architraves are generally of the domestic Palladian type pioneered in the early-eighteenth century and established by the 1740s. The details of the stairs also show not the slightest influence of Neo-classicism – the balusters are composed of urn base, slab and attenuated column in the conventional Palladian manner, and the dado to the stair is designed as a vertical section of the stair handrail as was common in the early-eighteenth century (see p. 171).

The fire surrounds are also mostly free from Neo-classical influences. This determined adherence to the use of well-established decorative motifs is highlighted by the fact that the terrace opposite, undertaken in 1773,[46] is of a most avant-garde Neo-classical design. The developer here was a Michael Barrett, who obtained from Christ's Hospital a building lease of sixty-one years dated from Lady Day 1774. But it seems likely that the inspiration behind the advanced Neo-classical design of these houses was Samuel Wyatt. He was responsible for No. 14 Queen Anne's Gate (then No. 7 Park Street), which, according to the surviving building agreement,[47] was 'built for Charles Townley by Mr Barrett agreeable to plans made by Saml Wyatt'. The house was to be completed by 29 September 1776 for the sum of £3,650. This house was about six times the cost of the houses opposite because it was much larger, particularly in its depth, and much more richly fitted out.

Pattern-books provide a possible source for certain of the elements used in Nos. 5–13 Queen Anne's Gate. Certainly the Gothic fanlights are identical to those published by John Crunden in his *Joiner's and Cabinet Maker's Darling* of 1770 and the plan of the individual houses is very similar to a type published by Robert Morris in William and John Halfpenny's *Modern Builder's Assistant* of 1747. Morris was adapting an unusual, but not unknown, plan type that in its fundamentals is illustrated by Joseph Moxon in his 1703 edition of *Mechanic's Exercises*, but with fireplaces arranged as a central stack between the back and front rooms and not set separately against the party wall.

TAX AND RATES

The national and local taxes and rates for which the owners and occupiers of these houses were liable in the 1770s are well recorded. These charges were made up by the payment of national taxes – land and window taxes – and parish rates, including those for the relief of the poor, and for watching, lighting, cleansing, repairing and paving the highway. Taxes and rates were calculated on an assessed value, or 'rent', of each house. Non-payment was a serious offence, with the commissioners for the various taxes and rates having power of distrain upon the property of the offender.[48] An unusual element of the tax status of Nos. 5–13 Queen Anne's Gate is the fact (mentioned in several of the quoted documents) that Christ's Hospital took upon itself the responsibility for paying the land tax, when this was usually an expense left for the tenant to pay along with the other taxes and rates.[49] It can be assumed that the basis on which Christ's Hospital let the houses (rather like furnished lodgings on short leases) obliged it to take responsibility for the land tax.

The first relevant assessment for these houses was carried out on 26 April 1773 for the 'poor rate'.[50] This established a 'pound rate' (that is, determined how much per pound value) or 'rent' each resident of the parish should pay towards the relief of the poor. This was usually the key local tax, for its commissioners established the 'rent' of the houses, which was then used for all other rate assessments.

The poor rate was explained in the document of assessment: 'upon all and every person and persons who inhabit, hold, occupy or enjoy any land, house, shop, wharf, warehouse or other building in the parish'. The assessment was undertaken by church wardens and vestrymen with, in this case, the connection between the 'relief of the poor' and 'repairing the highways and cleansing the streets' made very clear, because all these activities were covered by the same instrument: 'Puisant to the directions of the Act of Parliament made and passed in the 25th year of George the Second' the commissioners in April 1773 resolved upon a rate of 1s. 11d. in the pound for the relief of the poor; 2d. in the pound for cleansing the streets; and 1d. in the pound for the repair of highways. These monies were to be collected quarterly. On this basis Thomas Watson Ward, the occupant of what is now No. 11 Queen Anne's Gate and which was then valued as worth '£49 rent', had to pay £1 6s. 6½d. quarterly. This total was reached by adding up the three rates – 1s. 11d., 2d. and 1d. – and then multiplying the total by 49 – the assessed 'rent' or value of No. 11 Queen Anne's Gate. The total, £5 6s. 2d., is four times the quarterly rate of £1 6s. 6½d. The occupant of No. 9 Queen Anne's Gate, Thomas Jones, and of No. 7 Queen Anne's Gate, Thomas Gilbert, were also charged £5 6s. 2d. annually for the relief of the poor, cleansing and repairing the highway.

Lighting and paving were covered by an additional rate of 1773.[51] Existing 'by virtue of an Act of the eleventh year of George the Third', it called for a 'rate of 1s. 3d. in the pound upon all and every person inhabiting, occupying, possessing and enjoying any land, houses, building, tenement, etc.' in the parish. The number and location of lamps in Queen Anne's Gate is not revealed, though

a lamp report of 1808,[52] giving an account of lamps in operation in the parish on the night of 5 December, records that of the parish's 496 lamps, 52 were 'down', 5 were out of action for other reasons and that Queen's Square (the western half of the current Queen Anne's Gate) contained 8 lamps. The street now contains fourteen early-eighteenth-century houses and would have contained more in 1808, so that there was about one lamp between two to three houses.

The land and window taxes for 1773 and 1774 were raised together. In 1773 only Thomas Gilbert, the occupant until 1775 of No. 7, was mentioned; the other houses were marked on the tax ledger as empty. Gilbert's 'rent' for these national taxes was shown as £15, which made him liable to £2 5s. land tax, while the twenty-five windows recorded in his house raised an annual window tax of £2 13s.

It is puzzling that, despite Christ's Hospital's decision to pay land tax on Nos. 5–13 Queen Anne's Gate, the occupier is shown as liable; this may, of course, have been merely an administrative device, with the hospital actually picking up the bill. Gilbert's window tax payments were made according to a sliding scale that was used for assessment in 1773.[53] The only odd thing is that No. 7 Queen Anne's Gate was taxed for twenty-five windows when it contains only twenty-one back and front, including the basement windows. The glazed rear door and the roof light above the staircase may have been regarded as taxable, while the extra-wide window lighting the ground floor back room may have been taxed twice.

In 1774 Thomas Gilbert's 'rent' value was £16, which raised his land tax to £2 8s.[54] In this year Thomas Watson Ward in No. 11 and Thomas Jones in No. 9 were both in residence and marked as eligible for £2 9s. window tax raised on twenty-four windows. Neither was charged land tax. The position had changed by 1776, when all the houses were given a rent value, with the occupiers being made directly responsible for paying the land tax. In this year the tax book explains the legislation as 'an act for granting an aid to his majesty by a land tax to be raised in Great Britain for the service of the year 1776'. By this time Thomas Gilbert had been replaced at No. 7 by the Honourable Thomas Pelham. The rent value of the house was still £16, but its land tax contribution had been increased to £3 4s. – a hefty 16s. a year increase, showing that the rate-per-pound value had risen dramatically between 1774 and 1776. The window tax remained the same.

No. 9 was valued at £13 'rent' and the occupier, Thomas Jones, was responsible for the payment of £2 12s. land tax annually, and No. 13 was valued at £12 rent, which made the occupier James Tracey responsible for a £2 8s. land tax payment. Both Jones and Tracey paid £2 8s. window tax. Why No. 7 had a greater rental value than Nos. 9 or 13 is now impossible to determine, though this may be related to the fact that it is recorded as having twenty-five windows, while the other houses possessed for tax reasons twenty-four. Perhaps its internal fittings were of a much higher standard, though this is not supported by the surviving evidence. Only one of the houses possesses a mahogany handrail on the staircase, and that is No. 13.

Appendix Three

———◆———

Fire Surrounds and Staircases

Fire surround of 1725 in a house in Elder Street, Spitalfields. This is one of the common early-eighteenth-century types of surround: panelled lintel and posts, moulded impost, keystone and Baroque profile to lintel soffit. The shelf is probably a practical addition of 1800; originally the surround would have had a shallow, and functionally useless, cyma recta cornice.

Fire surround in first-floor front room in No. 27 Fournier Street, Spitalfields, of 1725. This type of eared, ovolo-moulded surround with marble slips formed the basis of many Palladian fire surround designs from the 1720s to the 1780s. The shaped frieze is, in this case, a later addition.

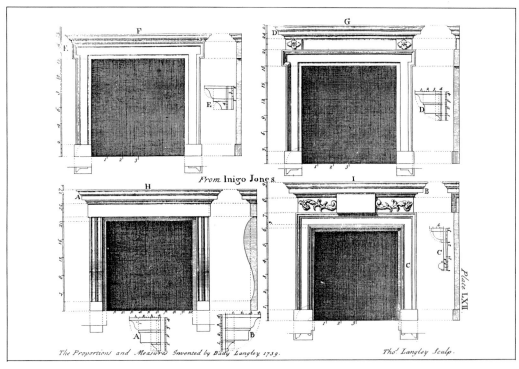

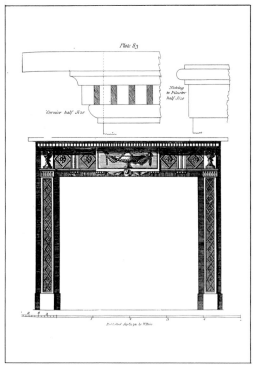

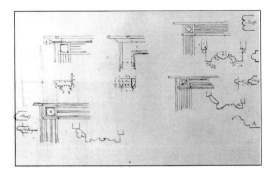

Sketches made in c. 1800–1810 by George Stanley Repton of fire surround details. This design, with reeded lintels and posts meeting at a roundel, square, quatrefoil and so on, was immensely popular from c. 1795 to c. 1825.

Opposite, top: *Plate from Batty Langley's* The City and Country Builder's and Workman's Treasury of Designs *of 1745. This shows the common eared ovolo type surround.*

Opposite, bottom left: *Plate from William Pain's* Practical House Carpenter *of 1789. The popular temple-front composition – pilasters supporting an entablature – is here dressed with a fine collection of Neo-classical motifs.*

Opposite, bottom right: *Design drawing of c. 1760–65 by Edward Stevens of Sir William Chambers's office, for the entablature of a late-Palladian design.*

Plate from William Pain's Carpenter's and Joiner's Repository *of 1778. The profiles of the mouldings and the embellishments are Neo-classical and typical of the 1770s. Notable are the astragal 'nosings' on the left that frame the fire opening and the quirked cyma reversa forming the top of the cornice mantel shelf.*

Second-floor flight in No. 46 Queen Anne's Gate, Westminster, of c. 1704. The design and construction are typical of the date; the balusters are formed from squat columns sitting on bulbous urns. The handrail is of a square section, as is the newel that has an inner edge embellished with a half baluster. All balusters are of the same size and placed on a continuous closed string embellished with an architrave.

Detail of second-floor flight at No. 14 Fournier Street, Spitalfields, of 1726. The stair arrangement here is more usual, with the open string treads rising on a diagonal stair carriage faced with carved tread ends and architrave mouldings. The three balusters per tread are each of a different height and are shown here arranged in the common manner: the bases of the urns align with the tread surface on one side and the square tablet (which separates urn from column) on the other. The capitals of the baluster columns, however, do not read in horizontal alignment but follow the diagonal of the handrail. A fourth type of column, of extra height, has been used for the landing balustrading.

Ground-floor flight in Nos. 4/6 Fournier Street of 1726. The treads are unusual: they are formed as boxes and so look like masonry blocks, with their stepped soffits exposed. The tread ends are inlaid with mahogany and walnut. The balusters are, like the handrail, of mahogany and are unusual in that they lack tablets between twisted columns and gadrooned urn.

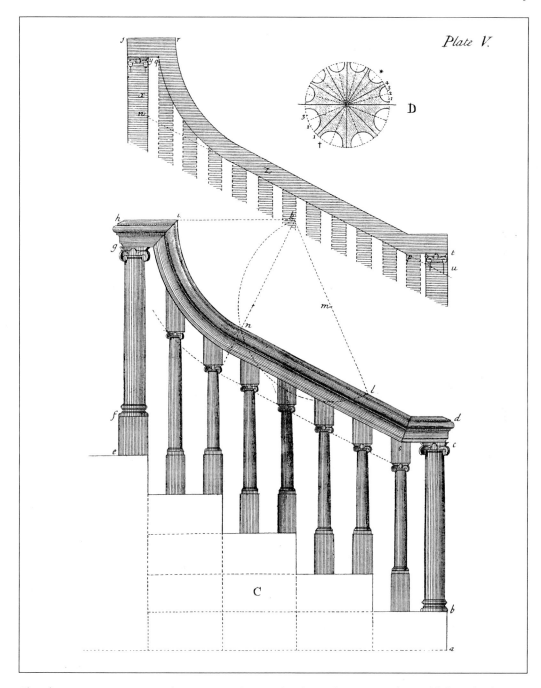

Plate from Francis Price's British Carpenter *of 1735. This shows the geometry for establishing the 'kneeing' of the handrail at the bottom and its ramp at the top. It also shows the manner of fixing the correct height for the balustrade capitals. This type of stairs, with balustrades formed from single columns, was a most logical application of classicism to function but not often used.*

Plate showing a dog-leg stair from Abraham Swan's British Architect, *or the* Builder's Treasury of Staircases *of 1745. This provides profiles for handrail, newel cap, stair nosing and also the means of ramping the handrail up to the newel.*

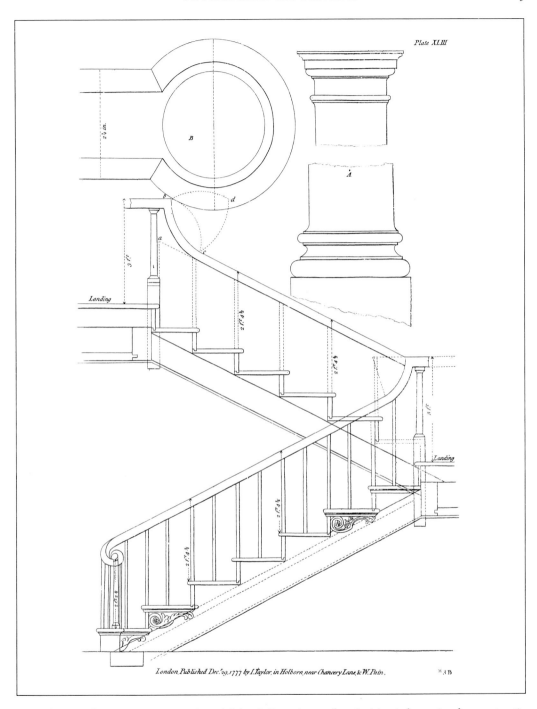

Plate XLIII

London, Published Dec.ʳ 29, 1777 by I. Taylor, in Holborn, near Chancery Lane, & W. Pain.

Plate from William Pain's Carpenter's and Joiner's Repository of 1778 giving information for constructing and detailing a dog-leg stair. As was common after 1770, the turned baluster has given way to plain balusters of square or oblong section.

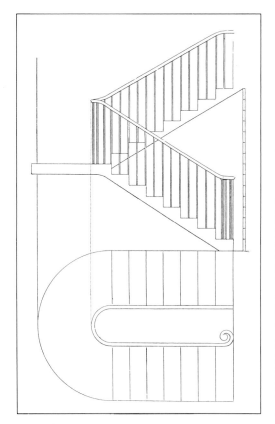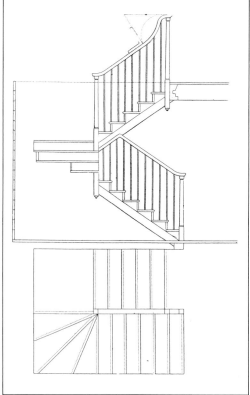

Plates from Peter Nicholson's book on Staircases *of 1820. Left: A semi-circular open-well stair. Right: A dog-legged stair with one quarter of a circle of winders that turn the first flight on to the half-landing. This was a device for fitting a staircase into a compressed space.*

Notes

PART ONE: LIFE IN THE CITY

Chapter One: Street Life

1. Louis Simond, *Journal of a Tour 1810–11* (ed. Christopher Hibbert, 1968).
2. Erik Gustaf Geijer, *Impressions of England 1800–1810* (trans. Elizabeth Sprigg and Claude Napier, 1932).
3. John Gwynn, *London and Westminster Improved* (1766).
4. Robert Southey, *Letters from England by Don Manuel Alvarez Espriella* (1807).
5. J.A. Anderson, *A Dane's Excursion in Britain* (1809).
6. Carl Philip Moritz, *Travels through England* (1782).
7. Cesar de Saussure, *A Foreign View of England* (1902 edition).
8. Richard Rush, *A Residence at the Court of London 1817–25* (1833).
9. J.A. Gotch, *Inigo Jones* (1928).
10. For example, J.T. Smith, in *Nollekens and His Times* (1828), related numerous anecdotes based on the price of coal. When coals were at an 'enormous price', those sitting for Nollekens to sculpt were forced to add the cost of coals to the price of the bust if they were to keep warm. Also, partly because of his miserly habits, Nollekens kept his precious coal locked in the wine cellar and would be caught taking coals off the fire after guests departed.
11. Francis Maximilian Misson, *Memoirs of Travel over England* (trans. John Ozell, 1719).
12. Jacques Henri Meister, *Letters Written during a Residence in England* (1799).
13. Jean Bernard Le Blanc, *Letters on the English and French Nations* (1745).
14. See M. Dorothy George, *London Life in the Eighteenth Century* (1925).
15. Tracts on London, 796 h21, 1–15, British Museum Department of Manuscripts.
16. James Peller Malcolm, *Anecdotes of the Manners and Customs of London during the Eighteenth Century* (1808).
17. Trustees' minute book 191, Liberty of Norton Folgate, Tower Hamlets Local History Library.
18. Notebook E1033, Westminster Central Library.
19. Lamp report E3306, Westminster Central Library.
20. Jos Hayling, lighting report, A2279, Westminster Central Library.
21. Pierre-Jean Grosley, *Tour of London* (ed. T. Nugent, 1772).
22. Johann Wilhelm von Archenholz, *A Picture of England* (1789).
23. Add. MS31325, British Museum Department of Manuscripts.
24. William Hutton, *A Journey to London* (1818).
25. William Matthews, *An Historical Sketch of the Origins, Progress and Present State of Gas Lighting* (1827).
26. Jos Hayling, lighting report, A2279, Westminster Central Library.
27. Add. MS18238, British Museum Department of Manuscripts.
28. Hermann Ludwig Püeckler-Muskau, *Tour of England* (1832).
29. Add. MS31325, British Museum Department of Manuscripts.
30. Trustees' minute book 191, Liberty of Norton Folgate, Tower Hamlets Local History Library.
31. François de La Rochefoucauld, *A Frenchman in England* (ed. Jean Marchand, trans. S.C. Roberts, 1933).
32. *Dyche's Dictionary* of 1765 contains an enlightening essay on the importance of the 'vivifying spirit' in air and how this spirit can be destroyed.
33. James Boswell, *London Journal 1762–3* (ed. F.A. Pottle, 1951).
34. Georg Christoph Lichtenberg, *Visits to England* (trans. W.H. Quarrell and M.L. Mare, 1956).

Chapter Two: Work and Play

1. Christian August Gottlieb Goede, *The Stranger in England* (1807).
2. Archenholz, *A Picture of England*.
3. Anderson, *A Dane's Excursion in Britain*.
4. Moritz, *Travels through England*.
5. *Sophie in London* (ed. Clare Williams, 1933).
6. Rush, *A Residence at the Court of London 1817–25*.
7. Simond, *Journal of a Tour 1810–11*.
8. Jane Austen, *Persuasion* (1818).
9. Grosley, *Tour of London*.
10. Malcolm, *Anecdotes of the Manners and Customs of London during the Eighteenth Century*.
11. La Rochefoucauld, *A Frenchman in England*.
12. Geijer, *Impressions of England*.

13. Boswell, *London Journal 1762–3*.
14. Southey, *Letters from England by Don Manuel Alvarez Espriella*.
15. Benjamin Franklin, *Complete Works*, vol. 1 (1806).
16. Susanna Whatman, *The Housekeeping Book of 1776* (intro. Christina Hardyment, 1987).
17. Z.C. von Uffenbach, *London in 1710* (trans. W.H. Quarrell and M.L. Mare, 1934).
18. J. Mackey, *A Journey through England in Familiar Letters* (1724).
19. Saussure, *A Foreign View of England*.
20. Goede, *The Stranger in England*.
21. Jane Austen, *Northanger Abbey* (1818).
22. Misson, *Memoirs of Travel over England*.
23. James Boswell, *The Life of Samuel Johnson*, vol. 1 (1821 edition).
24. John Macdonald, *Memoirs of an Eighteenth-century Footman* (1790).
25. Boswell, *The Life of Samuel Johnson*, vol. 1.
26. Jane Austen, *Emma* (1816).
27. John Trusler, *Honours of the Table* (1788).
28. J.T. Smith, *Nollekens and His Times* (1828).
29. Jane Austen, *Letters 1796–1817* (ed. R.W. Chapman, 1955).
30. Meister, *Letters Written during a Residence in England*.
31. Barthélemy Faujas de St Fond, *A Journey through England and Scotland in 1784* (ed. Sir A. Geikie, 1907).
32. Püeckler-Muskau, *Tour of England*.
33. J.E. Austen-Leigh, *Memoir of Jane Austen* (1870).
34. St Fond, *A Journey through England and Scotland in 1784*.
35. La Rochefoucauld, *A Frenchman in England*.
36. James Beeverell, *Pleasures of London* (1707; trans. W.H. Quarrell, 1940).
37. William Hickey, *Memoirs* (ed. Peter Quennell, 1960).
38. Boswell, *London Journal 1762–3*.
39. Goede, *The Stranger in England*.
40. Madame d'Avot, quoted in Malcolm Letts, *As the Foreigners Saw Us* (1935).
41. Lichtenberg, *Visits to England*.

PART TWO: LIFE IN THE HOUSE

Chapter One: The 'Common House'

1. Simond, *Journal of a Tour 1810–11*.
2. Grosley, *Tour of London*.
3. La Rochefoucauld, *A Frenchman in England*.
4. *Sophie in London*.
5. Saussure, *A Foreign View of England*.
6. Archenholz, *A Picture of England*.
7. Rents were dear in London for two reasons. First, building land was in short supply, with the centre of the city constrained by large, aristocratic estates to the west and north-west, and the river to the south. To the east, expansion was possible but undesirable to many because of its industrial and impoverished character. Second, protectionist policies were exercised by those who had already built and wanted to safeguard the value of their property by preventing new building. This problem was tackled as early as 1685 by the speculative builder Nicholas Barbon in his pamphlet entitled *An Apology for the Builder*.
8. Malcolm, *Anecdotes of the Manners and Customs of London during the Eighteenth Century*.
9. L6/6, RIBA Drawings Collection.
10. Rush, *A Residence at the Court of London 1817–25*.
11. Richard Neve, *The City and Country Purchaser and Builder's Dictionary* (1726 edition).
12. Houghton Hall, Norfolk, designed in 1721 by Colen Campbell, did not include a formal dining-room, but one was created between 1728 and 1731 by William Kent within one of the four three-room apartments on the first floor. The mahogany dining-table made for this room in 1730 was extendable, being formed from four separate gateleg tables. It is significant that dining-tables were not illustrated by Thomas Chippendale or his contemporaries in their trade catalogues, which suggests that tables intended specifically for dining were not usual even as late as the 1760s.
13. O.E. Deutsch, *Handel: A Documentary Biography* (1955).
14. *Survey of London: Vol. 39*.
15. ibid.
16. CHA13097, Christ's Hospital Archives, Guildhall Library.
17. First-floor dining-rooms are also recorded at No. 6 Grosvenor Square in 1757 (MSS8766, Guildhall Library) and at No. 9 in 1777 (MSS845, schedule 111, bundle 16, Wiltshire Record Office, Longleat).
18. For example, J.T. Smith in *Nollekens and His Times* gave an account of No. 14 Queen Anne's Gate, completed in 1776 and occupied by Charles Townley, in which the dining-room was the large ground-floor rear room overlooking St James's Park.
19. Southey, *Letters from England by Don Manuel Alvarez Espriella*.
20. HCW/1/1/1–8, RIBA Library.
21. L6/6, RIBA Drawings Collection.
22. *The Life and Letters of the Hon. Mrs Edward Boscawen 1719–61* (ed. Cecil Aspinall Oglander, 1940).
23. Wood, *Essay towards a Description of Bath*.
24. James Peacock (under the pseudonym Jose Mac Packe), *Nutshells* (1785).
25. In vol. 16, quoted in Joseph Jean Hecht, *The Domestic Servant Class in Eighteenth-century England* (1956).

26. Lease of house in Northumberland Row, Tottenham, June 1756, in possession of the Duke of Northumberland, Alnwick Castle.
27. Nicholas Barbon, *An Apology for the Builder* (1685).
28. *Survey of London: Vol. 39.*
29. ibid.
30. Watch book, 11 June 1736, D436 and 10 June 1737, D441, Westminster Central Library.
31. Census for Great Marlborough Ward, 1801, D1742, Westminster Central Library.
32. For example, at third-floor level between Nos. 15 and 17 Elder Street and at first-floor landing level between Nos. 17 and 19 Princelet Street.
33. Misson, *Memoirs of Travel over England.*
34. Moritz, *Travels through England.*
35. Francis Grose, *The Olio* (1793), quoted in M. Dorothy George, *London Life in the Eighteenth Century* (1925).
36. T.A. Murray, 'Remarks on the Situation of the Poor in the Metropolis', MS1932, Guildhall Library.
37. George, *London Life in the Eighteenth Century.*
38. Franklin, *Complete Works*, vol. 1.
39. Robert Campbell, *London Tradesmen* (1747).
40. MS1932, Guildhall Library.
41. Lease of house in Northumberland Row, Tottenham, June 1756, in possession of the Duke of Northumberland, Alnwick Castle.
42. Lease in possession of Messrs Simmonds, Church Rockham, Holborn.
43. CHA13097, Christ's Hospital Archives, Guildhall Library.
44. Watercolour view, in the British Museum Print Room, painted from memory in 1848. George Scharf moved into No. 14 Francis Street in about 1830. The house, now demolished, stood in present-day Torrington Place and had been built in 1772 on the Bedford Estate.
45. MS2701, Lambeth Palace Archives.
46. ibid.
47. Illustration in James Ayres, *The Home in Britain* (1981).
48. Examples can be seen in the kitchens of No. 18 Folgate Street, Spitalfields, 1725 and No. 27 Fournier Street, 1725. Both of these examples have been relocated from other Spitalfields houses.
49. Acc.349/293, Greater London Record Office.
50. MS14316, London Assurance Surveys, Guildhall Library.
51. Wood, *Essay towards a Description of Bath* (1749 edition).
52. For example, No. 29 Percy Street, London, built about 1765, where the ground-floor front room is panelled, while the first-floor front room and the rest of the house are embellished with plaster decoration.
53. Southey probably means crystal glass.
54. For example, in the second-floor front room of No. 58 Grafton Way, London, built in 1793. See also the plans of No. 28 Soho Square (L6/6, RIBA Drawings Collection).

Chapter Two: Servicing the House

1. Quoted in N.S. Billington and B.M. Roberts, *Building Services Engineering* (1982).
2. Benjamin Thompson, Count Rumford, *Chimney Fireplaces* (1796).
3. British Museum Prints Room.
4. Probate inventories, AM/PI(1), Greater London Record Office.
5. Benjamin Thompson, Count Rumford, *Essays Political, Economical, Philosophical*, vol. 3 (1802).
6. Peter Pindar (pseudonym of John Wolcot), quoted in Egon Larsen, *In America and Europe* (1953).
7. MS Soane Museum.
8. HCW/1/1/1–8, RIBA Library.
9. *Survey of London: Vol. 36*, Appendix 2.
10. G.T. Clarke, *Report to the General Board of Health on the City of Bristol* (1850), Bristol City Record Office.
11. *Report of the Select Committee on the Supply of Water to the Metropolis*, evidence of William Chadwell Mylne (1821), Parliamentary Papers, British Museum.
12. Francis Blomefield, *Essays towards a Topographical History of Norfolk*, 5 vols. (1739–75).
13. Documents 838 and 839, Coutts & Co.
14. D/EP/74219, Hertfordshire Record Office.
15. *Report of the Select Committee on the Supply of Water to the Metropolis.*
16. ibid.
17. This plan is now deposited in the Library, King's College, Cambridge.
18. P.F. Jones, *Whittington's Long House*, London Topographical Society, vol. 23 (1972).
19. Joseph Fletcher, 'A History of Sewerage in the Metropolis', *Journal of the Statistical Society* (1844).
20. HFCS, Greater London Record Office.
21. Southey, *Letters from England by Don Manuel Alvarez Espriella.*
22. *Survey of London: Vol. 39*, Appendix 2.

PART THREE: THE HOUSE

Chapter One: Construction and Speculation

1. Ware, *A Complete Body of Architecture.*
2. Grosley, *Tour of London.*
3. Malcolm, *Anecdotes of the Manners and Customs of London during the Eighteenth Century.*

4. Simond, *Journal of a Tour 1810–11*.

5. John Soane, *Lectures on Architecture* (ed. Arthur Bolton, 1929).

6. Batty Langley, *London Prices of Bricklayer's Materials* (1748).

7. Analysis of mortar from Spencer House, St James's, built in 1756, revealed a mix of three parts sand to one part lime.

8. Quoted in C.W. Chalkin, *The Provincial Towns of Georgian England* (1974).

9. John Wood [the younger], *Series of Plans for Cottages* (1781).

10. Tobias Smollett, *Humphry Clinker* (1771).

11. Building contract for the west side of Gower Street, the north side of Chenies Street and the south side of Store Street, 1 March 1777, Bedford Estate Office.

12. Roger North, *Autobiography* (ed. A. Jessop, 1887).

13. Campbell, *London Tradesmen*.

14. John Summerson, *Georgian London* (1969 edition).

15. N.G. Brett-James, *The Growth of Stuart London* (1935).

16. Misson, *Memoirs of Travel over England*.

17. Archenholz, *A Picture of England*.

18. MS14316, London Assurance Surveys, Guildhall Library.

19. MS8674/19 and MS8674/20, Hand in Hand fire policy register 1718/19, Guildhall Library.

20. *Survey of London: Vol. 39*.

21. Copy in author's possession.

22. *Survey of London: Vol. 39*.

23. John Eveleigh's ledgers, Bath Reference Library.

24. MS2701, Lambeth Palace Archives.

25. Elizabeth Waterman Gilboy, *Wages in Eighteenth-century England* (1934).

26. A.E. Richardson, *Robert Mylne* (1955).

27. *Survey of London: Vol. 39*.

28. Walter Ison, *The Georgian Buildings of Bath 1700–1830* (1980 edition).

29. *Survey of London: Vol. 39*.

30. Add. MS18, 238ff 30–32, British Museum Department of Manuscripts.

31. Building contract for the south side of Bedford Square between William Scott and Robert Grews and the Trustees of the Duke of Bedford, 6 July 1776, Bedford Estate Office.

32. Bedford Estate Office.

33. Lease assignment from Michael Searles, 1 August 1791, Southwark Local History Library. See also A. Byrne, *London's Georgian Houses* (1986).

34. Original lease for centre house and others in possession of Sam Anderton.

35. Quoted in A.J. Youngson, *The Making of Classical Edinburgh* (1968 edition).

36. *Survey of London: Vol. 39*.

37. Geijer, *Impressions of England*.

38. Püeckler-Muskau, *Tour of England*.

39. Goede, *The Stranger in England*.

Chapter Two: Proportion

1. Andrea Palladio, *The Four Books of Architecture* (1570; trans. Isaac Ware, 1738).

2. Leon Battista Alberti, *The Ten Books of Architecture* (1485; trans. James Leoni, 1726).

3. Building contract, 6 July 1776, Bedford Estate Office.

4. Robert Morris, *Lectures on Architecture* (1734).

5. Peter Nicholson, *The New and Improved Practical Builder* (1823).

6. William Pain, *The Carpenter's and Joiner's Repository* (1778).

7. See Arthur Stratton, *Interior Decoration of the Eighteenth Century* (1928).

8. Sebastiano Serlio, *Five Books of Architecture* (1537–47; Robert Peake edition, 1611).

9. Pain, *The Carpenter's and Joiner's Repository*.

10. Nicholson, *The New and Improved Practical Builder*.

Chapter Three: Elements of the House

1. Saussure, *A Foreign View of England*.

2. Richard Neve, *The City and Country Purchaser and Builder's Dictionary* (1703).

3. Moxon's *Mechanick Exercises* was published as a series of pamphlets from 1677.

4. Plate 76 of Batty Langley's *Builder's Jewel* of 1741 showed sketches of three panelled rooms. The simplest, with plain frame to panel and Tuscan cornice, he called 'Tuscan'; the next, with ovolo-embellished frame to panel and more complex bed mould to cornice, he called 'Doric'; the last, with compound-moulded panel frame (presumably ovolo and fillet) and more delicately moulded cornice, he called 'Ionick'. In all types the dado panel was flush.

5. For example, an inventory of 1720 for No. 11 Kensington Square, built in about 1702, mentions tapestry hangings. See *Survey of London: Vol. 42*.

6. E.A. Entwisle, *The Book of Wallpaper* (1970 edition).

7. Trade card in the Heal Collection, British Museum Prints Room.

8. *Letters of a Grandmother 1732–5* (ed. Gladys Scott Thomson, 1943).

9. *Survey of London: Vol. 40*.

10. Lease of house in Northumberland Row, Tottenham, June 1756, in possession of the Duke of Northumberland, Alnwick Castle.

11. Sir William Chambers's letter book, MS41133, British Museum Department of Manuscripts.

12. CHA13097, Christ's Hospital Archives, Guildhall Library.
13. RIBA WIR/1/1/1, RIBA Library.
14. *Letters of a Grandmother 1732–5*.
15. Ian Bristow, *The Architects' Handmaid: Paint Colour in the Eighteenth-century Interior* (catalogue to the 1983 exhibition at the RIBA Heinz Gallery).
16. *The Purefoy Letters 1735–53* (ed. George Eland, 1931).
17. BH(K) 1185, Northamptonshire Record Office.
18. William Salmon, *Polygraphice, or the Art of Drawing, Painting and Varnishing* (1672).
19. Peter Nicholson, *Mechanic's Companion* (1825).
20. Nicholson, *The New and Improved Practical Builder*.
21. I. and J. Taylor, *The Builder's Price Book* (1787 edition).
22. John Smith, *The Art of Painting in Oyl* (1738 edition).
23. Nicholson, *Mechanic's Companion*.
24. 'Joseph Emerton, Brother of the Late Mr Alexander Emerton, Colourman', broadsheet 89.55, Heal collection, British Museum Prints Room.
25. Taylor, *The Builder's Price Book*.
26. Ian Bristow, in his catalogue to the 1983 RIBA exhibition on paint colour in the eighteenth-century interior (see note 15), lists 'pigments in use during the eighteenth century arranged in approximate order of price'. From cheapest to most expensive, the order runs: whiting; common yellow ochre; native brown ochre; better-class red oxides of varying hue; ivory black; charcoal black; umber; red lead; cheap yellow lake; white lead; lamp black; cheap red lake; patent yellow; Scheele's green; raw sienna; Prussian blue; green verditer; burnt sienna; verdigris; blue verditer; vermilion; indigo; carmine lake.

    According to W.M. Higgins's *House Painter* of 1841, 'Prussian blue was discovered by accident in 1704' by a German chemist, while smalt is a blue formed by 'glass stained by oxide of cobalt and then ground'. Verditer, like indigo, comes from a plant.
27. Nicholson, *New and Improved Practical Builder*.
28. T.H. Vanherman, *Every Man His Own House Painter* (1829).
29. Nicholson in his *New and Improved Practical Builder* of 1823 put the opposite point of view. Graining, he wrote, would 'last ten times as long' as paint because it could be easily refreshed by being 'occasionally re-varnished without losing any of its freshness'.
30. James Peacock (under the pseudonym of Jose Mac Packe), *Nutshells* (1785).
31. *Sophie in London*.
32. Box J4, Sir William Chambers office, Edward Stevens Drawings; J49 and J4/11 RIBA Drawings Collection.
33. Lease quoted by Sir John Summerson in *John Nash* of 1949. Crown leases at the Public Office under Cres. 2, 22, 26 and 35 give much general, but little specific, information beyond 'paint three times in oil'. Regrain-ing of sashes is refered to in about 1840 in connection with Carlton House Terrace.
34. CHA 3/1/3, RIBA manuscripts.
35. Joseph Salway, 'Survey of the Kensington Turnpike Trust Road from Hyde Park Corner to Hammersmith' (1811), Add. MS31325, British Museum Department of Manuscripts.

Chapter Four: Town Gardens

1. *John Evelyn's Diary* (ed. W. Braun, 1903).
2. Lord Chesterfield, letter to Solomon Dayrolles, 31 March 1749, vol. 3 (ed. Mahon, 1845–53).
3. *Lady Mary Coke's Letters and Journals*, 3 June 1768 (1889–96).
4. John Harvey, *Early Nurserymen* (1974).
5. Pehr Kalm, *Visit to England* (1892).
6. J.L. Ferri de St Constant, *Londres et les anglais* (Paris, 1804).
7. *The Autobiography and Correspondence of Mary Granville, Mrs Delany*, vol. 1 (ed. Lady Llanover, 1861).
8. *The Life and Letters of the Hon. Mrs Edward Bos-cawen 1719–61* (ed. Cecil Aspinall Oglander, 1944).
9. Jean de la Quintinie, *The Compleat Gard'ner* (trans. John Evelyn, 1693).
10. Andreas A. Feldborg, *A Dane's Excursion in England* (1809).
11. MS Douce C.11. 20U–21R, Bodleian Library.
12. Add. MS23005, Bodleian Library.
13. Geijer, *Impressions of England*.
14. Hermann Ludwig Püeckler-Muskau, *Letters from Albion* (1814).

PART FOUR: APPENDIXES

Appendix One: Case Study – No. 15 Elder Street and No. 2 Fournier Street, Spitalfields

1. MLR1724/5/67, Greater London Record Office.
2. MLR1727/3/417, Greater London Record Office.
3. MLR1727/2/132, Greater London Record Office.
4. MLR1725/5/464 and MLR1727/5/404, Greater London Record Office.
5. MLR1727/2/132, Greater London Record Office.
6. MLR1727/2/133, Greater London Record Office.
7. Langley, *London Prices of Bricklayer's Materials*.
8. George, *London Life in the Eighteenth Century*.
9. MS2713, Lambeth Palace Archives.
10. MS2750/2, Lambeth Palace Archives.
11. MLR1726/1/277–85, Greater London Record Office.

12. As explained by Morris in his *Lectures on Architecture* of 1734 and 1736.

13. THC5162, Greater London Record Office.

Appendix Two: Case Study – Nos. 5–13 Queen Anne's Gate, Westminster

1. Christ's Hospital committee of rentors' minute book, CHA12806, Christ's Hospital Archives, Guildhall Library.

2. James Jennings's 1726 report on the estate says that £200 had to be spent on each of the seven large houses on the north side of Park Street and £60 each on the smaller houses on the south side (CHA13709). This analysis was supported by George Tullock's survey of 1752 (CHA13083). He found that four of the seven large houses on the north side of Park Street were empty and three of these 'untenable' and four of the houses on the south side were 'untenable' with collapsing rear elevations.

3. See Richard Horwood, 'Plan of the Cities of London and Westminster, the Borough of Southwark and Parts Adjoining' (1792–9).

4. Christ's Hospital committee of rentors' minute book, CHA12811, Christ's Hospital Archives, Guildhall Library.

5. For example, both Batty Langley's *London Prices of Bricklayer's Materials* of 1748 and I. and J. Taylor's *The Builder's Price Book* of 1776 and 1787 give the prices of old and new materials such as tiles.

6. In a building agreement of April 1770 for the construction of a dwelling and bakehouse in Fore Street, Limehouse (WIR/1/1/1 RIBA Library), in a building agreement of 1736 for houses in Essex Street, Strand (Acc. 349/293, Greater London Record Office) and in a building agreement for No. 10 St James's Square, where reference is made to 'reusing some of the old walnut … floor' with upper rooms to be wainscoted with the best of the old wainscot (HCW/1/1/1–8, RIBA Library).

7. Viewing subcommittee book, 19 June 1759, CHA12834, Christ's Hospital Archives, Guildhall Library.

8. CHA12853, Christ's Hospital Archives, Guildhall Library.

9. William Salmon, in his *Palladio Londinensis* of 1734, recommended a hundred and a quarter, while Batty Langley, in his *London Prices of Bricklayer's Materials* of 1748, recommended '41 quarter bags of lime' to a rod of stock bricks. A bag, as Langley pointed out, should contain a bushel of lime and twenty-five bushels equal a hundred of lime.

10. From 1729 to 1770 bricks made within fifteen miles of London were to measure $8\frac{3}{4} \times 4\frac{1}{8} \times 2\frac{1}{2}$ ins.

11. Langley, *London Prices of Bricklayer's Materials*.

12. Nicholson, in his *New and Improved Practical Builder* of 1823, reflected early-nineteenth-century taste by listing the Marl brick – another name for Malme – as superior to grey stock.

13. Salmon, *Palladio Londinensis*.

14. Langley, *London Prices of Bricklayer's Materials*.

15. Taylor, *The Builder's Price Book* (1787 edition).

16. William Pain, *British Palladio* (1786).

17. In *London Prices of Bricklayer's Materials* Langley suggested a 25 per cent saving by purchasing direct from the kiln.

18. Salmon, *Palladio Londinensis*.

19. Salmon, in his *Palladio Londinensis*, said baldly that a 'bricklayer will lay a 1,000 bricks a day', but Langley, in his *London Prices of Bricklayer's Materials*, pointed out not only that a rod can contain more than the 4,500 bricks recognized by convention but also that 1,500 place bricks could be laid in a day. Laying 500 grey stocks 'with great neatness' could also take a day. On this basis an average of 1,000 bricks a day seems reasonable.

20. Taylor, *The Builder's Price Book* (1787 edition).

21. Sir William Chambers's letter book, MS41133, British Museum Department of Manuscripts.

22. WIR/1/1/1, RIBA Library.

23. Christopher Wren had been Surveyor-General of the King's Works.

24. CHA12834, Christ's Hospital Archives, Guildhall Library.

25. ibid.

26. On the Grosvenor Estate, for example, a building agreement of the 1720s usually specified that building should be complete in six months, although for large houses such as those in Grosvenor Square twelve to eighteen months was allowed (*Survey of London: Vol. 39*).

27. *Survey of London: Vol. 10*.

28. For example, Thomas Barlow, the Surveyor to the Grosvenor Estate, acquired in 1721 about six acres of Grosvenor Estate land on a 99-year lease for a ground rent of £67 per annum. He sublet some building plots (on 60- and 80-year leases), developed others and consequently obtained about £280 per annum in improved ground rents over the £67 he had to pay, as well as £160 in rack rents from his new developments. See *Survey of London: Vol. 39*.

29. CHA12806, Christ's Hospital Archives, Guildhall Library.

30. CHA13097, Christ's Hospital Archives, Guildhall Library.

31. A specimen lease of 1724, MS18238, British Museum Department of Manuscripts.

32. *Survey of London: Vol. 39*.

33. Leases of 1784 for the south-west portion of Gower Street, Bedford Estate Office.

34. Lease of 1815 for No. 12 Park Street (now No. 13 Queen Anne's Gate), by which time the rent had risen to £63 per annum. CHA13097, Christ's Hospital Archives, Guildhall Library.

35. This safeguarding of fittings was even practised in more coventional speculative development. Among the 'Common and usual covenants' attached to Grosvenor Estate building agreements in the 1720s was one that required the surrender of the building at the end of the leasehold term with its fittings intact. See *Survey of London: Vol. 39*.

36. Richard Neve, *The City and Country Purchaser and Builder's Dictionary* (1726 edition).

37. When the site of No. 12 Folgate Street, Spitalfields (house built in 1724) was redeveloped in 1982, a deep, brick-lined well 2 ft in diameter was discovered at basement level. It was full of household waste such as broken dishes and chamber pots, and was located roughly where the staircase would have been. Also Smith, writing in 1828 in *Nollekens and His Times*, described Nollekens's basement kitchen in about 1785 as having a 'dust hole, which was infested with rats, the drains had long been choked up'. The space beneath the kitchen stairs was, in houses without areas and vaults under the pavement, a popular place for storing coal. The space was sometimes reached via a small trap-door located in the ground-floor entrance passage at the foot of the stairs, as in No. 5 Elder Street, built in 1725.

38. C.D. Andrews, *A Short History of No. 1 Queen Anne's Gate* (1980).

39. In the 1783 edition of Ralph's *Critical Review* it is noted that water was supplied three times a week and cost 14s. a year. Grosley, in his *Tour of London*, referring to a house rented for £38 a year, wrote, 'the landlord was ... obliged to pay a guinea a year for water ... besides two towards the Poor tax, and three for window light, scavengers and the watch'. The water was, confirmed Grosley, 'distributed ... three times a week'.

40. Area vault privies were provided at No. 10 St James's Square in 1734 (HCW/1/1/1–8, RIBA Library) and at No. 28 Soho Square in about 1770; the latter was described as a 'servants' privy' (L6/6, RIBA Drawings Collection).

41. Court orders, 27 March 1690, Westminster Commissioners of Sewers.

42. Court orders, 21 November 1690, Westminster Commissioners of Sewers.

43. George Tulloch's 1752 report on estate, CHA 13083.

44. An Act in the reign of William and Mary established that inhabitants who did not contribute towards the cost of public lights should hang out their own. See George, *London Life in the Eighteenth Century* (1965 edition).

45. Sir William Chambers's letter book, MS41133, British Museum Department of Manuscripts.

46. Tenancy agreement book, CHA12853, Christ's Hospital Archives, Guildhall Library.

47. Photocopy in possession of the author.

48. E2996/5, Westminster Library.

49. Mrs Purefoy, in a letter of 25 May 1740, regarding a house in Cursitor Street, Chancery Lane, on which she had the remains of a forty-year lease granted in 1710 and which she was trying to sublet, wrote, 'I never paid anything for shewers [sewers] in my life, it being, as I suppose, a tennant tax.' See *The Purefoy Letters 1735–53*.

50. E468, Westminster Central Library.

51. E1033, Westminster Central Library.

52. E3306, Westminster Central Library.

53. For example, the Taylors' *Builder's Price Book* of 1787 includes a table showing amounts of old and new window tax. For a house of twenty-five windows, the pre-1787 tax was £2 13s. per annum, with the new tax £6 13s. A twenty-four-window house rose to £6 4s.

54. E3148, Westminster Central Library.

Bibliography

(Place of publication is London unless stated otherwise.)

Ackerman, R., *The Microcosm of London*, 1808–10.

Adam, Robert, *Ruins of the Palace of the Emperor Diocletian at Spalatro*, 1764.

Alberti, Leon Battista, *Ten Books of Architecture*, 1485; James Leoni edition, 1726.

Anderson, J.A., *A Dane's Excursion in Britain*, 1809.

Archenholz, Johann Wilhelm von, *A Picture of England* (written in about 1780), 1789.

Austen, Jane, *Letters 1796–1817* (ed. R.W. Chapman), 1955.
Emma, 1816.
Northanger Abbey, 1818.
Persuasion, 1818.

Ayres, James, *The Home in Britain*, 1981.

Barbon, Nicholas, *An Apology for the Builder*, 1685.
A Discourse of Trade, 1690.

Beeverell, James, *Pleasures of London* (trans. W.H. Quarrell), 1940.

Boswell, James, *The Life of Samuel Johnson*, 1821 edition.
London Journal 1762–3 (ed. F.A. Pottle), 1951.

Brett-James, N.G., *The Growth of Stuart London*, 1935.

Bowles, John, *London Described*, 1731.

Bryant, Arthur, *The Age of Elegance*, 1950.

The Builder's Dictionary: or, Gentleman and Architect's Companion, 1734.

Butcher, William, *Smith's Art of House Painting*, 1821.

Buxton, Thomas Fowell, *The Speeches of T.F. Buxton*, 1816.

Campbell, Colen, *Vitruvius Britannicus*, 1715–25.

Campbell, Robert, *London Tradesmen*, 1747.

Carwithan, John, *Various Kinds of Floor Decorations*, 1739.

Chalkin, Christopher William, *The Provincial Towns of Georgian England*, 1974, Montreal and Leeds.

Chambers, William, *A Treatise on Civil Architecture*, 1759, 1768, 1791.

Colvin, Howard, *A Biographical Dictionary of British Architects 1600–1840*, 1978.

Cornforth, John and Fowles, John, *English Decoration in the Eighteenth Century*, 1974.

Craig, Maurice, *Dublin 1660–1860*, 1952.

Crunden, John, *Convenient and Ornamental Architecture*, 1767, 1770.

Crunden, John and Milton, Thomas, *The Chimney Piece Maker's Daily Assistant*, 1766.
Carpenter's Companion, 1770.
Joyner and Cabinet Maker's Darling, 1770.

Defoe, Daniel, *Colonel Jack*, 1722.
The Complete English Tradesman, 1727.

Deutsch, O.E., *Handel: A Documentary Biography*, 1955.

Dossie, Robert, *Handmaid to the Arts*, 1764.

Eland, George (ed.), *The Purefoy Letters 1735–53*, 1931.

Elsom, Robert, *Practical Builder's Perpetual Price Book*, 1825.

Entwisle, E.A., *Book of Wallpaper*, 1954, 1970.

Fairchild, Thomas, *City Gardner*, 1722.

Feldborg, Andreas A., *A Dane's Excursion in Britain*, 1809.

Fiennes, Celia, *Journal* (ed. C. Morris), 1947.

Foreigner's Guide through the Cities of London and Westminster, 1729.

Franklin, Benjamin, *Complete Works*, 1806.

Geijer, Erik Gustaf, *Impressions of England 1809–10* (trans. Elizabeth Sprigg and Claude Napier), 1932.

George, M. Dorothy, *English Social Life in the Eighteenth Century*, 1923.
London Life in the Eighteenth Century, 1925, 1965.
England in Johnson's Day, 1928.
England in Transition, 1931.

Gibbs, James, *Book of Architecture*, 1728.

Gilboy, Elizabeth Waterman, *Wages in Eighteenth Century England*, 1934.

Glossop, W., *The Stove-Grate Maker's Assistant*, 1771.

Goede, Christian August Gottlieb, *The Stranger in England* (written 1802–4), 1807.

Gotch, J.A., *Inigo Jones*, 1928.

Greig, J., *Farington Diaries*, 1922.

Grosley, Pierre-Jean, *Tour of London* (ed. T. Nugent), 1772.

Grose, Francis, *The Olio*, 1793.

Gwynn, John, *London and Westminster Improved*, 1766.

Halfpenny, William, *The Art of Sound Building*, 1725.

Halfpenny, William and John, *The Modern Builder's Assistant*, 1747.

Hartley, D.R., *Water in England*, 1964.

Hatton, Edward, *A New View of London*, 1708.

Heal, Ambrose, *London Tradesmen's Cards*, 1925.
London Furniture Makers, 1953.

Hecht, Joseph Jean, *The Domestic Servant Class in Eighteenth-century England*, 1956.

Hickey, William, *Memoirs* (written about 1810; ed. Peter Quennell), 1960).

Hoppus, Edward, *The Gentleman's and Builder's Repository*, 1737, 1738, 1748.

Hughes, Helen Sand, *The Gentle Hertford*, 1940.

Hutton, William, *A Journey to London* (written in 1784), 1818.

Ison, Walter, *The Georgian Buildings of Bath 1700–1830*, 1948, 1980, Bath.

Kalm, Pehr, *Visit to England* (written in 1748), 1892.

Laing, David, *Hints for Dwellings*, 1800.

Langley, Batty, *New Principles of Gardening*, 1728.
  A Sure Guide to Builders, 1729.
  Builder's Jewel, 1741.
  The City and Country Builder's and Workman's Treasury of Designs, 1745.
  London Prices of Bricklayer's Materials, 1748.
  The Builder's Complete Assistant, 1750.

La Rochefoucauld, François de, *A Frenchman in England* (written in 1784; ed. Jean Marchand, trans. S.C. Roberts), 1933, Cambridge.

Le Blanc, Jean Bernard, *Letters on the English and French Nations* (written 1734–7), 1747.

Letts, Malcolm, *As the Foreigners Saw Us*, 1935.

Lewis, Wilmarth Sheldon, *Three Tours through London in 1748, 1776 and 1797*, 1941, New Haven.

Lichtenberg, Georg Christoph, *Visits to England* (trans. W.H. Quarrell and M.L. Mare), 1956.

Lillywhite, Bryant, *London Coffee Houses*, 1963.

Llanover, Lady (ed.) *The Autobiography and Correspondence of Mary Granville, Mrs Delany*, 1861.

Loudon, John Claudius, *Greenhouse Companion*, 1829.

Lysons, Daniel, *The Environs of London*, 1792–6.

Macdonald, John, *Memoirs of an Eighteenth-century Footman* (1790; ed. Peter Quennell, 1985).

Mackey, J., *A Journey through England in Familiar Letters* (written in 1714), 1724.

Maitland, William, *History of London*, 1739, 1775.

Malcolm, James Peller, *Anecdotes of the Manners and Customs of London during the Eighteenth Century*, 1808.

Malton, Thomas, *A Picturesque Tour through the Cities of London and Westminster*, 1792–1801.

Matthews, William, *An Historical Sketch of the Origins, Progress and Present State of Gas Lighting*, 1827.
  Hydraulia, 1835.

Meister, Jacques Henri, *Letters Written during a Residence in England* (written in 1791), 1799.

Misson, Francis Maximilian, *Memoirs of Travel over England* (trans. John Ozell), 1719.

Mitchell, C.R. and Leys, M.D.R., *History of London Life*, 1963.

Montagu, Lady Mary Wortley, *Letters* (ed. Robert Halsband), 1965.

Moritz, Carl Philip, *Travels through England*, 1782.

Morris, Robert, *Essay in Defence of Ancient Architecture*, 1728.
  Lectures on Architecture, 1734, 1736.

Moxon, Joseph, *Mechanick Exercises*, 1677–83, 1700.

Neve, Richard, *The City and Country Purchaser and Builder's Dictionary*, 1703, 1726, 1969.

Nicholson, Peter, *Mechanical Exercises*, 1812.
  An Architectural Dictionary, 1819.
  Treatise on the Construction of Staircases, 1820.
  New and Improved Practical Builder, 1823.
  Mechanic's Companion, 1825.

Noorthouck, John, *New History of London*, 1773.

North, Roger, *Autobiography* (ed. A. Jessop), 1887.

O'Dea, W.T., *A Social History of Lighting*, 1958.

Oglander, Cecil Aspinall (ed.), *The Life and Letters of the Hon. Mrs Edward Boscawen 1719–61*, 1940.
  Admiral's Widow, 1942.

Olsen, Donald J., *Town Planning in London*, 1964, New Haven and London.

Pain, William, *The Builder's Pocket Treasure*, 1763.
  The Practical Builder, 1774.
  Carpenter's and Joiner's Repository, 1778.
  Practical House Carpenter, 1789, 1794.

Pain, William and James, *British Palladio*, 1786.

Palladio, Andrea, *The Four Books of Architecture*, 1570 (trans. Isaac Ware, 1738).

Peacock, James (under the pseudonym of Jose Mac Packe), *Nutshells*, 1785.

Phillips, Hugh, *Mid-Georgian London*, 1964.

Pillet, René Martin, *L'Angleterre à Londres*, 1815.

Pococke, Richard, *Travels through England*, 1754, 1889.

Powell, Rosamund, *Eighteenth-century London Life*, 1937.

Price, Francis, *British Carpenter*, 1735.

Püeckler-Muskau, Hermann Ludwig, *Letters from Albion*, 1814.
  Tour of England, 1832.

Quarrell, W.H., *The Pleasures of London*, 1940.

Quarrell, W.H. and Mare, M., *London in 1710*, 1934.

Richardson, A.E., *William Pain's Decorative Details*, 1946.
  Robert Mylne, 1955.

Rush, Richard, *Memoranda of a Residence at the Court of London*, 1833 (ed. Philip Ziegler 1987 edition).

St Constant, J.L. Ferri de, *Londres et les anglais*, 1804.

St Fond, Faujas de, *A Journey through England and Scotland in 1784* (ed. Sir A. Geikie), 1907.

Salmon, William, *Palladio Londinensis*, 1734.

Salmon, William, *Polygraphice, or the Art of Drawing, Painting and Varnishing*, 1672.

Saussure, Cesar de, *A Foreign View of England*, 1902.

Serlio, Sebastiano, *Five Books of Architecture*, 1537–47; Robert Peake edition, 1611.

Shebbeare, John (under the pseudonym Batista Angeloni, Shebbeare professing to be translator only), *Letters on the English Nation*, 1756.

Simond, Louis, *Journal of a Tour 1810–11* (ed. Christopher Hibbert), 1968.

Shirley, John, *The Accomplished Ladies' Rich Closet*, 1687.

Smith, John, *The Art of Painting in Oyl*, editions of 1676, 1687, 1705, 1738, 1788.

Smith, J.T., *Antiquities of London*, 1791.
  Nollekens and His Times, 1828.
Smollett, Tobias, *The Adventures of Roderick Random*, 1748.
  The Expedition of Humphry Clinker, 1770.
Soane, John, *Lectures on Architecture* (ed. Arthur Bolton), 1929.
Somerville, T., *Memoirs of My Own Life and Times*, 1741–1814
Southey, Robert, *Letters from England by Don Manuel Alvarez Espriella*, 1807.
Stratton, Arthur, *Interior Decoration of the Eighteenth Century*, 1928.
Stuart, James and Revett, Nicholas, *Antiquities of Athens*, vols. 1–4, 1762–1816.
Summerson, John, *Georgian London*, 1945, 1969, 1988.
  John Nash: Architect to King George IV, 1949.
Survey of London, 41 vols. published from 1900.
Swan, Abraham, *The British Architect*, 1745.
  A Collection of Designs in Architecture, 1757.
  Designs in Carpentry, 1759.
  Designs for Chimnies, 1765.
Swift, Jonathan, *Directions to Servants*, 1731, 1745.
Taylor, I. and J., *The Builder's Price Book*, 1776, 1787.
Thompson, Gladys Scott (ed.), *Letters of a Grandmother 1732–5*, 1943.
Tingry, Pierre François, *Painter's and Varnisher's Guide*, 1832.

Trusler, John, *Principles of Politeness*, 1778.
  Honours of the Table, 1788.
Townley, James, *High Life below Stairs*, 1759.
von Uffenbach, Z.C., *London in 1710* (trans. W.H. Quarrell and M.L. Mare), 1934.
Vanherman, T.H., *Every Man His Own House Painter*, 1829.
Ward, Mary, *The Complete Cook-Maid*, 1766.
Ware, Isaac, *A Complete Body of Architecture*, 1756.
Welldon, William and John, *The Smith's Right Hand*, 1765.
Wendeborn, Beghardt Friedrich August, *A View of England*, 1791.
Whatman, Susanna, *The Housekeeping Book of 1776* (intro. Christina Hardyment), 1987.
Williams, Clare (ed.), *Sophie in London*, 1933.
Whittock, Nathaniel, *The Decorative Painter's and Glazier's Guide*, 1827.
Wood, John, *Essay towards a Description of Bath*, 1742, 1749, 1765.
Wilson, F.M., *Strange Island: Britain through Foreign Eyes*, 1955.
Wren, Christopher, *Parentalia*, 1750.
Wright, Lawrence, *Clean and Decent*, 1960.
Young, Arthur, *Six Weeks' Tour through ... England*, 1772.
Youngson, A.J., *The Making of Classical Edinburgh*, 1966, 1968, Edinburgh.

Index